FALLEN

The Vampire Syndicate

REBECCA RIVARD

Wild Hearts Press

Fallen: A Vampire Syndicate Romance
The Vampire Syndicate Series
Copyright © 2023 by Rebecca Rivard

This book is a work of fiction. The names, characters, places, and incidents are products of the author's imagination, or have been used fictitiously and are not to be construed as real. Any resemblance to actual persons living or dead, locales, or events is entirely coincidental.

Cover design by Jacqueline Sweet
Editing by Tiffany Winters
All rights reserved.

The uploading, scanning, and distribution of this book in any form or by any means—including but not limited to electronic, mechanical, photocopying, recording, or otherwise—without the permission of the copyright holder is illegal and punishable by law. Please purchase only authorized editions of this work, and do not participate in or encourage electronic piracy of copyrighted materials. Your support of the author's rights is appreciated.

Fallen/ Rebecca Rivard. — 1st ed.

❀ Created with Vellum

FALLEN
THE VAMPIRE SYNDICATE

"A must-read series!" - Paranormal Romance Guild

TWILIGHT

To save a friend, I stake my alpha in Slayers, Inc. and disappear, hoping my superiors will believe I died along with my alpha.

But you don't quit Slayers, Inc. until you're too old to fight...or dead. A member of SI's shadowy Board of Directors tracks me down. One last job, he tells me, and he'll make things right with the organization.

The catch? I have to go undercover as a blood thrall in the dangerous world of vampire syndicates.

BRIEN

Twilight shouldn't be up for sale. She made it clear she'd never be anyone's thrall.

But there she is, the main attraction at a private auction. The woman I'd do anything, pay any amount to have. So I buy her.

But is she who she's pretending to be—or have I brought the means of my own destruction directly into my lair?

"Kept me on the edge of my seat!"-Vine Voice

Want to be the first to hear about my vampire romances and other steamy paranormal books?
Sign up for my newsletter! In return, I'll gift you with a sexy short story.
https://rebeccarivard.com/newsletter

❦ I ❦

TWILIGHT

A vampire had me in their sights.

Le Dahlia Noir was crowded with humans, some seated, others dancing—but I *felt* those inhuman eyes on me, sizing me up. When you've been a slayer for over a decade, you develop a sense about these things.

A chilly finger tripped up my spine.

My voice faltered on the sultry lyric I was singing. "In the middle of the night..."

I swallowed hard and kept going. *It's okay. You* want *them to notice you.*

It was the reason I'd taken a job as a singer at a posh Quebec City nightclub.

I whisper-sang, "Just call my name," and swept a look around the dark room.

Make that *two* vampires: a darkly beautiful male in a pricy suit and a golden-haired female in a purple off-the-shoulder dress. They gazed intently at me from a black velvet couch against the back wall, their faces shimmering, moonlike, in the low lighting.

I kept my eyes moving, hoping they wouldn't guess I'd made them as vampires. But they knew, all right. The woman's tongue flicked out to taste her full lower lip.

My mind blanked. For a panicked second, I couldn't think of the next line. Then my training kicked in and I finished the song with a throaty flourish.

Thank God for the harsh education I'd undergone at the Slayers, Inc. camp, even if at the time I'd wanted to take the damn rules and shove them up the nearest trainer's ass.

But you're not a slayer anymore, are you?

Although technically, I was AWOL, so maybe I was still a member of SI; I wasn't sure. Two years ago I'd staked my alpha while on a top-secret black op, then disappeared, hoping I'd be presumed dead along with Crow. I thought I'd gotten away with it—until a member of the SI Board had tracked me down and blackmailed me into taking the job at the Dahlia. If approached by a vampire, I was supposed to play along and await further orders.

I smoothed sweaty palms down my tight cherry-colored skirt—if you want to attract a bloodsucker, wear something red and sexy—and somehow made it through the next two songs without glancing their way again.

Three more vampires entered and made their way to the back of the room, taking seats on either side of the first two. Heads turned. A ripple went through the club. The humans shifted in their seats, uneasy and yet helplessly drawn to the gorgeous predators lounging on the velvet couches.

I wrapped my hand around the mike. "Thank you for listening," I said to a polite round of applause. "We'll be back later."

The three men in the house band put down their instruments and headed backstage, me following. Behind us, canned music came on and a stagehand hurried to move my mike to the side of the stage.

I paused for a moment to watch as a trapeze dropped from the ceiling. Three women and a man, their faces and leotards painted to resemble fantastical plants, emerged from different doors around the club. They cartwheeled and flipped their way to the stage for a Cirque-du-Soleil-inspired performance.

Backstage, the tiny breakroom was too hot. Quebec City was in the middle of a rare heat wave and DeGarmo, the club owner, hadn't sprung for air-conditioning back here.

The men in the band went outside to smoke, but I needed time to regroup, so I got a soda from the fridge and sank onto the ratty brown couch.

Somehow I had a feeling tonight was the night. The Dahlia Noir was connected to the Quebec City Syndicate and was a known funnel for blood thralls.

I'd been singing at the club for three weeks. Word would've gotten out that the new girl was looking to stay in Quebec City because she didn't have any family back in the States—and no real friends in Quebec City, either, who might make things awkward if I disappeared.

Down the hall, a door opened, and someone approached the breakroom—DeGarmo. I recognized his soft, rapid tread.

My stomach did a nervous flip. This was why I was here, even if I wished with all my heart that I could just disappear again. But Kuro or someone else would only find me, and this time, there'd be no second chances.

I'd broken too many rules.

I took a gulp of soda as DeGarmo appeared in the doorway.

"Ah, there you are." He spoke in French, a thin man with a smile that didn't reach his eyes. "We have some guests who'd like to meet you."

I pressed the cold can to my forehead. "And if I don't want to meet them?" I responded, also in French.

Better not to appear too eager. Besides, let the prick sweat. He deserved it for how he treated his employees. The Dahlia made DeGarmo a boatload of money; the man could afford air-conditioning —or at least a damn fan—and decent furniture for his staff.

His smile hardened into something dangerous. "I suggest you hear what they have to say."

I lifted a shoulder, let it drop. "If you insist..."

Back in the club, the performers had entwined themselves into a human ball that slowly unfolded into a four-sided flower. They raised their arms, petal-like, to a silver spotlight standing in for the moon. The male hoisted one of the women onto his shoulders. She grasped the trapeze and swung herself up on the bar in a single graceful movement.

The five vampires, all of whom had neck tats linking them to the Quebec City Syndicate, eyed me like they were calculating my worth on the open market. The black walls pressed in on me. The vampires' enticing scent swirled around me like a dangerous caress.

I straightened my spine, channeling my inner Lucy Liu. "You wanted to see me?" I asked in English.

I also spoke fluent Spanish and some Korean, but I was still learning French. If this was to be a negotiation, I wanted it to be in English so I knew exactly what I was agreeing to.

DeGarmo sucked in a furious breath. "Pardon Mademoiselle Lee, if you please," he told the vampires. "She forgets herself."

"It's of no matter," said the dark-haired man sitting beside the blond female. "Introduce us."

"Of course. My apologies." He indicated the couple. "This is M'sieur Lemaire and Madame Fleur."

"*Enchanté*," they murmured.

I pulled my lips into a smile. "Likewise."

"*Asseyez-vous.*" Lemaire nodded at the leather armchair across the table from him.

DeGarmo pulled it out, and I lowered myself into it.

"That will be all," Lemaire told DeGarmo, who shot me a be-good glare and left, leaving me with five hungry-eyed vampires.

Still in Lucy-Liu mode, I raised a finger at a server named Claire. "A French 75, *s'il te plaît*." In the three weeks I'd worked here, I'd developed a taste for the lemony cocktail. "You don't mind buying me a drink, do you, M'sieur?" I smiled at Lemaire.

"It's my pleasure," he returned. "*S'il vous plaît*," he told Claire. "And bring us another bottle of blood-wine."

While we waited for our drinks, I lifted my long hair from my shoulders both because I was hot and because I wanted to draw attention to my neck. "Is this your first time in the Dahlia?"

Lemaire's gaze locked on my throat, and Fleur licked her lips again. Her irises, an eerie yellow that was almost an exact match for her hair, gleamed like dull suns.

A couple of nearby humans cast me envious glances, clearly wishing they could be in my place. If they only knew...

"No," said Lemaire. "But it's been a few months."

I released my hair, letting it settle on my shoulders again. "I didn't think I'd seen you before." I lowered my voice, an eager wannabe thrall. "I would've remembered you."

"Would you, now?" Lemaire's smile sent ice shivering over my skin.

Claire brought my cocktail and the blood-wine. She opened it and topped up the five vampires' glasses.

I took a gulp of my drink. The French 75 packs a kick—gin and champagne will do that—and right now, I needed a kick.

"You're alone in Quebec?" asked Fleur.

"I am, yeah. I'm hoping to stay, though. Otherwise I have to leave when my ninety days are up."

Lemaire's eyes hooded. "And when is that?"

"End of August."

"You would like to remain in Canada?" asked Fleur.

"Yeah. I really like it here. Quebec City, especially."

"*Ah, bon?*" Fleur exchanged a look with Lemaire.

"Perhaps we can help," Lemaire said.

I forced a big smile. "Are you serious? That would be awesome."

"Call me." Fleur produced a plum-colored business card and put it on the table. "We're always looking for beautiful girls."

I eyed the card without taking it. They'd expect me to negotiate. "What kind of money are we talking about?"

"You'll make more in a week than you can make at Le Dahlia in a month." She nudged the card in my direction. "In addition, we'll provide you with a place to live. You'll have a clothing allowance, too."

And all I'd have to do was allow them unlimited access to my body and blood.

"The work's not hard," Fleur added. "Many of our employees have been with us for years. You'd have to sign a contract, of course."

"For at least a year," Lemaire added.

"And you can get me a work visa so I can stay in Canada?"

"This is not a problem," he said.

Fleur reached for my hand, smoothing a finger down my wrist. A quiver went up my arm.

Her mouth curled, catlike. "Such smooth, pretty skin. You'll be popular. I will offer you a twenty-five percent signing bonus."

I opened my mouth, but she shook her head. "Call me. This is not the place to discuss details." She released me and put the card in my palm.

I tucked it into my bra and stood up. "My break's almost over. I have to go backstage."

Lemaire sat forward. "Call us. Soon." He put a touch of compulsion into his voice, the bastard.

I pretended it worked. "I will."

Lemaire sat back, lips tilted in a cat-who-caught-the-canary smile.

"We'll be expecting to hear from you," Fleur said.

I nodded and made my way back through the tables. The skin between my shoulders itched. I wanted to break into a run, but I didn't.

No, I sauntered, hips swaying, like a model on a freaking runway.

Crow would've been proud of me.

❧ 2 ❧

BRIEN

It was sheer luck that I was at the auction. I'd never bought a blood slave in my life.

Maybe that made me soft. Maybe it made me too "human," as my father said, even though I was a pureblood vampire, and, unlike him, I'd been born a vampire, not made. But I preferred feeding from—and fucking—a thrall, i.e., someone who'd chosen the lifestyle, not been forced into it.

I was in town to negotiate with Régis Dussault, the Quebec City primus, about an investment in his lavish new riverfront casino. After the lawyers and accountants had their say, we'd hash out the final details tomorrow night and hopefully, sign the agreement.

As I rose to leave, Régis put a paternal arm around me. "I have something special planned for tonight."

"Oh?" I swallowed a grimace. My plan for the rest of the evening had been to return to my rented chateau and kick back with Cain, Talon and a few of our favorite thralls.

"An auction," the primus added. "Some new females. Fresh and *très belle*. An Italian, a pretty little Asian, and a couple of Irish girls straight from the country."

I couldn't refuse without insulting Régis. I'd just have to make sure I was outbid.

"You honor me," I said.

"Not at all. It's my pleasure." He guided me outside into the cool August night. "You can ride with me."

Cain and Talon trailed at a short distance. Maritime enforcers, they weren't just my best friends, they were my bodyguards, turned by my mother when I was a teenager to be my personal security.

Régis's limo pulled up. "The auction is at Le Dahlia Noir," he told me. "There's an aboveground club, if you want to mix with the humans after. The syndicate owns the building."

We got into the limo and pulled out, Cain and Talon following in a rented SUV.

The underground version of Le Dahlia Noir was done up like a British gentleman's club—leather and wood-paneled opulence. A heavy satin curtain concealed a small stage, and bluesy jazz emanated from hidden speakers.

The Quebec City Syndicate vampires stood around, talking in small groups or lounging on the leather couches. Régis introduced me, Cain, and Talon to those we hadn't already met, then he and I settled onto a pair of club chairs in front of the stage. Cain and Talon took seats on a couch at the back along with a QCS enforcer.

A miniskirted server poured two glasses of blood-wine, then set the bottle on the black lacquered table between us.

I sipped my wine. "It's very good," I told Régis. "One of yours?"

He offered me the thin-lipped smile that was about as pleased as he ever got. "A red from my own vineyard. The secret is the terroir."

"Terror?"

"No, *terroir*. It comes from the French for *land*, but it means so much more than that. Soil, climate, topography. The vines high on the hill give us grapes that taste different from the wines lower."

I eyed the dark red liquid in my glass. "No kidding."

"*Oui*. The higher elevation keeps the vines cooler at night, for example, which helps the grapes conserve their acidity. The wine will be more elegant, and it lasts longer." The primus turned his glass in his long fingers. "I'm a farmer at heart. Sometimes at sunset, I walk my vineyards. It's so peaceful."

I swallowed a chuckle. Régis, a farmer? The man was as cutthroat as they came.

"Tell me about making wine," I said. "My father is thinking of investing in a couple of local vineyards."

Actually, it was my idea. These days, Jules thought only of blood and death. But he was officially the Maritime primus, and I pretended he was still calling the shots. In reality, his lieutenant and I had been running the syndicate for the past year.

"*Ah, bon?*" asked Régis. "He should. He can control the blood-wine process from start to finish."

"We do own some vineyards in California."

"Then you must add some Canadian wines to your portfolio."

Régis launched into an explanation of the different red wines his vineyards produced. I'd finished my first glass of wine before he circled around to his real reason for inviting me here tonight.

"The loss of Lenore must have been a blow to you and Jules. She'll be missed."

My hand tightened on the wine glass's fragile stem. My mother had been slain a little over a year ago by an unknown assassin just steps from our castle on Lilith Island.

"Thank you. And yes, it was a blow."

You have no idea.

My mother hadn't been exactly warm and fuzzy, but she and my father had been a mated pair. Losing her had ripped his heart out.

"Your father—he's well? I've heard talk..."

I shrugged. "Lies. Put about by our enemies."

"Hm." Régis arched a skeptical brow, but he didn't push me on it. "Still, if you should require an ally, you've impressed me this week."

"Thank you. I appreciate the vote of confidence. But as you know, my father is still the Maritime primus."

Régis inclined his head. "Of course."

I sipped my wine. Did Régis mean it, or was he probing for weaknesses?

My father's time as primus was rapidly coming to an end. When that happened, I wanted his allies to know me in my own right. In fact, I'd agreed to invest a sizeable amount in the QCS casino for just that reason.

The piped-in jazz stopped and the satin curtain fluttered.

"Ah." My host settled back. "The auction is about to begin."

I nodded absentmindedly. The rumors about my father were spreading. I had to do something before the other syndicates realized how bad he'd gotten and moved on us.

The curtain parted to reveal a woman in a slinky black dress, her back to the audience, her rich brown hair swept forward over one shoulder. The dress dipped to her waist, an erotic frame for the rose-and-dagger tattoo that ran the length of her spine like a crimson scar.

I eyed her without really seeing her, my mind on my father. Then my jaw dropped. A shock of recognition pierced me like a nail to the chest. My already slow-pumping lungs simply...stopped.

Carefully, without taking my gaze from the woman being auctioned, I put my glass on the table at my elbow.

What. The. Fuck?

I took in the thrall's narrow, deceptively delicate body; her toned arms; the red, do-me heels. Returned to the scarlet tattoo.

It's not her.

It couldn't be. Lainey Q had short silver hair. And what in the name of Lilith would she be doing at a private auction?

It's been two years. She could've grown her hair out, dyed it brown.

But she hadn't had that tattoo. I'd seen her in a skimpy dress at my friend Zoe's birthday ball, and I would've noticed it.

Besides, slayers didn't have tattoos.

It's not her.

After Lainey had disappeared, I'd moved heaven and earth trying to locate her—which hadn't been easy, since I couldn't let anyone, especially my parents, know how badly I wanted to find her.

I'd even wondered if she'd died, because she'd stopped posting to Instagram around the same time she'd disappeared. Her five-million-plus followers had been as baffled as I was.

I'd sent Talon and Cain to look for her, made discreet inquiries of my allies in other syndicates. I'd even hired a human private investigator. She was the one who'd discovered that the woman known as Lainey Q had never really existed. She was a front for a slayer, one who'd infiltrated the Tremblay Syndicate before vanishing. My friend Zoe, the new Tremblay Prima, had told me straight out that Lainey was a slayer, but I hadn't believed it.

She'd seemed so genuine. I'd danced with her. Kissed her. Buried myself deep inside her.

The woman had fucking screamed for me. No one was that good of an actress.

Except clearly she was, and I was a jackass for thinking she'd actually wanted me. I'd told myself I'd dodged a bullet and stopped searching...only to stumble across her at a goddamned blood-slave auction.

Régis leaned across the table. "I told you the Chinese girl was a beauty."

She's not Chinese, you ass. She's Korean. Korean-American, actually.

I finally remembered to breathe. "She is." I kept my tone bored and hooded my eyes, hiding the blue I felt flickering in my irises.

No one could guess I was *this* close to going full-out vampire and ripping out Régis's fucking heart. But there were a dozen of them and only one of me, even if you counted Talon and Cain.

So I'd have to win the bidding.

A human in a chic white dress, her auburn hair twisted into an elegant bun, walked to a mike on one side of the stage and aimed a practiced smile at us.

"Bidding starts at twenty-five thousand dollars," she said in French. She nodded at Lainey Q. "Turn around."

Lainey Q—or whoever the hell she was—turned to face us. Her mouth curved up, but her dark, feline eyes were dead. They traveled over the seated vampires, snagged on me and widened, then quickly moved on.

The auctioneer walked around Lainey, pointing out features like she was a prime piece of cattle—her silky skin, her youth, her obvious good health.

Something sparked way back in Lainey's eyes. She lifted her chin and stared proudly back at us. So she hadn't lost all her spunk.

Unfortunately, that made the roomful of blasé vampires sit up and take notice. My kind craves a challenge.

"Do I have a bid for twenty-five thousand?" asked the red-haired auctioneer.

A silver-haired vampire raised his bidding paddle.

I settled back into my armchair, biding my time. She shouldn't have been up for sale. She'd made it clear she'd never be anyone's thrall.

But now here she was, the main attraction at a blood-slave auction. The woman I'd do anything, pay any amount to have. And now someone with enough cash could take her and do whatever they wanted with her?

No. Fucking. Way.

She wasn't leaving with anyone but me.

Another man, Nazaire, entered the bidding. Lainey's price topped a hundred thousand, then two hundred, then five hundred. The silver-haired vampire dropped out.

Nazaire, the bastard, gave a smug smile.

I raised my paddle. "One million dollars."

Nazaire's smile withered. He turned heavy-lidded eyes upon me. Menace saturated the air.

I stared back steadily.

"Two million," he ground out.

I lifted my paddle again without taking my eyes from Nazaire. "Four million."

The auctioneer rubbed her hands together, a gleeful smile on her face. "Four million dollars. Do I hear four and a half?" She looked at Nazaire.

He glanced at me, jaw working. But I was the Maritime Syndicate heir. It would take a richer man than him to outbid me.

He shook his head at the auctioneer. "*Non.*"

"Anyone else?" When no one raised the bid, she nodded at me. "Sold for four million dollars to Prince Brien."

Régis looked positively jovial. A large percentage of that four million would go into his treasury. At least it would put him in a good mood for tomorrow's negotiations.

He gave me a sly, man-to-man smile. "She *is* tasty, isn't she?"

At my side, my fingers clenched. I grunted noncommittally.

Do not *smash your fist into his face. Remember the endgame.*

Lainey stared down at the stage, fingers knitted together. She didn't look proud now.

She looked...desperate. Resigned. And maybe a little afraid.

Which was a punch to the gonads, but then, what did I expect? That she'd be grateful, even happy, that I'd been the one to buy her?

At the auctioneer's nod, she stepped back and the curtain closed. I came to my feet.

"I believe I'll take ownership now," I told Régis.

He stood as well, and we shook hands. "Enjoy her. I wouldn't mind a taste myself." When I just stared back, his smile faded. "Tomorrow night, then."

"The usual time?"

"Yes." His smile returned. "I believe we can come to a final agreement, don't you?"

"I'm counting on it."

❈ 3 ❈
TWILIGHT

Brien's green glare stabbed into me like an ice pick.

Damn him anyway. What was the Maritime crown prince even doing in Quebec City? He should be 500-some miles away in Nova Scotia.

I'd known he was searching for me. I'd also known I couldn't let him find me.

He was a weakness, the only vampire I'd ever wondered *What if?* about. The vampire who still turned up, uninvited, in my dreams.

But things had gone too far. I couldn't stop now if I wanted to, and I did *not* need the Perfect Prince effing things up for me.

I kept my eyes downcast, playing the terror-stricken human, which wasn't all that hard. This wasn't like going undercover for Slayers, Inc.

Yeah, those assignments could be risky. You never knew when things might go south. Take my last couple of jobs, for example.

But those ops had been planned weeks in advance. I'd felt in control, my cover note-perfect, and I'd always had a switchblade or two concealed somewhere on my body.

This felt like being shoved onto a tightrope with no training...and no net to catch me if I fell.

Backstage, Madame Z—that's how she'd been introduced, with the

Z pronounced the French way, *Zed*—waited. "Get ready. The prince wishes to leave *tout de suite*."

I knew better than to ask if I could change out of the dress and heels. I nodded and hefted the small bag which was all I'd been allowed. It held makeup, a toothbrush, a nightgown and a change of underwear.

I suppose I was lucky. Some blood slaves aren't even allowed shoes.

"Your tattoo," said Madame Ze. "It's most unusual."

I glanced over my shoulder, even though I couldn't see the tattoo from this angle. I didn't have to see it, though.

The image haunted my dreams, the horror of receiving it still bright in my mind.

A dagger and a rose in blood red.

The needles had hurt, but the real pain had been knowing that I'd been betrayed by one of my own. That I'd been set up. Lied to.

And that when I got off that table, I'd be Kuro's creature to move around like a pawn on a chessboard.

"What does it mean?" she asked.

I smiled thinly. "Vengeance."

Her plucked dark brows lifted. "I see. Come, then." She turned and led the way down a short hall. When we reached a closed door, she touched a pad and a camera scanned her face.

As the door unlocked, she bent her willowy neck to murmur in my ear. "Obey the prince, and you'll be fine. Just don't fight him. He's a quiet one, you comprehend? They are often the most dangerous."

Obey him?

A year ago—even three months ago—I would've laughed in her face. But tonight, I simply nodded. I'd learned to choose my battles.

"Now smile," she said, and waited until I obediently stretched my lips before pushing the door open.

Brien Leclerc stood on the other side, tall, blond and intimidating in a sharkskin suit.

Seeing him in the flesh for the first time in two years was an emotional punch. I sucked in a breath and stilled like my spike heels had been glued to the floor.

He looked even better than I remembered, as if one of the

vampire's dark gods had come to life. Same lean, sculpted face. Same full, sensual lower lip. Same incredible eyes, like frost-covered grass. The only change was that his dark blond hair had grown long enough to be pulled into a short ponytail.

"She's ready, my lord," Madame Z said.

"Thank you." Brien's eyes glittered into mine. His scent curled around me, dark and delicious.

My stomach tightened. It wasn't fair. The Perfect Prince was...perfect.

And I was still susceptible to him. My heart had sped up and my stomach fluttered like a teenager talking to her first crush.

"Let's go." Brien jerked his chin at the elevator.

Madame Z nudged me, and I lurched into motion, catching a heel on the doorjamb. Brien's fingers clamped around my upper arm, saving me from face-planting on the granite floor.

My cheeks heated. "Thanks," I muttered.

I wasn't usually this clumsy. My last cover as a stylist and Instagram influencer had meant I spent a lot of time in dresses and high heels. Besides, I was naturally graceful. At least, that's what my halmoni—my grandma—had always said.

As he steered me toward the elevator, two vampires flanked us—Talon and Cain. I hadn't even noticed them, I'd been so busy gaping at Brien. The GQ twins, I'd nicknamed them.

My gaze returned Brien. As long as I was his captive, I might as well look my fill. It fed a part of me that had longed to see him just one more time.

Not all vampires are pale. Like humans, they come in a variety of skin tones. Brien had a honeyed, surfer-boy tint that made me want to lick him all over. Beneath the hand-tailored suit, I knew he was tattooed and hard-bodied—at least, his upper body was.

Two years ago, we hadn't gotten completely naked. Just damn close.

The whole time I was examining him like he was Adam and I was Eve, Brien kept his gaze forward, a muscle ticking in his cheek.

I lowered my voice. "What are you doing here, anyway?"

He slanted me a sleet-cold look and didn't answer.

Okay. So he *was* pissed off at me.

I suppose he had a reason to be. When we'd met in Montreal, I'd been undercover at the Tremblay Syndicate, acting as a stylist for the then-Prima's daughter Zoe.

Brien had seen me at Zoe's birthday ball and pursued me with a single-minded focus. I'd had vampires chase me before. It's part of the job for slayers who work undercover. Once a vampire fixates on you, they can be hard to shake loose.

But this time had been different.

I hadn't wanted to shake this vampire loose.

Brien had intrigued me. As controlled as he was handsome, he had an edge that made you wonder—when you unwrapped him, would you find that urbane elegance was a cover for something dark, primal?

The stars in my eyes had made me stupid. Princess Zoe had escaped from the ball with Rafe Kral—and I hadn't even known for over an hour, because I'd been locked in a bathroom with Brien, sexing my brains out. Both Prima Victorine and Crow had been furious with me.

Brien had tried to see me the next day, but Victorine had informed him that I'd left. When he'd asked where I'd gone, she'd lied and told him she didn't know. Further events had left my Lainey-Q cover completely compromised. I'd jettisoned it and with it, any hope of further contact with Brien.

I'd only seen him once after that, a few months later in Maryland. I'd been undercover as a forty-something caterer, and I'd made sure he hadn't seen me. I'd even disguised my scent with a heavy perfume.

The elevator arrived. Brien and I stepped into it along with the GQ twins, who, like him, were lean and model-handsome. The pair weren't actually twins, of course.

Talon was darker with deep-set brown eyes and thick curls cut short on the sides and long on the top. Cain could've been Talon's photographic negative: light-skinned with pale blue eyes and cropped white-blond hair. I eyed the shark tattoo on Cain's neck, the mark of a "made" man in the Maritime Syndicate. Talon had a matching one.

Brien had a similar tat himself, only his was two intertwined sharks swirling around his upper right arm.

Locked in that bathroom, we'd only had time for a fast, explosive fuck—although I had made time to bite that sensual lower lip. While I'd caught my breath, I'd traced the tat's charcoal outline with my fingertip, acting impressed because Lainey Q would've been. But deep down, I *had* been impressed.

So Prince Brien had killed for his syndicate.

It shouldn't have turned me on, but it did. I had a dark side myself.

The elevator let us out in a private foyer near the main entrance of Le Dahlia Noir. Setting a hand on my lower back, Brien guided me outside.

A black SUV waited on the narrow cobblestone street. Talon opened the door, but Cain stopped me before I got in. "Your backpack."

I shrugged it off and handed it over. He looked through it, examining even the lining before giving it back. Then he crouched and examined my shoes, sliding a finger over each heel and fingering the toes.

He came to his feet. "She's clean," he told Brien.

I opened my arms with a twisted smile. "You sure you don't want to frisk me?"

Brien made a low, angry sound. "No. Put your arms down, damn it."

I brought them to my sides, aware that didn't mean he trusted me. You'd have to be damn creative to conceal a blade beneath this dress.

"Inside." Brien put a hard palm on my ass and practically shoved me into the SUV. He climbed in next to me, his body crowding mine. Talon took shotgun in the front seat, and Cain sat next to Brien.

The driver was a wide-shouldered, stern-faced woman around fifty. "Where to, sir?" she asked in a Canadian accent.

"The chateau," said Brien.

The chateau was a short way out of the city. We drove up a private lane lined on either side by vineyards. Despite its name, the chateau wasn't a castle but a large country house, with white-washed walls and an orange terracotta roof—although it did have two turrets, a separate winery, and a couple of other out-buildings including one labeled "Carriage House" in French.

I glanced around. The Maritime Syndicate's territory covered New Brunswick and Nova Scotia. How had the Maritime prince ended up at a Quebec chateau complete with its own winery?

"I rented it for the week," Brien informed me, seemingly reading my mind.

"A vampire owns it?"

A curt nod.

That meant it would have an underground lair. Brien was only in his mid-thirties, too young to take more than a minute or so of sunlight without being badly burned.

The driver dropped us at the door along with Talon, then continued to the carriage house. We entered the chateau through a small outer room that opened into a large, homey kitchen with brick-red cabinets and a French country table with blue legs and a scarred wood top.

A third man with a shark tat on his neck was waiting for us. Brien jerked his chin at me. "Take the woman downstairs."

"Your suite?" he asked.

Brien's mouth pulled into a nasty half-smile. "Of course."

I lifted my chin and stared down my nose at him like I was a vampire princess like Zoe Tremblay, not the woman he'd bought at an illegal auction.

"You have an objection?" he asked in silky tones.

"No, sir."

I kept my voice neutral; I knew better than to push Brien too far in front of his men. However, even calling him *sir* was a provocation, and we both knew it. But it backfired on me, because his smile simply grew darker, an expression that made my blood spark and fizz.

Damn the man anyway. He still pushed all my lady buttons.

The guard urged me through a door and down a narrow staircase carved out of bedrock. He opened the first door on the right. "Inside."

I complied, and he shut and locked it, leaving me alone. Panic squeezed my throat. The walls seemed to close in on me. The prick hadn't even turned on a light.

I jerked the door handle, but the door was vampire proof—thick wood reinforced with silver. I discovered that when I dropped my bag and slid my hands over the door and the silver bands that crisscrossed it.

I felt for a light switch but came up empty. My lungs locked. I slammed a fist against the door.

"Let. Me. Out."

The panic increased. The room felt airless. I couldn't seem to fill my lungs.

Breathe.

Slayers have to be tough. When my squad leaders had realized I had a phobia about dark, confined spaces, they'd locked me in rooms like this countless times. I had to either learn how to control my fear —or break. And I was damned if I'd let them break me.

I gritted my teeth and drew a slow inhale.

There's a light. There must be.

This wasn't a tiny room in a bunker beneath the SI training compound. This was a chateau, retrofitted for vampires and their thralls, and even a vampire required a small amount of illumination to see. There *would* be a light switch.

I ran my hands along the wall near the door again. This time, I found the light plate. I flipped the switch and an overhead light came on.

My shoulders sagged with relief. I exhaled loudly.

I was in a wall-papered parlor furnished with a couch and armchairs in a vintage red brocade. Behind the couch was a wet bar stocked with wine and liquor. I moved my bag to the nearest chair and switched on a couple of Tiffany-style floor lamps. Still shaky, I started opening doors to distract myself from the fact that I was locked underground.

The first door belonged to a large bathroom with a glassed-in shower and a pretty blue-and-white mosaic floor. I splashed some cold water on my face, feeling more myself now. If Fleur hadn't confiscated my phone, I might've taken a photo.

The master bedroom was behind the second door. The bed was covered with a black silk duvet embroidered with gold flowers. The only personal items were a wooden hairbrush and a couple of leather hair ties on the dresser.

I pulled drawers, searching for a weapon. When I didn't find one, I rifled through the suits in the walk-in closet. I had no luck there, either, but then, I didn't really expect to. Brien wouldn't be that careless.

The suits smelled like him. I rubbed a sleeve against my face, drawing his earthy green scent into my lungs. I was acting like a lovesick ass, but I couldn't seem to help myself.

Back in the bedroom, I sat on the bed, running a palm over the duvet. Something curled through my lower belly, something hot and needy. If things had been different, I'd have been more than willing to lie down on the big silk-covered mattress and wait for Brien...naked.

Hell, I'd fantasized for the past two years about doing something just like that.

But things had changed. The SOB thought he owned me—and in his world, he did, even if it was illegal. The treaties between vampires and humans stated clearly that a vampire couldn't enslave a human, but there were always places like Quebec City where the syndicates paid the humans in charge enough to look the other way.

I came to my feet. That's when I saw a door concealed in the black-and-gold wallpaper. I opened it to find a small room barely large enough for a dresser and a single bed. The tiny bathroom had a sink, a toilet and a shower. Like the outer door, the connecting door was thick, silver-reinforced wood with the lock on the master-bedroom side.

My chest tightened. The room was a prison, a place to keep a thrall locked up during the hours when the vampires were deep in their day sleep.

No. Hell, no.

Closing the door, I stalked back to the parlor and the wet bar, where I poured myself a shot of whiskey and downed it in a couple of gulps. Heat filled my belly. False courage, but right now I'd take any courage I could get.

I had to get a hold of myself. From the time I'd seen Brien at the auction, I'd blanked.

That wasn't like me. Twilight always had a plan.

The lock on the outer door disengaged. The fine hairs on my nape lifted, although not from fear—or at least, not only from fear. This feeling was more primitive, like the electric thrill you get right before a thunderstorm hits.

Brien entered the parlor, closing the door behind him. "Drinking, sweet?" he murmured with a glance at the shot glass. "Am I that bad of a lover?"

The shock of seeing him after all these months had worn off. Instead, I was disappointed. Angry.

He shouldn't have been at that auction; he was the last vampire I'd have figured to be involved in the slave trade. Apparently, all that blond perfection hid a slimy worm of an inside.

I slammed the whiskey glass down on the wet bar. "Don't call me 'sweet.' And you're not going to be my lover at all."

"No?" His eyebrows were darker than his hair, a light but definite brown. He quirked the left one. "I have a four-million-dollar receipt that says you're wrong. But...are you worth it?"

I flinched. I tried to cover it, but he saw. Something flickered across his face. Remorse...maybe even pity.

My fingers tightened on the shot glass. I smoothed my expression, like Brien and his pity didn't have the power to hurt me.

"Fucking isn't making love."

"True." Shrugging out of his jacket, he dropped it on an armchair and prowled closer; a powerful, tawny cat of a man, like Daniel Craig in his first James Bond movie. "But then, I thought we did something more than fuck."

This time, I managed not to flinch.

Still, he was right, it had been more than fucking. We'd... connected, in some primal way I couldn't explain. A connection that had scared the crap out of me, because he was a vampire and I was a slayer. I couldn't, *wouldn't* let this thing between us develop. And so, when my mission had required it, I'd left Montreal without contacting him.

And after the mission ended, it was too late. Lainey Q no longer existed, and I couldn't risk meeting a syndicate vampire as Twilight...

even if it felt like in leaving Brien, I'd left behind something vital, like a lung—or my heart.

A few months later, I'd staked Crow and the only way to survive had been to erase Twilight completely. Not even my halmoni knew for sure if I was dead or alive. I hadn't dared contact her.

I filled my chest with a deep breath. "What are you doing in Quebec City, anyway? Aren't you supposed to be in Nova Scotia in that bat-cave of a castle?"

The broody black castle on an island off the coast of Canada. And no, I'd never been to Castle Leclerc. I'd looked it up because...reasons.

Brien tilted his head, considering me. "You googled me."

I set the shot glass on the bar. "I got bored one night."

"Yeah?" He was only two feet from me now. Loosening his tie, he drew it over his head and dropped it on the couch. "You should be happy I won the auction. The vampires bidding against me are both dark SOBs. Whips, handcuffs, gags...that sort of stuff."

I briefly closed my eyes. What had Kuro sent me into? There hadn't even been a plan for extracting me.

"Thank you. I—I'll pay you back somehow."

"I don't want your goddamned money."

"Then what do you want? You don't keep blood slaves."

"Don't I?"

"No." I folded my arms over my chest, refusing to let him frighten me.

The more I thought about it, the more it didn't make sense. I'd bet my scary-low bank balance that Brien Leclerc didn't keep blood slaves.

His fingers went to his shirt. I watched, distracted, as he undid the top two buttons, exposing the strong column of his throat.

"The auction." I forced my gaze back to his face. "You were sitting with the QCS primus. That's why you were there, weren't you? Business."

Suddenly, he was right in front of me, so close my nipples nearly touched his chest. They hardened and pressed against my bra.

I moistened my lips. "I'm right, aren't I?"

A shrug of his broad shoulders.

"What kind of business?" I asked, unable to resist probing.

"Syndicate business, and that's all you need to know." He rubbed a thumb over my lower lip, sending a lick of heat up my spine. "It's been a long and tedious week, but Quebec City just got way more interesting."

"Enough." I tilted my head to the side. "I know you're going to let me go."

"Do you now, Lainey?" He coasted a finger down my throat, his smile slow and dark. "Maybe you don't know me as well as you think you do. Or should I call you Twilight?"

My gaze snapped to his. Only a handful of other slayers had known my code name, and two of them were dead.

His eyes were jewel-bright in his too handsome face. He released my chin but remained close, crowding me against the bar.

"You're not the only one with access to information. You shouldn't have left Montreal like that. When you didn't show up the next day, I was worried." His mouth twisted. "I thought something had happened to you, that maybe some other vampire kidnapped you. That idiot Olivier, maybe. He was all over you at Zoe's ball."

"Prima Victorine knew I was okay."

"That occurred to me—so I went to her and asked. Not that with Zoe missing, she gave a fuck about where you were. But she said you were okay, so I went back home. The party was over anyway after Zoe disappeared with Kral."

He caught a lock of my hair, rubbing it between his thumb and first finger.

"But when I thought it over, I wondered if Victorine had forced you to stay in Canada and become a thrall. I sent Talon and Cain to look for you, but they couldn't find anything. Zoe was the one who told me you were a slayer, that I should forget about you. But I kept looking—I even hired a human investigator. Because I'm a goddamn fool."

I bit my lower lip. "No, you're not."

He scoffed. "Yeah, I am. A damn, trusting fool. It took months, but the PI came through, including the intel that you're known as Twilight to your squad."

"She shouldn't have been able to—"

"Sweetheart. For enough money, people will tell you just about anything. But no one knew where you were. Until tonight, I wasn't even sure you were still alive."

He took my chin in a hard grip. A fiery blue line shimmered to life around his irises.

My heart tripped. He wasn't just angry, he was furious, despite his outward calm. That thin blue line said he was fighting his vampire.

"So, *Twilight*. You're a slayer—or were, anyway. So what are you doing here in Quebec City? And why the *hell* were you being auctioned off?"

I tried to hold his gaze but couldn't. "Fuck off," I told his chin.

He nudged my chin higher. "Look at me."

When I obeyed, his gaze locked on my exposed throat.

The sensitive skin tingled. They'd fed from me, every few nights. They hadn't even granted me the aphrodisiac's hot rush; they'd wanted me to feel the pain. Fleur herself had drunk my blood just a few hours before the auction—to settle me down, she said. Make me docile.

Brien exhaled, a raw, angry sound. "Who did this?"

He touched the twin marks Fleur had left. The makeup I'd applied to conceal it must've worn off. The bitch hadn't had the decency to lick my throat to heal the punctures.

I jutted my chin to hide my humiliation. "A Quebec City coven."

"Who?" A muscle jumped in his cheek. His hand moved to my shoulder. "I want names."

Lemaire and Fleur had tried to compel me not to reveal anything else about them and their coven, and I'd pretended to go along. But through some quirk of genetics, I can't be compelled. It runs in my family, was what made me valuable to SI.

"I don't know," I lied, because what was the point in naming them? It wasn't Brien's syndicate.

"Then where did they take you?"

"I don't know."

"You're protecting those bastards?"

I shrugged him off and stepped back, arms hugged around myself.

The surge of adrenaline at seeing Brien had worn off. I was tired and hungry and just...done.

"I don't know," I said, hard-voiced.

His ice-green eyes narrowed. "You're good."

"What d'you mean?"

"I can sense your emotions, but they're faint, like you have them behind a locked door. Still, I can tell you're lying to me. What I don't know is why."

"Well, you're wrong. I don't know where I was." That much was the truth. "When they brought me to their nest, I was blindfolded, and again when they took me to the Le Dahlia Noir. All I know is that I was somewhere in Quebec—the province, not the city. Maybe an hour from the club? When they let us outside, I saw vineyards."

"When they let you outside?" The blue rimming his irises flared again.

I lifted a shoulder. "You know, for exercise."

And sunshine. It had been the highlight of my day. The thing that had kept me going.

"Sweet Lilith."

My stomach growled. I couldn't have come up with a better distraction, because Brien scowled.

"You're hungry. They didn't feed you, either?"

I rubbed my palms up and down my bare arms. "I wasn't hungry."

Not after Madame Z had appeared around sunset to dress me. I'd known then that I'd be auctioned off that night. "In fact," she'd informed me, "you're the main attraction."

"Sit." Brien pointed at the couch. "I'll order some food from the kitchen."

My hackles raised. No one ordered me around. But I was exhausted, mentally and physically—that part was no act.

I sat.

❧ 4 ❧

BRIEN

Something was...off.

Now that the fury hazing my brain had cleared, I could tell that Twilight had lost weight since I'd last seen her. Too much weight.

Yeah, she'd been wiry, but not like this. In Montreal, she'd been high-energy, taut-bodied. Now she looked like a strong wind would level her.

What had they done to her?

Her stomach growled again.

Okay. This I could fix.

The chateau had come with a chef for the human and dhampir employees. I texted a soldier to have the chef put a tray together for her, then rounded the couch and crouched on my haunches in front of her.

"I ordered you some food—it should be here in a few minutes. Meanwhile, I'm going to take a shower." I wrapped my fingers around her nape, caressing her jaw with my thumb. "Don't try to run—you'll just piss me off. There's a guard in the hall and more outside."

She sliced me an *are-you-kidding?* look through those tip-tilted feline eyes. "When I leave, it won't be at night."

Ah, that was my Lainey Q. I dropped a kiss on her insolent mouth and released her chin. "You won't be leaving at all, *Twilight*."

Her chest jerked. "Stop calling me that."

"Then what should I call you? Lainey Q? She vanished, remember? Her followers are still searching for her. Have you seen the wild conspiracy theories they've cooked up?" Some of which I'd had the PI investigate...just in case.

"Yeah?" Her mouth quirked. "Huh. I deleted my social media accounts. And then after, I couldn't go online or they'd find—" She clamped her lips together and shook her head.

"After what? And who's *they?*"

She lifted a slim shoulder. "Fine. Call me Twilight then."

My jaw tightened; I wasn't used to being brushed off like that. But her eyes had shuttered, and it was clear I wouldn't get anything more out of her.

"Twilight," I repeated, this time without the irony. "It fits, some-how." Like her, the twilight was layered, mysterious. Beautiful.

She just shook her head.

I waited for her to say something else. When she didn't—just stared at a spot over my shoulder—I headed into the bathroom, stupidly disappointed that she wouldn't tell me more.

Behind me, she said, "It doesn't matter anyway—what you call me," so low that if I hadn't been a vampire, I wouldn't have heard her.

Brow furrowed, I shut the bathroom door and stepped into the shower. There was a puzzle here, one I intended to solve. But not tonight.

Twilight had no reason to trust me. Pushing her wasn't going to get me anywhere.

No, better to back off for now. I'd take her back to Lilith Island, feed her up, give her time to recover. I wanted her to see me as the good guy—and then I'd lower the boom.

And if that made me a ruthless bastard, then I was happy to own it.

I made my shower short, afraid she'd try and escape despite what I'd told her. She was smart; she might be able to evade the first level of security, and I didn't want a confrontation with her. Not when she looked like hell.

But when I left the bathroom on my way to the bedroom for a

fresh set of clothes, Twilight was still in the parlor. She'd taken off her high heels and stood next to the bookcase, flipping through an issue of French *Vogue*.

She glanced at my naked body and did a doubletake. Her cheeks sucked in and her eyelids fluttered. Then she looked me over a second time, bold as hell. Taking her time about it.

My dick loved the attention. It twitched and started to harden. "Like what you see?"

Her gaze fixed on my growing erection. She licked her lips and I swallowed a groan.

"Fishing? You know you're hot."

"I still like to hear it." *Especially from you.*

"Then I'll be sure and stroke...your ego every day."

I exhaled a bark of laughter. She blinked like she was surprised I had a sense of humor.

I prowled toward her. "You can stroke my ego right now. You can even squeeze it. Or maybe lick it."

Yeah, I'd love to see that pretty mouth opening to take my dick.

She slid the magazine back onto the shelf. "Is that what you want?"

Her tone was velvet. Whatever blood was still left in my head headed south.

A knock sounded on the door. "What?" I snapped without taking my gaze from her.

"It's me," Cain responded. "With the food."

Twilight's cheeks creased like she was holding back a laugh. "Guess your ego will have to wait."

I set my teeth. "Come in," I ground out and kept going into the bedroom, where I dragged on a pair of jeans and a worn black linen shirt, leaving it unbuttoned.

Back in the parlor, a tray piled high with food—a baguette, cold chicken, foie gras, a trio of fancy French cheeses, a bowl of strawberries, a pot of cream—was on the coffee table.

Twilight was still next to the bookshelf. Cain's gaze flicked from her to me. "Can I talk to you?"

"What's up?"

He tipped his head at the door. "In the hall."

I nodded. Cain wouldn't bother me if it wasn't important.

"Eat," I told Twilight and followed him out the door.

The chateau's basement had been built to withstand a vampire attack, with thick walls and heavy wood doors. I pulled the door closed so Twilight couldn't overhear us.

Talon opened his door, curly hair damp from a shower. "Why don't you guys come in here?" he asked with a glance at the guard a few yards away.

As soon as we were alone, I folded my arms over my chest. "Let me guess. This is about the woman."

My friends exchanged a look. Then, as usual, Cain spoke first. "What the fuck, Bri? Since when do you buy blood slaves?

"I couldn't leave her there. Not with Nazaire bidding on her."

Nazaire—he went by one name—was a sadistic SOB. Enslaving his thralls was only the tip of the iceberg. He kept it on the down-low, but before we'd come to Quebec, Cain had done a deep web search on the Quebec City Syndicate hierarchy. When negotiating, the more intel you have, the better.

The QCS was old-school, treating their human servants more like slaves. They got away with it because most of the city's politicians were in their pocket. And Nazaire was the worst of the sorry bunch.

"So you're going to release her?" Cain asked.

"That's between me and her."

He blinked. This wasn't like me, and we all knew it.

"Think, Brien," said Talon. "What if SI finds out you bought a slave? They could use it as an excuse to put a contract out on you."

"Fuck SI. How would they find out, anyway? As soon as we're done here, I'll take her back to the island. We won't allow her access to a phone or the internet. As far as the rest of the world is concerned, she's a new thrall."

"Holy Dark Lady." Cain's eyes narrowed. "She's that woman, isn't she? The one you've been looking for—Lainey Q."

My jaw tightened. A primitive part of me wanted to hide her, even from my best friends.

"Yeah. But we're calling her Twilight now."

"I thought she looked familiar," said Talon.

"Well, damn." Cain scratched his cheek. "Guess you have the bitch right where you want her, don't you? A goddamn slayer."

Talon shook his head. "I don't know about this."

"I think it could work in Brien's favor," Cain said. "We admit nothing, but if a rumor spreads that he's keeping a slave, we let it stand. It will impress those old assholes who say he's not enough of a bastard to become primus."

"Exactly." My smile would've made those ruthless old vampires sweat—if a vampire could sweat, that is. "But only the three of us can know she's a former slayer. I don't want the syndicate wondering why I'm showing a slayer mercy."

"That tattoo on her spine should do it," said Cain. "No slayer would deliberately get one, especially a tat that large. It makes her too easy to identify."

Talon pursed his lips. "Something about this doesn't pass the smell test. She could've gotten the tat to make us think she's left SI for good."

"Maybe so," I said, "but she'll be in my territory. What can she do with no phone or weapons? But this isn't up for discussion—I've made up my mind. She stays."

He shrugged. "You're the boss."

"So that Lainey-Q thing in Montreal," said Cain. "It was all an act? Even you and her—?"

I trained a hard stare on him, and he broke off.

What had happened between me and Twilight was none of their damn business. And I refused to believe she'd been acting we'd had sex. The woman had scratched her nails down my back, her pussy squeezing around me as she moaned my name.

On the other hand, maybe she was an Oscar-level actress.

Or maybe she got off on fucking vampires before she staked them.

I scowled.

"When you think about it," Talon said, "that Lainey-Q alias is a perfect cover."

I nodded. "She really was a stylist, a good one, with over five million followers on Instagram. And Prima Victorine wasn't the first vampire who'd hired her for a special event."

"Smart," said Cain. "She'd be invited into her clients' private spaces. She must've heard and seen things. But how did she get away with it? Eventually, someone would've connected the dots."

"Maybe all she did was reconnaissance," I said. "She could provide schedules, the layout of the buildings, other intel. Then she leaves and a month or two later, someone turns up with a silver blade in their heart. Who'd suspect an airhead fashionista?"

"Or maybe," Talon pointed out, "the prima knew she was a slayer. Remember what people said, that Victorine had bribed some of SI's top people to intervene in her blood feud with the Krals."

I'd wondered that myself. "It's possible. I'm fairly sure Victorine hired her to spy on Zoe. Not that Zoe would say anything."

"And you're taking the woman back to Nova Scotia with us?" Cain shook his head. "You'd better lock up the knives and keep her chained to your bed."

I shrugged. "I can handle her."

"Don't forget she's a slayer, not a ditzy Instagram influencer—and she had everyone fooled. Even you."

"She's a human," I returned. "You really think she can take me? And if she gives me any trouble, I'll confine her to a cell. Now if we're finished here—?"

Talon was closer to the door. He put a hand on the handle but didn't turn it.

"What?" I asked.

"Your father can't know she means anything to you," he stated. "He has to think she's just another thrall."

"Or he'll want her for himself," Cain added. "And then—"

"Yeah," I replied grimly. "I know. He might grab her like he did Gwen."

Jules had seized the thrall one night after she'd left me. He'd locked himself into his apartment with her and remained there, abusing her and drinking from her until she died from the beatings and the blood loss.

And I hadn't been able to stop it. Jules was the primus. He could do whatever he damned well pleased.

Maybe he'd believed Gwen was special to me, even though she wasn't. I didn't let myself get attached to thralls.

But as I'd stared down at Gwen's broken, drained body, I finally accepted the truth. My father was going blood mad.

Back in my suite, Twilight was curled up on the couch, a half-eaten plate of food on her lap. She glanced at me and put the drumstick she was about to bite into back on the plate. "What's wrong?"

"Nothing that concerns you."

"Right," she said flatly. She sipped some water, looked me up and down. "First time I've seen you in jeans."

"I don't always wear suits."

"But even when you wear jeans, they're designer. Those are Balmain, aren't they? Uber-trendy and they cost something like fifteen hundred dollars."

"So I have money." I took the armchair next to her and stretched out my legs. "What's your point?"

Actually, I didn't know what brand the damn jeans were, or how much they cost. My personal assistant Avril bought most of my clothes.

"Not that you're rich. That even when you wear jeans, they're the perfect choice. Like the 'Perfect Prince.'" She made air quotes around the phrase.

She was starting to get to me. "I'm not perfect," I said in a voice as flat as hers. "And I fucking hate that hashtag." If I ever discovered who'd started it, I was going to mess them up.

"It fits," she muttered.

"Finish your dinner," I growled. "You look like you need it."

With a shrug, she reached for the drumstick again. Her pearly teeth sank into the meat, delicately greedy.

I didn't usually watch humans eat. When you're born a blood drinker, the foods that humans find delicious can turn your stomach.

Fried bird parts? Mashed-up goose liver? And don't get me started on tofu...

But seeing Twilight bliss out over her dinner was better than fore-play. I couldn't stop looking at her. The blood craving awoke, a low thrum in my veins.

Finishing the drumstick, she spread foie gras on a piece of the baguette and took a bite. Her eyes closed in pleasure.

"This is so good. Everything is."

I grunted, my mind's eye seeing those soft, warm lips closing around my dick instead of the bread. I shifted on the chair, looked away. I *would* keep the upper hand this time around...even if it killed me.

"So." She glanced at where my unbuttoned shirt gaped open over my abdomen and trailed off like she'd forgotten what she'd meant to say.

Maybe this thing wasn't as one-sided as I'd believed.

"So." She took a sip of wine. "What happens now?"

My gaze flicked to her throat. The craving increased.

I went to the wet bar for a glass of blood-wine. "I have to be here another night. You'll be allowed out during the day, but only with a guard."

"Fuck you, too," she muttered.

"You don't think I know you'd leave as soon as we fell asleep?"

"You could try trusting me."

I simply looked at her.

Her mouth thinned. Leaning forward, she plucked a strawberry from the bowl on the tray, exposing her back and the rose-and-dagger tattoo.

That tat was the biggest mystery of all. How had she fallen so far? What had happened to turn a slayer—and a good one, according to the PI—into a blood slave?

Twilight glanced at me over her shoulder and caught me staring. She straightened and turned sideways so I couldn't see her back.

"And then what happens—after tomorrow night?"

I took my wine around the couch and sat down beside her. "Then we leave here."

She put the strawberry down and set the plate on the coffee table. "To go where?"

"You don't need to know."

"Why not? Who would I tell?"

"I'm not worried about that. You're not going to have access to any communication devices."

"Then why not tell me?"

Setting my wine on the table, I reached for her hair. She seemed calmer now, but I sensed the fear beneath the sass. A better man would try to ease her fears.

But I wasn't feeling nice. Not tonight.

"Your hair grows fast." I wrapped the silky dark tresses around my palm, turn by turn, forcing her to scoot closer to me on the couch until our hips were touching.

"Stop it." She put a hand on my chest. "I know you're going to let me go."

"Am I?"

I tightened my grip on her hair, half-expecting her to try and shove me away. Maybe I would've let her and maybe I wouldn't. Like I said, I wasn't feeling particularly nice.

But she didn't try to push me away. Instead, she slid her hand up, stroking a thumb over my collarbone, although stopping short of my throat. She knew not to touch a vampire's throat without permission.

I tugged on her hair, drawing her head back so her long, pretty neck was exposed to my hungry gaze. Her muscles worked, and my fangs tingled.

After all, holding off—being *nice*—had gotten me nothing.

That night in Montreal, she'd held me so tight, like I meant something to her. Said things—*I want you, so much*; *I'll see you tomorrow*; *yes, I promise I'll be there*—and then vanished like the earth had opened up and swallowed her whole.

Nice wasn't my natural inclination. I was, after all, vampire-born.

A predator.

A rare pureblood born to two vampire parents. Raised on blood, not milk. Tutored with blows and harsh words, not kindness. Taught to take, not ask.

And I was starving. For her.

Only for her.

My fangs lengthened. I scraped the sharp points over her creamy beige skin. A single drop of blood welled. I licked it, taking her flavor into my mouth, savoring my first taste of her.

She was...perfect. Sexy, spicy, feminine.

Twilight shuddered. Her hand gripped my shoulder.

And she still hadn't tried to push me away.

I licked my way to her ear and nibbled the lobe. "You want the truth?"

"Yes." A single, breathy word. She gulped and spoke again, more firmly. "Yes."

I retracted my fangs. I *would* feed from her. My vampire wouldn't let her go now.

But not tonight. She needed to recuperate, gain some weight. I might be hungry, but I wasn't a monster. And even if she were in good health, something was funny about this whole setup. I didn't need Cain and Talon to point that out.

"You're mine now." I gave her hair a slight tug. "I own you, love. All you need to know is you'll be with me. You'll go wherever I say, do what I tell you to do. Or weren't you paying attention when I bought you for four mil?"

She sucked in a shocked breath and drew back as far as she could with my hand in her hair. A small part of me was ashamed, but the rest felt an unholy satisfaction, wanted to hurt her just a little for leaving me like that.

Then her mouth pulled into a twisted smile. "Of course, sir."

She grabbed the wrist of the hand I had twined in her hair and lowered herself to her knees in front of the couch. Startled, I went along with it.

Brushing my shirt tails out of the way, she undid the button of my jeans. My hand tightened in her hair, my eyes locked on the fingers skillfully undressing me. My anger still simmered, but my dick didn't care. Hell, the anger was like a lit match to my hunger, adding to the heat lapping at my spine.

She eased the zipper down over my erection. I'd gone

commando after my shower, and it pushed out of the opening, blood-engorged and straining toward her. She fisted me and licked the slit.

Her tongue was hot and wet. I made a sound: part sigh, part groan.

She cast a look up at me, lips still twisted. Somewhere in my lust-drenched brain a lightbulb flashed.

She wasn't turned on. She wasn't doing this because she wanted to. She was treating me like a goddamn job.

My fingers tightened on her hair. This time I didn't intend to hurt her, but I did. She winced but remained where she was, gazing up at me scornfully.

"Stop." My voice was a raw scrape in my throat.

"Isn't this what you want?" She stroked a palm down my hard length. "Sir."

I swore. A sharp, foul word. My dick loved her calling me *sir*, but not like this.

"Stand up, damn you."

She started to scramble back up. I helped, grabbing her arm with my free hand and dragging her ungently to her feet.

I unwound my hand from her hair and jerked my chin at the couch. "Sit."

She swiped the back of her hand over her mouth, eyes narrowed with challenge. "What's wrong?"

"Just sit the fuck down."

"Or else what?"

"*Now*," I snarled, and her sense of self-preservation finally kicked in. She sat, although on the armchair, not the couch.

I came to my feet, pulling up my jeans but leaving them undone. Crossing the small space between us, I leaned over and wrapped my fingers around her nape.

"Don't *ever* check out on me like that again."

"You *own* me, remember? As long as you get off, why do you care?"

My back teeth set. "It's not like that. Between us."

"It is now, *sir*."

"Do *not* call me 'sir.' Not unless you mean it."

"Then what should I call you? My lord?"

Goddamn her anyway. How had she managed to turn the tables on me? To make me feel guilty for treating her like property?

But I'd realized one thing. I might want to own Twilight, but I wanted her to like it.

And yeah, I knew that was fucked up. That I wasn't being rational.

But I couldn't help myself.

She opened her mouth to say something else and I stopped her with a furious kiss. She made a soft, mewling sound.

Hades. I'd hurt her.

My gut clenched. I lifted my head.

But she grabbed me by the shirt and pulled me back to her. Our kiss this time was raw, needy. Real.

Somehow, we were both on our knees. Still kissing her, I released her chin and cupped her face between my palms. She pushed my shirt down my shoulders and our bodies aligned, her nipples hard against my bare chest, my erection against her warm belly.

It wasn't enough. Not what I wanted, needed. To be inside her again after two long years.

Her pelvis rocked against me. She tore her mouth from mine. "Touch me, damn you."

She wanted me. She couldn't hide her racing heart, her needy gasps.

Something in me settled. Shrugging off the shirt, I traced a finger down her throat.

Claiming it. Claiming *her*, even if she didn't realize it yet.

She licked her kiss-swollen lips. "Brien?" Her eyes were darker, sultry, just as I remembered.

"That's better."

I moved my hands to her shoulders, nudging off first one strap, then the other. No bra. The silky black dress slipped down her torso, catching on the tips of her breasts, which was erotic as fuck.

My hands raised of their own volition. I covered her breasts with my palms, teasing the nipples with my thumbs. Her head fell back and I couldn't help myself. I nipped her throat.

She moaned, and the vibration went straight to my balls.

I jerked her dress down to her thighs and cupped her mound over her tiny red panties. She was hot, the silky material soaked.

Triumph surged through me.

She really did want this—me. That much wasn't a lie.

I rubbed her swollen clit through the panties.

"Jesus," she said hoarsely and brushed my hand aside so she could shove the dress and panties the rest of the way down.

They stuck on her ankles, and I lifted her with one arm and dragged them off with the other hand. Then her legs were wrapped around me, the wet heat of her pressed against my dick.

I prided myself on my self-control, but Twilight had undone me with nothing more than a kiss and a scrap of red satin. Her arms wrapped around me and her heels dug into the backs of my legs.

I put an arm around her waist, arching her over the armchair until her shoulders almost touched the cushion. Rocking my dick against her. My scruples were all that stood between me and a powerful, all-consuming physical gratification.

Gods, I wanted to drown myself in her. To forget my father and the syndicate and all the other issues banging around in my brain, like why Twilight had been offered up at auction on the very night Régis had invited me to attend.

And how to protect her from my father.

Her long, tip-tilted eyes were closed, the lashes dark crescents against her cheeks. Her breasts were small and firm, the nipples a tight plum-brown.

I nuzzled her cheek. She smelled like wine and strawberries, and I was starving for her. So damn turned on, my muscles straining toward her like I was a runner and she the finish line, the only goal that mattered in my straitjacket of a life.

I drew a slow breath, ignoring the ache in my balls. Holding back, just to be sure I had myself under control.

Her eyes opened. A perplexed line appeared between her brows.

But I'd mastered myself, enough to know that I wasn't going to finish this, not tonight. I'd stick with the plan.

Take her back to Nova Scotia, install her in the castle with the other thralls. Buy myself time to figure out what to do with her.

Because I *would* own Twilight—and not just her body.

I wanted her soul.

That didn't mean I wasn't going to let her come tonight. I wanted to see her climax, to have her understand that it was me giving her pleasure. A mind-blowing, see-what-you've-been-missing orgasm.

I lowered my head and drew a tightly furled nipple into my mouth. That drove her crazy, I recalled. I remembered everything about the one time I'd had her, including that when you toyed with her tits, she got so hot she almost came.

I sucked hard, enjoying how she arched into my mouth and, with a raspy *Oh, God*, gripped my skull, holding me against her.

With my left hand, I teased her other nipple, rolling it between my fingers and pinching it.

Her free hand pushed at my waistband. "Take off your jeans."

I released her nipple. "I don't think so." I moved my mouth to her other breast, giving it the same treatment.

She snaked a hand between us and tried to stroke my cock, but I pushed it away.

She made a small, needy sound. "Brien. I want this. I'm not pretending now. *Please*."

Damn, I liked hearing her beg. In fact, I fucking loved it.

If I had my way, she'd be doing a lot of begging in the future.

I raised my head and kissed her, then hooked an arm beneath her hips and set her ass back on the chair. Her lip gloss had worn off, leaving her mouth a soft rose. Her long dark hair tumbled over her breasts and shoulders, and her thighs were splayed open, her heels on the seat cushion, her pussy bared to me, the lips plump and glistening.

I shoved my jeans down my thighs, unable to stand even the soft brush of the open zipper against my cock any longer.

She shot my erection a greedy look, then licked her lips.

It was like she'd tongued me. Slowly.

My groin tightened. Pre-cum coated the head.

I fisted myself, giving myself a few hard strokes to take the edge off. Then I gripped her open thighs and swiped my tongue up her center. Her salty woman scent filled my nose, my lungs, my brain.

She hissed with pleasure and moved restlessly against my mouth, tunneling her fingers into my hair, tightening her strong thighs around my head.

I sucked on her clit and her hips bucked. I held her down against the chair and kept it up, at times swirling my tongue around her swollen bud, at times drawing it into my mouth.

Her head thrashed against the seatback. "Fuck me, fuck me, fuck me."

My lips moved against her swollen bud. "Come for me. *Now*."

I gave it a hard suck, and she broke, crying out my name, low and hoarse.

It was the sound of *Brien* on her lips that made me crack. My fangs pressed against my gums, the blood craving—the hunger for this one woman of all the women I'd ever known—too strong to resist.

Flipping her around, I bent her over the chair, her hair spilling over her shoulders and across the embroidered red cushion, then dug a condom from my jeans, the one I'd put in the pocket after my shower. I supposed I'd known how this would end up.

I stood and shoved my jeans the rest of the way off, then worked the condom on. Taking hold of her hips, I rubbed myself against her, bending my knees and pressing between her thighs. Not entering her, just teasing her until she was moaning and pushing back against me.

Wrapping a hand around her throat, I lifted her chin, forcing her to arch her back. Her firm ass pressed against my thighs.

"I'm going to take you," I said against her ear. "So hard. To make you hurt so you know who owns you. And you're going to let me, aren't you?"

Her throat worked beneath my hand.

"Answer me." I nipped her ear.

She hissed. "Yes, damn you. Yes."

She was a good half-foot shorter than me, and even with her legs straight we didn't line up, so I lifted her and draped her over the couch arm instead. She braced her forearms against the arm, and I stroked into her. She closed around me, tight and hot.

At last.

I gritted my teeth. Needing this and yet angry—with her, with myself—at how easily she'd shredded my self-control.

She tightened around me even more. *"Now,* Brien."

I withdrew and thrust back into her. Giving into instinct and burying myself deep inside her. Taking her as I wanted, no holds barred.

Dimly, I was aware that she'd reached her hand between her legs to pleasure herself.

"That's it." I cupped a small, firm breast, taking a nipple and giving it a hard pinch that made her moan. "Make yourself come. I want to feel you squeezing around me."

She turned her head to one side, her hair flowing over one shoulder in a silky midnight waterfall that exposed the side of her throat. "More. Harder. It feels so good..."

My gaze locked on her soft skin. My fangs lengthened.

The darkness in me salivated.

Drink.

Take.

Conquer.

But I wasn't so lost in the blood craving that I'd forgotten they'd fed from her earlier tonight. I couldn't take more blood from her, so I closed my eyes and focused on the sensation of fucking her.

"Oh God, oh God..." Twilight constricted around me as she came a second time.

Pleasure punched up my spine. My balls drew up tight and my hips jerked, hard and fast. I kept thrusting, drawing it out as long as possible, until what felt like a bolt of lightning split apart my brain and I emptied myself into her with an agonized groan.

❧ *5* ❧

TWILIGHT

I hung over the couch arm, a limp, satisfied noodle, my cheek on the brocade cushion. Brien touched his lips to my nape, and a final, heated quiver went over my body.

Holy crap on a cracker.

I was in trouble—big trouble. Sex with him had been even better than I remembered, and I'd remembered plenty. The man had a magic mouth, magic hands, magic...everything.

Two years ago he'd been self-assured, even cocky, with the confidence of a man who'd been born a prince. But the cockiness had an edge now. He'd matured into a tough, top-of-the-food-chain alpha male, and it was sexy as fuck.

Brien straightened and lowered himself into the armchair, pulling me onto his lap. I rested my head on his shoulder, toying with the wiry brown hair on his chest.

I was so tired, and his strength was seductive. It would be too easy to fall for him, to surrender to the electricity that crackled to life whenever we were within ten yards of each other.

It had been eons since I'd felt truly safe. You don't take the slayer's oath if you're looking for things like security and peace of mind.

After I'd staked my alpha, I'd had to hide from everyone, even SI.

Crisscrossing the Americas, picking up odd jobs when and where I could. Suspicious of anyone who looked at me twice.

Then somehow Kuro had found me and strongarmed me into taking the job singing at Le Dahlia Noir. Yeah, I'd had food and a place to sleep, but I'd known it was only temporary. He'd placed me there so I could attract the attention of a Quebec City coven.

"They'll ask you to come work for them," he'd said, "and you'll accept."

Then he'd smiled, and I'd known I was screwed.

At first, I'd been puzzled at how well the coven treated me. They hadn't touched me, except to feed—and even that had been just a few times. And they'd refrained from injecting the aphrodisiac in their saliva into me.

Most of the other thralls were blood addicts—they were too thin, with an addict's glassy zombie eyes. Finally, another thrall had explained they were probably saving me for the next auction.

I'd swallowed sickly at the pity on her face. "When?"

She'd thrown a look over her shoulder at the guards. "I don't know for sure," she whispered, "but I heard something about August third."

My stomach knotted. "That's next Thursday."

"Yeah." A guard headed our way, and she moved off with a muttered apology.

The hell with Kuro. I'd decided right then to escape and take my chances with SI, but it had been impossible. The thralls were locked in the coven's underground lair except for an hour each afternoon when we were allowed outside.

Brien combed his fingers through my hair. "I like it long. It suits you."

My eyes flew open. I shrugged and gave him a truth. Blame it on my exhaustion and that sense of safety.

"I hate it. I only grew it long as a disguise. I can't wait to cut it off."

He stilled. "No. I forbid you to cut it."

He what?

I pulled back to look him in the eye. "Try and stop me, *sir*."

His eyes hooded. "I could, you know. Stop you." The threat was clear.

"Yeah." My smile was razor-thin. "You could. But sooner or later, someone will slip. And I can be all kinds of creative with sharp things."

He drew me back against his chest. I could've fought him, but I was drowsy and wallowing in the afterglow, so I let him. But I held myself stiff, my fingers curled into fists so I wouldn't forget and begin petting him again.

"I don't want to fight with you," he said, low-voiced.

"Then don't threaten me or give me orders."

"I should've known you'd be difficult."

"Then why buy me?"

"I told you. I couldn't leave you there—your life would've been hell with either of those other two bidders. And it wouldn't have been a long life."

I scoffed. "So this was you rescuing me."

"I thought you needed it," he said simply.

I lifted my head and made sure he saw my curled lip, but inside, my stomach bottomed out, because I *had* needed to be rescued—and I hated it. Hated feeling helpless like that. But without Brien, right now I'd belong to a sadistic vampire, a man who apparently would've used me until I died a cold, painful death.

Brien didn't even know the worst of it, that I'd killed Crow and thought I'd gotten away with it...until that night at a Costa Rican bar when someone had tapped my shoulder and I'd turned to see a stranger with prominent, all-seeing eyes. An Asian-American like me, although not of Korean descent. Japanese, maybe, since he'd told me to call him Kuro.

But he'd known me: my slayer code name, Twilight. Known that I'd been born in San Francisco but had grown up in LA. However, it was when he'd let drop that he knew both my mother and grandmother had been slayers, too that all the blood drained from my cheeks. He even knew it had been my mom who'd pushed to get me accepted at an SI training camp when I was twelve, a year earlier than most slayers-in-training.

Only a member of SI's Board of Directors could've known all that.

I was still reeling when Kuro dropped his final bombshell. He knew about Crow. That I'd staked her—the North American alpha—after she'd ordered me to kill my best friend Ridley.

Brien traced a finger down the red dagger on my spine.

I stiffened. The skin had healed, but even after four months, it was sensitive. Maybe because I still hadn't accepted how drastically my life had changed.

"One thing I've been wondering," he said.

"What?"

"Your tattoo." His fingertip followed the stem of the rose twined around the dagger's blade. "A slayer doesn't have tats."

I tossed him a taunting smile. "Don't tell me you haven't figured it out."

"I can think of two explanations. The most obvious is you're not a slayer anymore. Maybe you've even been disgraced—kicked out. That would also explain why you ended up singing at Le Dahlia Noir. The PI told me you had some money put away, but I'm guessing it ran out."

My smile faded. He was within spitting distance of the truth.

I'd been forced to accept that tattoo. Kuro had said that if I fought back, he'd handcuff me to the table and the end result would be the same.

So I'd obeyed, each prick of the needle reminding me that I was no longer a slayer—and might never be again.

I hadn't moved or made a sound the whole time. Not even when my back had grown slick with blood and my mouth filled with the taste of bitter iron from the hole my teeth had torn in my lower lip.

I was Twilight. Daughter of Shade, granddaughter of Ghost.

I'd survived SI training camp. I was damned if I'd let this bastard break me now.

Brien's eyes narrowed.

"Or?" I asked to wipe that considering look from his face.

His face hardened. "Or you're still a slayer, and this is an elaborate ruse—the auction, the tattoo. A way to insinuate yourself into my life and my syndicate."

My laugh held zero humor. "You nailed it." I pushed off his lap and turned to face him. "I got the tat and let myself be ensnared by that fucking Quebec City coven, because I somehow knew you were going to be at the auction last night. Five hundred miles from where you live."

But Kuro could've known, muttered a small voice.

Brien came to his feet and loomed over me. "And yet, there you were. The woman I've been searching for. The one woman I would've never let go to another vampire."

I stared up at him, a crater-sized lump filling my throat. "You were still searching for me? It's been two years…"

I meant that much to you?

His face shut down like I'd pushed a button. "You—I wasn't finished with you. And I don't like it when people make promises they don't keep."

"Oh, I see." I snorted. "*I* left *you* instead of the other way around. Perfect Prince Brien couldn't stand knowing that a woman might not want to stick around for a second act."

His mouth turned down. "Don't. Call. Me. That."

"What? Perfect Prince Brien? That's what they call you on social media, you know."

Okay, I'd started that hashtag myself. But it had stuck because it fit.

"Fuck social media. But you—" He ran his fingers through his hair. It was almost dry now, with strands of gold and bronze mixing with the blond. "Just don't, okay? I am *not* perfect."

His expression was oddly naked, like it mattered that I understand he wasn't perfect. It tugged at my heart, something I couldn't allow.

"Fine." I grabbed my dress and shimmied into it. "Whatever. You're the boss, right?"

He watched me pull up the straps and smooth down the skirt. "Twilight…"

"What?"

"Why are you here? Really?"

I nailed him with a fuck-you smile. "Because you bought me, *sir*. And as you keep saying, you own me now."

He waved that aside. "Not here with me. Here in Quebec. If you're not a slayer anymore, why are you singing in Canada? You're from California, right?"

I swallowed. Beneath that supermodel exterior, the man was smart. What's more, he was close to the truth. Too close.

The tattoo had been to punish me for staking my alpha, but now that I'd ended up with Brien, I had to wonder if Kuro had had another, hidden reason. Maybe he'd wanted to allay suspicions that I was an undercover slayer.

I wasn't. At least, I wasn't with Slayers, Inc. any longer. My strings were being pulled by one man, Kuro. But if Kuro really was a member of the BOD, then maybe, just maybe, he was my way back into the organization.

"Haven't you figured it out yet? I'm on the run from SI. The first place they'd look for me is LA or San Francisco. I've stayed away from the West Coast. This is the first time I've even been back to North America in over a year. I mean, who'd look for me in northern Quebec?"

Every word was true, and I knew Brien would sense that.

What I'd left off was the part about Kuro finding me in Costa Rica and sending me to Quebec City and Le Dahlia Noir.

"I see." Brien rubbed a hand over his face. His eyelids dropped, reminding me of how young he was for a vampire. The approaching dawn was tugging him into the day sleep.

"You don't believe me?" I asked. "Then send me away."

That made his eyes open wide. The rim around his irises flashed a dangerous blue. "You'd like that, wouldn't you?"

"Maybe." Instead of moving back like a sane person would when faced with an irate vampire, I stalked closer, trailed a finger down his chest. "Maybe not. There are some...benefits, I guess."

His breath caught. He caught my hand and brought my wrist to his lips. "I'll see you tonight," he said against the tender skin. "I suggest you get some sleep. I'll be keeping you busy."

"Yes, sir." I said it to irritate him, but he simply grinned, a wicked curve of his mouth, and then scraped his teeth over my inner wrist.

The tremor that went over me was purely sexual. I jerked my hand from his, hating how easily he could turn me on.

His mouth flattened. "Inside." He indicated his bedroom.

"You want me to sleep with you?"

"I'd have to trust you to allow that. No, I'm going to lock you in there."

He indicated the door in hidden in the wallpaper. The one hiding the small, windowless bedroom.

Panic smacked me in the chest. My lungs constricted, and for a frightening few seconds, I couldn't get enough oxygen.

"No." I took a step back, shaking my head. "Please. I swear I won't try anything."

"Too bad I don't believe you." He grabbed my arm, and I broke, twisting out of his grip and running for the door, desperately trying to figure out the code to unlock it.

When I couldn't, I pounded the wood with my fists. "Let me out!" My breath sobbed in. "Let me out! Please, somebody, *let me out*."

"Twilight." Brien took me by the shoulders, and I exploded, twisting and fighting to get away. "Hey, hey," he said, but I didn't really hear him.

I slammed my heel down on the metatarsals of his right foot, and although he swore under his breath, he didn't release me, so I went for his balls with my right hand. He was too fast for me, though, knocking my clawed fingers aside with his knee. The next thing I knew, I was enveloped in a bear hug, my arms against my sides.

"Sweet Lilith." Lifting me off my feet, he gave me a hard squeeze. "Calm the fuck down. *Now*."

I thrashed wildly, kicking back at him until he wrapped a powerful leg around both of my legs, restraining me.

I kept struggling, face hot, chest jerking, even though I knew it was hopeless. "*No*. Don't do this. *Please*."

"Twilight." He pitched his voice low, soothing. "Chill out. I didn't understand, all right? Settle down, and we'll talk about it."

I shuddered and stopped fighting, hanging in his arms, tears streaming down my face. He waited until I drew a ragged breath.

"You okay?"

I sniffed and nodded. "You can put me down now," I mumbled, ashamed and humiliated at my loss of control.

"You sure?"

"Yes."

He put me on my feet and turned me around. "You really are afraid to be locked in there." He ran his hands up and down my arms. "I can feel it. It's not an act."

I jerked a shoulder, keeping my gaze on his chest. His sternum had a red mark from where I must have jabbed him with my elbow. More shame washed over me.

"All right," he said. "I can't let you stay in here, not while I'm asleep, but there's an empty suite next door that you can have. But you'll be locked in—that's non-negotiable."

"Okay." It wouldn't be easy—I hated being locked in at all—but as long as it wasn't a dark, cramped box like the room he'd ordered me into, I could deal.

He lowered me into an armchair and handed me a glass of water, then pulled on his boxers and sent a text to someone. While we waited, he dampened a washrag and wiped the tears from my face, so gently I felt my eyes sting again.

A knock sounded on the hall door. "It's Talon," said a deep voice.

Brien invited him in and told him to put me in the empty suite for the night. "Lock her in and put a guard outside her door."

Talon's brows climbed, but he nodded. "No problem."

"Tomorrow," Brien added, "she's to be allowed as much time as she wants outside. And have Avril order her some clothes—she needs something besides that evening gown."

"Will do," said Talon.

Brien stroked the backs of his fingers down my tear-damp cheeks. "I'll see you tomorrow night."

I caught his wrist. "Thanks."

"Don't thank me. You're mine now. And I take care of what's mine."

The suite they put me in was similar to Brien's. Talon waited until I'd turned on the light before locking the door.

I still had a spurt of panic as the door locked behind him, but this time, I was prepared. I set my jaw, fisted my hands and took several deep breaths. Then I took a long, hot shower before crawling into bed.

When I woke up, I had no idea what time it was. No clocks, of course; vampires can sense the passing of time.

My empty stomach announced it was time for breakfast, or maybe even lunch. The first thing I did was to try the outer door again. It was still locked.

I hammered my fist on the door. "Hey, I could use a little food here."

"I'll inform the cook," said a voice from the other side.

"Thank you," I called back.

That's when I saw the packages piled on the couch. I forgot my hunger and made a beeline for the couch. Yeah, Lainey Q had been a cover, but the best disguises contain something of yourself, and I have a weakness for pretty, quirky clothes and these were just what I would've picked out for myself if I had the money for expensive, one-of-a-kind pieces.

I may even have squealed when I saw the red patent-leather Christian Louboutin stiletto heels. And I gasped when I unboxed the silver Prada high-tops.

I found everything I needed, including underwear, and all in my size. I shimmied into a pair of silver shorts and a trendy black tee with a lace-up neckline.

I was pulling on a pair of pink socks when a woman knocked on my door, calling in French, "May I come in?"

"*Oui, bien sûr*," I returned.

The lock disengaged and a woman in black pants and a crisp white shirt entered with a tray of food holding a typical French breakfast: buttery croissants, three small quiches and fresh fruit. She'd even brought a pot of coffee and a tiny pitcher of cream.

My stomach growled as she set it on the coffee table. "This looks great," I said. "Thank you."

"I am the housekeeper here," she informed me in English. "Do you have need of anything else?"

I shook my head. "No, thanks. This should be enough."

She didn't return my smile. "I'll return when you have finished."

Which meant they were observing me through a hidden camera. I cast an involuntary look around. Had they watched me change? Then I mentally shrugged. I didn't mind being naked in front of other people, although I'd rather it be on my terms.

I folded my arms over my chest. "When I'm done eating, I want to go outside."

The housekeeper inclined her head. "Of course."

As soon as the door closed behind her, I fell on the food. When I'd eaten my fill, I brushed my teeth and laced on the Prada high-tops, then set a pink baseball cap on my head and went to the door, prepared to make a nuisance of myself until they let me out.

But as I reached the door, it opened, and I was greeted by a tall man in a royal blue Maritime Syndicate uniform with a silver shark embroidered on the lapel. "Good afternoon, miss. I'm here to take you outside."

"Awesome." I grinned up at him. "I'm ready."

He, at least, returned my smile. Then his lips pressed into a thin line, like he'd been ordered not to engage with me.

He waved a hand for me to proceed him down the hall. "This way."

6

BRIEN

"Régis asked about Jules," I told Cain and Talon. "At the auction last night. He said he's heard rumors that he's not well."

We'd gathered in my suite at the chateau after the final meeting with Régis. I hadn't seen Twilight yet that night, but according to Avril, she'd eaten three substantial meals and spent most of the day outside, walking through the vineyards and swimming in the chateau pool.

"Fuck." Cain's lean, almost-pretty face darkened. He rose from a leather armchair to prowl restlessly around the parlor. "I thought we'd have more time."

"I told him it wasn't true, of course, but—" I sank into the armchair Cain had abandoned.

Talon was sprawled on the couch across from me, arms folded behind his head. He appeared relaxed, but I knew his analytical mind would be sifting through the implications.

"Someone in the syndicate must've leaked it," said Cain. "There's no other explanation."

"Yeah." My mouth tightened.

Jules had been going steadily downhill ever since my mother had been staked in the woods near the castle. No witnesses and no weapon left behind. Just a ruby bracelet, her gold mate-ceremony ring, and a pile of ashes.

My father was a vicious SOB, but my mother had been his other half. They'd ruled as a pair, unusual in the syndicate world, but they'd shared such a close bond it was as if they spoke with one mind.

He'd thrown everything he had into finding who had sent her to her final grave. People had been bribed. Tortured. Murdered.

But her slayer had never been identified.

Meanwhile, I'd taken over running the syndicate—temporarily, I'd believed.

However, something in my father had broken. All he thought about was avenging my mother's death, and when he'd been unable to find her killer, his health had deteriorated.

Then, a few months ago he'd attacked Gwen. Cain and Talon had helped me spirit the body out of the castle and bury it deep in the forest. The official story was that she'd slipped off a cliff, hit her head and drowned. My father's lieutenant, Prosper, had paid a visit to Gwen's parents to keep them from asking questions, and I'd followed up with a large cash "gift."

One death, we could cover up, but not two. I had to do something about my father, and soon. But it was tricky.

Jules was my sire. Stake him, and the hierarchy might turn on me. To a vampire, staking your own sire is a taboo you didn't break.

I hadn't even wanted to come on this fucking trip but Prosper had said I couldn't insult Régis by cancelling at the last minute. He'd keep an eye on things, he told me. So I'd gone, even though I wasn't sure whose side Prosper was on these days.

Talon stirred. "The best way to counteract the rumors would be to have your father appear in public. He hasn't started to smell yet —we still have a little time before it's obvious he's going blood mad."

"It's too risky," I said. "He's too unpredictable—you never know how he'll be from one night to the next. And sometimes when you talk to him, it's like he's not all there. He just stares at you without saying anything."

A fixed, psychopathic stare.

Cain scrubbed a hand over his short white-blond hair. "What does Prosper say?"

"Nothing. You know him. He plays his cards close to the chest."

"Yeah." Cain's mouth bent down, and I felt my own do the same.

The alliance between Prosper and my father dated to when my father had first arrived from France. Prosper, an indigenous Canadian who knew both the local terrain and the politics of the various groups jockeying for power—the English, French and assorted First Nations governments—had been key in helping Jules found the Maritime Syndicate.

Within a decade, Jules had turned Prosper and brought him into the syndicate as a soldier. Prosper had shot up the hierarchy, eventually becoming Jules's lieutenant and righthand man, and there he remained, my father's most loyal ally.

But not mine.

Talon sat up. "He'll challenge you the minute the primus is in his final grave. He'll never accept you as his dominant."

"I know. But hell, if the situations were reversed, I'd probably do the same thing." I gave a wolfish grin. "And I say, bring it on—because I *will* win. I know all his tricks, and a few he won't be expecting."

Talon's answering smile was as toothy as my own.

"You're faster than him, too," said Cain. "You'll win, all right, which is why you have to watch your back. He might take you out the same way they got Prima Lenore. I've never been sure that he wasn't behind her attack, anyway."

I shook my head. "I don't think so. To him, my mother was part of the team, someone he respected. And he may be an SOB, but he's not a coward. If he had a problem with my mother, he would've confronted her to her face, not ambushed her."

"Whatever goes down, you know we're with you," said Cain, and Talon grunted assent.

"I know." I cast them both a grateful look. "And I'm grateful as hell that you two are on my side. But a challenge from Prosper could be a good thing—the tension between us is making the upper hierarchy edgy. Take him out, and the other high-ranking vampires will fall into line. Otherwise, I could find myself fighting multiple challenges."

"True," said Talon. "But that's the future. First, we have to do something about Jules."

I grimaced. "Yeah. But—"

A knock on the door interrupted us. "We'll finish this tonight," I said as my PA said, "It's me, Avril."

Cain opened the door. "The thralls are ready?"

"They are," Avril said. "The jet is on standby and the cars are in the courtyard. I've given the order to load the luggage."

Talon and I came to our feet. "Tell the thralls we're leaving in ten minutes," I told her. "Cain and Talon will meet them in the courtyard. But not the new thrall—I'll escort her outside myself."

"Very good, my lord." Avril left.

Cain frowned. "You sure you want to bring Twilight to the island? You could give her some money and put her on a plane to the States."

I didn't have to look at Talon to know he was nodding agreement.

Fuck that. I was damned if I'd leave Twilight behind now that I'd finally found her.

"I'm sure." I brushed past them into the hall.

7

TWILIGHT

By the time we got to Nova Scotia, the coming dawn had smudged the horizon a hazy pink. We broke through the clouds, flying low over the ocean. The jet banked to the right and Lilith Island came into view.

My stomach gave an uneasy flutter.

I'd known the island, named after the vampires' Dark Lady, was a dozen miles off Nova Scotia's coast, with no way on or off except by boat or aircraft—controlled, of course, by Brien's syndicate. Still, you had to see Lilith Island from the air to understand how isolated it was. A jagged chunk of land surrounded by the North Atlantic's cold, inky waters.

I wasn't leaving until Brien allowed me to leave, and without a phone or other device, I couldn't contact anyone for help, either.

Not that I had anyone *to* contact.

Brien eyed me from the comfortable leather seat next to mine. He'd loosened his tie and undone the first couple of buttons of his shirt, and something about his expression made me think he was recalling last night.

Heat swirled through my lower abdomen. I squirmed on the seat, and a corner of his mouth kicked up.

I dragged my gaze back to the window. I could see Castle Leclerc now, its four black towers rising from a wispy fog like something out of a gothic novel.

Brien spoke into my ear. "The ocean here has wicked currents."

I snorted. "You must think I'm an Olympic-class swimmer."

"The ocean's too cold for humans to last for more than a few minutes, anyway—and the water is infested with great whites. We encourage them." He sat back, his mouth curved in a very sharklike smile. "Oh, and by the way, the castle grounds are patrolled by wolf-dogs and their handlers."

"You're worried I'll try and escape." I dredged up my best Lucy-Liu grin, all badass confidence. "How...cute."

"What the fuck's that supposed to mean?"

"It means, this isn't you. You don't keep blood slaves. You're going to let me go."

His green eyes hooded. "Will I?"

I swallowed. Maybe I didn't know him as well as I thought I did.

I lifted my chin. "Yes. You can start by allowing me to have a phone. It's medieval, keeping me incommunicado like this."

"A phone?" His look said I was out of my freaking mind. "I'd have to trust you to give you a phone."

I rolled my lips in. He was right not to trust me, but it still hurt.

"Whatever." I ran my fingers up his thigh, taking a savage satisfaction in how his gaze followed the movement. "I can wait." I stopped just short of the erection pressing against his zipper. "Like I said, the perks aren't bad."

He lifted his eyes. I gulped at the heat in them. He caught my hand and brought it to his lips, scraping his teeth over the wrist.

"I hope," he said, "that I can do better than *not bad*."

I moistened my lips, searching for a comeback, but my mind was picturing what could be better than last night.

His expression was darkly amused. "Later." He put my hand back in my lap.

I swallowed dryly. *Later.*

I couldn't wait, damn him. He could seduce me with a few words and a touch. I was loose-limbed and wet, just thinking about *later*.

Brien turned to say something to Cain and Talon, and I settled deeper into my seat. That's when I felt the crinkle of paper in the back pocket of my chinos.

WTF?

When we'd left for the airport, my pockets had been empty. I surreptitiously touched the pocket and confirmed there was what felt like a folded piece of paper in it.

The pilot aimed the small jet for a narrow landing strip in the forest near the castle. As the plane descended over the thick trees, I mentally tallied everyone on board other than Brien and myself—Cain, Talon, a trio of thralls, Brien's PA, and two Maritime soldiers. In addition, there was a pilot, co-pilot and a flight attendant.

I could rule out the pilot and co-pilot; they remained in the cockpit for the entire flight, and when they'd greeted Brien before takeoff, they'd been several feet away.

Cain and Talon appeared loyal to Brien. Although with vampires, especially syndicate vampires, you never knew for sure; their first loyalty was usually to themselves. Still, they seemed close to Brien, and as "made" men, they'd have sworn an oath of loyalty to the Maritime Syndicate.

That left seven possibilities: the thralls, the flight attendant, the soldiers and Brien's PA. The thralls—Eden, Lesa and Pinky—were all curvy model-types who didn't seem interested in anything but money, sex and clothes. But then, no one knew better than me how easy it is to fake that kind of thing.

The flight attendant, Russell, was a smiling, let-me-entertain-you kind of guy, which could also be a cover. People tend to assume there's nothing beneath the upbeat veneer.

Then there was Avril, Brien's red-haired, thirty-something PA. She'd worked for Brien for years, and, from the way she eyed him when he wasn't watching, she was half in love with him. I couldn't see her agreeing to work for Kuro for any amount of money, unless, of course, he'd blackmailed her into doing it.

And the soldiers were both Canadian dhampirs who, like Cain and Talon, would've sworn an oath of loyalty to the syndicate.

Could Kuro's reach extend into the Maritime Syndicate itself? SI had spies everywhere in the vampire world.

I stifled a sudden, inappropriate urge to laugh. *Girl, you are* so *fucked.*

I shifted on my seat. Crossed and uncrossed my ankles.

"Hey." Brien put his hand over mine. "You're under my protection. No one's going to touch you."

I drew a slow breath. He shouldn't have picked up on my agitation; I was trained to hide my emotions from vampires. That Brien had sensed I was upset (even though he'd misunderstood the reason why) was disconcerting. I was losing my edge. Two years out of the game did that to you.

"Except you," I muttered to piss him off. Better that than have him guess something else had upset me.

But he didn't seem pissed off. Instead, he interlaced his fingers through mine in silent reassurance.

My heart lurched. His kindness touched something deep inside me, a lonely, needy corner that I'd learned to ignore.

I curled my fingers around his and stared out the window as the jet touched down. What would he do if I confessed why I was really here, telling him about Kuro and asking for help? Would he believe me, or figure it was a story I'd made up to get him to release me?

He could sense a lie in most humans—it came with a vampire's ability to detect human emotions. But as a slayer, I'd been trained to fool a vampire in the same way a person can learn to trick a lie-detecting machine by suppressing their autonomic nervous system responses. Brien would know that.

The jet rolled to a halt. I pulled my hand from his.

Because in the end, if I was going to somehow fix this mess and be allowed back into SI, Brien was the enemy. A syndicate prince.

He had no reason to believe me, and it might make him even more suspicious. If he decided I was still a slayer, he might lock me up and throw away the key—if he didn't slit my throat and feed me to those sharks he'd tried to scare me with.

The pilot came on the intercom. "My lord, ladies, gentlemen. We've arrived on Lilith Island. Welcome home."

The cabin door opened. Brien grabbed his laptop from the overhead compartment and guided me toward the exit where the crew was lowering the stairs.

Three SUVs and a pickup truck pulled up alongside the jet. Under Russell and Avril's supervision, the passengers were quickly sorted into the vehicles, and we set off for the castle, our luggage following in the truck.

Brien and I were in the lead car along with Cain and Talon. They were silent as we bumped along a cobblestone road through the forest. More fog covered the road and coiled, snakelike, around the dark castle hunkered on the cliff above the trees.

I glanced at Brien and found him staring broodingly back at me. I had to force myself not to fidget.

Not good. Not good at all. If you let him spook you, you're fucked.

"Impressive." I gave him a perky, Lainey-Q smile and waved a hand at the massive black building looming above us. "How long has your family lived here, anyway?"

He shrugged a powerful shoulder. "A couple hundred years."

"They own the island," Cain added.

His tone made it a threat, not a piece of information, but I simply nodded. "I know."

We drove through a stone arch smothered in ivy and came to a halt in a cobblestone courtyard. Brien exited and helped me out. The air was damp with salt spray, and somewhere far below, the surf boomed.

Avril hurried up as the ornate wood doors creaked open. "Can I help you, sir?"

He nodded. "Order Twilight some more clothes, would you? Have them expressed to the island. And make sure you get her a winter coat and other things—sweaters, gloves, whatever—for when it gets colder."

Her brows scrunched together. "She's here to stay, then?"

"Yes." He started up the worn granite steps, the GQ twins on his heels.

Okay, that put me in my place. The entire conversation with Avril had been conducted as if I weren't standing right there, and now he'd entered the castle without bothering to see if I'd follow.

But then, he knew I had nowhere to go.

Avril stared after Brien, her expression wistful, until he was inside the castle. The soldiers and other thralls followed, and Russell got back into one of the SUVs.

Avril flicked me a look and started, like she'd forgotten I was standing there. She straightened her fitted gray suit and touched a hand to her neat red bun.

"Go on in. Kerry—the housekeeper—will show you to your suite."

"You don't live in the castle?"

"Actually, I do—I have an apartment on the second floor. But I want to say hi to my mom and dad. They're just up the road."

"So you're from the island?"

"Born and bred."

I nodded, my mind on the piece of paper in my pocket. This felt like my last chance. Enter the castle, and I was committed to whatever Kuro intended to force me to do. I slid my hand into the pocket, fingering the folded scrap.

The SUVs exited the courtyard, following the road around the castle that the pickup had taken with our luggage.

"Go." Avril made a shooing motion with her hand. "Brien will wonder where you are."

"Right." I lurched into motion, because I was already committed.

Sometimes the only way out is through.

The foyer was large enough to hold a good-sized party in. A mosaic of a curved shark was set into the polished granite floor, illuminated by pearly lightbulbs held in the mouths of sea-serpent sconces. Tapestries depicting each of the four seasons unfurled down the rough stone walls, and the arched ceiling was covered by a painting of the crescent moon in a star-filled night sky.

The thralls and soldiers had scattered, presumably to their own quarters, but Cain and Talon remained near Brien, protecting him even in his own family home. Either they were being extra-cautious, or Brien didn't trust his own people.

A tall, angular woman and a hulking man with a buzzcut, both in blue Maritime uniforms with shark insignias, were waiting to greet the three of them.

Brien gave them an easy smile. "Kerry. William."

A cat, all white except for a single black ear, trotted out of a side door, meowing loudly. "Demon." Scooping the cat up, Brien cradled it to his chest. "Have you been a good girl while I was gone?"

I stared, charmed despite myself, as Demon butted her head against his chin. He scratched her behind her jaw, and she settled deeper into his arms with a contented purr.

"Welcome home, my lord." Kerry's pleased expression transformed her narrow face from plain to intriguing. "Your business went well?"

"It did."

"Good, good." She beamed like a proud mother.

He waved a hand at me. "We have a new thrall—Twilight. I want her in the garden suite."

"The garden suite? Very well." The housekeeper sent me a speculative look.

"I'm going to bed," he told the couple. "Take care of Twilight for me. And William? She can go anywhere she wants, but I want a guard with her at all times."

"Very good, sir," said William.

Kerry's brows raised in surprise. I suppose she was wondering why I required a guard. All I cared about was that I wasn't going to be locked in.

"Thank you," I mouthed at Brien.

He gave a curt nod and strode out of the foyer along with Talon and Cain. As they entered the hall, a man in black pinstripe Armani stepped out of the shadows, intercepting them. Demon hissed and jumped out of Brien's arms, streaking down a side passage.

Jules Leclerc. I would've known Brien's father anywhere. He was a little shorter and thinner than Brien, and he had dark hair, not blond, but the two shared the same handsome, chiseled features.

"Father." Brien inclined his head cooly.

An unpleasant smile warped the older vampire's face. "Where have you been?"

William stepped in front of me, using his broad body to conceal me. "Stay back," he ordered out of the side of his mouth.

My brows climbed, but I was happy to comply. Something about the primus made my Spidey-senses tingle.

"In Quebec City with Régis Dussault," Brien told him. "He agreed to our terms, by the way."

"Negotiating?" asked Jules. "With Régis?" Then he inhaled audibly. "Who's that behind William?"

A chill went over me. My Spidey-senses went from wary to a five-alarm alert.

I instinctively went for the blade I always had hidden in my left shoe before I remembered I didn't have any weapons. I swallowed a curse and brought my hand back to my side.

"No one important," said Brien. "Here, let me tell you about Quebec City. We could've used you there."

Jules snarled. "You shouldn't have gone without my permission. You take too much on yourself."

"My apologies," Brien said tonelessly.

Their footsteps receded. I peeked around William in time to see Jules shake off the hand Brien had placed on his lower back and stalk off ahead of his son. Brien and the other two men followed.

I stared after the four of them. WTF?

Jules was supposed to be an intelligent, ruthless primus, but he'd sounded more like a sulky five-year-old. And where was his mate, Lenore?

Combined with the way the GQ twins had hovered protectively around Brien, something was very wrong at the top of the Maritime Syndicate. Because if I had to guess, I'd say Primus LeClerc was in the early stages of blood madness.

I fingered the folded slip of paper thoughtfully.

"This way, Miss."

Kerry led the way down the side passage that Demon had taken, a stone corridor with slits for windows and only a few doors. Gas torches burned at intervals along the walls, barely penetrating the gloom. It was like I'd been transported back to the time when vampires like Jules Leclerc had ruled their territory with absolute power.

The helplessness I'd felt in Fleur's lair flooded back into me. My steps slowed. I'd thought anything would be better than staying with that cold bitch and her coven. Now, though, I wasn't so sure.

Kerry glanced over her shoulder. "Come with me or not," she said matter-of-factly. "But you should know it's best not to be out and about when Prince Brien takes his day sleep. The primus is old enough to be awake even during the daylight."

That got me moving again. No way did I want to become prey for a blood-mad vampire.

"Thanks for the heads-up," I said.

She hmphed. "Don't thank me. The prince seems taken with you, and it would be more than my job is worth to let harm come to you."

We went down two flights then wound our way through a series of tunnels. If I hadn't had a good sense of direction, I would've been hopelessly lost.

Somewhere beneath the back of the castle, Kerry stopped at a thick, silver-reinforced door. She opened it and gestured for me to precede her into the suite.

My eyes widened. "This is the garden suite?" I'd braced myself for something dark and gothic, but the living room had a relaxed, beachy vibe: warm tropical woods, creamy yellow upholstery, sea-green walls.

"Yes." She nodded at a French door off the living room. "You can access the garden through there."

The door's glass was darkened to protect a vampire's sensitive eyes and skin. But still, it was a window.

I peered through the bedroom doorway at the king-size canopy bed. "Where does Brien sleep?"

Kerry's thin lips pursed. "If the prince wants you to know, he'll tell you."

Oh-kay. Apparently, I wasn't going to find a friend in Kerry.

A man appeared with my two suitcases, and she directed him to put them in the bedroom closet. She waited for him to leave, then told me, "Someone will come for you this afternoon to take you for a walk. Are you hungry? I can order you breakfast."

"No, thanks. I think I'll just lie down for a while. I'd like lunch around one, though," I added, testing her.

"As you wish. The floors are heated for the thralls. It's set on low, but feel free to adjust it. The thermostat's next to the intercom." She indicated the box on the wall next to the door. "If you need anything, use the intercom. Push 2 for me, and 3 for the kitchen."

Apparently, I was to be treated like a guest...or a prisoner in a velvet cage. I could work with that.

"Come to the door," she told me. "I'll add you to the people allowed access to this suite."

I obeyed, and she added my fingerprint to the biometric recognition pad.

"You're in," she said. "If I were you, I'd lock the door at all times. Only Brien and a few of his most trusted people have access to this suite."

My spine tingled. Again, that hint of a warning, that something was wrong at the castle.

"I will," I promised.

She gave a tiny nod and left. I locked the door behind her and slipped off my shoes. The paper was burning such a hole in my pocket now, I was surprised my pants weren't smoking.

I padded into the bathroom. The suite didn't appear to have any video cams, but just in case, as I slid off my pants, I palmed the piece of paper and unfolded it, glancing at it sidelong.

Two words—*Prince Perfect*—with a rough picture of a dagger through their center.

It took me a few seconds to take it in. Then it hit me.

Kuro wanted me to slay Brien, not Jules.

It was the only possible interpretation. Hell, I'd coined the term "Prince Perfect" myself.

A sick sensation clogged my throat. I risked a second, longer look, but the message hadn't changed. I crumpled the paper in my hand.

Robot-like, I finished undressing and lowered myself onto the toilet seat. I peed. Flushed the slip of paper along with the toilet paper. Got into the shower.

No.

My throat closed, my breath coming in jagged gasps.

Not Brien.

It didn't make sense. If anyone in the castle needed to be put out of their misery, it was his father.

I shampooed my hair, digging my fingers into my scalp to ground myself.

Not Brien.

I can't.

The sob erupted from that deep, lonely part of me. I pressed the heels of my hands to my eyes, gulping oxygen as the shower rained down on my head.

I didn't want to stake Brien.

Not even if it was the only way I'd ever be a slayer again.

You. Are. So. Fucked.

※ 8 ※

BRIEN

As we headed below the castle to our lair, Jules seemed to come back to himself. He shot me a look as cunning as the great white shark he'd chosen as the Maritime Syndicate emblem.

"My office," he said in clipped tones.

My nape tightened. It had been a long time since Jules had beaten me—he didn't fucking dare. Still, I couldn't help reacting when he ordered me to his office in that particular voice.

"Of course," I said expressionlessly, mindful that other vampires would be watching from the shadows.

Prosper, definitely—and probably a couple of others.

We'd kept Jules's decline a secret from the outside world, but everyone in the castle knew he was losing it. The vampires high in the hierarchy were circling like wolves closing in on a wounded alpha, waiting and watching. Eyeing me for weaknesses.

Behind me, Cain and Talon crowded closer, uncaring that it might draw my father's attention—and anger.

Fuck, I loved these guys. They had my back, always—my only real allies in the spiderweb of intrigue that was Castle Leclerc.

Jules's office was attached to his private apartment. We followed him down the long, winding flagstone stairs to the underground lair where the castle's resident vampires resided.

As we descended, the air grew damper, its scent a mix of salt water and dirt and the musky aroma of vampires that hurtled me back to my boyhood. Happy memories, of running through the tunnels and spying on the older vampires during a rare hour of freedom from my tutors. I'd had three—one for schoolwork; one for physical education and martial arts; and one for everything else, including piano, dance lessons and etiquette.

And later, after Cain and Talon had been turned, of slipping into the shadows with them and escaping castle to go to a pub or even a campfire on the beach with the other island kids.

As we reached the first landing, Prosper stepped out of the shadows. Jules nodded at him as if he'd known his lieutenant was there all along and kept going down the stairs.

Prosper was built like a midweight boxer, lean and muscular, with short dark hair, fuzzy caterpillars for eyebrows, and permanent pouches under his eyes like a TV cop who's seen too much. Combined with his love of camp shirts, it was the perfect cover. Most people, even other vampires, never realized he was a vampire until it was too late.

He blocked my descent and raked his hard brown eyes over my face. "How did it go in Quebec City?"

"Good," I said.

Prosper raised an eyebrow, silently demanding I expand. In the year since my mother's passing, he'd become bolder, subtly pushing me to acknowledge that he was dominant to me.

I brushed past him. I was the crown prince; I didn't report to him. He could hear my report along with Jules.

And the question of dominance had yet to be settled.

When we reached the lower level, we turned right, following the torchlit passage to Jules's apartment. Prosper's quarters were next to my father's. The rest of the rooms in that section were taken by Jules's thralls and his top people.

My own apartment was on the opposite side of the castle, something I'd made happen the day I turned twenty-one.

Jules's apartment had been furnished by my mother. The living room was an opulent space of leather and velvet and rare objets d'art.

A half-dozen candles flickered on the inlaid-marquetry coffee table, and a young, scared-looking thrall waited at the sideboard with an open bottle of blood-wine.

"Close the door," Jules ordered her and she hurried to obey. "You," he barked, stabbing a finger at Cain and Talon. "Wait in the hall."

They hesitated, but they had no choice but to obey.

Jules jerked his chin at me. "In my office."

I pressed my lips together and complied. Prosper followed, closing the door so I was trapped in the office with the two of them and Jules's large ebony desk. I stared at the shiny black surface.

Once, my fear and anger would've been fighting to get out. I'd have known I was about to be bent over the desk for a beating. But now I felt nothing except an icy lump where any family feeling for Jules might've resided.

My father made a low, angry sound. "Look at me."

I turned—and he lunged, closing a claw-like hand around my throat. A deliberate insult, his way of telling me he owned me and could do anything he wanted. Grab my throat, beat me with a belt.

Anything.

And just like when I was a child, no one would interfere, not even my mother.

Over his shoulder, I saw Prosper watching us, his expression wiped of any emotion. He must know that Jules was going blood mad, but if he did, he didn't show it by even a flicker of an eyelash. Outwardly, he remained the loyal lieutenant.

"Where have you been?" Jules demanded in the old-world French of his boyhood.

I replied in the same language. "In Quebec City. Negotiating with Régis, as I told you."

"You lie!" He shook me like a dog.

A killing fury flamed to life in the icy lump that was my heart.

I was no longer the boy who had to obey my father and primus. I was a man, and a pureblood, whereas Jules was a vampire who'd been turned. Now that I'd come fully into my powers, I was stronger—and we both knew it.

I grasped his wrist, digging my nails into the tender place between the tendons on the inner side. "Let me go," I said, soft and dangerous.

A vivid blue flared to life around Jules's irises, so bright it looked like his eyes had caught fire.

"Like fuck I will." He shoved dagger-line fangs into my face. "I'm your primus. You will treat me with respect."

The switchblade in my back pocket practically leapt into my free hand. I pressed the button, releasing the sharp silver blade. I felt my own eyes go vampire, my fangs lengthening even faster than his. I pictured sinking them into his jugular, distracting him long enough to stab the blade into his chest.

I drew a slow breath through my teeth.

He's your sire. You can't stake him in front of his own lieutenant.

"Jules." Prosper put a hand on my father's arm. "He went to Quebec City for you, to negotiate with Régis's syndicate. Now come, it's time for you to feed."

Dumbstruck, my gaze flicked to the lieutenant's broad face. Prosper had never taken my side against Jules. Not even last month, when Jules had threatened to slash up my face with a silver dagger. That time, Talon had intervened, reminding Jules that silver wounds left scars. Even my father's confused mind had understood that a scarred heir would make him look weak, and he'd lose face.

"Let him go," Prosper told me in an undertone. "I can handle this."

I waited another beat, then retracted the switchblade and returned it to my pocket. But I didn't let go of my father's wrist until Prosper tugged at Jules's arm.

"Come, my lord."

Jules released my throat. Bewilderment flashed across his face.

He brushed a hand over his mouth, the vampire still shining in his eyes. "Hungry."

"I know. You need to drink." Prosper put an arm around my father's shoulders and turned him away from me.

Rattled, I took a deep breath. Jules had grown worse in the short time I'd been away. I couldn't put off acting much longer.

Prosper's thick black brows drew together. "*Go*," he told me.

To my father he said, "We'll get Carly for you. You like her, don't you?"

"Yesss." Jules's voice was a hiss, his grin evil—and not him.

My father was a brutal SOB who rarely even smiled, let alone grin like a cruel child.

"You'll watch him with Carly?" I asked Prosper. "We can't afford another fuck-up like with Gwen."

Most of our thralls had been born on the island, members of families that had worked for the syndicate for generations. One "accident," our people could forgive, but if it happened again, we might have a revolt on our hands.

"Yes," Prosper said without looking at me, and urged Jules deeper out of the office and toward the door which led to the quarters occupied by his personal thralls.

Prosper pulled the door shut behind them with a quiet click. I stared at it for a long beat, then left.

In the hall, Talon and Cain scowled at the fingermarks on my throat. Talon rumbled angrily, and Cain cursed under his breath.

"Not here," I said tightly. "Tonight."

They nodded, still visibly upset. But we all knew that this wasn't the time or place to talk about my father.

The day sleep tugged at me. The summer nights were short this far north, and it was even worse for Cain and Talon. Although a half-dozen years older than me in human years, they were young for vampires, having been turned when I was already a teenager. If we didn't get to bed soon, we'd drop where we stood.

I dragged a weary hand over my face. "Let's get to bed," I said, and we set off at a jog for the other side of the castle.

When we reached my apartment, Talon and Cain went inside to do a quick sweep for bugging devices, a precaution they took whenever we left the island. Meanwhile, I slipped around the corner to the garden suite.

I didn't go inside, just listened at the door. From somewhere in the apartment came the steady drone of running water. Twilight was taking a shower.

Something settled in me. She was here in my lair, where she

belonged. I listened for another minute, then returned to my own apartment.

Cain and Talon had the apartments on either side of mine. Cain gave me the all-clear and wished me a good sleep before heading for his place. Talon simply grunted, then disappeared, yawning, into his own apartment.

I engaged my security system and peeled off my clothes, dropping them next to the bed. Outside, I sensed the sun pushing above the horizon.

Twilight would be finishing up her shower. Reaching for a towel.

My dick hardened.

Her skin would be slick from the water, her hair a wet dark rope. Her nipples would be puckered, her throat clean and sweet-smelling.

Craving obliterated my common sense—for her blood, her tight little body. My fangs lengthened and I actually took a step toward the hall. Then my eyes glued themselves shut.

I'd never resented the sun so much. The vampire's curse.

But there was no fighting it.

I turned back to the bed, fell sideways onto the mattress, and was out.

❧ *9* ❧

TWILIGHT

I had a bad night. It seemed like I'd barely fallen asleep when I was awakened by a cat meowing.

I groaned and dragged a pillow over my head to shut out the sound. It came again, too piercing to ignore.

I pushed up on an elbow and growled, "Go away."

"*Mee-rroww.*" The cat was getting upset now.

Grumbling to myself, I threw off the covers and padded into the living room, dressed in the ribbed tank and sleep shorts I'd worn to bed.

Demon pawed at the French door, meowing furiously.

"Hang on," I muttered and let her in. Judging by the sunlight pouring into enclosed garden, it was ten or eleven o'clock. I must've slept six or seven hours, although I'd been so twitchy, it felt more like three.

The little white cat butted her head against my leg until I picked her up. I rubbed her behind her ears, half-expecting her to bite my hand. Instead, she settled deeper into my arms, a purr vibrating her small body.

I glanced up at the garden's high stone walls. "Where'd you come from, anyway?"

"Meow." She slanted me an inscrutable look through her yellow eyes.

Still holding her, I stepped over the threshold—and into a fairytale. Vines flowed down the weathered walls, and fruit trees raised their branches among potted herbs and other greenery. Butterflies flitted from flower to flower, and in a pint-sized apple tree a fat sparrow was singing its heart out. From somewhere nearby came the tranquil sound of a waterfall.

"It's like a freaking Disney movie," I muttered to Demon.

She flicked her black ear, which I took for agreement.

"For vampires," I added, because it was a moon garden, with silvery green foliage, and pale blue, lavender, pink and white flowers seeded throughout the fruit trees and herbs.

A secret garden—or almost—because there was another entrance catty-corner to mine. Another French door, reinforced with silver, the glass too dark to see through. There was also a narrow wood door to my right that I assumed was used by the gardeners.

No cams—that I could see, anyway.

Demon wriggled out of my arms and trotted down a flagstone path, and I followed. A narrow, man-made stream meandered through the garden's center, ending in a low waterfall that spilled into a pool stocked with koi. They swam unhurriedly back and forth among waxy pink lotuses, trailing their fins and tails behind them like colorful gold, yellow and black scarves.

I helped myself to an apple from one of the trees and sat on a cast-iron bench to eat it. Demon stalked past me to the pool's edge to stare, tail twitching, at the fish, who regally ignored her.

My fingers tightened around the apple. Kuro had sent me on a suicide mission.

Even if I could bring myself to stake Brien, there was no way off this island without the Maritime Syndicate's permission.

And if Brien knew I was a slayer, then the GQ twins did, too. Slay Brien, and I'd be their chief suspect.

I set the half-eaten apple on the bench.

You have a little time. Kuro won't expect immediate results.

For one thing, I had to get my hands on a weapon. Right now, no one in the castle was going to let me near anything silver, even a butter knife.

And just as important, I needed to come up with a plan for escaping this godforsaken island after I'd staked Brien.

Assuming I could bring myself to stake him in the first place.

I pressed the heels of my hands to my eyes.

Why couldn't SI just leave me alone? I wasn't a threat to them. Yeah, I knew things, but I was a low-level operative. I couldn't name more than a few other slayers, and even those I knew by code names or aliases. Just as no one knew my real name, the one I'd been born with. I hadn't told even my friend Ridley, aka Princess Renata.

On our last op, Ridley and I had been forced into the middle of a vendetta between two syndicates. At the time I'd blamed Crow. She was a fanatic, consumed by her deep hatred of vampires. She didn't give a fuck about collateral damage as long as she could hurt the syndicates.

But Crow was dead—and if Kuro actually was speaking for the BOD, then nothing had changed.

I moaned lowly and put a hand to my stomach. It felt like I was being ripped in two, with one half reminding me that I was a slayer, that I'd sworn an oath, damn it.

Meanwhile, the other half argued, *But it's Brien.*

Invisible walls closed in on me. An acid fury at Kuro burned in my chest. He'd boxed me into a cell as dark and confining as anything at training camp.

Jumping to my feet, I headed back inside. I had to move around, take a walk or something.

I changed into a T-shirt and cropped jeans and was lacing up the new high-tops when a woman in a royal-blue Maritime Syndicate uniform arrived with my lunch. I'd lost my appetite, but I made myself eat a few bites of everything.

A touch of my finger to the biorec pad, and the door unlocked.

In the hall, a guard with freckles and spiked strawberry-blond hair straightened from the wall. "Good afternoon, miss."

I dipped my chin in a stiff nod. "I want to go outside."

"No problem. I'll show you to the courtyard."

I nodded and followed him. I was pretty sure I knew the way, but why let them know?

Outside, I filled my lungs with the salty ocean scent as my companion put on a pair of sunglasses.

"You're a dhampir, aren't you?" I asked.

He nodded. "Name's Jasper. Prince Brien found me on the mainland and invited me to join the syndicate." His expression was close to hero-worship.

"Nice to meet you." I put out my hand. "I'm Twilight."

"A pleasure to meet you." He gave an easy grin and pumped my hand.

It was impossible not to smile back. "So, Jasper. Which way should I go?"

"That way." He pointed through the archway at the cobblestone road. "There's a trail down to the beach in fifty meters or so."

"Sounds good." I'd started off when I heard my name being called.

I turned back to see Eden and Pinky hurrying toward me across the courtyard. They came up on either side of me.

Eden's gaze raked over me. She was basically a Valkyrie: tall, shapely body; yellow hair pulled into a ponytail; sharp cheekbones; sky-blue eyes. All she lacked was a sword and a breastplate.

"So you're the new thrall," she said.

"That's me." I gave her an easy, Lainey-Q smile. "And you're Eden —and Pinky."

Pinky gave me a wide smile back. She was petite, with a nicely rounded body and a pretty oval face framed by a short black Afro. "We're going to the beach if you wanna come along."

Eden's narrow-eyed scrutiny relaxed; apparently, she'd decided I wasn't a threat. "Yeah, you should come."

"I'd like that," I said, and we headed through the arch. "So you're both from the island?" I asked.

And did either of you happen to slip a note into my pocket?

Eden answered. "Yeah, we're locals. The syndicate marked us as thralls when I was fifteen, and Pinky was what—?"

"Sixteen," said Pinky.

"But we didn't sign a contract until we were twenty-one," Eden added.

"You're okay with that?" I asked.

Pinky shrugged. "It's more money than we could make doing anything else on the island."

"FYI," said Eden, "I'm Talon's main thrall, and Pinky is Cain's favorite."

"Oh." *Don't ask, damn it.*

But I had to know. "What about Brien?"

Eden shook her head. "He doesn't play favorites—doesn't want anyone getting ideas."

"But Lesa was in Quebec City for him," said Pinky.

Of course. Why else would she have been there?

My heart constricted. I tightened my jaw. I was jealous, which was insane. Brien wasn't mine, and he never would be.

And I was fine with that.

Absolutely, freaking-ass fine.

"Don't worry," said Eden. "You're new—Brien will be all over you for a while."

All over me.

My body liked the sound of that. My nipples tightened and my belly heated. And God, that was fucked—that I was hot for Brien, even knowing he was my target.

"But don't get attached," Pinky said. "Like we said, he doesn't play favorites."

"And you're okay with that?"

Eden shrugged. "It's a job. The best money you can make around here."

Pinky glanced sidelong at Eden. "Your sister turned them down."

"Because she was in love," said Eden.

"Some guy she met on the mainland," Pinky told me.

Eden pointed a thumb to her chest. "Me, I wanted to be a thrall. After three years, I can opt to leave—"

"Or the syndicate can let her go," said Pinky.

"Sure, but why would they?" said Eden. "New thralls aren't that easy to find, especially thralls willing to move to an island for three years. Anyway, my three years are almost up. As soon as my time's up, I'm getting the hell out—I want to travel for a year, and then I'm going to open my own business."

"Yeah?" I'd never met a pair of thralls like these two—or a syndicate like this, to be honest. Most of the thralls I'd met were trapped, even if they didn't admit it. Vampires are possessive SOBs; once you signed a contract with one, they usually worked things so you didn't leave until they were done with you.

Pinky lowered her voice. "You did sign a contract with Brien, didn't you? Because it's better...safer. Sometimes, the primus takes you anyway."

"Seriously?" I dropped my voice as well.

"Pinky," murmured Eden and tipped her head at Jasper. Which was all the answer I needed.

Pinky eyed me, concerned.

"Yeah," I lied. "I signed a contract."

"Good. Just be careful, you know?"

"There's the path to the beach." Eden turned down a steep, rocky trail, easily navigating it with her long legs.

Pinky rolled her eyes as we followed. "She's an effing mountain goat."

I chuckled and she grinned back. I had a feeling I'd made a friend —unless she was pretending to like me. Because if she was working with Kuro, wouldn't she try to befriend me? But then, I was pretending, too.

My stomach twisted. Sometimes I hated my life.

You're not here to make friends. Focus on surviving.

The beach was raw and beautiful, all wet sand and jagged rocks and heaving ocean. The wind whipped my hair around my face, and seagulls screeched and wheeled overhead.

A royal blue boat with a shark insignia zoomed past. "That's the ferry to the mainland," said Eden.

Corralling my hair, I plaited it into a makeshift braid. "There's a ferry?"

"Twice a week," she confirmed.

"Tuesdays and Saturdays," Pinky added. "We don't really get nights off, but you can go off-island for a day or two if you clear it with the guys ahead of time."

"Good to know," I said.

Eden sent me a sidelong look, like she suspected I was more interested in the ferry than I was acting. Or maybe I was just being paranoid.

My shoulders felt like they were hunched up around my ears. I exhaled, so damn tired of suspicion and lies. Of wondering if everyone I met had a hidden agenda.

We picked our way over the rocks to a crescent of smooth beige sand. I removed my shoes and socks and waded into the icy water. Behind me, Eden and Pinky were still talking, but I'd stopped paying attention.

Lifting my face to the sun, I dug my toes into the sand and let the ocean ebb and flow around my ankles.

❧

I ate supper alone in my suite, then curled up on the couch with a sexy romance that Pinky had lent me, eyeing the sky through the French door and wondering when Brien would send for me.

At the rap on my door, my heartrate kicked up. "Who is it?"

"Talon." The lock disengaged and the tall, broad-shouldered vampire entered.

I dropped the book on the coffee table and sat up. When I'd arrived back from the beach, the walk-in closet off my bedroom had been filled with the new clothes Brien had asked Avril to get me. I'd taken a shower and changed into one of the new outfits.

Talon took in my cropped tee, suspenders and tiny red shorts without visible emotion. "The prince wants you."

"'Kay." I gave him a cheery smile just to piss him off.

He gazed back stone-faced.

I shoved my feet into my silver Pradas and followed him into the hall. We turned down a short passage with just three doors in it. Talon stopped at the door in the middle and touched his index finger to the biorec pad. The door opened and he ushered me inside.

"The prince will be with you in a few minutes," he said and closed the door, leaving me alone in the living room.

I waited for Brien to appear, but the door to what I assumed was his bedroom remained shut, so I glanced around. The living room was decorated in an urban-loft style—wood and metal furniture, a plank floor, industrial copper lighting. A French door faced the secret garden, its glass darkened like the one in my suite.

Three large oil paintings hung on the wall opposite the French door. I recognized the style. People said the artist was a dhampir, although no one knew for sure because she sold her work through intermediaries.

Powerful and sensual, the paintings sucked you in. I found myself moving across the room so I could examine them more closely.

A golden-eyed jaguar prowled through a shadowed rainforest. Sharp-toothed, iridescent snakes glided through an overgrown garden. And in the third—and largest—painting, a black-haired vampire in a glittering tiara lounged on a throne surrounded by her court, a bloody dagger dangling from one hand.

They were like a window into Brien's mind. More evidence that the buttoned-up, Perfect Prince had a dark, sensual side.

A finger touched my nape, sending electricity zinging down my spine.

"Hello." Brien's voice was smooth, golden whiskey.

"Hello," I said without turning around.

Brien's scent enveloped me, earthy and green and tempting. He brushed my braid out of the way. Cool lips touched the sensitive skin beneath my ear. "I hear you've been good today."

My breath caught. "Define good."

"All the staff are still alive, and you made friends with Eden and Pinky. Plus, you didn't do anything to piss me off...like trying to escape."

I huffed a laugh. "By that definition, I guess I was good."

He cupped my throat, and my head dropped back against his shoulder.

"I like it when you're good," he said against my temple. "It makes me think you want to please me."

My heart swooped in my chest like a seagull through the blue sky. I swallowed thickly. Because I did want to please him—or a part of me did, anyway.

"Twilight." His grip tightened on my throat—not hurting me, just showing me who had the power here.

My limbs grew heavy, and my knees would've buckled if his free hand hadn't come to my stomach to press me against his body. He was going to feed from me, sink his fangs into my throat.

And I wanted it. Lord help me, I wanted it.

A wave of heat flushed my skin. My body strained toward his.

I shouldn't want it so much. I was so messed up.

This—us—was so messed up.

But I did want it. That was my guilty secret. I fucking loved a vampire's kiss. That aphrodisiac they have in their saliva can make sex so hot.

I wasn't the only slayer who felt that way, either. We might not like to admit it, but for some of us, sex with a vampire was a definite perk. Just like some of us wondered what it would be like to be turned...

And this wasn't just any vampire, it was Brien. The man who'd starred in my dirtiest fantasies for the past two years.

I was desperate to feel him naked against me. Over me. In me.

He caressed my throat with long fingers warmed by my skin. His other hand cupped me through my shorts.

With a ragged moan, I pressed back against his erection. He bent his knees, aligning the hard ridge with the crack of my ass, and ground against me, his dick burning hot even through the layers of material separating us.

I reached back, grabbing his thigh through his cut-off jeans. I ran my hand down to the coarse hair of his inner leg above his knee.

He pulled me tighter against his hard body. "Sweet bloody Lilith, I want you."

I melted into him. "Yes."

A single, softly spoken word that felt like surrender. Hell, it was surrender. This was wrong, and I knew it—the man was my target, for God's sake—but I couldn't fight both him and myself.

Brien exhaled a breath, stroked a possessive hand up my belly to my breasts, palming one and teasing my nipple through the soft black tee.

"No bra." He pinched my nipple, making me arch against him. "You *are* being good."

"Mm." I rubbed my ass against him, and his hand went to my other nipple, pinching it as well.

"Or is this all a lie?" He turned me around and put me a few inches away from him.

Eyes half-closed, I murmured in protest and reached for him.

He caught my wrists and brought my arms to my sides. I forced my heavy lids open. His eyes were narrowed, his mouth twisted skeptically.

I jerked against his hold. "Let me go, damn you."

He tightened his grip on my wrists, keeping me where I was. Frost-green eyes searched mine. "I *will* learn to read you. You're good, but I'm starting to get little glimpses. Right now you're upset...angry. Why, Twilight? What are you hiding?"

I glared back, but it was hard to hold his gaze when I was fighting the conviction that he could read my mind.

He can't. That's your guilt talking.

However, he could sense my emotions, and despite my training, mine were apparently leaking out. Anger, agitation, sadness—and at the center, a hopeless sort of emptiness.

Tell him.

But my mouth remained firmly shut.

Slayers, Inc. had let me down in so many ways. Still, other than my halmoni, they were all I had. My family. My friends.

Without SI, what was I?

I couldn't go home. My halmoni would be so ashamed of me. She'd been a top slayer in her day, the famous Ghost who'd notched over a dozen kills.

And my dad had checked out years ago. He didn't even live in Los Angeles anymore; after Mom had been killed, he moved back to Korea. I hadn't seen him since her funeral.

Brien's lips thinned. "That's what I thought. But you're mine now. Try anything, and I'll make you sorry you were ever born."

Anger flared. I allowed it to fill me, knowing such a strong, hot emotion would obliterate everything else—the fear, the yearning.

"Yes, *sir*."

He muttered something dark and released me. I stepped back, rubbing my right wrist.

He scowled. "I hurt you."

I lifted a shoulder. "It's okay."

"No. It's not." He pinched the bridge of his nose. "Just go," he said without looking at me. "You have the night off."

I stared at him. He'd gotten me all worked up, and now he was sending me away? I should be grateful but fuck that.

"What if I don't want the night off?"

His nostrils flared. His head swung in my direction like a beast scenting prey. "*Go*," he repeated in a low, goaded tone.

I went.

❊ 10 ❊

BRIEN

"So." Cain fingered the shark tat on the side of his neck. "What's the plan?"

We'd turned on a sound-cloaking device, an invention of Cain's. Anyone trying to listen in on our conversation would hear only white noise...loud, irritating white noise, especially to a vampire's ultra-sensitive hearing.

Still, out of habit we'd formed a tight circle in my living room and were speaking in low voices. You get that way when you live in a viper's pit.

I scrubbed a hand over my hair and tried to focus on Cain's question, but I was still horny and on edge from the encounter with Twilight. I could feel that taut body pressed against mine, taste her soft skin...

I should've never brought her back to the castle. She was a distraction. A sexy, too-tempting distraction—the last thing I needed right now.

So take her. She's yours. What are you waiting for, an engraved invitation?

But even with the craving riding me hard—even though I *owned* the woman—I hadn't been able to bring myself to fuck her again. Not if she wasn't totally on board.

And she wasn't.

She wanted me—that much hadn't been a lie. She'd been wet for me, her heart beating fast, her breath coming in eager rushes.

But she didn't *want* to want me, and that was a gut-punch.

Because she had wanted me, once. In Montreal, she'd been as hot for me as I'd been for her.

Or had that just been part of the act?

I scowled. The woman had me twisting on her strings like a demented marionette when I should be focused on my father and consolidating my power in the syndicate.

Cain's phone buzzed. He glanced at the screen. "Jasper says Twilight is at the Bite Club with a few of the other ladies. You want me to tell him to confine her to her suite?"

"No. Let her stay." What was the point in keeping her locked up? She'd be safe enough with the other thralls. "But make sure she doesn't go anywhere else."

Cain nodded and sent a text, then pocketed the phone. "So about Jules..." He glanced at Talon, who took over.

"He's worse, Brien. In just a week—" He shook his head.

"I know," I said. "He forgot that he agreed to the trip to Quebec City—and then he went for me. I would've staked him if Prosper hadn't stopped me."

"Sweet Lilith," muttered Talon. "That would've blown everything sky-high."

"Yeah," I said grimly.

"Or maybe it would've been a good thing," said Cain. "We've been covering for Jules for too long."

"Because he's Brien's sire," Talon reminded him.

Cain heaved a breath. "Then let's contact SI, let them handle it. Much as I hate to bring them into our private business—"

Talon shook his head. "Jules hasn't been off-island for months. We'd have to give a slayer free run of the castle. They'd use the opportunity to get all the intel they can on us."

"Forget it," I said. "I'll be damned if I'll let one of those bastards on my island."

Cain opened his mouth, then closed it again.

"What?" I asked.

"Twilight's a slayer," he said. "Maybe we should use her."

"No. She's not a part of this, understand?"

"But—"

I gave him a hard stare and he shrugged and subsided.

"Unless they sent her," Talon said. "I know she says they kicked her out, but that's what she would say, isn't it? Tattoo or no tattoo."

I shook my head. Yeah, I thought Twilight was hiding something, but... "How would she have known I'd be at the auction? Régis didn't invite me until that night. And other than you guys, no one but Jules and Prosper even knew I was going to be in Quebec City."

"Avril knew," Talon said. "And the three thralls we took with us."

"Not until the night before we left," I returned.

Talon moved a big shoulder. "Prosper could've told someone. Or Jules, for that matter."

"Still," said Cain, "Brien has a point. Even if SI somehow found out he was planning to go to Quebec, how in Hades could they have predicted he'd be at that auction? No, if Twilight is still a slayer, her target was probably someone in the Quebec City Syndicate—like Nazaire. If anyone needs snuffed, it's him."

Talon lifted his brows. "If that's true, you threw a wrench into the works by buying the woman."

"I don't know," I said. "She could still be a member of SI—I'll give you that much. But the rest doesn't add up. If Nazaire had bought her, she'd have been fucked. She had no weapons and no way to contact anyone. A blood slave has no rights, no protection. He could've turned her into a fucking blood addict and no one would've stepped in to save her. I know SI expects their operatives to work independently, but if she was there to slay someone, she would've had to be a cross between Houdini and a ninja."

"Why don't we offer her a deal?" Cain asked. "One last job—her freedom in return for staking Jules. If she's here to slay him anyway, even better—all we have to do is allow her access to Jules. Best-case scenario, she succeeds, and you become primus. And if something goes wrong, she takes the fall, not you."

My hands were around his throat before I'd realized I'd moved. "I said, 'She's. Not. A. Part. Of. This.'"

Cain's pale eyes widened. He dropped his gaze and raised his hands in surrender. "Got it. Sure."

I glanced at my fingers on his throat, cursed, and released him.

"Shit, Bri," he said. "I'm sorry. I didn't—"

I jerked my chin in acknowledgment. Hating that I'd lost control and grabbed him like Jules had grabbed me. It was like my SOB of a father had taken over my brain for a few seconds.

Still, I would *not* drag Twilight into this, even if she was the perfect fall guy. Jules was too dangerous. Not to mention Prosper.

"The woman's out of the slayer game," I said. "Permanently. Even if I have to chain her to my bed to keep her safe."

"Understood," said Cain.

Talon spoke, his deep voice calm. "So what's our alternative? Another nameless assassin?"

"Like the slayer who took out my mother?" I frowned. "I don't think so. The syndicate already looks weak. If it happens a second time, we'll look like fools, vulnerable to attack. No one will want to deal with us."

And my long-range plans included expanding the syndicate's influence, which meant brokering more deals like the one I'd made with Régis and the QCS.

"Then we need a fall guy," said Talon. "Cain's suggestion has merit." At my growl, he raised a staying hand. "Not your woman. Someone else, someone to take the blame."

"Or," said Cain, "we say to Hades with the subterfuge and let it get out that Jules is blood mad."

"And then," Talon added softly, "we slay the SOB ourselves. We just engineer things so it looks like he went to his final grave without any help."

I looked from him to Cain. Rubbed a hand over my face. "I don't know."

This was the jagged rock that our last few discussions had run aground on. The man might be a monster, but he was my father. It wasn't only that he was my sire. It was that taking him out in this underhand way didn't sit right, even though I knew he'd never accept a direct challenge from me. He'd have me staked out in the sun rather than chance me besting him.

Talon pursed his lips. "It's time, Brien. If he attacks another thrall…"

"Or worse," muttered Cain. At my questioning look, he added, "Fuck, Brien. You have to realize he could go for you next."

"He won't."

"Are you sure?" Talon gave my neck a pointed look, reminding me of the marks Jules had left on it.

I set my hands on my hips and dropped my head. "No," I admitted. "Not after last night."

"We know you're waiting for the right time," Talon said. "But the syndicate enforcers have started whispering among themselves. That you're not ready. That you're vulnerable."

That brought my head back up. "Prosper?"

"No. At least, not that I've heard. Still, if you wait much longer, we could lose control of the situation."

"It's okay," said Cain. "You don't have to do it. We will."

I growled. "The hell you will. My decision, my responsibility."

Talon heaved a breath, but we'd had this discussion before. They both knew my mind was made up.

"Then do it already," Cain gritted. "The man's a goddamn time bomb. He could blow any night now and become a danger to everyone on the island."

My jaw hardened. "You think I don't know that?"

A vampire in the final stages of blood madness was basically a rabid animal, constantly craving blood and not caring how they got it.

Frustration twisted Cain's good-looking face. "So why are we here? I thought you'd made up your mind. The locals have been uneasy ever since Gwen died. They know something's fishy about her death. My dad took me aside to ask if my sisters were safe. He's talking about sending them off-island until Jules is dealt with."

"Fuck." I sank into a chair. "It's gone that far?"

Talon and Cain took seats on the couch facing me. Talon leaned forward, hands on his thighs.

"None of this is your fault," he said. "We know that. Hell,

everyone does. But if you don't do something, the next death will be on your head."

My stomach tightened. "I know."

"And there's Prosper," Cain added. "He'll never accept a demotion. If he doesn't challenge you for primus, he'll expect to be your lieutenant, and I'm betting he'll arrange to have you slain within the year. Frankly, I'm surprised he let you live to adulthood."

Talon drew an index finger across his throat. "If he causes any trouble, he goes."

They weren't saying anything I hadn't considered myself. Still, it was one thing to think it, another to hear it stated aloud.

I massaged the bridge of my nose. How in Hades had things come to this?

Most vampires don't survive for long after losing their mates. They either walked into the sun or shoved a stake into their own heart. But my father had clung to this world, consumed by his desire to avenge my mother before going to his own final grave.

And now it was too late. He was too far gone to realize how bad off he was.

I brought my hand down, squared my shoulders. This was what I'd been raised to do—take charge. Maybe my parents hadn't foreseen things turning out in quite this way, but they were the ones who'd tried to beat the softness out of me. Or rather, my father had, but my mother had stood by and let it happen.

"Okay," I said, "here's how we're going to handle it. If we keep a constant guard on Twilight, Jules might fixate on her." I hadn't forgotten his expression when he'd scented her last night in the foyer. "Plus, we need to give her some rope. If she's a plant, sooner or later she'll make a mistake. So call off the guards but keep an eye on her through the video cams."

"Will do," said Cain.

"And make sure she doesn't get her hands on anything she could use as a weapon," I said, "even a goddamned spoon. She's liable to sharpen it into a dagger."

"What about during the day?" asked Talon. "Should we have Jasper stick with her?"

"Jules is never up and moving until late in the evening, but just in case, have Jasper keep an eye on her anyway, especially if she leaves the castle. He doesn't have to conceal himself—I want her to know he's watching whenever she's off the grounds. And she's not to leave the island under any circumstances."

Talon nodded. "I'll let him know."

"As for my father—" I instinctively lowered my voice even further —"I want you both to call one or two people—vampires you're already friendly with so it doesn't raise suspicion—and let it drop about Jules being blood mad. Cain, you can knock out the cameras in his section for a few minutes?"

"I can."

"Good. We'll wait a few nights, and then—" I lifted my hand, slashed it downward. "I help him into his final grave."

❧　II　❧

TWILIGHT

Brien had left me with the female equivalent of blue balls. I felt itchy and out of sorts. I started back to my suite, then halted. My guard had disappeared.

Okay, then.

I turned right instead of left, figuring I'd see what the other thralls were up to. Anything was better than spending time alone with my thoughts.

Heels clicked on the stone floor and Eden came around the corner, her hourglass curves poured into a red bodycon dress. "There you are! I was coming to see if you were free."

"Yep. I even lost my babysitter."

"Oh, they're always watching." She tipped her head at the camera tucked into a metal torch.

"Yeah, I figured that. But—" I shrugged. Why tell her Brien had decreed that a guard was to be with me whenever I left my suite?

"So." I flashed a big smile, partly for Eden, partly as a middle-finger-salute to anyone observing us. "What do you guys do around here for fun?"

"That's why I came to get you."

She drew me around a corner and down a short passage. We

92

turned left, then left again. A couple more turns and we reached a shiny red door.

"Welcome to the Bite Club," Eden said with an ironic little smile and pushed it open. Dance music spilled into the hall.

I snort-laughed. "The Bite Club?"

"Yeah." Eden's smile widened into something more genuine as she urged me inside. "It's where we hang out until the guys want us."

"Wow." I gave a low whistle. "This is—"

"Nice, huh?"

Jasper slipped in the door after us. The other thralls said hi, then ignored him, so I did the same.

"Very nice," I agreed with Eden.

Actually, the club was a decadent fantasy world in scarlet and purple and black. Small colored spotlights roamed over a large dance floor encircled by couches and other furniture, including a round velvet couch wide enough to have an orgy on. There were a number of dark nooks partially concealed by heavy silk curtains, and a bartender stood behind a hammered-metal bar.

Lesa rose from a fainting couch and sauntered toward us in a clingy gold dress that set off her olive skin. A matching gold headband was wrapped around her short dark curls.

"Want a drink?" she asked me in a faint French-Canadian accent. "Chad here makes the best margaritas." She smiled at the hunky blond bartender.

"Yeah?" Resting my forearms on the bar, I grinned at him. "Hi, Chad. I'm Twilight, and I'd love a margarita."

"Nice to meet you," he said with a wink. "Strawberry jalapeno? I was just mixing up a batch."

"Perfect."

Pinky appeared from another corner of the room in a glittering sequin mini dress. She draped an arm around my shoulders and told Chad, "Make one for all of us. This is a welcome party."

Lesa was right about Chad's margaritas. The first one was practically a mouthgasm. I drank it down a little too fast, letting the sweet but spicy beverage coat my worries.

"Another one?" Chad asked when I set my glass on the metal bar.

I started to refuse. A slayer needs to keep a clear head. But then, I wasn't a slayer anymore, was I? I could get as wasted as I wanted.

"Why not?" I returned. "I'll help."

I joined him behind the bar, and he put me to work washing and de-stemming the strawberries, which I accomplished along with a great deal of laughter.

When we were finished, I bumped my hip against his. "Thanks."

"Have a taste," he said.

I complied, then licked my lips. "Yum."

His gaze went to my mouth, and I blinked and edged back. Okay, maybe I had been flirting, but that was the margaritas talking. I hadn't expected him to take me up on it, especially under the video cam's watchful eye.

He stiffened and turned away, busying himself with refilling Pinky, Lesa and Eden's glasses. More thralls arrived, a half-dozen women and a trio of men. Eden introduced me around, and we started dancing. I learned that there were about two dozen thralls in the castle altogether.

"We almost never see the primus's thralls, though," a tall redhead named Hanna said. "He doesn't allow—"

Another thrall frowned and shook her head at Hanna, and she bit her lip. "Anyway, this is pretty much everyone."

I pretended I hadn't noticed the awkwardness. "Seems like a fun group."

"You have no idea," drawled another woman.

"Then show me," I returned, and they all grinned. Someone turned up the music and we stopped trying to talk, just danced.

The night passed in a haze of music and laughter and dancing. I finished my second margarita and took a break to use the bathroom.

Someone was in the other stall; I could hear ragged breathing. Then, as I dried my hands, I heard a sniffle.

"Hey," I called softly. "You okay?"

"Yeah." Eden's voice. The toilet flushed but she didn't exit the stall.

I hesitated. "I can get someone else if you want me to."

"No. Please." She exited the stall, cheeks streaked with muddy mascara tears. "I'm good. Really." She gave me a tight smile.

"You sure you don't want me to get Pinky? Or Lesa?"

"No." She washed her face and walked past me into the anteroom, where she sat on a poufy pink stool in front of a large mirror and took out her makeup. Her red, swollen eyes met mine in the mirror. "Go away, Twilight. This doesn't concern you."

"Right." I touched her shoulder anyway.

Her eyes squeezed shut. "Please. Just go."

Back in the main room, a half-dozen vampires had arrived. They prowled through the kaleidoscope of sexily dressed thralls, drawing their chosen human into the shadowed nooks or onto a couch.

I helped myself to another margarita and was standing at the side of the bar, talking to Pinky, when my nape tightened. I glanced over my shoulder to see a dark-haired vampire in an expensive designer suit and skinny red tie heading straight for me. He stopped a foot away and looked me over without speaking, lean and sharp-toothed as a hungry coyote.

I gave him a vague nod when what I really wanted to do was give him the finger, and turned back to Pinky, praying he wouldn't ask me to dance. Because I wasn't sure if I was allowed to refuse.

The seconds ticked by. My neck crawled. I was about to turn back and ask what he wanted when he moved off.

My breath whistled out. "Jesus."

"That's Matthew Smith," said Pinky in an undertone. "An enforcer. Stay away from him if you can—he's not a nice man. And if he can use you to hurt Brien, he will. He's Team Prosper all the way."

"Don't worry, I will. Prosper's the Maritime lieutenant, right?" I knew, of course, but a new thrall might not.

"Yep." Her mouth curved in a brilliant smile. "Smile back, okay? I don't want them to know we're talking about them. It's not like we thralls don't know what's going on, but..."

I nodded and grinned.

"Everyone knows the old primus will be in his final grave soon." Her voice was practically a whisper now.

"But why?"

She fake-laughed. "Because he lost his mate. It's been over a year now."

"Ah." That explained why I hadn't seen or heard anything of Lenore Leclerc. And it was bad, because losing a mate was enough to drive a vampire blood mad.

"Anyway, when he passes, Brien will take his place as the new primus—unless Prosper challenges him."

"I see." A heavy lump settled in my stomach.

The Maritime lieutenant was rumored to be a ruthless, stone-cold killer. If Prosper challenged Brien, it would be because he believed he could win.

"Smile," Pinky said under her breath, and I obediently arranged my lips into an upward curve. "Good. Let's dance."

I set my drink on the bar and joined her on the dance floor. "But Brien's the crown prince," I said in her ear.

She slid an arm around my neck and touched her lips to the corner of my mouth, putting on a show for the vampires.

"A thrall died a couple of months back," she said in an undertone. "You don't want to be the next. They say it was an accident, but we're not so sure."

A shock vibrated up my spine. I pulled back. "For real?"

"Smile," she hissed, and I immediately obeyed.

Pinky nodded at someone behind me. "Mademoiselle Dumas."

I turned to find a vampire with the face of a 1940s movie star—powder-pale skin, pouty scarlet mouth, deep blue eyes. Her wavy brown hair was parted at the side and brushed forward over one shoulder, and the keyhole neckline of her tight black dress showcased full white breasts.

Dumas looked at me down the length of her narrow nose. "You're different from his usual, I suppose."

"His usual?" I dredged up a clueless Lainey-Q expression. Better than punching her in the throat.

"The prince. He usually goes for women. Not someone who dresses like a slutty schoolgirl."

"You don't like my clothes?" I ran a hand down my bare abdomen and over the tiny red shorts. "I have to admit," I added, eyeing her plump white cleavage, "that I don't have the tits to pull off a dress like that."

A frown pinched her perfectly plucked brows, like she was trying to decide if I was mocking her.

"I'm Twilight." I unleashed a thousand-megawatt smile on her and stuck out my hand.

"Clarisse Dumas." She eyed my hand without taking it.

With a shrug, I brought it back to my side. "Nice to meet you, Clarisse."

Her nose lifted another notch. "You will call me Enforcer Dumas." She stalked off, hips swishing in the snug black skirt.

I swallowed a grin and started dancing again.

Lesa danced up. "Ignore her," she said under her breath. "She's jealous because the prince picked you up in Quebec and rushed you into a thrall contract."

"That's unusual?"

"Hell, yeah. First time he's ever done it."

"Huh."

If only Clarisse knew what had really happened—that Brien had bought me at a blood-slave auction. I watched the curvy vampire over Lesa's shoulder. She'd taken the hand of a male thrall and was leading him to an empty nook.

I mean, let's face it, the woman was hot. As a human, I couldn't compete.

Maybe I should've throat-punched her while I had the chance.

"But don't make too much of it." Lesa pretended to fix my hair. "First rule of being a thrall is don't fall in love. You'll just get your heart broken."

"Don't worry," I said. "I don't intend to." But my chest gave a funny little twist.

"Good." Lesa stepped back and smiled at the dark-skinned, curly-haired vampire approaching us.

"*Bon soir*," he said to me.

"Hello," I said and tensed, but he wasn't there for me.

Cupping Lesa's ass with one powerful hand, he jerked her up against his body. "I've been looking for you, little one."

She twined her arms around his neck. "I've been right here, gorgeous."

He scraped his teeth along her throat and her eyelids closed in pleasure. His eyes stayed open though, catching me staring. He licked the scrapes, staring at me boldly.

My stomach tightened, my body recalling all over again how Brien had left me unsatisfied.

I faded back into the crowd, though. If I didn't, I had a feeling I was going to be joining Lesa and her vampire for a threesome, and I didn't want that. I wanted Brien.

I danced for a few more minutes, then headed back to the bar. My head was spinning. Maybe that last margarita hadn't been a good idea after all.

Chad found a bottle of mineral water for me and I stood near the bar, sipping it and watching the dancers.

Clarisse and the male thrall had disappeared. With any luck, he'd keep her busy for the rest of the night—and away from Brien.

And why did I care so much about who Brien fucked?

I frowned and smacked the green bottle down on the bar.

Chad appeared. "Something wrong?"

"No." I gave him a brilliant smile. "I changed my mind. I think I would like another margarita."

He grinned back. "Coming right up!"

I was gulping the margarita when Jasper approached with another man. "Hey." He gave me one of his shy smiles. "You having fun?"

I raised my glass to him. "Sure am."

"This is Eugene." He nodded at the elegantly dressed, dark-haired man.

I raised my glass to him as well. "Nice to meet you, Eugene."

His blue eyes met mine in an intense, William-Dafoe stare. "And you."

"You settling in all right?" asked Jasper

"I am, thanks. It's a beautiful place."

"Good, good."

We talked for a few minutes with Eugene standing silently by. Even when I asked him a direct question, his response was a curt *yes* or *no*. It was awkward AF; when they finally moved off, I heaved a relieved exhale.

Pinky popped up at my elbow. "Jasper's cute, isn't he?"

"Yeah. But I'm not so sure about Eugene."

"He has to warm up to you. They were both born to thralls. Eugene's been around as far back as I can remember, but Jasper's only been a Maritime man for five years or so."

"Team Brien?"

"Yeah. Jasper's mom didn't want him to be part of the syndicate, so she never told his father about him. Brien found him working in an office and hating it. He's kinda like a big puppy, isn't he?"

"Yeah." My mouth twitched. "I like him."

"Me too. With him, what you see is what you get."

That's how the next hour went, with the syndicate's enforcers and soldiers giving me the onceover and then either moving on or welcoming me to the island.

One by one, the other thralls were claimed for the night. The word must've gone out that I was Brien's. That probably shouldn't have sent something hot and fizzy bubbling through me, but it did.

I blamed it on the alcohol.

Eden returned from the bathroom and started dancing again. No one but me seemed to notice how her partying seemed feverish, like a woman who was holding herself together by a thread. Or maybe she was always like that.

Talon came for her soon after and they left the club, but Pinky stayed, and Lesa reappeared with faint bite marks on her throat. We three were the only ones still on the dance floor. I'd taken off my shoes and was dancing barefoot. Only a few other thralls and a couple of vampires were left in the club.

Pinky pulled Chad out from behind the bar to dance with us. Everything—the music, the lights, the alcohol, my desperation—had combined to tumble me into an exhilarated, reckless headspace. We formed a circle with Pinky and Lesa to either side of me and Chad across from me.

The music slowed, became dark and sexy. I closed my eyes and turned in a circle, running my hands down my torso.

Imagining it was Brien, touching me.

When a man's hands covered mine, it seemed part of my fantasy—until cool fingers guided mine to my breasts.

My eyes flew open. I didn't have to glance behind me to see who it was; I knew. I'd recognize Brien's touch, his scent, anywhere.

His lips touched my ear. "Hello, Twilight," he said in a dark voice.

Chad was dancing only a couple of feet away. Brien didn't say anything, just looked at him over my shoulder.

The other man's Adam's apple bobbed. "Sorry, my lord." He backed up, slowly at first, then faster until he was practically jogging across the floor to the bar.

Brien brushed my right hand from my breast and covered it with his own fingers. Firm. Possessive.

"Stay away from him."

"Or what?" I asked, fueled by that reckless, fizzy feeling. "You'll lock me in my room, *sir?*"

His growl vibrated down my spinal column. Liquid heat slicked my thighs. I pressed them together.

I'd poked the vampire and he was pissed off. Maybe I should've been wary, but I wasn't. I was turned on.

His mouth went lower. He closed his teeth over the tendon at the turn of my shoulder, and I shuddered.

"I wouldn't push me, if I were you." Silky tones. "Not tonight."

"Yeah?" I snaked my hands up to his neck, twining my fingers around his nape and pressing myself back against him. His dick pressed into the small of my back. "I'm not afraid of you."

His hand went to my throat, squeezed. "Maybe you should be."

Lesa and Pinky had disappeared. I hadn't even seen them go, I was so focused on Brien.

Chad wiped down the bar, gaze carefully averted.

"Leave." Brien jerked his chin at him. "You're off for the night."

"Yes, sir." Chad set down his rag and disappeared out a side door.

Brien raised his voice. "Everyone else leave, too," and the few people still in the club cleared out.

His hand slid over my breasts to my bare stomach. His fingers spread out, covering me from my navel to my mound.

"This is mine, Twilight. No one else touches you. If I find you flirting with Chad again, I'll rip his goddamn head off."

He said it so calmly, the threat took a moment to register.

I shivered, part excitement, part shock. The recklessness urged me to keep teasing him. But Chad didn't deserve to be dragged into this.

I feathered my fingers over the short hairs at Brien's nape. "I wasn't flirting. Just having a little fun."

"The only fun you're going to have is with me. I thought I made that clear. But if you didn't understand, I'll be happy to explain exactly what I meant." He turned me sideways so he could smack my ass, two hard slaps.

My bottom tingled at the words and the dominance.

"Understood." I touched my lips to his jaw. "It won't happen again."

I honestly hadn't meant to set out to make him jealous—or had I? Maybe a part of me had hoped he was watching, had wanted to see how he'd react.

Jesus. I was turning into one of *those* women.

He acknowledged my apology with a grunt, then spun me around so my back was against his chest again. Undoing my shorts, he shoved his fingers into my panties. His middle finger teased my clit, dipped lower.

He exhaled audibly. "You're so wet. So ready."

My head fell back against his chest. "I've been ready half the night."

"Because of me?"

"What do you think?"

He slipped a hand under my bra and tugged at my nipple. "Be good, or I'll spank your ass red."

"Should I be scared?"

He chuckled—and cupped me roughly. "You never say what I expect you to."

"At least I'm not boring."

"No. Never that. Sweet Lilith, I missed y—" He broke off mid-word, but we both heard what he'd almost said.

A sense of my own power welled up in me. I wriggled my ass against him.

I missed you, too.

But I didn't say it because it felt like the final surrender. The absolute, no-turning-back split with my life before this.

He slid his finger back to my clit, slippery now with my own juices. I swallowed, and he hummed against my throat.

"You like that, don't you, baby?"

I swallowed a groan. "Yeah."

"How much?" He toyed with the swollen flesh.

"A lot. Or, you know—you could use your mouth."

He chuckled and removed his hand from my shorts.

I caught his wrist. "Don't tease me. I'm so worked up..."

"Patience isn't your strong suit, is it?"

I brought his hand to my mouth and touched my tongue to his palm, licking the center like a cat. "I can be patient...if I know it's worth it."

"A dare?" He turned me around and gave me a hard kiss on the mouth, then, keeping me against his body with a firm hand to my back, took out his phone and issued a series of voice commands. "Cameras off. Spotlights off. Pocket lights and music on."

The spotlights ceased their dizzying passes over the room, replaced by a dim, sunset glow from lights set into the lower walls. The music changed to something low and sensual.

Returning the phone to his pocket, he released me and lowered himself onto the nearest couch. He'd showered and changed into a dark blue button-down shirt in a soft rayon that draped over his upper body, hinting at the sinewy muscles beneath. His streaked blond hair brushed the top of his shoulders and his eyes gleamed in the low light.

Spreading his legs, he put his hands on the plush red cushions on either side of his hips and eyed me like he owned me. A heated, *you're mine and I'm going to fuck you* look.

Which didn't bother me nearly as much as it should've.

"Get naked." A soft command.

I hesitated. This Brien wasn't the one I thought I knew. Hot AF, yeah, but unpredictable. I didn't have a handle on him.

"I'm waiting." His gaze stroked down my body. "Or didn't you mean it?"

I focused on the ridge pressing against the zipper of his soft, well-worn jeans and flashed back to how he'd felt inside me, long and firm and delicious. A honeyed heat spread through my lower abdomen. I licked my lips in an unconscious gesture I didn't realize I'd made until he focused on them.

His eyes darkened. The corner of his mouth ticked up. *I dare you.*

I lifted my chin. *You're on, Prince.*

Keeping my eyes trained on him, I pulled my tee off and dropped it on the floor. His fingers dug into the red cushion.

Encouraged, I stepped out of my shorts. That left my panties, a filmy, see-through black silk. I was still a little drunk and a lot reckless.

I started to dance, swaying my body to the low music, turning around and wiggling my bottom at him. Hooking my thumbs in the sides and drawing them partway down my hips until they were a thin strip across my ass.

When I turned back around, Brien had gone completely still as only a vampire can. I hadn't even seen him take a breath since I'd started my little striptease.

A neon blue circle had flamed to life around his irises, a warning that I was playing with a dangerous man. But I was kind of a danger junkie. The implied threat only amped up the thrill.

I strutted forward, hips swinging, stopping just out of his reach.

He jerked his chin at me. "The panties, too."

"These?" I drew it out, sliding my hands over my breasts, playing with the nipples...moving a hand down my belly and between my legs so I could touch myself through the panties.

The heat in Brien's eyes seared me. I was so turned on I was about to self-combust.

"The panties," he repeated. Without looking away, he reached down and adjusted himself.

My skin prickled with a buzzing, humming anticipation. The sense that I was dancing along a razor's edge increased.

But I was committed now. Pushing the panties down over my legs, I stepped out of them and straightened back up.

His throat worked. "Fuck, you're beautiful."

"Now you." I undid the button of his jeans, easing the zipper down over a truly impressive erection. The tip pushed out of his boxer briefs. I rubbed my fingertip over the slit, smoothing his pre-cum around the sensitive head.

He sat up and dragged off his shirt, then removed the rest of his clothes in a flurry of too-fast-to-see moves. The last thing he removed was an ankle sheath with the ebony head of a dagger poking out of it.

Our eyes met as he put it on his clothes out of my reach. Then he snaked a powerful arm around my waist and dragged me between his legs.

12

BRIEN

I pulled Twilight close and fastened my mouth on her nipple, so turned on that right then, she could've told me she was here to stake me and I would've answered, "As long as I get to fuck you first."

I wasn't supposed to be in the Bite Club, or anywhere near Twilight. I'd decided to stay away from her for the rest of the night.

Then, as our meeting ended, Talon had glanced at his phone and done a doubletake.

"What?" I asked.

"Your new thrall."

"What's she up to now?"

Talon showed me and Cain the scene in the Bite Club: Twilight, surrounded by our three favorite thralls, Pinky shaking her lush bottom, and Eden and Lesa forming a sandwich with Twilight in the center. When Eden spun away, Twilight turned and ground her ass against Lesa's.

I nearly swallowed my tongue. My dick sprang to attention, pressing against my shorts.

"Holy Dark Lady," Cain said in a hushed voice.

Talon put the phone back into his pocket. "I think I'll go shower and then get Eden," he said with a small smile.

He left, and Cain and I changed into workout clothes and went to the gym to pump some iron. In between reps, I obsessively checked the camera feed.

Clarisse Dumas approached Twilight.

That wasn't good. Clarisse was power hungry. It made her a good enforcer; she'd do anything my father ordered, including sleeping with his son. When I'd been a few years younger and a lot dumber, I'd let myself be lured into her bed for a few nights.

Clarisse was a beautiful woman with the tits of a porn star. I'd been more than willing to fuck her...until she'd started making noises about setting a date for our mating ceremony. I'd told her as diplomatically as I could that I didn't intend to mate with anyone for at least another fifty years.

Anger had tightened her face, but she'd swallowed it to say, "I can wait."

I'd inclined my head and left. I couldn't afford to straight-out reject her. I needed every ally I could get.

To my relief, Clarisse moved off after a short exchange with Twilight.

I returned the phone to my pocket and put in a hard forty-five minutes on the elliptical before checking on Twilight again. This time, she was laughing with Chad.

My fangs pricked at my gums. The man was eyeing her with way too much interest.

Cain snorted. "Go get her, for fuck's sake. She's a new thrall. Jules and Prosper won't think anything of it. In fact, they'll wonder what's up if you stay away from her these first few days."

He had a point, one I was more than willing to accept.

"Maybe I will," I said, and headed for the showers.

As soon as I was dressed, I aimed for the Bite Club, no longer giving a rat's ass if Twilight was all-in or not.

She was here. She was mine.

And I was going to take her the way I'd wanted to ever since she'd pulled that disappearing act two years ago—rough and raw and deep.

Now Twilight grabbed my shoulders and moaned. "Please, Brien."

I flicked my tongue over the aroused bud of her nipple and sucked harder. She wanted to know if I was worth it? I'd have her on her knees and begging before I was through.

Her slender body writhed against mine, supple as a yoga instructor. My mind filled with all the positions I could take her in.

Moving my hand to her ass, I gave the taut muscles a squeeze.

Sweet Dark Mother. I needed her more than blood itself. I ached for her—her touch, her taste, everything.

A part of me rebelled against the need, wanted to punish her for making me feel like that. She deserved it, for fucking me in Montreal, for making me believe we'd begun something new, something special, and then vanishing from my life.

I shifted to her other breast, scraping my teeth over the soft skin, hurting her…just a little. Putting my mark on her as the most primitive part of me craved.

She shivered and arched her back.

I kept her against me, controlling her, and relishing the fact that she was mine to control. I was an alpha vampire, and she was my catnip.

Sassy, but vulnerable.

Independent, yet willing to let me take charge—when it came to sex, anyway.

Beautiful, but in an understated, *who cares?* way.

Her right hand drifted from my shoulders to my head, holding me against her breast, wordlessly telling me she wanted this as much as I did. My dick butted between her thighs, eager to bury itself in her wet heat. I released her nipple and allowed myself a few strokes against her smooth skin. Pleasure tugged at me like a rip current, dragging me deeper into a swirling sea of sensation.

Her eyes closed. She rubbed her clit over the head of my dick. The base of my spine tingled. The urge to bend her over and push inside her was nearly overwhelming, but I beat it back.

Not yet.

She hadn't begged nearly enough yet.

She whimpered. "I need…"

She reached down, stroking me while I watched, the visual of her capable fingers on me increasing the pleasure.

My balls tightened and drew up. I was close to exploding, so hard I hurt.

"That's enough," I gritted, stopping her with a hand on her wrist.

Her brow puckered. "You don't like me touching you?"

"I like it fine. Now let go." I waited until she released me, then lifted her up and laid her face down over my knees.

She didn't fight me. Instead, she braced herself with her hands on the floor, her braid falling forward over her shoulder. "You're going to spank me?"

She didn't sound afraid or pissed off. She sounded...intrigued.

My dick got even harder. "Sometimes."

Placing a hand on her back, I pushed her thighs apart and wrapped a leg around her calf. With my free hand, I traced the lower part of the red dagger to where the point ended just above her ass.

A shiver went over her. The salty perfume of her arousal filled my nostrils.

I waited for her to ask another question—or to object.

When she didn't, I said, "And yeah, I'm going to spank you. Because I think a part of you wants it, and even if you don't, I want it. I've wanted it for two goddamn years. Then I'm going to keep you here and pleasure you until you're begging me to let you come, and right now, I'm not sure if I'll let you."

"Brien..."

I smacked her ass a couple of times. "It's too soon to beg."

"I wasn't beg—"

I shut her up with a couple of harder smacks. She pushed her bottom up at me, wordlessly asking for more.

I slid my fingers between her legs. She was dripping wet.

Yeah, she wanted this all right.

I gave her another hard spank. This time she moaned with pleasure.

Her muscular butt was pink from my hand. I ran my palm over the heated skin.

"You like this, don't you?" I smacked her again. "Bad girl."

She groaned. "Brien..."

"Quiet. I'm just getting started here."

Her swallow was audible.

My mouth curved. Revenge sure was sweet.

I dipped my fingers between her legs again, spreading her juices up to her clit, swirling around the sensitive bud without touching it. She stood it for a minute or so, then started wriggling her ass, trying to get me to touch her where she wanted.

"Hold still." I pressed a hand to the small of her back, forcing her to still, and gave her another smack. "You're not in charge here, I am."

Her breath sobbed out. "*Please*, Brien."

I slipped my hand under her throat and cupped her chin, forcing her head back so I could scrape my teeth down the side of her neck.

"You left me." The words pushed their way out of my lips, harsh with pain.

Fuck. I hadn't meant to say that.

She stilled, probably as stunned as I was at the hurt in my voice. "I had to. You know I couldn't—you and me..."

"Then you shouldn't have let it go that far." My mouth thinned. "Or was I just a part of the job? A distraction, so no one would notice when Zoe left the ballroom with Rafe."

"No!" A shake of her head. "Jesus, no. I almost blew everything by fucking you. My mission had nothing to do with you. I tried to stay away from you, damn it. You're the one who chased me."

She was telling the truth. I *felt* it, along with her remorse. That was something at least.

And she was correct—I *had* chased her, like a big cat who'd scented his mate. She'd been flirting with another vampire, a Tremblay Syndicate soldier, and I'd sent him off on some fool's errand so I could make a move on her myself.

She pressed against my legs, trying to turn over. I released her head but kept her where she was.

"I didn't think it meant anything to you," she told the floor.

I straightened and slapped her ass to shut her up. "It didn't."

But I think we both knew that was a lie.

"Brien—"

Another smack. "You're talking too much."

"But—"

"I said, *be quiet*." I slid a couple of fingers into her cunt to change the subject.

She moaned and constricted around me. She was so wet and hot, I could've come just touching her. I finger-fucked her, slow and deep, then toyed with her clit, stopping when I sensed she was close to climaxing.

Then I did it again.

The third time I removed my hand from her, she swore at me and tried to slither off my lap.

"Oh, no you don't." I caught her and flipped her onto her back on the couch.

She scowled up at me, breasts rising and falling in time to her ragged breaths. "God, you can be a prick."

I smiled and knelt between her thighs. Her nipples were dark and aroused, her knees bent up so I could see the glistening pink heart of her.

I slicked a finger over her sex, and she groaned and rocked her hips up toward me, so close, a couple more touches would probably do it.

I played with her until I drew a few more whimpers and a gush of hot liquid. I showed her the dew. "I guess you like pricks, then."

Her mouth bent in a rueful smile. "I guess I do."

She watched as I licked my finger. She tasted as sharp and salty as the ocean outside the castle.

"I like *you*, anyway," she admitted, low-voiced.

A look passed between us. I didn't answer, but my anger eased.

I drew a finger down the center of her throat. Her pulse fluttered, causing my fangs to tingle with the urge to lengthen. The craving pulsed in me.

Her gaze slid from mine. "I don't want to. But some things you can't help."

"I know."

Our gazes tangled. We stared at each other, arrested.

You feel this thing between us, too?

Yeah.

Then she turned her head and closed her eyes, deliberately shutting me out.

A harsh growl vibrated in my chest. She could try to shut me out; that didn't mean she'd succeed.

I traced my finger through the slight cleavage formed by her small, perfect tits and continued down to circle her navel. I toyed with her clit. Her thighs tensed and she caught her breath.

I removed my hand and combed my fingers through the neatly trimmed hair on her mound. She squirmed on the velvet cushions.

"Damn you! Do it already. This is me, begging. I need to come."

I nearly laughed aloud. She wasn't begging. No, she was practically ordering me to get her off.

And damn if it didn't turn me on. She *was* a badass, after all. Her strength challenged the alpha in me, made the erotic game we were playing even more enjoyable. Easy women bored me.

I'd take this complicated, secretive, former—or not-so-former—slayer over any other thrall in the castle.

Hell, I'd take her over any thrall I'd ever had, period.

I moved lower, putting my mouth to her sex. "I think you can do better," I said against her slick pink flesh.

"Better?" She sounded dazed.

"Mm-hm." Getting up, I snagged a condom from my pants pocket, then came back to stand over her.

She sat up and reached for me, but I shook my head as I rolled it on.

"Lie down and spread your legs," I told her.

Her beautiful almond eyes flared. For a few moments I thought she'd refuse, then she lay back down, propping herself on her forearms. Holding my gaze, she slowly spread her thighs in invitation.

I knelt between her legs and stroked her throat, locating the plump jugular vein. It pulsed beneath my fingertips; sweet, dark seduction. My mouth watered.

She caught my wrist, holding me still. "Are you going to feed from me?"

"Not tonight." She still needed to gain back that weight she'd lost. "But I will take a sip."

She licked her lips. "All right."

I eyed her, unable to read how she felt about my feeding from her. Guilt niggled at me. The syndicate thralls always signed a contract spelling out the agreement between us before anything happened, but I wasn't willing to enter a thrall contract with Twilight. The dark part of me liked owning her, didn't want to give her any kind of an out.

I tugged my wrist from her fingers and went back to stroking her —her throat, her breasts. "It doesn't hurt. The thralls love how it makes them feel."

She nodded. "I'm not worried." A short pause, in which her gaze slid from mine. "You're not my first. And I don't mean Fleur's coven. That was against my will, and those SOBs knew it and didn't give a fuck."

"There were others? While you were on a job?"

"Yeah—and I liked it, okay? A couple of times, I volunteered for a job because I—you know." Her expression dared me to say anything.

That animalistic possessiveness arose in me again. The alpha beast —the vampire—wanted to punish her for not waiting. For letting some other vampire taste her, fuck her.

I moved lower and slid my hands under her ass. "Yeah, you're going to have to beg for a long, long time before I let you come."

She actually curled her lip at me. "Fuck. You."

I smothered a grin and nipped her mound. "Now you're really in trouble."

"Brien..." She moved her hands restlessly over her body, like when she was dancing—touching her tits, her belly, her thighs.

I hadn't thought I could get any harder. I was wrong.

My breath whistled in through my teeth. When her hands came to her mound, I caught them, pinning them on either side of her hips, and brought my mouth to her center, blowing a stream of warm air over her sensitive flesh.

"Beg me, sweetheart. Beg me to finish this. Beg me to let you come."

"Go to hell." She tried to jerk her hands from mine, but I tightened my grip and rubbed my lips over her sex.

Light, teasing touches that I knew wouldn't be enough. I could be patient. It was no hardship; I could've licked and sucked her all night.

It wasn't long before she released a small, agonized sound. *"Brien."*

I gave her a wolfish grin. "Beg me," I reminded her and touched the flat of my tongue to her clitoris.

She cursed—and broke, begging and pleading in a way that the primitive part of me fucking loved.

I might not be her first, but I was determined to be the one she never forgot.

It would be my face she'd see when she touched herself, even years from now.

My body she'd feel moving between her thighs.

My name she'd moan as she climaxed.

When I finally took pity on her, it took two swirls of my tongue before she shattered, sobbing my name in a way that was music to my ears.

She was still saying it when I slid inside of her.

So. Damn. Good.

Every nerve in my body lit like I'd been hit with a jolt of electricity. I stilled, head thrown back in ecstasy, as my fangs slid out. Still deep inside her, I scraped the sharp points over the pulsing vein until a few drops of blood welled.

I lapped it up, taking her special, unique taste onto my tongue, and giving her the aphrodisiac in my saliva back.

Her lungs heaved and her back bowed as the potent chemicals raced through her bloodstream. I licked the small wound again until it healed, then started thrusting into her.

"Yes..." She dug her nails into my shoulders, bucking wildly beneath me.

I pressed her down to the couch, controlling her movements, and continued stroking in and out of her.

"More." She rubbed her pelvis against mine.

I angled my hips so that I brushed over her clit with each pass. "Like this?"

"Yes. Oh, God. Yes..."

And then she was coming again, her pussy clenching around me like a hot fist.

Sparks shot up my spine. I slowed my strokes, fucking her hard and deep and raw.

Exactly as I'd pictured that I'd take her when I finally tracked her down.

And I would have tracked her down. I knew now I would've never given up, never stopped searching for her. My vampire wouldn't have let me.

A savage possessiveness engulfed me.

Mine.

I stroked in, then out.

You're mine now.

Then I stopped thinking and simply felt, each thrust better than the one before.

My world narrowed to her. Her scent. The grip of her smooth thighs around my hips. The heated clasp of her sex.

Her feline eyes opened, captured mine.

I gripped the base of her braid and gave her a rough kiss, licking and sucking at her lips, her tongue.

We were still kissing when my climax overtook me. I dragged my mouth from hers and pressed deep, giving myself over to the explosive pleasure. When I was finished, I hung over her, wrung out and satiated.

A minute, maybe more, passed, then Twilight heaved a breath and straightened her legs alongside mine.

"Okay," she said with a cheeky smile, "that was definitely worth my while."

I nipped her ear and rolled onto my back, drawing her into my arms. "You're such a bad girl."

"Guilty." She snuggled into me and rested her cheek on my chest.

I caressed her neck and shoulders, heart full.

I'd never felt like this before. I wanted to kiss her. Worship her. Offer her the moon and the stars if she would promise to stay with me.

Gradually, uneasiness crept in. I didn't want to feel like this. I *couldn't* feel like this.

I stopped stroking her.

Jules snarled in my brain. *You're soft, boy. She's nobody—a human. You don't need her fucking permission to keep her. She's already yours.*

She combed her fingers through the hair on my chest. "What are you thinking?"

The tenderness in her voice, the *caring*, somehow grated. I didn't want her to care for me.

This wasn't about love or affection. It was about sex and blood and power.

All the reasons why I shouldn't trust Twilight poured back into my mind.

"Get dressed." I smacked her bottom, a reminder to us both that she was just a thrall. Hell, she was lower than that. She was my slave.

She stiffened, and my heart constricted. I opened my mouth to say I was sorry, then shut it again.

A Leclerc prince doesn't apologize to a thrall.

Another lesson Jules had beaten into me.

Without a word, Twilight slid from my arms, gathered her clothes and disappeared into the women's restroom.

I tossed the condom in a trash can and got dressed. When she emerged, I was waiting.

"If you're finished with me, my lord?" Her voice dripped with ice.

So I was "my lord," now. Well, I'd asked for it.

I jerked my chin at the exit. "Yes. Return to your suite."

"Yes, my lord." She turned to leave, then swung back around.

Her eyes flickered, and for a fraction of a second, I saw the vulnerable person behind the badass. The woman who'd snuggled against me after sex as if she really did like *me*—not the prince.

I grimaced. "Twilight..."

Lucky for me, she regained her inner badass before I said anything further. Striding back to me, she grabbed the front of my T-shirt and planted an open-mouthed kiss on my lips. Then she went to the door.

The last thing she did was fling me a kiss-my-ass smirk. "Thanks for a good fuck, *Prince*."

Then she was gone, leaving me alone in the empty club.

13

TWILIGHT

I sauntered back to my suite as if Brien hadn't sent me away like a plaything he'd grown tired of. Head high, shoulders back, a smile on my lips.

But the moment the door closed behind me, I slumped against it. Damn Brien anyway for making me feel something for him.

In that moment I hated him a little.

A tear slipped down my cheek. I scowled and swiped it away.

I should've known better than to believe he still felt the same connection I did, that whatever was happening between us was honest, even if nothing else was.

I'd seen enough vampires lie to their thralls, pretending the thrall was special, when they were only looking to add another notch to their bedposts.

Some even laughed about it after with their friends.

My nails dug into my palms. *If he dared...*

With an angry toss of my head, I headed into the bathroom for a shower. Washing off Prince Brien's scent sounded like a helluva good idea right now.

I pinned up my hair and set the temperature to hot, choosing the lower showerheads so my hair would stay dry. Heated water pummeled me from five directions. I closed my eyes and let it wash me clean.

By the time I stepped out, I had things in perspective.

I mean, it *had* been a good fuck.

No complaints there. I was still humming.

So what if the man who'd provided it was a prick? Maybe that was for the best. At least I wouldn't do something stupid, like fall in love with his cold-hearted ass.

This situation was already a shitshow. The last thing I needed was to get all warm and fuzzy about Brien.

I toweled off and put on a sleep shirt. I had a TV, even if I didn't have the internet, so I curled up on my couch and put on an old movie.

An hour later, I awoke with a start and stumbled sleepily into the dark bedroom. Dragging the covers down, I crawled into bed and laid my head down.

And stilled.

My pillow had an odd lump.

Uneasiness snaked over my nape. I slipped my hand into the pillowcase—and touched a closed switchblade.

My breath sucked in. I jerked my hand back out like I'd been burned.

I pushed up on my forearms and looked around the room.

But I was alone. You get an instinct for things like that, and I *knew* no one had been here when I first entered, and after, I'd been in the living room. No one could've come into the suite without waking me up.

No, the blade must've been placed in my pillowcase earlier tonight.

I lay back down, aware that I might be under surveillance. Still, even a vampire needs some light to see, and the bedroom was pitch dark with no windows. The camera might have detected some motion, but they'd just figure I'd rolled over.

Gingerly, I slid my hand back into the pillowcase and felt around.

There was something else... There. I had it—a slip of paper about two inches square.

Leaving the switchblade where it was, I palmed the piece of paper and went into the bathroom. A couple of low lights came on, one above the sink, the other above the toilet. I closed the door and tilted the paper until I could see it in the light.

This time, it wasn't a note, it was a photo—of my halmoni exiting her LA condo dressed in her trademark black T-shirt, jeans and white sneakers. A recent picture, because her short brown hair had gray streaks in it. She must've stopped dyeing it.

My stomach clenched. The message was plain.

Kuro knew where my halmoni lived. Had her under surveillance.

Stake Brien, or she'd be hurt, even killed.

Blood pounded in my ears. My fingers closed on the photo, crumpling it.

You lowdown son of a bloodsucker.

It was bad enough that Kuro was blackmailing me, but to drag my seventy-eight-year-old grandmother into it? A respected former slayer?

Shaking with anger, I sank onto the toilet seat. For a long moment, I simply sat there, jaw working, fist clamped around the photo.

Then my training took over. Ripping the photo into tiny pieces, I lifted the seat and flushed them before sitting down again.

I stared down at my knees, stomach knotted. The last of the strawberry margaritas pressed against my throat, threatening to come up.

Three things were overwhelmingly, terrifyingly clear.

One: Kuro was in this for himself. No way the SI Board would've approved a threat against my halmoni. Me, yes.

But not my grandmother. Not the legendary Ghost.

Two: Kuro must be here on Lilith Island. Maybe even inside the castle itself, although from what I could tell, all the castle's human employees were members of families that had lived on the island for decades, even centuries. Either way, Kuro was close. Close enough to send me a message. Close enough to slip me a switchblade.

But it was number three that had me jumping off the toilet and running to throw up into the sink.

If I didn't slay Brien, my halmoni would pay.

My second day started out a lot like the first, except I woke up with a headache and a mouth that tasted like cotton.

At least I'd slept. I'd lain awake for hours until exhaustion finally took me under. It was afternoon before I opened my eyes again.

I palmed the switchblade and took another shower, washing my hair even though it didn't really need it so I could hide the blade in the shampoo bottle. When I emerged from the bathroom, I found breakfast waiting for me in the living room. I carried the tray into the garden, and after two cups of coffee and an egg sandwich, felt marginally less sluggish.

I toyed with a croissant, ripping off pieces without eating them.

Now that I had a weapon, it was up to me to get Brien alone, preferably outside the castle so I could escape and stow away on the ferry. My stomach curled in on itself. The thought of staking Brien made me physically ill, but what choice did I have?

If only I could get a message to my halmoni. She was resourceful, and she still had friends in SI.

I put down the mangled croissant and, leaving the tray on the coffee table, headed upstairs for a walk. As I left the castle, Jasper was waiting in the courtyard. I nodded at him and kept going, but when I glanced back, he was ten yards behind me.

So Brien didn't trust me. Smart man.

I spent a half hour sunning myself on the beach and trying not to think. When I climbed back up the cliff, Lesa was coming down the path, a funky scarf wrapped around her brown curls.

"Hey, Twilight," she said with a smile.

"Hey."

She started to walk past, then stopped and swung back. "I'm on my way to Bluebeard's Cove to visit my mom. Wanna come?"

"I'd love to."

"It's on the other side of the island, but I'll show you the shortcut."

The shortcut was a dirt path through the forest. As trees closed around us, cool and green, I glanced at Lesa. "Bluebeard's Cove?"

Her left cheek creased in amusement. "Half the island's descended from pirates."

"Pirates? You're shitting me."

She put a hand over her heart. "It's true, I swear."

I chuckled and shook my head.

Lesa grinned. "You don't wanna mess with a Lilith Islander."

"I'll remember that."

The hike to Bluebeard's Cove took about fifteen minutes. We descended through the trees, coming out on a low cliff. The town was spread out before us, postcard-perfect: colorful clapboard houses, neat green lawns, a pair of slate-topped churches. In the harbor, brightly painted boats bobbed, protected by moss-covered cliffs that hugged the cove like a pair of arms.

"Wow," I said.

"It's pretty, isn't it? And it's all for us. No outsiders allowed without the syndicate's approval."

To get to the town, we had to walk down the winding stone steps cut into the cliff. As we reached the bottom, I noted the location of the ferry terminal at the end of a pier.

Lesa followed my gaze. "The ferry's free," she told me, "a service provided by the syndicate."

I considered the sleek blue boat. "How fast does it get you to the mainland?"

"To Halifax? About two hours."

"Has this island always belonged to the Maritime Syndicate?"

"Yeah. Primus Leclerc bought it from a pirate—or stole it," she added, her dark eyes twinkling. "The story's a little unclear on that point."

"And the humans stayed?"

"The primus offered steady jobs and a chance to turn all that pirate gold into businesses they could pass down to their children. An early form of money laundering. My great-great-whatevers took the deal, like a lot of other islanders."

"That's my mom's café." Lesa indicated a small, white-washed restaurant with a red roof and bistro tables shaded by striped umbrellas. "You want a coffee?"

"No money," I said with a rueful shrug.

"Didn't anyone tell you? You can tell the shops to bill the syndicate —just let them know you're a new thrall. Actually, they probably know already. It's a small island."

"Then I'd love some coffee."

We ordered coffee and blueberry pie, which arrived still warm from the oven.

"Mom bought the café with syndicate money," Lesa told me.

"She was a thrall, too?"

Lesa nodded. "I suppose it seems strange if you didn't grow up here, but where else can you make enough money in a few years to buy your own business? Besides—" her mouth curved—"it's no hardship to fuck a vampire, is it?"

"No." I squeezed my thighs together, the memory of Brien moving inside me still fresh. "It isn't."

"Hey, you guys." Eden spoke behind me. "Tell me there's still some blueberry pie left, or I may have to do you some damage."

"I don't know," said Lesa with a grin as Eden and Pinky took the chairs across from us. "Twilight here had two slices already."

"I regret nothing," I shot back and we all laughed.

The server bustled up. "Of course, there's enough pie," she said with a frown at Lesa. "Your mom baked a half-dozen just this morning."

"I'd like a slice, then," Eden said. "A large one."

"And coffee," Pinky added.

"Somebody was up late," murmured Eden.

"Mm." Pinky's mouth curled in a cat-who-ate-the-cream smile.

More pie and coffee arrived, along with bite-sized pastries that Lesa's mom asked us to test, and that we pronounced delicious. By the time we rose to leave, I realized I was actually enjoying myself, even if the whole time my brain had been ticking away in the background, gathering facts and impressions about the three women and wondering if any of them were working for Kuro.

Back at the castle, we scattered to our own apartments. I couldn't help noticing that no one else was located as close to Brien as I was. Apparently, he wanted me where he could keep an eye on me.

Jasper had taken off as soon as we arrived back, so after a short stop in my suite to freshen up, I headed out to explore the castle. Might as well test my limits.

The level where my suite was located was a twisty, poorly lit labyrinth. I kept running up against locked doors and having to retrace my steps and try another passage.

Definitely the vampires' level.

I was at the opposite end of the castle from my own rooms when I came upon a door guarded by a hard-faced soldier. He folded his arms over his blue uniform and glowered at me like I was a roach he'd like to crush beneath the heel of his combat boots.

"This section is forbidden to unaccompanied thralls. Leave."

"No problem," I said with a shrug and turned back.

I felt his gaze boring into the space between my shoulder blades until I went around the bend. So that's where the primus's apartment was. Why else post a guard outside the door?

I made my way back to the center of the labyrinth again. This time, I climbed the stairs to the ground floor. From the air, I'd seen that the castle was basically a rectangle with a tower at each corner and a curtain wall running around the top. Now, I explored the long corridors between the towers.

The rooms were beautiful, with marble floors and furniture that would have been at home in the palace at Versailles, but strangely empty. They'd clearly been set up for show, not actual living. Other than Avril, huddled over a laptop at a table in the large, book-filled library, the only people I ran into were Kerry, who gave me a short, unsmiling nod before continuing on her way, and a couple of maids.

A ballroom filled the entire north wing, its tall windows draped in red silk curtains that were a lush contrast to the black-and-white checkboard floor. A half-dozen chandeliers dangled from the high ceiling, their crystals polished to a fierce shine. Gilded mirrors hung at intervals along the walls, and a pair of black marble fireplaces with sharks carved into their surrounds stood at opposite ends of the dance floor.

I wandered around, taking everything in. I could almost hear the music playing, see the room filled with vampires and thralls dressed in all their finery, like they had been that night I met Brien.

Then I was turning myself, arms curved in a dancer's pose. My mirror images spun with me, an endless series of Twilights in pink tees and silver high-tops, their long dark braids whipping around their faces.

I crouched and brought my fists up, mock-fighting with my reflections, leaping and kicking in a martial arts sequence that came as naturally as breathing, one I'd learned from my halmoni as a kid. I'd missed working out; missed the ebb and flow of the familiar sequence; missed pushing my body to go harder, faster, higher.

It felt good to move, to remember that I was a trained fighter, not the helpless thrall I was pretending to be.

Mindful of the cams above a couple of the entrances, I added a few dance moves here and there, pretending I was doing one of those body-combat workouts. Exercise, not training.

I kept it up until I was bent over, gasping, then jogged slowly around the ballroom to cool off. As I slowed to a walk, a spidery awareness crawled up my spine.

Someone was watching me.

Wiping my face on the hem of my shirt, I darted a look around.

The side door opened. I glimpsed a lean, dark-haired male dressed in a T-shirt and cargo pants, then he was gone.

Kuro.

There was something about that smooth, gliding gait—the gait of a martial arts expert, which I assumed Kuro was. You didn't graduate from an SI training facility without a black belt.

I flew across the marble floor and threw open the door, only to find myself in a windowless passage, at the end of which were two more doors. I tried the door on the right first. It led to a staircase landing, with steps going up and steps going down, both empty as far as I could tell.

The door on the left opened onto the back lawn. When I jerked it open, the man was hurrying around the corner of the castle. I dashed across the grass, skidding to a halt a few feet from the edge of cliff, but he'd disappeared.

I peered over the cliff. Sixty feet below, waves crashed and foamed over the sharp rocks at the bottom. The drop was nearly straight down, too steep for anyone to have gone over unless they were a freaking rock climber. And if Kuro had gone over the side, I should've been able to see him.

Unless he'd disappeared into the shadows.

Most slayers were dhampirs, after all. As a human, I was the odd one out. SI had only recruited me because of my ability to resist a vampire's compulsion, and because my mom had vouched for me. You could say it was the family business.

"Hey!" A soldier loped toward me, a wolfdog at her side.

I ignored her to jog along the narrow strip of grass between the castle and the cliff. I found another door about ten yards down, but when I tested it, it was locked.

That crawling awareness tightened the back of my neck.

I spun around, but there was no one there—that I could see, anyway. My hands fisted. "What the hell do you want from me?"

But of course, I knew.

He wanted me to know that he was watching. That I was his creature, dancing to whatever tune he played, and I'd better remember it.

The soldier rounded the corner. The dog snarled lowly, but at a sharp command from her, it settled onto its haunches, its hazel wolf-eyes fixed on me.

The soldier's gaze jumped from me to the cliff. "Is something the matter, Miss?"

"No," I said, aware Kuro was probably nearby, listening. "I was just —" I came up blank. "Jogging," I muttered and brushed past her and the wolfdog to go back inside.

❧ 14 ❧

BRIEN

"You." Twilight's mouth turned down as I let myself into her suite through the French door.

She was kicked back on the couch, her braid falling forward over a red satin bustier in a shiny espresso rope, reading a book and nibbling on a chocolate from the box I'd had delivered along with a crate of romance novels I'd had expressed from the mainland.

It was an apology of sorts; I'd mishandled things last night. I was never going to win her trust if I kept pushing her away.

"Me." I gave her a crooked smile and reached out a hand. "I came to get you."

She looked at my hand, then popped the candy into her mouth and chewed. Slowly.

"No hurry," I added.

Her eyes narrowed like she thought I was being sarcastic, but I meant it. It was no hardship to wait, not when she was reclined on the cushions that tight red bustier and a black-and-silver pleated skirt that exposed a length of smooth thigh. She could've been posed for an erotic painting: *Woman Eating Chocolate*.

Just looking at her made my dick stir.

Finishing the chocolate, she dropped the book on the table and rose to her feet.

125

"Thanks for the chocolate," she said, arms crossed over the bustier like expressing gratitude was painful, but something she felt she had to do. "And the books. I've missed reading."

I allowed myself a small smile, pleased she'd enjoyed my gifts. "I figured you needed something to do."

Actually, she'd been a busy woman that day. I'd reviewed the security footage of her with Cain, and she'd covered a lot of ground, visiting the village and surveying a good amount of the castle.

The scene in the ballroom—part dance, part martial arts—had been like watching my own private dancer. I'd found myself picturing all the ways that strong, supple body of hers could move for me.

The bit at the end had been puzzling, as if she'd spotted someone else in the ballroom with her, but if so, they hadn't shown up on the video feed. Cain had promised to dig deeper, but it wasn't difficult for a syndicate member to avoid the cams, especially aboveground, where they served mainly as backup for the wolfdogs patrolling the grounds.

After all, no one could approach the island without us knowing. Even a vampire concealed in the shadows had to arrive by some kind of vehicle. The only aboveground cams were at entrances and in a few public rooms like the ballroom—and everyone in the syndicate knew that.

"Well, thanks." She looked me up and down. "So. I suppose you're here for another round? My lord." Her lip curled.

Hell, yeah.

I prowled closer, stopping a foot away from her. Inhaling her clean feminine scent.

A tiny shiver ran over her body, but being Twilight, she squared her shoulders and glowered back.

I fingered her silky rope of hair, letting the backs of my fingers brush her nipple. It hardened beneath the red bustier.

"I wouldn't say no to another round—" I wound the braid around my palm and tugged, forcing her to step closer—"but that's not why I'm here."

"No?" Her throat worked. Her gaze went to my mouth. "Then why?" Her tone thickened.

"You'll see."

With my free hand, I rubbed my thumb over a smear of chocolate at the corner of her mouth and held it to her lips. She raised her eyes to mine and sucked my thumb inside.

Her mouth was hot...wet. I could almost feel it closing around my dick.

"Mm." Her lids lowered. "My favorite kind of chocolate."

"I know."

"You knew? How—?" She shook her head. "Never mind."

I bent my head and licked the seam of her mouth, taking the chocolate's sweet, dark flavor onto my tongue.

"I'm here for a reason," I murmured.

"Yeah?" Her throat worked.

"Um-hm." I nibbled her soft lower lip. "I have something I want to show you."

Her eyelids drifted lower, then shut altogether. She forced them open with a visible effort. "Sure. Whatever you say, *my lord*."

I tightened my grip on her braid. "If you're trying to piss me off, it's not working. You can 'my lord' me all you want. I'll also answer to 'sir' or 'master.' Actually, I prefer *master*."

Her breath hissed in. "You—"

I grinned against her lips. "Or you can call me Brien. Your choice, love."

She opened her mouth, and I kissed her, swallowing her growl.

Her hands came to my chest. A second ticked past, then another. I slid my tongue deeper, tasting her the way I'd craved ever since waking up.

Another few seconds passed. I waited for her to push me away, or simply freeze and leave me kissing a block of ice. When she didn't, I cupped her cheek with one hand and eased back.

Not breaking the kiss. Tempting her with leisurely strokes of my tongue.

Her breath sighed out. Her hands fisted in my shirt. She leaned into me, sucking my tongue deeper.

I rumbled approval, gathering her closer with an arm around her waist. She was like liquid wax against me, warm and pliable, making sexy little sounds that I drank in like a drug.

I ached to bend her over the couch, lift that tiny excuse for a skirt and thrust inside her, but I'd come here to make up for my asshole behavior last night. Jules was still directing my moves, and that had to stop.

More than that, I had a deep-seated urge to get to know her better. Yeah, I had a comprehensive file on her, but that didn't tell me who she really was. The woman beneath the sass and sharp edges.

I planted a last kiss on her sweet, chocolate-flavored lips and pulled away. She blinked up at me, eyes so dark I could've drowned in them.

I unwound her braid from my hand and arranged it in the center of her back. "Come." I paused, then added, "Please."

Her breasts heaved. "Let me put on my shoes."

At least she'd stopped "my lording" me. Small steps.

She disappeared into the bedroom and returned wearing blue over-the-knee socks and silver high-tops. Paired with the short skirt, she looked hot as hell, Harley Quinn without the pigtails.

I opened her door and reached for her hand. She glanced down at our joined hands, brows scrunched together, but she didn't try to pull away.

I took a firm grip on her hand and stepped into the shadows. We walked through the passage, unseen, until we reached a tunnel that no one but me, Talon and Cain used anymore. I'd left the door slightly open so we could slip through.

I stepped back out of the shadows, pulling her along with me, and closed the door behind us.

"Jesus," she whispered. "It's dark in here."

I tightened my grip on her hand. "It's a straight shot from here—fifteen yards or so. And you don't have to whisper."

"Oh. Then why the secrecy?"

I started walking. "It's a surprise." Plus, I didn't want my father—or any of the older vampires—to see me favoring her more than I would any new thrall.

We wound our way up the west tower's spiral staircase, me in the lead. Twilight halted, and I glanced back to find her eying the night sky through the narrow window between the second and third floors.

"Tell me you're not going to toss me off the roof."

A huff of laughter escaped me. We reached the top, and I wrapped a hand around her nape.

"Not," I said against her mouth, "unless you're very, very bad."

We exited onto the curtain wall that connected the castle's four towers and I locked the door behind us. When I turned around, Twilight had her forearms on a parapet and was gazing at the silver trail the crescent moon had painted on the ocean.

"Wow." She smiled at me over her shoulder. A genuine smile. "This is—" She shook her head.

I moved behind her and caressed her shoulders. "We're alone up here. No cams. It's my private place. The thralls are allowed up here during the day, but at night, everyone has orders to stay away."

"I can see why you'd want to keep it to yourself." She relaxed back against me. "Thanks for bringing me up here."

I wrapped my arms loosely around her waist and kept talking so she wouldn't remember who she was leaning against and stiffen again. "I used to beg to come up here. Sometimes, if I got my homework done early"—and with zero mistakes—"Ferguson let me come up here."

"Who's Ferguson?"

"My tutor. A human. He retired and went back to the mainland when I was in my teens. I had two other tutors—for physical education, martial arts, piano and dance, etiquette...that sort of stuff. But Ferguson was my main teacher from the time I turned four until I was sixteen." I still visited him every few months, checking that he was well and had everything he needed.

She turned her head to look up at me. "What about your mother and father?"

"What about them?"

"Didn't they care about your homework?"

"No. As long as I exceeded expectations, they left me alone."

"My life was pretty scripted, too. Oh, things were okay up until I turned twelve, although my halmoni trained me in martial arts for two hours a day from the time I was four. But after I was sent to the training camp, every minute of every day was accounted for, even our downtime—exactly thirty minutes after supper, no more, no less. But at least I had those first twelve years with my family. I went to public school and had friends, sleepovers—normal kid things, you know."

"No, I don't know."

"What d'you mean?"

I looked over her head at the ocean. "I didn't have any friends until Talon and Cain were turned. I was fourteen then. Not a kid."

"Jesus." She turned in my arms. Soft palms framed my face. "You had it kind of rough, didn't you?"

"I'm the crown prince. My parents had to toughen me up—otherwise, the other vampire spawn would've turned on me like a pack of wolves."

"Oh, Brien." Sliding her arms around my waist, she rested her cheek against my chest. "You want to know a secret? I used to wish I was a vampire. You're stronger, faster. Like real-life superheroes. I wanted so bad to be turned."

"You?"

"Yeah." A self-mocking chuckle. "When I was a little girl, I used to play vampire and slayer with my dolls. My mom and my halmoni thought it was cute how bad I wanted to be a slayer. But I was pretending to be the vampire, not the slayer. The vampires were rich, powerful. And they live for hundreds of years. Who wouldn't want to be a vampire?"

I had no power.

Instead, I'd had fear.

Duty.

And the crawling sense that whatever I did, however hard I tried, I was still going to fail—and be punished for it.

Because the Maritime heir had to be perfect.

I gathered Twilight closer, craving her warmth. Her very human, very beautiful imperfections. "Money and power isn't everything."

She nodded. "I know that now."

"I guess you do. You've been a slayer long enough."

"Yeah." Her arms tightened on my waist. "We're a pair, aren't we? I knew I had to train hard and learn everything they threw at me—mental and physical—or end up dead or a blood slave as soon as I was sent on my first mission. And they don't care. Not really." A rueful laugh. "The Board doesn't fucking care. If we can't handle it out there, we might as well be dead, because we're no use to them—and a dead operative tells no tales."

"To Hades with them. You're never going back to that." Sliding my fingers into the silky hair at the base of her braid, I drew back her head. "I'm keeping you."

"Brien—"

"You'll have anything you want. Money, diamonds, clothes..."

"Except my freedom, right?" Her lips compressed. "Because you're asking me to stay as your thrall, aren't you? Or will I still be basically your slave—with no contract, no real rights? Hell, you won't even let me have a goddamn phone."

I covered her mouth with mine to stop the questions.

This thing riding me, this feeling I called lust—because I couldn't let it be more—wouldn't allow me to grant Twilight her freedom until I was sure she'd never leave me.

She interested me like no other woman. I wanted to dance with her, coax her to laugh with me like she'd laughed with Chad. Wanted to get inside that clever brain and learn all her secrets.

And I wanted—no, needed—to fuck her, over and over, hard and deep until I'd imprinted myself on her very cells.

Gods, I was an SOB. When you came right down to it, I wasn't any better than my father.

Because if it was the only way to prevent Twilight from leaving me again, then yeah, I'd keep her on the island as my blood slave.

15

TWILIGHT

I kissed Brien back, the switchblade I'd shoved into my high-top a cold weight against my inner ankle.

Do it, damn it.

It was the perfect opportunity to take him out. We were alone, his defenses down.

The man had practically handed me his ass on a silver platter. No cams, and no one knew we were up here.

I could stake him, toss the switchblade into the ocean and sneak back through that tunnel he'd brought me through. No one would be able to pin this on me.

But...he'd trusted me, brought me to his special place. Shared something of himself, which couldn't be easy for a man brought up with only a tutor for a friend—and that's why I couldn't do it.

On top of that, the more I saw of Brien, the more certain I was that SI had no business slaying him. It was a replay of Victorine Tremblay and the Krals, only this time, I didn't know who had it out for Brien.

But someone did, that was for damn sure.

I turned my face and took a gulp of oxygen. His mouth followed, pressing kisses to my cheek, the corner of my lips.

"You're so beautiful," he said hoarsely.

I pushed against his chest. "You still haven't answered me. Would I have my freedom?"

I asked more to buy myself time than because I cared. Brien couldn't hold me prisoner forever. If I really wanted to escape, I would.

His lungs heaved. "Because I don't want to lie to you. Ask me for anything but to let you go."

"I see. Points for being honest, at least." The flippant answer covered my confusion.

This was serious. *He* was serious—about me. Yeah, in a fucked-up, kind of obsessive way, but I could be obsessive myself.

My heart gave a curious little skip.

You could be his.

Longing filled me. My eyes squeezed shut. I tried to think of my halmoni, but all I saw was Brien, his expression open and earnest.

You could be his, and to hell with Slayers, Inc.

I'd been drifting ever since staking my alpha. Searching for a place to call home.

But maybe I hadn't been searching for a place at all. Maybe I'd been searching for a person, someone who'd make wherever I was feel like home.

"I mean it." Brien pressed a kiss to each of my eyelids. "Stay with me and you'll never have to work again."

I swallowed over a prickly lump and opened my eyes. "I—"

"Don't say anything right now. Think about it, okay?"

I exhaled. "Okay."

"I promise I'll make it worth your while."

"Stop it." I shoved at his chest. "I don't want your damn money or jewelry or whatever."

"Who said I was talking about money or jewels?" he asked with a wicked smile and, bending me over his arm, put his mouth to the bustier to suck on my nipple.

A thrill zinged straight to my core. I clutched his head, holding him to my breast. He dragged up my skirt and palmed my ass, squeezing and caressing it. I wrapped a leg around his lean hips and rubbed myself against him like a cat in heat.

The crescent moon emerged from behind the clouds. Brien glanced up at me, his face moonlight-bright, his pale green irises encircled by an unearthly blue.

His fingers dove into my panties, testing my wetness. "This," he said in guttural tones. "This is what I'll give you. More pleasure than you can handle."

His fingers teased and stroked me, driving me into a fast, white-hot orgasm. Stars burst behind my eyelids. I clung to his shoulders, gasping for oxygen.

He pressed me back against the stone parapet and undid his pants. "Take off your panties."

I placed a palm against the rough stone to ground myself. "Not yet." I pushed his shoulder, trying to turn him. "Back against the wall."

His brows drew together in confusion. Then understanding dawned, and he allowed me to move him so his back was to the parapet.

I lowered to my knees on the hard stone in front of him and eased his pants and briefs down his thighs. His erection sprang free. Cupping his balls, I slid my tongue up his length until I reached the cap. I tongued the slit, taking his saltiness on my tongue, breathing his musk.

"Sweet Lilith," he said in thick tones. He grabbed my head and nudged the crown against my lips. "Open up."

Taking control almost before I'd begun.

I smiled against his hot flesh. We'd see about that.

"Not yet," I said, wrapping my hand around the base of his cock.

I licked up his length again, a languorous slide of my tongue.

Showing him that he didn't have all the power. That he was as much at the mercy of this thing as I was.

"Suck me." His fingers tightened on my head. "Take me inside."

"Soon," I said with a wicked glance up at him. "I want to make sure you're ready."

"I'm going to spank you so hard," he warned.

My ass tingled and my insides heated. "You can try," I said against his slick skin.

"Now." He pressed himself against my lips and I opened for him.

He pushed inside and I sucked him deeper. My knees would be bruised tomorrow, but I didn't care. The pain seemed right, somehow. Necessary.

He swallowed audibly. "That feels so good."

He thrust into my mouth, slow and easy, careful not to overwhelm me, when he must've wanted to press hard and deep.

I hummed against his cock. He kept going, an easy, unhurried rhythm, alternately praising me and commanding me, until he broke, fucking my mouth in short strokes. A minute passed, then he stilled and groaned, coming in hot spurts.

Lifting me up, he licked my lips clean, telling me what a good girl I was and that it was my turn now. He set me on the rough stone behind me. Taking hold of my panties, he ripped them down the center. He was already hard again.

He nudged my thighs wide and stepped between my legs, rubbing the blunt head of his cock over my sex. "I have to be inside you."

"Yes." I reached for him.

"Wait." He pulled away and fumbled in his back pocket. "A condom."

He toed off his shoes and dragged off the rest of his clothes. As he rolled on the rubber, I snaked a hand between my legs, so turned on, so wet, just from sucking him, that my fingertips set off sparks. I moaned and rubbed harder.

Brien stood in front of me, watching and fisting himself. "Don't stop," he ordered when I lifted my hand. "I like seeing you touch yourself. Put on a show for me, angel. Show me how much you want me."

I hummed assent and leaned back, still touching myself, heedless of the drop behind me. A hundred feet below, the ocean hurled itself against the cliff. My free hand was on the parapet, but the wall wasn't that wide. A single shove would send me over the edge.

Somehow that made the pleasure even sharper.

Brien grabbed me, anchoring me with strong fingers around my thighs. "What the hell are you playing at?"

"You won't let me fall."

I leaned back even further. My braid swung free, brushing the stone. Gravity tugged on me.

If Brien let go now, I *would* go over. No shove required.

I didn't care. It was my crazy way of showing I trusted him.

"For the Lady's sake." His grip tightened on me. "You like to take risks, don't you?"

I laughed up at him. "I wouldn't be here if I didn't."

"Gods." He wasn't laughing. He shook his head, saying, "What am I going to do with you?"

My smile faded. Taking my hand from between my legs, I brought myself upright so my face was a few inches from his.

"Fuck me," I whispered. "Hard. Make me forget everything but you, in me."

Make me forget I'm supposed to kill you.

His curse was low and vicious. In a swift move, he reached down and tore my panties the rest of the way off. Then he lifted me from the stone perch and lowered himself to a low bench against the wall a few feet away, arranging me so I faced him, my thighs on either side of his, my heels against his ass.

The wind picked up, lifting his shoulder-length blond hair and whipping it around his face. In the moonlight, he appeared impossibly handsome. An emerald-eyed, silver-skinned god.

I rubbed myself against him. "Give it to me."

"First, I want this off." Reaching behind me, he unzipped the bustier and pulled it over my head. The skirt he left on, bunching it around my waist so he could look at me spread open in front of him, his cock pressing against my mound. "That's better," he said, toying with my clit.

I sucked in a breath, and he kept up the teasing touches until I started to climb again. I squirmed on his open thighs. "Now, Brien. *Please.*"

"Oh, I like it when you beg." Lips peeled in a feral smile, he pushed inside me. When he was deep inside, he lifted me and brought me down hard on him.

A shock of pleasure radiated from my center outward. My toes curled in my high-tops. "Oh god, oh god."

"Take it, angel." He did it again, sending a wave of delicious shivers through me.

"Yes." I tightened my grip on him. "Harder."

His lips covered mine in a hungry, open-mouthed kiss. We settled into a rhythm, him lifting me and bringing me down forcefully onto his cock. I was spread open, helpless to stop him. I had to take whatever he gave me, and I loved it. Loved feeling him so hard and deep inside me.

Chills chased up and down my spine. I clung to him, kissing him back until he tore his mouth from mine. His gaze zeroed in on my throat, and his fangs elongated, the points glinting in the moonlight.

Gripping the base of my skull, he turned my head, exposing my throat. He rocked his hips slowly against mine, his focus on the side of my neck.

"So fucking sexy," he said.

I dug my nails into his shoulders. "Do it. I want to feel your teeth."

He rumbled in approval and scraped his fangs down my skin. The pleasure/pain sent a shudder over me.

His mouth came down on my throat again. This time, he sank his fangs deep.

My body arched in pain. I moaned lowly and scrabbled at his back. "Please," I said, not sure if I was asking him to stop or asking for more.

He murmured something soothing and tightened his grip on my skull, keeping me in position for him to feed. He thrust harder, fucking into me.

The pain morphed to a sharp pleasure. When I moaned a second time, it was a blissed-out, don't-ever-stop sound.

He didn't feed long—a minute, maybe two. I was coming before he finished, an intense, incredible orgasm that started deep inside and reverberated through me like a gong.

My mind blanked with the pleasure. The aftershocks kept coming, wave after wave of them. I clung to Brien, chanting his name in a broken voice.

He withdrew his fangs and, without breaking his rhythm, licked my throat clean, healing the tiny puncture wounds. His fingers dug into my hips and he thrust into me, fast and hard, then stilled and groaned, "*Twilight*," as his own climax shuddered through him.

After, he lifted me enough to disengage from me, then turned me so I was sitting on his lap, my legs to the side. I kept my arms loosely around him, my head against his shoulder.

He toyed with my braid. "You didn't cut it off."

"It's not like anyone's letting me near a pair of scissors."

"Like that would stop you."

I shrugged. Okay, maybe I hadn't cut it because he liked it. That didn't mean I was going to admit it.

"I'm pretty sure I could know you a hundred years and never fully understand you, but thanks for not cutting it." He feathered his fingers over my nape. "I can't let it look like I favor you, Twilight. When we're in sight of the cameras or my father's men, I may act like an ass sometimes."

"I figured that," I said, lifting my head. "But what about last night when we were alone in the club? You sent me away like I was a goddamned toy. Someone to be used, then thrown away."

He glanced away. "What about you? Are you going to tell me the truth about why you're here?"

I pushed off his lap and picked up my bustier. "You know why—" I broke off because I didn't want to lie to him, either.

He rose to his feet and we got dressed in silence.

"But thanks," I added, because I couldn't stand how the silence was building. "For bringing me up here." For giving me a glimpse of the real you. "It was...special."

Suddenly he was right in front of me. He tucked a strand of hair that had escaped my braid behind my ear. "Are you in trouble? Is that it? Because I can help."

I stiffened. I'd almost forgotten the switchblade. Suddenly, it felt like a ten-pound weight in my shoe. Then I recalled I'd been wearing my high-tops when I'd wrapped my legs around his hips, and my body broke out in a cold sweat.

What if he'd felt it through the shoe? A vampire's senses were incredibly sensitive, a human's amped by a factor of ten.

"Why would I be in trouble?"

"And now you're hiding something." His hand tightened around my nape. "You should know I'm getting better at reading you all the time. It happens that way between vampires and humans sometimes."

I swallowed. If Brien was finding it easier to read me, it meant we'd formed a personal connection, one he could use to track me.

He angled his head to one side, as if listening to something I couldn't hear. "You're worried—afraid, even. Don't be. You're safe with me, love. I promise."

I tried to push away from him, but he only allowed me to put a few inches of space between us.

I stubbornly kept up the pressure. "Let go. I want to go back."

"I could make you tell me why you're here." His tone was contemplative.

I narrowed my eyes. Actually, he couldn't, since I couldn't be compelled. But he didn't know that.

"Try it," I said between my teeth, "and I *will* take off. First chance I get. You'll have to watch me every second of every day."

He ignored me to continue, "I don't know how you engineered it, but it's too much of a coincidence that you showed up at that auction the one night I attended."

My gaze slid from his. I'd wondered about that, too. Had Kuro arranged for Brien to be there? But how?

Brien scrutinized me. I could almost *feel* him digging into my soul, urging me to spill all my secrets.

Anger. The most effective shield against reading more subtle emotions.

I didn't even have to work at it. I was still furious and humiliated at what had been done to me.

I knocked his hand away from me. "They tattooed me. You think I'd have let them do that if I had a choice? It's like a big fat target on my back. Once the word got out, all a vampire would have to do was rip off my shirt, and they'd have proof it was me. If I was still a slayer, I wouldn't last a year in the field."

"They threw you to the sharks, didn't they?" He touched my cheek. "So why won't you trust me? Tell me what's wrong—what hold they have over you—so I can help you."

I stared at him for a heartbeat, maybe more, so fucking tempted to tell him everything.

Why not? What's stopping you?

Enough had changed between us that I was pretty sure he'd believe me.

He could protect my halmoni from Kuro, and if Kuro *was* on Lilith Island, Brien could track him down. The island was Brien's home turf, after all.

But in saving my halmoni, I'd betray her in the worst possible way. Slayers, Inc. was her life. Her only daughter had been sacrificed to the cause.

And I didn't even want to think about what my mom would've said if she were still alive and found out I'd left SI to become a vampire's thrall. She might've even terminated me herself.

And you'll never be a slayer again.

Bring a syndicate prince into this, and I wouldn't have just burned my bridges with Slayers, Inc. I would've torched the whole freaking city.

"You *are* in trouble." Brien rubbed the pad of his thumb over my lower lip. "I don't have to read you to know that. Let me help, damn it. Let me keep you safe."

Safe? I hadn't felt safe in a thousand years, it seemed like.

I turned my face. "I don't know what you're talking about."

He exhaled through his teeth. Then he stepped back, his expression wiped clean of any emotion.

I felt the loss like a blow to the solar plexus. In sharing those stories, Brien had gifted me with something more precious than money or jewelry or pretty clothes.

But now he'd closed back down again, and it was my fault.

"We should go back," he said.

I hugged my arms around myself. "Yeah. Okay."

❦ 16 ❦

BRIEN

"Where's the prince?" Prosper's voice.

I exchanged a glance with Cain.

After escorting Twilight back to her suite, I'd come straight to my office and buried myself in my work. Better that than dwell on how she was willing to give me her body…and nothing else.

Cain and I had been going over the plan he'd worked out for temporarily taking down the video cams in my father's wing. I intended to make it look like Jules had gone insane and staked himself. Yeah, people would be suspicious, but without proof, no one could pin it on me.

"What the fuck's he doing here?" muttered Cain. It had been years since Prosper had come to my side of the lair.

"Let's find out." I rose and went to my door.

Prosper was in the large natural cavern that had come to be known as my war room. It held weapons, video screens and other security apparatus controlled by me. I had three offices built in a half-circle around it for me, Talon and Cain.

Behind me, Cain shut his laptop.

In the war room, Jasper had risen from his computer station to answer Prosper. "Prince Brien is in his office, sir."

"What can I do for you?" I stepped forward, Cain behind me.

To my right, Talon had already exited his office. He joined Cain, the two standing a little behind me.

Prosper swung to face me, his big arms folded over a navy-blue camp shirt, his TV-cop of a face unyielding. "We need to talk."

I nodded at my office. "Come inside, then."

He shook his head. "Not here. Somewhere we can be private."

I considered the lieutenant. *What did he know?*

Behind me, Talon and Cain had stilled. I didn't have to be a mind reader to know they didn't want me to go off alone with Prosper. But if I refused, it would make me look weak and add fuel to the rumors that Prosper and I were feuding.

I tipped my head at the hallway. "Walk with me."

"Not here when anyone can hear us. My quarters." He strode off as if I was one of his flunkies.

I gritted my teeth and followed. I had no choice if I wanted to know why he'd sought me out.

Prosper's apartment was basically a cave divided into two rooms. The walls were bare rock, the chisel marks still visible. The floor was made of rough stone and the sturdy oak furniture had been built sometime in the previous century.

The only spot of color came from the faded Navajo rug in front of his living room couch. Prosper stopped on one side of the red, yellow and black rug, and I took a stance on the opposite side, facing off like a pair of fighters about to enter the ring.

The lieutenant spoke first. "I think you know what this is about."

Still uneasy about why Prosper had come looking for me, I went on the attack. "Father's worse. We both know it."

"No. He's...about the same."

I noted the slight hesitation and kept hitting. "No, he's not. I was only gone a week, and he didn't even remember where the fuck I went."

"That was just one night."

"So you're saying that he's better? Then where is he? I haven't seen him since I came back from Quebec."

Prosper's mouth tightened—and then he hit back. "You're planning something."

I lifted my brows. "Am I?"

"He's still the primus," Prosper reminded me softly. "And your sire, the man who gave you life. You'll lose the hierarchy's respect if you take him out—and set a dangerous precedent."

Guilt sank sharp teeth into me. I shook it off to respond, "We can't have another death like Gwen's. The humans won't stand for it. And the other syndicates are starting to ask questions. Régis asked me straight out how Father was."

Another hesitation. "I've had a few private messages about him myself."

"And?"

"I refer them to the primus."

"Does he respond?"

"No," Prosper admitted.

"But someone replies. You."

Prosper dipped his chin.

I shook my head. "How long do you think that's going to work?"

His shoulders sagged. He dropped his gaze to the Navajo rug as if looking for answers in the pattern.

I was still taking in how defeated he seemed when he straightened and took a step toward me. "I have a proposition for you."

I nodded for him to continue.

He moistened his lips, like what followed was difficult for him to say. "What if Jules consents to be confined to his apartment twenty-four/seven?"

A beat passed while I replayed what he'd said. "He'd agree to that?"

"I'll make sure he does." His expression didn't change, but his fists clenched. He saw my glance flick to them and quickly smoothed out his fingers, but the small movement was telling. He was genuinely upset at having to ask this. "He knows something's wrong—in his lucid moments, anyway. And if he doesn't agree, I'll lock him in a cell."

Shock held me silent for a few seconds. "You'd do that?"

"Yes." Prosper's chest heaved. "If it were me, he'd do the same."

"What about his thralls? We can't expect them to continue to service him."

"He can drink blood-wine. If he needs more than that, I'll supervise him and a thrall myself."

"He'd remain as primus?"

"In name only."

"With you running things," I said flatly.

"No. I swear on my honor that we'd go on as we have been."

We'd been sharing duties, with neither completely in charge. That Prosper wanted to continue with an arrangement that didn't satisfy either of one of us was a declaration of sorts. He *would* challenge me at some point down the road. If not, he would've conceded to me now.

Still, it might be best for the syndicate to continue as we were for the time being. It would also give me more time to form alliances and convince the older vampires that I was capable of taking my father's place.

And I wouldn't have to live with the shame of staking my own sire.

"No one else has to know," Prosper said.

"That would probably be for the best." I'd tell Cain and Talon, of course, but they knew how to keep a secret.

He let out an almost soundless breath of relief. "So we have an agreement?"

"Yes. But I want your oath that he won't be allowed out of his apartment for any reason. The thralls must be protected."

"You have my word. I'll inform the primus of our decision."

I nodded. "I'll come with you."

"No," he said firmly. Then he sighed. "You...agitate him. It's better if I do this alone. He trusts me."

Hurt jabbed me, quick and sharp. You'd think I'd know better than to expect anything from Jules, especially these days. But apparently, the boy who'd wanted more than anything to please his father could still be hurt.

"It's better this way," Prosper added, and I hated that he saw that little boy.

"Fine. I guess you'd know." I shrugged as if we were discussing someone else's father.

Outside Prosper's apartment, I found Cain and Talon in the hall.

Cain was pacing, but Talon was propped against the wall, outwardly relaxed. I knew better; he was as tense as Cain.

"Everything okay?" Cain asked.

Talon pushed off the wall, his gaze moving between my eyes.

Inside my head, Jules sneered. *Traitor. I always knew you'd do something like this.*

My father had never wanted my love—but he had demanded loyalty.

When you got right down to it, I was conspiring with Prosper to pull off a bloodless coup, something that to my father, would be the worst sort of disloyalty.

But fuck if I was going to feel guilty about it. Jules had wanted a ruthless SOB of a son. In other words, he'd wanted a son just like him.

Well, he'd gotten his wish.

"Everything's fine," I told my friends.

🎋 17 🎋

TWILIGHT

"**H**ey, girlfriend." Eden sauntered around the bend as I closed the door to my suite.

My spine prickled. Her again. It seemed like every time I stepped out of my suite, the tall blond thrall popped up.

"Hey," I said and started walking.

A cold, heavy fog had settled over the island. After sleeping in, I'd spent a couple of hours lying around in my suite, reading, with Demon curled up next to me. Now I'd decided to continue exploring the castle. You never knew when that kind of intel might come in useful.

Eden fell in beside me. "Where are you going?"

I hesitated. My gut said not to trust her, but if she was spying on me, better to have her where I could see her than sneaking around behind my back.

I gave her an easy smile. "Nowhere in particular."

She glanced at my joggers and sleeveless tee. "You're not on your way outside, are you? It's like fucking pea soup out there." Her mouth compressed. "Hell, the fog's even inside the castle. Just one more thing I hate about this goddamn island."

I blinked, taken aback by her bitterness. "Why don't you leave, then?"

"I'm going to. As soon as my contract is up." She let out a breath and gave me a half-hearted smile. "Don't mind me. It's the fog—it gets to me."

I flashed to her crying in the Bite Club. Something was bothering her—something more than the fog—but I was pretty sure that if I pressed her, she'd brush me off again.

"I wasn't going outside," I said. "I figured I'd do laps around the upper floors of the castle."

"Why not go to the gym?"

"There's a gym?"

"You didn't know?"

I shook my head. "I've been working out in my suite."

"Get someone to show it to you. It's big, with plenty of equipment. The vampires use it at night, but in the day it's mainly just us thralls. But I was on my way upstairs to do laps around the curtain wall—wanna come?"

I agreed, and we headed up the stairs and down the hall to the south tower.

Lesa joined us, dressed in joggers and sneakers, her curly black hair pulled into a messy bun. "You going up to the curtain wall? So am I."

"Suit yourself," said Eden with a shrug. As we entered the south tower, she called, "Race you to the top!" and took off with me and Lesa on her heels. The worn stone steps were too narrow to pass anyone, so I kept just behind Eden with Lesa following me.

When we reached the top, Eden high-fived me. "You made it."

I dragged in a laughing breath. "Barely. I'm out of shape."

Lesa emerged from the tower and bent over, hands on her thighs, sucking oxygen. "You two are insane."

Eden just chuckled and jogged off into the mist, blond ponytail bouncing.

"Sometimes I want to smack her," Lesa grumbled as we followed. "She's just too perky to be true."

It's fake.

But I didn't say it aloud, just smiled and shrugged.

We passed the place where I'd had wild monkey sex with Brien yesterday evening. My stomach constricted.

It had been so good...and that was bad.

The man was making me question everything I believed about myself. Being a slayer was in my goddamned DNA. So why hadn't I staked Brien when I'd had the chance?

I'd spent half of the night tossing and turning, my brain like a hamster on crack, racing in circles and never getting anywhere.

Suppose I did tell him the truth and he thought it was just another lie? I hadn't even kept the notes. Even the switchblade wasn't proof— I could've swiped it from somewhere.

I accelerated, racing after Eden until I caught her. She sped up too, and we ran together until we lapped Lesa.

I made an apologetic face at her. "Sorry. I need a workout."

Lesa flapped a hand at me. "Go right ahead."

Eden and I kept going until sweat dripped down our faces.

The second time we lapped Lesa, Eden flashed a tight grin at me. "You seem like you're in pretty good shape to me."

"I haven't had much chance to work out lately."

She grunted. "Where're you from, anyway?"

"LA."

"Jesus, why'd you leave?"

"I went off to school."

"And you never went home?"

My chest tightened. *A slayer doesn't go home, they hole up for a few weeks' vacation and then move on to their next assignment.*

"Not to live," I said.

We kept running. "What about Brien?" she asked. "Where did you meet him?"

I gave her a version of the truth. "I was singing in a club. He saw me and—" I lifted both my shoulders.

"In Quebec City?"

"Yeah."

She shook her head. "You're lucky you got out of there. Some of the covens in the QCS are hard-core."

It was my turn to grunt.

Eden picked up the pace until we were running full-out, unable to talk.

The fifth time we lapped Lesa, we slowed and kept pace for

her. There was just enough room for the three of us to run side by side.

As we passed the monkey-sex parapet, Lesa nudged me. "The prince really likes you, you know."

It was as if she'd read my mind. My stupid heart gave a happy little skip. "You think?"

"Yeah. He almost never comes to the Bite Club for a thrall."

"Work it all you can," advised Eden. "Get him to settle some money on you—extra money, above your contract." Her lips twisted, the bitterness back in her tone. "Before he gets tired of you. And whatever you do, don't fall for him."

On my other side, Lesa nodded.

I didn't inform them that I wasn't under contract and wasn't getting paid. "I wouldn't take extra money from him."

"I see—you have 'principles.'" Eden made air quotes with her fingers. "Or maybe you do think you're in love with him."

Maybe.

I swallowed hard.

"Oh, Twilight," said Lesa.

I pretended I hadn't heard her. "I thought you liked it here," I said to Eden.

"I do." She gave a short, *you actually took me seriously?* laugh. "I'm just in a bad mood. This fucking fog, you know."

I had to ask. "Did Brien get tired of you?"

"Brien?" She did a doubletake. "No. I told you; he doesn't have favorites."

"So it's Talon?"

Her mouth trembled, so quickly, I almost missed it. "Let it go, already," she growled. "I told you, I'm not myself today."

We rounded the east tower, and abruptly, we were in the sunlight, with the North Atlantic and much of the island still covered in patchy fog. I sucked in a breath and halted, taking in the view, and they stopped with me.

In the forest surrounding the castle, treetops poked out of the cottony white stuff. Further away, wisps floated over the fat cows in a meadow near a weathered red barn.

"This island is so beautiful." I rested my forearms on the parapet. "Like something out of a movie."

"I guess so." Lesa swung a heel up on the wall and leaned forward, stretching the back of her leg. "When you grow up here, it's just home."

Eden rested her arms on the parapet beside me. "When I was a kid, I used to look up at the castle and wonder what it was like to be a thrall and live here with all these rich, hot vampires. The women seemed like princesses to me with their fancy clothes and jewelry. And now I know." The corner of her mouth hitched in a self-mocking smile. "We're not princesses, we're dolls. Pretty things with no brains."

"You can't leave?" I asked.

Her laugh held no amusement. "I signed a contract with a vampire syndicate. What d'you think?" She pushed off the parapet without waiting for me to answer. "You know what? I've had enough. See you guys at dinner."

"Wait for me!" Lesa called. To me, she muttered, "Don't mind her. She likes to come off like she doesn't give a fuck, but I'm pretty sure she's in love with Talon. But please don't tell her I said so."

I nodded. "I figured it was something like that."

"Too bad he treats her like just another thrall. I mean, he likes her, but..." Lesa shrugged. "She should've known better. Anyway, see you later." She jogged after Eden.

I gazed after them. I knew better, too. Too bad my heart didn't.

I scowled and, resolutely putting everything from my mind but exercise, went through an extended martial arts sequence. I cooled down with a leisurely jog around the castle wall.

The sun had started its slow slide down the sky. Sunset wasn't far off. Brien would be waking up soon, and he wasn't going to back off forever. He suspected something. He was going to keep pushing.

I had to make a decision, come up with a plan.

I sped up, taking each lap faster and faster, and then I was running full out, my brain back on the hamster wheel.

Brien. My halmoni.

And Kuro. This had all started with him.

God, I ached to take him out. He was using me, and I fucking hated it.

I didn't halt until my lungs were screaming. I doubled over, gasping for breath, no clearer now on what I should do than I had been when I'd woken up this morning.

The north tower door creaked open. My head jerked up.

No one was there. No one I could see, that is.

I straightened slowly. "Who's there?" I called out.

No answer.

My jaw set. Damn Kuro anyway. It wasn't enough to use me, the prick had to stalk me as well.

The shadows shifted, and suddenly I wasn't so sure it was Kuro. The presence felt...different.

The fine hairs on my arms lifted. I recalled what Pinky had told me about a thrall dying last month and backed up, heart crashing against my rib cage.

Someone *was* there. I felt him watching—and somehow, I knew it was a *him*. A vampire, and not a young one, because the sun was still above the horizon.

And my switchblade was five floors below in a freaking shampoo bottle.

Adrenaline spiked in me. My primitive brain screamed: *Run. Hide.*

I drew a breath and forced myself to move slowly.

You don't run from a vampire; it triggers their hunting instincts. Hell, they want you to run. They enjoy the chase.

I backed up another few yards. I would've sworn something brushed against me, even though you shouldn't be able to feel a vampire when they're in the shadows.

I drew in a shaky breath. "Look, what do you want?" Except to scare the crap out of me, that is.

A loud meow made me jump. Demon trotted toward me, tail high and proud.

My lungs emptied in a whoosh. "What are you doing up here?"

She let out a *there-you-are* cry and twined around my legs.

I scooped her up. "Sorry, but I'm on my way down. You'd better come with me, or you might get locked out."

She flicked her black ear and butted her head against my chest, demanding I pet her. When I obliged, she relaxed, purring.

I rubbed my cheek against her fur. "You're a big softie, aren't you? That hard-ass thing is just an act."

The fog had drifted back. Misty fingers curled over the battlements.

As I started toward the tower, cat in my arms, it descended like a curtain dropping. I couldn't see the door five yards away.

Fuck. I tightened my grip on Demon and continued forward, using the stone wall on my left as a guide.

It's only fog.

Until it wasn't.

Jules Leclerc coalesced out of the gray mist. "Hello, *ma petite*."

I recoiled, heart in my throat.

He was dressed in head-to-toe black Armani. He peeled his lips at me in what was meant to be a smile but didn't quite succeed. He was showing too much gum, and his gaze was the fixed stare of a predator.

"You're my son's new thrall."

"Yes." Hugging Demon closer, I straightened my spine.

Never let a vampire see your fear.

He tilted his head to one side. "What's your name?"

I hesitated, but he probably knew the answer anyway. "Twilight."

"Twilight." In his thick French accent, my current alias sounded almost pretty.

And Leclerc wasn't bad looking, really. He was handsome in a sharp-boned, aristocratic way, and he smelled almost as good as Brien.

I swayed toward him, then caught myself. The motherfucker was messing with me, amping up his vampire allure.

I wrenched my gaze from his, my fingers twitching on Demon's fur. I wanted to stake him so bad I could taste it.

Somehow, I dredged up a smile and started to edge past him. "Well, nice meeting you, but I was on my way down."

He blocked me. "I didn't say you could leave."

I instinctively shifted to clueless Lainey Q, pursing my lips like I didn't know what he was talking about. "I'm sorry, but I really have to go. Brien's expecting me."

I tried to edge around him again, but he trapped me between his body and the parapet.

"Brien can wait." Bony fingers touched my face.

My skin crawled. I sidled along the wall toward the open door.

He brought his other hand up and tried to close it around my nape. I ducked and dodged away, but in evading him, I crushed Demon to my chest. She yowled and erupted, slashing his hand with her claws.

He hissed and grabbed my shoulders. "Bitch." He gave me a shake.

Demon hissed back. I somehow managed to keep hold of her.

"It's okay, it's okay," I murmured, afraid that if she attacked Leclerc again, he'd wring her neck and toss her into the ocean.

Leclerc shoved me up against the hard stone. His scratched hand was bleeding. His fangs glinted whitely in the murky light.

My mouth dried. I shoved at his chest with one hand, but he had me trapped.

"Hungry," he said hoarsely.

His pupils had filmed over. It was like he wasn't really inside there, just a mindless, ravenous monster.

Demon flung herself out of my arms and escaped along the wall. I twisted and turned, fighting to break free of him. He grabbed my braid and jerked my head back, exposing my throat. Somehow, I managed to get my knee between us. I brought it up sharply, but he knocked it away with his free hand.

His bleeding hand came back to my throat. Blood trickled down the side of my neck, cold and sticky. His blood.

His gaze snapped to his injured hand. His eyes flared blue, and he let go of me.

I staggered backward with Demon, coming up hard against the stone wall.

Leclerc grabbed his bleeding hand and dragged it toward his mouth. I watched, horrified, as he sank long, razor-sharp fangs into his own hand. He snarled like a dog and tugged, tearing off his own flesh, and sucking eagerly at the spurting blood.

For a couple of beats, I stared at him, too shocked to move, as he gnawed at his own hand like a dog with a juicy bone. Then my breath shuddered in. I backed away.

He didn't even look at me.

I took off for the tower. As I dragged the door open, Demon shot out of nowhere and raced down the steps. I slammed the door shut, hoping it would stop him long enough for me to get away, and hurtled after her.

18

BRIEN

It was done. Prosper had notified me that Jules had agreed to our terms and was confined to his apartment. We'd had to bring Kerry and William in on the secret—someone needed to see to my father's needs—but they'd sworn a blood oath not to tell anyone else.

Now, though, I could turn my attention to Twilight. It had been two nights since I'd last seen her. I'd deliberately stayed away to focus on syndicate business, and to prove to myself that I could.

But my craving for her hadn't eased. No, I'd woken with my fangs extended and a hard-on that wouldn't quit.

Starving, but only for her. Her blood. Her body. Her touch, her scent...hell, even her smile.

I showered and dressed in worn jeans and a black linen shirt. As I slid a dagger into my ankle sheath, I glimpsed Twilight in the garden through the French door's darkened glass.

I crossed the apartment and opened the door. She stood the other side, fist raised to knock on the glass.

"Brien." With an uncertain smile, she brought her arm back to her side.

I knew the uncertainty was because of the way we'd left things the other night, but that was fine with me. I liked her a little off-balance. The gods knew, she had the same effect on me.

"Twilight."

She looked fuckable in black fishnets, patent-leather Doc Martens and a lipstick-red dress that was the next thing to being naked. She'd slicked her hair into a ponytail and painted her mouth the same red as the dress.

My gaze returned to her mound, clearly visible beneath the tight dress.

Did she have on any panties under that tiny excuse for a skirt?

Folding her arms under her breasts, she cocked a brow at me. "See something you like, Prince?"

"Yeah. Turn around."

"Say please."

"Do it," I ordered.

Her eyes narrowed. Then a slow smile curled over her lips and to my surprise, she sashayed in a small circle, showing off her ass for me.

My dick pressed against my jeans. Damn, she was beautiful: strong and supple and vibrant. I couldn't wait to feel all that fiery energy wrapped around me while I pounded into her.

"Remind me to give Avril a bonus," I muttered.

"She has good taste. It's like she knows me."

I forced my gaze from her legs to her face. "I told her you were a sexy badass."

"Yeah? That's how you see me?" The badass looked...shy.

Charmed despite myself, I smiled. "Yeah."

"I mean, I *am* a badass, but I don't know how sexy I am."

"Trust me. You're sexy." Wrapping my hand around her ponytail, I tilted her head back so I could kiss her. Her mouth was petal-soft and yielding beneath mine. I nibbled my way to her earlobe. "Want to know a secret?"

"Depends. Is it a good secret?"

"Yeah." Releasing her hair, I skated my palms down to her hips, urging her up against my pelvis so she could feel how hard she'd made me. "I have a weakness for sexy badasses."

"Sure you do." She rolled her eyes at me. "All those supermodels you hang out with are secretly black belts."

"Says the 'Stylist to the Stars' who was secretly a slayer."

The corners of her mouth twitched. "You have me there."

I turned her in the direction of the French door. "Wait for me in the garden," I said with a hard tap to her ass. "I'll get us something to drink."

Outside the crescent moon shone down on a mist ghosting over the plantings, and tiny lights twinkled along the winding flagstone path. To my vampire sight, the shadowed scene was a living painting of pale, shimmering flowers, dark-branched trees and silvery leaves.

I followed Twilight's scent to where she was seated on a cedar bench near the koi pool, one lean, fishnet-clad leg crossed over the other. The waterfall flowed softly into the pool. On the other side of the outer wall, a wolfdog whined, and a guard quieted it with a word.

"Hold these, will you?" Handing her the two glasses of prosecco I was carrying, I took out my dagger and cut a single pink rose for her, trimming the thorns. I slid the dagger back in its sheath and placed the rose on her lap. "For you." I sat on the bench beside her.

Yearning flickered across Twilight's face. She bit her lip. "Thank you."

She handed me one of the glasses and picked up the flower, inhaling its sweet fragrance.

Her eyes met mine over top of the petals. "I don't want to fight with you, Brien."

"Then don't. Just for tonight, let me romance you."

"Romance me?" She gave a short laugh, like she was sure I was joking, but I'd seen that flash of yearning when I'd given her the rose. She touched the flower to her lips, then put it back on her lap.

"Yes." I touched my glass to hers, holding her gaze as we sipped the dry, bubbly wine.

Suddenly, that was exactly what I wanted to do—romance her. I wanted to forget all the secrets and half-truths and treat her like the quirky, sexy, special woman she was.

Any thought of keeping her off-balance faded from my mind and I found myself speaking from the heart. "I like you, Twilight. I want to get to know you better."

"I'd like that, too, but—" She rolled her lips into her mouth.

"Only what you want to tell me," I added. "A truce, okay?"

She gave me a quick, searching look, then nodded. "It's a deal."

She moved closer until her hip touched mine. Putting my glass on the flagstone path, I slid an arm her shoulders.

She relaxed into me, her fingers toying with the rose. "I love this garden. I've been coming here every day. And it *is* romantic, especially tonight, with the mist and that moon." She glanced at the silver crescent hanging low in the sky.

I rubbed a cheek against her shiny dark hair. She smelled like fresh air, as if she'd spent the day outside. "Zoe designed it."

"The prima?" She took another look around. "Color me impressed. Although, I remember that conservatory in the Tremblay Chateau..."

"She designed that, too."

"That's what I figured. She spent a lot of time there."

I grunted. Zoe was a good friend but I wasn't out here to talk about her. "Tell me about yourself. Was your father a slayer, too?"

The detective I'd hired had said that he and Twilight were estranged.

"No. I'm not even sure how they met. Maybe it was an arranged marriage. I don't know. I haven't seen him in years. He was born in Korea, and he moved back after...after my mom passed."

"I'm sorry."

A small, sad shrug. "We weren't that close. He pretty much washed his hands of me after I stayed with SI even after what happened to my mom. She was killed while on a job, you know."

"The PI put that in the report, but I don't know the details."

She gave a humorless laugh. "Neither do we. It was in South America—I don't know which syndicate. Even my dad doesn't know exactly what happened. All he got from the SI Board was a fat check. Like we wanted their fucking money."

I pulled back to scrutinize her. "You really loved her."

It was like encountering a person from a foreign country, a country you'd heard about but had never visited. One with different customs and a language you knew you'd never be able to learn.

Jules had discouraged affection from me. To keep me strong, he said. I wasn't even allowed to call him "Father."

And my mother had been very beautiful and very demanding, a

woman who'd expected perfection in everything. The gods knew I'd tried, but no matter how hard I worked, it was never good enough.

I wasn't good enough, and I never would be.

I'd almost preferred Jules's beatings.

Twilight finished her prosecco and put the glass on the ground next to mine. The rose she set on the bench beside her.

"I didn't really know her. Mom was always gone, you know? She dropped me off at training camp when I was twelve, and she was captured pretty soon after that. My halmoni—my grandmother—was the one who raised me. But yeah, I loved my mom. Hell, I wanted to be her. She's a legend in SI, you know. The Shade."

"Your mom was the Shade?"

Twilight was right; her mom was a legend. Strong, relentless, incorruptible.

"You've heard of her."

"Oh, yeah. I wouldn't want her on my island, but from what I heard, she had integrity."

"She did." Twilight's smile was pleased.

I laid my cheek against her temple. We fell silent, watching the fish trace shadowy loops in the dark pool. The night was filled with sound: leaves rustled, the waterfall burbled, a cricket's insistent chirp.

We spoke each other's names at the same time.

"Twilight..."

"Brien..."

She turned her head, chuckling, and our mouths met.

"You wanted to say something—?" I asked against her lips.

"Nothing." She slipped a hand around my nape, urging me closer. "It's nothing."

I'd been half-hard ever since I'd seen her in that red dress, but I felt no hurry. I slid my tongue over her soft, slicked-up lips. Even when they opened, I didn't put my tongue inside.

She wasn't in a rush, either. She gave me teasing, shallow kisses—my mouth, my jaw, my cheek. Her other hand came to my chest and nuzzled the hollow of my shoulder.

I gathered her closer, somehow both aroused and content. Being with her like this—holding her—filled an emptiness inside me. A hole in my soul that I hadn't even known existed.

I stroked her inner thigh through the fishnet. Still not in a hurry; just needing to touch her.

She dropped her head back, staring up at the crescent moon. Her chest heaved. "Sometimes I wish I'd never become a slayer."

I drew a small circle on her knee. "Why?"

She huffed a laugh and raised her head. "I don't—" She made a pained sound. "Don't listen to me. I'm in a mood."

But I was curious now; frankly, I couldn't picture her doing anything else. "What would you have done instead?"

"That's the thing—I don't know. It's the family business. And when I showed...an aptitude for it, it was basically a done deal."

"An aptitude?"

She shook her head. "It's a slayer thing."

That made me even more curious. But I'd promised not to push her, and if I did, she'd probably just lie anyway and our fragile truce would be broken.

"But I'm glad now," she said without looking at me. "Because if I hadn't, I never would've met you."

My heart squeezed. Then my whole chest constricted. I felt like I was suffocating.

I released her thigh and massaged my sternum with the heel of my hand, trying to make this painful, needy emotion go away. "Let's go inside." I stood up, drawing her to her feet.

The rose fell to the ground. She ignored it to cup my face.

"I mean it," she said and touched her lips to mine.

I stilled. Emotion flooded me, an overwhelming wave of want and need that was impossible to beat back.

I closed my arms around her supple body and kissed her back, a little too hard. She moaned low in her throat and melted into me, rubbing herself against my dick. I cupped her ass and hitched her higher so I could grind myself against her mound while I ate at her mouth.

She wrapped strong thighs around me and kissed me back with an enthusiasm that made me forget everything but getting inside her.

Her hands were all over my body. Touching my shoulders, sliding under my shirt to stroke my waist.

I walked with her toward my apartment.

She tore her mouth from mine. "Wait. My rose—."

"I'll buy you a truckload of roses." I reached around her to open the door. "Now kiss me."

She laughed into my eyes and obeyed. I kicked the door shut behind us and carried her into the bedroom.

I set her on the edge of the bed and still kissing her, knelt between her legs. I framed her face in my hands, licking into her mouth like she was ambrosia and I a starving man.

It wasn't enough. I needed more. I ached to sink into her, to satisfy this powerful, never-ending craving.

I dragged my mouth from hers and slid my hands down her legs, removing her Docs. She placed her hands on the mattress and watched, legs open enough for me to tell that she wasn't wearing panties—and the fishnets didn't have a crotch, either.

I swallowed a groan.

Taking off my shirt, I undid my jeans and eased the zipper down. Leaving the jeans on for now, I ran my hands up the fishnets to her hips.

She took a short, aroused breath. "Jesus, I want you."

Her thighs widened even more, and her tongue poked out, moistening her kiss-swollen lips. Most of the color had worn off, and her hair was escaping from the ponytail. She was as sensual as Eve, mussed and hazy eyed from my kisses.

I tugged the hair tie off and combed my fingers through her hair, arranging it around her shoulders. "You still didn't cut it."

Her mouth flattened. "You're going to make me say it, aren't you?"

"Say what?" I asked.

That got me a men-are-clueless look. "I didn't cut it because you like it this way, okay?"

My chest tightened with a complicated blend of humility and arrogance.

Sweet Lilith, this woman...

"Don't get too puffed up about it," she grumbled.

I bit back a smile. I was pretty sure that if she realized I was amused, she'd knee me in the balls.

Instead, I set out to show her how much I liked that she wanted to please me, stroking a hand between her thighs and up to where she was slick and hot for me.

"You're such a bad girl." I slid two fingers into her, enjoying her gasp. "I'll turn your ass red if I find you running around the castle like this. No panties and no crotch."

She smirked at me. "It worked, didn't it?" she responded with a pointed look at my erection.

I rubbed my thumb over her swollen clit and her smirk faded. Her eyelids lowered in pleasure. "Don't stop. God, don't stop."

I kept stroking until her breath sped up and her head dropped back. Then I dragged up her skirt, pulling the dress over her head. Her bra was a black cobweb, see-through in strategic spots.

I palmed her breasts over the thin lace, then gave her nipples a hard pinch. "Definitely going to smack that ass of yours."

She gasped, then gave me a sultry, up-beneath-the-lashes look. "C'mere."

She hooked a hand around my nape and leaned back, bringing me with her so I had to come off my knees. She kept going until her back was on the mattress, her feet still on the floor, me leaning over her.

Our eyes met and we both stilled.

I touched her cheek. "I can't get enough of you." A confession ripped from the deepest part of me.

"Brien," she rasped.

Just my name, nothing else. But it felt like she was addressing the deepest part of me, the person that no one, even Cain and Talon, ever saw.

She kissed my bare chest, then brushed her lips over my throat—a light, barely-there touch. It was a no-go zone for vampires, and she knew it, but I allowed it.

I wanted to feel her mouth there. Wanted to grant her this special, intensely personal intimacy.

I wrapped my hand around the back of her skull, holding her mouth to my throat. "Bite me."

She made a hungry little sound and complied, a sharp nip that sent a spike of pleasure straight to my groin. She licked and sucked at the mark, reaching down with her hand to fist me at the same time.

I stood it as long as I could, then set her away from me so I could get undressed. The last thing to come off was the dagger and ankle sheath. I dropped them on top of my pants, and she glanced at it but didn't say anything.

I crawled back on top of her, then halted. "Condom." I started to push off her.

"It's okay. I had a birth control shot about a month ago. It's good for another eight weeks."

She wriggled on the bed, removing the bra. But when she reached for the fishnets, I stopped her.

"Leave them on."

Kneeling between her legs, I spread her thighs. The black netting framed her neatly trimmed mound.

Her gaze followed mine. "God, that's hot." She gave me a one-sided grin. "Even if it's my own cunt."

I pushed her thighs even wider and lowered my head. "Let's see if I can make you even hotter."

Her breath snagged. The blood pulsed enticingly in her veins.

Keeping my mouth on her thigh, I swiped my thumb over her sex. "How's that?" I asked against her fragrant skin.

Her swallow was audible. "Works."

I didn't need her confirmation. I could see it myself, scent her salty musk. I smoothed the moisture over and around her clit and put my mouth back on her inner thigh, seeking the vein that thrummed near the surface.

Her fingers dug into the blue silk duvet. "Do it."

A feral growl rumbled out of me. I tore the netting, baring her thigh, and sank my fangs into her soft skin.

Twilight's back arched. She groaned something unintelligible.

I drew hard, touching my tongue to the wound to make sure the aphrodisiac entered her bloodstream. She moaned and writhed beneath my mouth as the drug raced through her veins. I wrapped my fingers around my cock, stroking myself while I drank my fill.

Her breath sobbed in. "Fuck me. *Please*."

I licked the wound until it closed, then gave her clit a hard suck. She whimpered and begged me again to fuck her.

I was as eager as her. Rising over her, I took her wrists and pressed them to the mattress on either side of her head.

Our eyes met. I knew my vampire must be shining at her: hot blue lust. Some women would've been afraid, wouldn't have been able to hold my gaze.

But not Twilight. She gazed directly into my eyes and said, "Fuck. Me."

Yes.

I bared my fangs and sank into her wet heat.

"Jesus." She gave an agonized groan and bucked beneath me, fighting to pull her hands free.

I forced her back down onto the mattress, dominating her with my greater weight and strength. Her thighs tightened around me.

"Harder."

I fucked in and out of her. Firm, almost punishing strokes.

Wanting to hurt her for making me want to please her.

For making me feel emotions I had no business feeling for a thrall.

And most of all, for making me *need*.

Her eyes closed. She threw her head back, exposing her throat to me in unconscious invitation.

I scraped my fangs over the skin. Not breaking it, just letting her know that I could if I wanted to. That she was mine to take however I wanted.

She turned her head, her mouth seeking mine. Our lips melded together, and I tumbled through a black, starless space.

Time dropped away. The room ceased to exist. My problems—my father, Prosper, Twilight herself—were mere pinpricks.

The only real, true things in the universe were our two bodies, moving together in a sensual dance.

My balls drew up tight as the pleasure ratcheted to an almost unbearable level.

My fingers were threaded through hers now. I slowed down,

changing the angle of my thrusts so I brushed against her clit with each stroke.

She wrenched her mouth from mine. "Please...I'm so close."

I captured her gaze. "Say my name."

She stared up at me, eyes glazed, like she didn't understand. Her inner muscles constricted around me. A tremor went over her body.

"Say it." I pushed deep and stilled. "*Brien*. Beg me to make you come."

Comprehension flitted over her face. She lifted her head and scraped her teeth down my jaw, a wild thing I'd probably never tame... and the primal part of me liked that, was both challenged and aroused.

I didn't want a woman I could easily tame. The pleasure came in fighting her for control.

Small, sharp teeth sank into my earlobe, making me groan. When she spoke, her voice was a gritty purr.

"Fuck me, Brien. Make me come."

I pulled out and flipped her onto her stomach. She scrambled onto her hands and knees, her hair spilling around her shoulders. On her spine, the rose twined around the dagger like a crimson question mark —or a map to the mystery that was Twilight.

I gripped her hips and thrust in again. "Take me, then." With each word, I thrust hard, my thighs slapping against her ass.

With a needy moan, she slid a hand between her legs and rubbed her clit.

"That's it, angel." I wrapped a hand around her throat. Letting her feel my possession. "Feel how slippery you are against my cock. I want that tight pussy squeezing me until I can't see straight."

She drew a jagged breath and put her free hand on the slatted black headboard. The position arched her body in a beautifully erotic pose.

"Brien. Oh, god, oh god..."

The pleasure increased to a white-hot level.

"More," she begged.

I tightened my grip on her throat, careful not to hurt her. With my other hand, I tugged at her nipple. "Come," I commanded.

She made a high, needy sound.

As I thrust back in, I released her throat to pull her hips hard against me. Jagged white lightning exploded through my brain. She moaned and convulsed around me, dragging me over the edge after her.

❦

The next week passed in a haze of sex, wine and chocolate. The vampire trifecta.

I did the minimum of work, letting Cain and Talon handle the rest. I knew I'd shocked them. Hell, I barely recognized this new, irresponsible Brien myself.

But this Brien woke up smiling each night.

This Brien was...happy.

I knew it wasn't forever. People were going to start asking questions—about Jules, about who was in charge. And the uneasy peace between me and Prosper would probably break sooner than later.

Meanwhile, though, I was having the best week of my life.

In between having Twilight in every position I could think of, I coaxed her to tell me about herself. I especially enjoyed hearing stories about her childhood. I could just picture a tiny, dark-eyed, pigtailed Twilight playing vampire and slayer.

"I'll bet you were a baby badass," I'd told her, and she'd snort-laughed.

"Yeah," she'd deadpanned. "I came out of the womb kicking butt."

I toyed with the idea of asking if she'd meant it about dreaming of becoming a vampire. Would she be willing to be turned? And did I want to risk losing her?

Because it *was* risky—some humans didn't make it through the transition.

As for Slayers, Inc., she didn't volunteer any information about the organization or what her work had entailed, and I didn't ask. In return, I didn't talk about syndicate business in front of her.

As far as I was concerned, she was never going to work for those

SI bastards again anyway, especially after she shared why she was so terrified of being locked up a dark, windowless space.

One night I arranged a lobster bake in a secluded cove—just a fire, the ocean, and the two of us on a soft plaid blanket spread out on the sand.

As the lobster cooled, we sipped glasses of dry white wine and gazed out at the water. "I used to come here with Cain and Talon and some of the other teenagers," I told her.

"Yeah? Sounds fun."

"It was." I smiled, remembering. "But before that, I used to come with my father."

"To do what?"

"Swim. He's the one who taught me. He was...more relaxed in the water. We'd race each other around the island."

"What about those great white sharks?"

My mouth quirked. "That was part of the fun. Great whites are fast and sneaky as fuck. I could outswim them, but it wasn't easy."

She eyed me like I was insane. "That's your idea of fun?"

"Jules's way of toughening me up. But we both enjoyed it." My smile faded. "But that was a long time ago—twenty, twenty-five years."

And even though it had been a game, it had also been a test of my strength—mental and physical. A vampire wasn't easy to kill, but we still felt pain.

Twilight slid me a look. "The primus—he's okay?"

I instinctively smoothed out my expression. She'd broken our unspoken agreement not to talk about our respective professions. "Why do you ask?"

She compressed her mouth. "Because he more or less attacked me, up on the curtain wall."

I straightened from where I'd been lounging on the blanket. "When?"

"Last week. He didn't hurt me, but he scared the shit out of me."

"Last week? Why didn't you tell me then?"

"I didn't want to cause trouble. I figured you couldn't do anything about it anyway. Since then, I've been careful."

My stomach tightened. She shouldn't have had to deal with Jules at all, but at least he hadn't hurt her. "I'm sorry he scared you. I promise that he won't bother you again. He's been confined to his apartment."

Her brows raised. "I...see. That's good, then."

I waited for her to ask why he'd been confined, but she didn't. Had she guessed or heard that Jules was going blood mad? But I didn't press her. Frankly, I was glad to let the subject drop.

Going to the fire, I crouched on my haunches and ladled clams, corn and potatoes onto a plate. "It's cool enough to eat now."

I handed her the plate, and while she started eating, cracked the lobster claws open with my bare hands. Dipping the tender white meat into melted butter, I fed it to her between bites of the other food.

"Mm." Her face had the same expression as when she climaxed: eyelids lowered, mouth rounded in pleasure. "You don't know what you're missing."

"Let me taste." I lifted her onto my lap so I could lick the lobster-flavored butter from her lips.

She laughed at me and reached for a corn cob. "Back off, Prince. I'm still eating." Her small white teeth sank into the plump corn.

"Now you're in trouble." Taking the plate from her, I put it on the sand, unfastened her jeans and slid my hand into her panties.

"What are you going to do?" she asked around a mouthful of corn.

I took the cob, tossed it into the fire and laid her down on the blanket.

"I'm going to eat you." I pulled her jeans over her bare, sandy feet.

"That's punishment?"

I slanted her a wicked smile. "It is when you're not allowed to come." I drew her panties down her legs and teased the seam of her sex with my thumbs.

She propped herself on her forearms, hair tumbling over her shoulders. "That's harsh, even for you."

I slid a finger through the gush of liquid heat that my words had produced. "You like it, though."

Her smile was rueful. "You know I do."

I put my mouth to her. "Tell me a secret and maybe I'll let you come."

Her eyes flickered as if I'd made her uneasy, but her smile never faded. She shook her head slowly from side to side.

"I think I can make you." I lapped at her clit.

Her head fell back. "Do. Your. Worst."

So I did, and when I'd decided I'd tortured her enough, I did let her come, then pulled her astride me. We finished like that with her riding me in time to the slap of the waves against the shore.

Afterwards she collapsed onto my chest, her heart beating double-time, while I stroked her back. She shivered, and I murmured, "You're chilly. We should go."

"Not yet." She lifted enough so that I slipped out of her, then draped herself back over me with a satisfied murmur.

I felt around for my T-shirt and draped it over her, and she murmured her thanks.

The moon was almost full. I watched a cloud pass over it.

Twilight kissed my shoulder. "I have a secret for you."

"Yeah?" I'd forgotten about my teasing demand, but now I came alert.

"If we could go back to Princess Zoe's ball and do it over, you know what I'd do?"

"What?" I slid my hand beneath her hair, caressing her nape.

"I wouldn't have disappeared like that. I had to leave with Victorine—I would've been dead otherwise—but I would've found a way to get a message to you. Maybe we could've met up now and then."

I shook my head. "No."

"No?" She sounded disappointed.

"It wouldn't have been enough."

"Oh." Pushing on my chest, she lifted enough to see my face. "Really?"

"With you, it's all or nothing for me. You're different from my other thralls. Special."

Mine.

She rested her head on my shoulder again and toyed with the ends of my hair. "So where does that leave us? You're going to keep me here as your slave?"

My hand tightened on her nape. I knew she wanted me to deny it, to tell her that she was free to go if that's what she really wanted. But I couldn't bring myself to lie to her.

"For now, yes."

She tensed and pushed away. I resisted for a few seconds, then forced my fingers to open. She rolled onto her back and dropped her arm over her eyes.

"I should've known better than to fall in love with a vampire," she said under her breath.

I shook my head, certain I'd misunderstood. "You love me?"

"Maybe. I'm still making up my mind."

I came over top of her and nudged her arm off her eyes so I could see her expression. "You love me," I stated firmly.

Her dark brows snapped together. "Yes, damn you. Maybe not that first night, but I felt something even back then. Leaving you was the hardest thing I ever did."

Awe slashed at my heart, filled it with a raw, burning hope.

She meant it.

She didn't want to mean it, but she did.

I cupped her face, carefully, gently. Trying to show her without words how precious she was to me. "Thank you." I rested my forehead against hers.

"It's not something you thank someone for."

"To me, it is. You have to stay with me now."

She sighed. Her fingers came around my wrists. "Oh, Brien. It doesn't work like that."

The awe fled, leaving a jagged, painful space where hope had flamed. I pulled away from her. I thought again of how she was still keeping things from me.

"I see."

Her grip tightened on my wrists. Her eyes moved between mine. "What do you see?"

That you 'love' me like you love chocolate or sex or your silver Pradas. Because if your 'love' doesn't keep you with me, what the fuck is it good for?

"Nothing." I lifted her off me and reached for our clothes. "We should go back."

❧ 19 ❧

TWILIGHT

I was used to keeping my secrets.

Telling Brien things about my life had left me feeling more exposed than sex or offering him my throat.

That was my body. My secrets were my soul.

And it wasn't enough. He kept pulling back, even after I'd told him I'd loved him.

"You have to stay with me now."

The man didn't want love, he wanted to own me.

Back in his apartment, we took a shower together. Not talking. Not touching. Sticking to opposite sides of his big-ass shower stall.

Seeing his set face, something in me snapped. I wrapped a towel around my body and slapped a hand on his chest.

"Enough. I want my passport back. And my phone. And some money, while you're at it."

Brien's expression shut down in that way I hated. He dropped his towel and stalked to his walk-in closet.

I followed. Knowing I'd made a huge mistake, that he'd think this was why I'd told him I loved him, but unable to stop myself. "Answer me, damn it."

He pulled on a pair of navy boxer-briefs. "You don't need money or a passport. You have everything you need."

"Except my freedom." I curled my lip. "You're so fucking perfect, aren't you? You do everything by the book. Loving a human isn't in 'The Plan,' is it?" I made air quotes around 'The Plan.'

His green eyes iced over. "Don't say that."

But I was on a roll now. I fisted my hands to keep myself from bloodying that straight, perfectly symmetrical nose.

"That's it, isn't it? I don't fit into 'The Plan.' You probably have it written down somewhere. Step 1: Take over my father's syndicate. Step 2: Mate with a vampire princess. It must've been a tough blow when Zoe picked Rafe Kral over you."

His breath hissed in. "Zoe is a friend. Nothing else."

I made a scoffing sound. "That's what you would say, wouldn't you? And I'm not finished. Step 3: Rule the whole goddamn world."

I'd started keeping a few changes of clothes in his closet. I grabbed a sleeveless shirt and cargo pants and stomped back into the bedroom to put them on.

He appeared a few seconds later dressed in a T-shirt and jeans. He folded his arms over his chest and leaned against the doorjamb, watching me.

I zipped my pants and put my hands on my hips, waiting for him to say something, anything. Even a lie to make me feel better would be preferable to his closed-mouth stare.

But when his mouth finally moved, what came out of it was, "Where do you think you're going?"

A cold, demanding question that put me in my place, making it clear that even after this past week, I was nothing but a thrall to him.

I felt like he'd sliced me off at the knees. I had to brace my feet apart to steady myself. I should've known the Perfect Prince was too straightlaced—too *honorable*—to lie, even to make me feel better. But would it hurt him to show me a little tenderness?

"Back to my own suite." I inhaled a jagged breath and lifted my chin. "Unless you have a problem with that, *my lord*."

His mouth tightened. "No."

"Okay, then." I grabbed my high-tops and sat on a chair, lacing them up with sharp, angry movements.

He swore under his breath.

"Goodbye," I muttered and headed for the door.

His arms were still folded over his chest. He looked sexy and unattainable, mouth stern, eyes burning. A godlike being who could be worshipped but not loved.

He inclined his head, in full Prince-Brien mode. "I'll see you tomorrow."

All the fight went out of me. Suddenly, I was exhausted.

I rubbed a hand over my face. "Yeah. Whatever."

❦

I stayed in bed until the next afternoon. For the past week, I'd been buzzed on sex and the adrenaline that comes with falling in love. That had worn off right around the time Brien told me I didn't need my own money or a passport. Because I was his slave. And no matter how special he said I was, he was a prince, and he saw me as thing to be owned, not his equal.

I felt like I'd jumped off that castle wall and crash-landed onto the rocks.

Time to get real. My heart was bruised, that was all.

It would recover. Someday.

Meanwhile, I needed to wrap up the feelings I had for Brien and shove them into a box with a tight lid. They weren't important, not compared to my halmoni and why I was here in the first place.

For some reason, Kuro had backed off. I hadn't seen him since that day in the ballroom, which was over a week ago—maybe because he simply hadn't been able to get close, since I'd been spending every moment with Brien and sleeping during the day. I also hadn't received any other threatening notes.

How much longer would he hold off, though?

Ignoring the breakfast tray in the living room, I dragged on joggers and a cropped shirt and went for a walk with Pinky, who was fast becoming a good friend.

Today, though, even she couldn't cheer me up. "Is something the matter?" she asked.

I shrugged. "Just tired, is all."

Her warm brown eyes crinkled at the corners. "Brien keeping you up all night?"

"Well, yeah."

She nudged me with her elbow. "Tell him you need some sleep, girlfriend," she said, grinning. "He'll wear you out otherwise."

I somehow managed an answering smile.

We were supposed to eat lunch with some of the other thralls, but I begged off, grabbing some bread, cheese and an apple from the kitchen instead so I could eat in my suite. After lunch, I tried to read, but I couldn't get into the book. I closed my eyes and the next thing I knew I was asleep.

When I woke up a couple of hours later, I was still tired, but I made myself get off the couch. I brewed myself a cup of coffee and carried it into the secret garden.

While I was napping, thick rainclouds had moved in, throwing dark shadows over the castle. I was still in the same cropped shirt and joggers I'd worn for the walk with Pinky. I told myself that's why I felt chilled, all the way to my silly, wanting-something-it-could-never-have heart.

I lowered myself onto a flat rock next to the waterfall, legs folded yoga-style, gazing at the koi and sipping coffee.

God, I was such a cliché. The slayer who'd fallen in love with a vampire.

But it was time to stop fooling myself. While I'd been falling in love, Brien had been fucking his shiny-new thrall.

Demon padded up and crouched next to my leg, staring at the fish, tail twitching. I stroked her narrow back, and her throat rumbled in a surprisingly loud purr for such a small animal.

I smiled. The little white cat had wormed her way into my heart. She reminded me of my friend Renata. Neither took any crap from anyone, but once you won their trust, you had a friend for life.

If only I could talk to Renata, ask what she'd do if she were me. But I already knew the answer, because she'd done it when SI had sent her after Zaq Kral. Rather than slay an innocent man, she'd risked everything to help him.

You have to tell Brien the truth.

The voice in my head sounded a lot like Renata.

"Yeah, yeah," I said under my breath. "I know."

Demon's black ear twitched, although she remained focused on the fish. I felt a sliver of envy. If only life were that simple. She was a predator; they were prey. If she ever caught one, she'd show no mercy.

But I wasn't like that.

He needs to know why you're really here.

"But what about my halmoni?"

I knew the answer to that, too. Brien wasn't a monster. He'd send people to protect her.

And if she saw that as a betrayal—after all, I was outing her current alias to a syndicate prince—well, I'd just have to live with her anger and disappointment. She wasn't unreasonable. Once she knew why, she might even agree I'd done the right thing.

Slayers, Inc. wouldn't be so forgiving, though.

I'd never be a slayer again—and that was assuming they let me live.

I put the coffee cup down and knuckled my eyes.

I knew the rules. The most likely scenario was that they'd send an assassin to take me out. I'd have to watch my back for the rest of my life.

Well, so be it. Dying wasn't the worst thing that could happen to a person. Sometimes you had to take a stand if you wanted to be able to live with yourself.

A peace descended over me. I couldn't wait for sunset so I could go to Brien.

This was one secret I couldn't wait to share with him—a gift from me to him.

I don't know how long I sat there, listening to the waterfall and watching Demon, when a flash of lightning made me jolt. When I glanced up, thunderclouds had blotted out the sky.

I was reaching for my cup when I caught a whiff of something rotten. I froze, eyes darting from side to side.

The shadows next to a pot of roses stirred, then solidified into Leclerc, a long black cloak around his shoulders. He was so emaciated, his nose a beak in his bony face, that he looked more like an enormous vulture than a man. Beneath the cloak, he wore his usual

Armani, but the suit coat was unbuttoned, his pants sagging around his hips.

Demon hissed and arched her back, then streaked up a tree. Leaping to the wall, she scrambled up the vines and out of the garden.

The primus prowled toward me, silent as fog, eyes burning, demon-dark, in his sallow face. This close, the sickly-sweet odor was overpowering.

I stared at him, taking shallow breaths so I wouldn't gag. For a few seconds, all I could think was: *You're not supposed to be here. You're supposed to be locked up in your apartment.*

But clearly, he'd escaped—or someone had let him out.

Slowly and carefully, I unfolded my legs and put my feet on the rock's flat surface.

"Twilight." His mouth stretched in a predatory smile. "I've been looking for you."

"Well, you found me." I kept my voice low and soothing, as if a lethal, out-of-control vampire hadn't fixated on me.

This time, though, I was prepared. Except for when I was with Brien, my switchblade was always with me, tucked into the inside ankle of my left sock. I palmed it and came to my feet, my thumb on the catch.

He was almost to me now.

I glanced past his shoulder. "They can see you," I bluffed, even though I'd never found any cams.

"There are no cams. My son didn't install them." He sneered. "He likes his privacy."

"You're sick," I said in the same soothing tones. "Let me call someone."

I edged toward my suite. The primus moved with me.

My stomach heaved. He smelled so bad, I could barely stand to be this close to him. The man was decaying from the inside out, the disease attacking his internal organs.

I couldn't help feeling a twinge of compassion. He had to be hurting, and he'd be constantly thirsty, constantly craving blood.

Above us, thunder rumbled. I took another step toward my suite, and again, he kept pace with me.

Stalking me like a nightmare come to life.

I dropped the soothing tone and showed him the switchblade. "Back off, you sonuvabitch."

He bared sharp white fangs. "Stupid human." He circled right, the cloak swirling around his body. "You think you can win against a vampire? Fight me, and your blood will taste all the sweeter."

I touched the switchblade's catch and the long silver blade slid out. "You know how many arrogant pricks I've sent to their final graves?"

He was almost on me now. Spinning on my heel, I sprang over the stream.

He leapt a split-second later, landing in front of me. I backpedaled, slamming up against a tree trunk. A pear plopped to the ground beside me.

Leclerc's eyes bored into mine, his dark irises rimmed an impossibly bright blue. "On your knees, girl."

I backed around the tree and kept moving until I was on the flagstone path. He followed, so close I was smothered in his stomach-turning odor.

"On. Your. Knees."

His will beat at mine—and holy crap, he was strong.

Blood pounded in my ears. Sweat beaded on my temples. For a terrifying few seconds, I was afraid I wasn't going to resist the compulsion to obey, and I'd never met a vampire who'd been able to compel me. The switchblade dropped from my nerveless fingers.

It was the clatter of silver against the flagstone that slapped me awake.

You're Twilight. Daughter of Shade, granddaughter of Ghost.

You don't kneel to anyone, especially a vampire.

The urge to obey receded, but to throw him off guard, I pretended it had worked. "Yes, my lord." I started to bend my knees.

Another overpowering wave of his scent rolled over me. I sipped a small breath through my mouth.

Lightning crashed, and rain began to fall. He glanced up, distracted.

I risked a look down at the switchblade. I'd have one chance to stake him. I had to make it count.

One, two...

His face pulled into an evil smile. He reached for me. "Such a good girl."

...and NOW.

Scooping up the knife, I shoved it with all my strength in the space between his fourth and fifth ribs. There was resistance as it hit his heart and then it was through. I twisted my wrist, pushing the blade even deeper.

His shriek filled the air, ending in a gurgle. Blood dripped from his mouth.

A bony hand scratched at my throat, then he dropped to the ground, the switchblade handle sticking from his ribs.

I stared down at him, breathing hard.

His flesh blackened and started to smoke. He glared up at me, mouth working. More blood trickled out of the corner of his lips. Then his eyes glazed over.

He whispered a name. "Lenore."

Unearthly flames danced over his body. More skin blackened and turned to ash. The rotten scent was replaced by the odor of burning flesh.

"Lenore." A smile lifted his lips as if his mate were there beside him, and then he went still.

I waited another minute or so, then crouched on my haunches and wrenched the switchblade out of his body, wiping the blood and charred flesh on the grass. I came back to my feet, watching as his body disintegrated.

I gazed at the ashes numbly.

What the fuck had I done?

I retracted the blade and glanced at it, lungs heaving.

No one could know I'd stabbed Leclerc, especially Brien.

He might say he wanted me. He might promise to give me anything I asked for.

But I knew how syndicates worked. He couldn't let a thrall get away with staking his father and primus.

On top of that, I'd pretty much outed myself as a slayer. An untrained human would've never been able to stake the primus. If it came out that Brien had known all along I was a slayer, I might take him down along with me.

I gave myself a shake and sprang into action. First, I had to get rid of the damn switchblade. I darted back to the koi pool and pushed it into the stones forming the pool's perimeter.

A bolt of lightning split the sky, followed by a boom of thunder so loud it shook the castle. Rain sheeted down, drenching me and the primus's ashes.

At least it would wash the scent away.

I scooped up the wet black mass, scattered it around the rosebushes and patted mulch over it. For a long moment, I stared down at Leclerc's final resting place.

"You really fucked things up for me, you know." I blew out a breath. "But may you find some peace."

Wiping my hands on the grass, I rose back up and set out at a jog for my apartment.

Prosper met me on the path a few yards from the door. My heart kicked into overdrive.

I pasted on a bright, thrall-like smile. "Can I help you?"

He brushed past me and kept going straight to where I'd hidden the primus's ashes, while I followed more slowly.

He crouched beside the rosebushes and sniffed the ashes. Then his shoulders slumped. He scraped a hand down his face.

I halted a few feet away, the rain stinging my cheeks, staring at him with a hopeless desperation. We remained like that for what was probably only a few seconds. But it felt like an entire day passed.

The lieutenant rose and turned to me, eyes flinty, mouth a harsh slash.

"I knew you weren't who you said you were."

20

BRIEN

I started awake at the instant the sun set.

Twilight's in danger.

Ten seconds later I was dressed and out of my apartment. Hurtling around the corner, I slapped my palm on the pad next to her door but the lock didn't disengage.

I swore under my breath, waving my hand back and forth until the camera recognized it. The lock clicked and I wrenched the door open.

I knew immediately she wasn't there. Even if she'd been hiding, I would've *felt* her. Smelled her. Sensed her heartbeat.

I went through the suite anyway, opening the bathroom door, checking the closet. I even looked under the goddamned bed.

When I couldn't find her, I checked the garden. A light rain was falling, but I called her name anyway.

Demon appeared like a white wraith out of the darkness, meowing in agitation.

"Hey, girl." I hunkered down, rubbing her behind the ears. "Where is she? Where's Twilight?"

Demon ran past me into the living room, where she crouched on her haunches and stared fixedly at the front door. When I opened the door, she darted into the hall, then stopped and looked up at me with another distressed meow.

My throat closed.

Maybe Twilight wasn't in trouble. Maybe she'd left me.

"She's in the castle?" I asked Demon.

The little white cat just stared up at me. We started toward the castle's center, me jogging, her trotting alongside.

It occurred to me I might be able to locate Twilight by using the connection that had sprung up between us. I opened all my senses, trying to nail down her position. But all I could determine was that she was close, probably still in the castle.

My throat unclosed with a swoosh of relief. *She was still on the island. She hadn't left me.*

I slowed to a walk and texted Cain and Talon.

Me: *Where's Twilight?*

Talon responded first. *Just woke up. Checking with security.*

Cain's text came a second later. *On my way to your apartment.*

Me: *Not there. I'm outside*—I glanced around—*the Bite Club.*

Cain: *Stay where you are. I'll be right there.*

My hand clenched on the phone. Something was definitely wrong.

Cain raced around the bend, Talon right behind. They skidded to a halt.

My heart stumbled.

Jules.

Gwen's drained, beaten body flashed before my eyes. Every muscle in my body locked. I'd never felt this afraid, not even when he'd tortured me with silver to toughen me up. It would be just like my father to harm the only woman I'd ever cared about.

But if he had, if he'd *dared*, then he was dust.

"Talk," I barked.

"She staked your father," Cain said.

I recoiled. "Twilight?"

He nodded grimly. "Prosper caught her practically in the act. He's holding her in the lower level."

I dragged a hand through my hair, wondering if I hadn't woken up after all because this felt like some kind of nightmare. "Twilight staked Jules."

"It's true," Talon confirmed.

"But how the fuck did she get into his apartment?"

Talon's mouth bent down. "He got out somehow. She was in your garden—the one outside your apartment."

I shook my head in disbelief. "But Jules hasn't gone out during the day in close to a year."

"He did this time," said Cain.

I started for the stairs at a run. "And Prosper threw her in the fucking dungeon?"

She's afraid of dark, enclosed spaces.

"Rein it in, bro." Talon jogged alongside me. "We need to find out exactly what happened first."

"Oh, I intend to," I said, jaw tight. "But first, I want to see her. Talon, you talk to Prosper, get his story. Cain—you go with me. I don't care what the fuck she did, I want her out of there."

Talon sloped off in the direction of Prosper's quarters.

Cain hesitated. "And if she's guilty?" he asked.

I just looked at him, then took off at a run.

Cain caught up to me just before I reached the dungeon. "What I'd like to know," he muttered, "is how the fuck Jules got out of his apartment."

Blackness stirred in me. "That," I said, "is a very good question."

The dungeon held five cells. Four of the heavy, silver-reinforced doors stood open. Nathan, a dhampir soldier, stood watch outside the fifth.

"Sir," he said with a respectful nod.

"Open the door," I ordered.

He hesitated. "The lieutenant said no one's allowed inside without his say-so."

My eyes flashed vampire. Apparently, Nathan had forgotten whom he was talking to. "Open the fucking door."

Cain shoved the young soldier up against the wall. "His father is in his final grave, you ass. That makes Lord Brien the acting primus. When he gives you an order, you obey."

The soldier's Adam's apple bobbed. "Yes, sir. Sorry, sir."

Cain released him, and he fumbled with the key chain hanging from his belt loop before inserting the key in the lock. The deadbolt slid open.

I threw the door back on its hinges. "Wait out here," I told Nathan and stalked inside.

Behind me, Cain instructed Nathan to leave the door open and move to the end of the hall. "No one else gets in here, understand?" he added. "Unless it's Talon or Prosper."

Nathan replied, but his voice faded to nothing as I caught sight of Twilight.

She was huddled against the wall in the unheated cell in nothing but damp pink joggers and a cropped gray T-shirt. Her feet were bare, her arms twined around her bent legs. Shivers racked her slender body, and her throat had acquired three deep-red scratches.

My nostrils flared. The blackness took on a hot, angry tinge.

She scrambled to her feet, eyeing me warily. "Hey."

My gaze went to her bare feet. Prosper had her shackled to a wall like an animal. A heavy silver cuff was clasped around one slender ankle. A thick chain led from the cuff to the wall, allowing her only a few feet of movement in any direction. She couldn't even use the toilet unless a guard released her from the cuff.

"Get Nathan," I told Cain without taking my gaze from Twilight. "I want the key to that cuff."

Her throat worked. Fear radiated off her.

Fear of *me*.

My jaw worked. After the past two weeks, did she really think I'd hurt her?

Smoothing her palms down the outside of her joggers, she straightened her spine. "I guess you heard what happened."

"Yeah." I ached to go to her, to gather her up and promise her everything would be all right.

But I couldn't. I had to act like a primus. In fact, Prosper might've thrown her in the cell in part to undermine me.

Another shiver shook Twilight.

I swore. "You're cold."

"Well, yeah. I'm not a vampire. I feel the cold."

Her rueful smile trembled at the edges. Still trying to be the badass.

I stripped off my T-shirt and handed it to her. "Here," I said gruffly. "Put this on."

When she didn't take the shirt fast enough, I pulled it over her head myself, then took her hands and shoved them through the armholes.

"Thanks." She pulled the T-shirt tighter around her body, still shivering.

My teeth ground together. It fucking killed me not to take her into my arms. Or, even better, get her out of this damn dungeon.

But I couldn't. Not yet.

I stepped back and nodded at Cain, who'd returned with the key to the silver cuff and leather gloves to protect his skin from the poisonous metal.

He knelt on one knee and unlocked the cuff. It fell open and Twilight stepped out of it. Cain came to his feet, stripping off the gloves, and stood next to me.

Twilight shifted her weight to the opposite leg, rubbing the ankle that had been cuffed against it. The heavy ring of metal had left a red mark.

My mouth tightened. "Tell me what happened," I told her. "Starting with my father. He attacked you first, didn't he?"

I eyed her scratched throat. My anger rose again. That was on me. I hadn't done a good enough job of hiding from Jules what she meant to me, especially after she'd told me he'd attacked her once.

But then, Jules should've been locked safely away in his apartment.

She dipped her chin. "I—he must've been watching me from the shadows. I didn't see him until he was there."

"Hades." I pinched the bridge of my nose. "Self-defense isn't an excuse. Not when a thrall stakes a vampire."

That's how the syndicate would see it, anyway—the older vampires, especially. They'd demand I make an example of her.

She lifted a shoulder, let it drop. "I understand."

I growled. "You understand nothing."

"Brien," Cain said in an undertone. "We don't have time for this."

He was right. I considered Twilight.

In the oversized T-shirt, she appeared to be a large-eyed waif who wasn't capable of swatting a fly, let alone taking out my father. But I'd run my hands over every inch of her body. That delicate appearance was deceptive. The woman was pure muscle.

"Is that why you're here?" I asked. "To slay Jules?"

"No." She twisted her hands in the hem of the T-shirt I'd given her. "But I'm not sorry I did. He was blood mad—and don't tell me you didn't know. He *smelled*. The man was sick. I did him a fucking favor." She threw a look at both me and Cain. "I did you all a fucking favor."

Her words slashed at me. I'd screwed up, and now we'd both have to deal with the consequences.

Cain narrowed his eyes. "That's not an answer."

Her brow furrowed. "What?"

"The prince asked why you're here," he said. "If you're not here to slay his father, then why? And don't give us any bullshit about the auction. You were in that club for a reason. You must've known Brien was searching for you."

She shrank into herself. "That's not true. I didn't know he was looking for me. I swear I didn't—"

"Answer the question," Cain said in a hard voice. "Including how you managed to get your hands on a silver blade."

Suspicion scraped at me. "Yes. Answer him."

She briefly closed her eyes. Then she looked me straight in the face. When she spoke, her voice was barely above a whisper, but it hit me with the force of a shout.

"You. I was here to slay you."

My stomach clenched. Everything that had happened between us took on a different shade.

The connection I'd thought I'd felt.

That *I love you*.

Maybe she'd even been faking how much she liked the sex.

"So it was all an act," I said flatly.

21

TWILIGHT

Brien's face shuttered. I felt his withdrawal like a physical thing, and it *hurt*.

"No," I said hoarsely. "It wasn't like that."

I hadn't even been sure he'd come for me. At first, I'd been certain he would, but the time I'd spent locked in that windowless cell had done a number on me. As the hours went by, I'd begun to wonder if he'd abandoned me here.

What better punishment than to chain me in a dank, airless box and leave me to rot?

I'd come close to losing my shit. But I hadn't.

No, I'd survived the way I always had—by closing my eyes and pretending this wasn't happening. A bad dream.

And if it was my dream, then I could pretend I wasn't even here, that I was actually outside with nothing but blue sky and sunlight as far as I could see. This time, though, I visualized a very specific place, the beach where I'd walked almost every day since arriving on Lilith Island.

I dug my toes into the sand, inhaled salty air, splashed in the surf. Flew with the seagulls above the endless cobalt ocean.

Now, though, I'd come back to the here and now with a thump— and it felt like my heart was breaking apart, piece by piece.

I moistened my lips. "I'm sorry. I should've told you before. I was going to tell you tonight."

Cain shook his head. Brien looked at me like I was a snake beneath his feet.

Worse, I deserved it. I'd lied to him by omission.

Yeah, I'd had a good reason. And maybe in the end, it had even worked in Brien's favor. But guilt still ate at me. He'd started to trust me, and I guessed he didn't trust easily.

"It's true," I said. "I was planning to tell you everything. But I want you to know I never wanted to do it in the first place. I was blackmailed—they threatened my grandmother."

Cain snorted.

I briefly closed my eyes. Even I had to admit it sounded like something I'd made up to save myself.

"It's true," I repeated.

"Who was blackmailing you?" Brien asked.

"Someone from Slayers, Inc.—a man named Kuro. A member of the Board—or at least that's what he told me. He forced me to take that job at the Dahlia. I didn't know then who they wanted me to slay."

"So this Kuro gave you the weapon?" asked Cain.

"I think so—I found it under my pillow."

"Your pillow," he repeated neutrally.

I raised my chin. "That's right. One night it was just there."

"Really," said Cain.

Brien's face hardened. "Tell us the truth, damn it. I can't help you if you lie to us."

"But I'm not lying! One night I came back to my room—that first night, after we all went to the Bite Club—and found the switchblade under my pillow along with a note. You said yourself you can read me. Well, do it, then. You'll see I'm telling the truth."

Cain sneered. "You're a slayer. You think we don't know that you're trained to dampen your ANS responses?"

"Look, I'm not saying I didn't stake the primus. But if I were you, I'd at least check out my story. Because if I'm telling the truth, that means someone in the castle slipped me a switchblade. The Quebec

Syndicate took everything from me—you know I didn't have anything but a change of clothes. And I also received two notes. One on the flight from Quebec, and one with the switchblade."

Brien folded his arms over his chest. "Start with the notes. When and where did you find them? And what did they say?"

"The first one was in my dress pocket. I have no idea how it got there, but there was no note, just a drawing—a dagger through the word *Perfect*. But I knew they meant you, not your father."

"And the second?"

"It was a photo of my grandmother—a picture of her coming out of her condo. A recent picture."

"So she really is in danger?"

"Yes! I swear it."

Brien's eyes flickered. I could tell he was remembering all the other things I'd told him that hadn't turned out to be true.

Despair welled up in me. I rolled my lips in, willing myself not to surrender to it.

"At least look into it," I said. "Not for me—for my halmoni. Now that you know why I'm here, he'll go after her."

Brien heaved a breath and exchanged a glance with Cain.

I held my breath. Maybe he was starting to believe me?

Footsteps sounded in the hall outside the cell, and Lieutenant Prosper strode inside, followed by Talon.

"Who released her?" he snapped at Brien.

"Me." Brien met him stare for stare. "As I'm sure you know."

"She's a slayer, damn it. She was undercover at that auction. She knew you'd buy her and bring her here."

"I know," Brien said.

Prosper's thick brows lifted. "Do you, now?" he murmured.

Something about his tone stirred the fine hairs on my nape. I glanced uneasily from him to Brien as three more men crowded into the cell: Jasper, my sometime guard; Matthew Smith, the enforcer I'd met in the Bite Club; and a vampire I'd never seen before. Matthew and the other vampire scrutinized me with a cold curiosity, like I'd already been tried and convicted and the only thing that remained was to sentence me.

I pulled back my shoulders. I was Twilight, daughter of Shade, granddaughter of Ghost. If I was going to die, I'd do it with my head high.

"I didn't come here to slay Primus Leclerc, and the only reason I staked him was in self-defense. He attacked me first. And if you're implying that Brien brought me here to slay his father, then you're wrong. My orders were to slay Brien, not his father."

Prosper's heavy-lidded gaze swung to me. "Did I give you permission to talk, woman?"

I shivered despite myself. I squared my shoulders. "It's the truth."

Brien moved between me and the lieutenant. Talon and Cain moved to flank him like broad-shouldered bookends, one dark, one light.

"She's my thrall," said Brien. "I'll determine her punishment."

"You released her from the cuff," Prosper said with a pointed look at my ankle. "That 'thrall' has got you by the short hairs."

My heart sank. He was going to use Brien's treatment of me against him, make it seem like Brien was weak.

"She's a human," Brien replied. "She has no weapons. What can she do even without the cuff? Or are you afraid she'll attack you, too?"

Jasper snickered and Prosper's gaze swung to him. The spiky-haired soldier dropped his eyes but moved closer to Brien, Cain and Talon, making his allegiance clear.

"She staked the primus," Prosper told Brien. "She's lucky I didn't rip her head off."

"No," he said, "*you're* lucky you didn't rip her head off. The woman is mine—and Jules attacked her. If I'd been there, I would've staked him myself. But what I want to know is how Jules got out of his apartment in the first place—when you swore you'd keep him contained."

Brien seemed to have gotten larger—his shoulders broader, his spine steel-straight. The other vampires shifted uneasily.

Only Prosper didn't look away. "I don't know," he admitted.

A corner of Brien's upper lip lifted, showing a fang. "I don't believe you," he said flatly.

Prosper straightened. "Careful," he said in ice-cold tones.

"We had a deal," Brien shot back. "I'm not the one who broke it. If he got out, this is on you."

Jasper, Matthew and the other vampire had turned into statues, their gazes darting between the two men.

"I agree," said Prosper. "And I intend to look into it."

Brien folded his arms over his chest. "You do that."

"But as for the woman," Prosper continued, "just so everyone here understands—you're taking responsibility for her?"

Cain winced, and Talon murmured, "Brien..."

Brien ignored them, his focus on Prosper. "I do."

I took a step toward Brien. "Please don't do this." I was pretty sure I knew where this was going, and I had to stop it. I swung back to Prosper. "Brien had nothing to do with this. I told you, I was sent here to stake him. He didn't even know I had a switchblade."

Brien flicked me a look. "Stay where you are, Twilight." A command that had the force of compulsion.

I halted as if it had worked. No one here knew that I couldn't be compelled, and I wanted to keep it that way.

It wasn't like Brien would listen to me anyway. I knew how syndicates worked. This wasn't really about me; it was a showdown between two dominant vampires. If Brien backed down now, the lieutenant would ascend to primus without striking a blow.

"She's mine," Brien repeated. "She agreed to accept my blood bond. Didn't you, Twilight?"

Startled faces swung in my direction—except for Talon and Cain. They didn't appear surprised; they looked resigned.

All the spit left my mouth. I was so screwed.

Accepting Brien's blood bond in front of witnesses would make me his slave in truth. It was like a thrall contract, but permanent—he'd own my body and blood for as long as he chose. And if I broke my word and tried to escape, he'd be legally allowed to hunt me down and force me to return.

But if I said no, I'd be calling Brien a liar in front of his syndicate's top men—and signing my own death warrant.

"Well?" Lieutenant Prosper asked silkily. "Did you agree to accept his blood bond?"

I moistened my lips. Lord knows, I didn't want to die.

But this was about more than me trying to save myself. I wanted this, wanted to stay here on Lilith Island with Brien.

Brien's eyes gleamed in the dark cell. He appeared confident, but his jaw had gone rigid, like he was steeling himself for rejection.

"Answer the question," he said.

He doesn't love you. This is insane.

Still, I was a risk taker, and if you aren't a little uneasy before upending your entire life, then you're probably not paying attention.

And something about that rigid jaw gave me hope.

"Yes," I told Prosper without taking my eyes from Brien. "I agreed to accept his blood bond."

Brien's tense posture eased. He held out his hand to me, and I went to him and took it.

Prosper was speaking. "If that's true," he told Brien, "then you won't mind making it official. We'll act as your witnesses."

"Of course." Brien gently urged me to face him.

My fingers tightened on his. "Now?"

"Now," he confirmed.

Over Brien's shoulder, I saw Matthew's mouth lift in amusement. The prick was enjoying this, like my dilemma was a show for his entertainment.

"It's the thrall's choice," Prosper said.

Yeah, like he'd given me a choice.

I turned a defiant smile on Brien. "Let's do this, then."

He went first, speaking the ritual words. "I, Brien Leclerc, offer you, Twilight, my blood bond. To bind yourself to me. To be mine, and mine only, for the rest of your life."

The cell receded. All I saw was Brien, his handsome face severe, his kryptonite eyes searing into mine. He had both my hands in his now, his fingers cool and firm.

My heart seemed too big for my chest. I'd never witnessed a blood-bonding ritual. In fact, I'd written them off as an amped-up, no-way-out version of a thrall contract. Another way vampires took advantage of thralls.

I'd been wrong. This felt almost like a wedding. But then, I was agreeing to bind myself to Brien for the rest of my life, a bond only he could break.

He didn't love me. I knew that.

But he felt *something* for me. I had the power to hurt him—I'd seen that, more than once. That wouldn't be true if I was just another thrall to him.

For now, that was enough.

I squeezed his hands, gave him a brilliant smile—and threw myself off the parapet.

"I, Twilight, accept your blood bond, Brien Leclerc. Binding myself to you, to be yours, and yours only, for the rest of my life."

Brien released my hands and stroked his fingers down my throat in a blatant, *you're mine* gesture. "Let it be so."

The air leaked out of my lungs. My pounding heart settled. "Let it be so," I echoed.

"So her actions are yours," stated Lieutenant Prosper.

"Yes." Brien sent a hard look around at the other vampires. "And as far as I'm concerned, she did nothing wrong. It was Jules's time to go to the Dark Lady. You all knew it. I'd decided to stake him myself, if necessary."

A shock wave passed over the small group. My own eyes widened.

"The woman did him a kindness," Brien added, "and the syndicate a favor. She has my full support. She won't be punished."

My stomach dropped. It was like watching a train wreck. You want to intervene, but there's nothing you can do. The train is too powerful to stop.

Prosper's chest expanded. "She staked the primus. She can't be allowed to go free."

"I'm the primus now." Brien cocked a brow. "Unless you're issuing a challenge?"

A small moan escaped me. It was like he was trying to provoke Prosper into challenging him.

"As you wish." The lieutenant's broad face arranged itself into stern lines. "Let everyone here be my witness. I challenge you, Brien Leclerc, for Primus of the Maritime Syndicate."

Brien had never appeared so coldly beautiful, even bare-chested and in jeans. His blond hair shone gold in the light shafting in from the hall, and his face seemed sculpted out of marble. The intertwined sharks on his arm stood out in sharp definition.

"And I accept your challenge, Lieutenant Prosper. May the best vampire win."

"May the best vampire win," echoed the others.

"The lieutenant is the challenger, which means Prince Brien chooses the place and time and weapons," said Cain.

"Understood," said Prosper.

"I choose midnight tomorrow," said Brien. "In the ballroom. Weapons will be daggers, and I call on Talon and Cain to act as my seconds."

"I accept," Cain said immediately.

"And so do I," said Talon.

Prosper gave Brien a tight nod. "Until midnight tomorrow, then. My seconds will call on yours." He left the cell along with Matthew and the other vampire.

Brien exhaled through his teeth. "Well."

Cain clapped him on the back. "You can take him."

"Not unexpected," murmured Talon, "but I thought he'd give it a little more time."

"We're pulling for you, sir," Jason stated.

Brien smiled faintly. "Thank you." Taking me by the arm, he told Cain and Talon, "We'll continue this upstairs."

"Maybe you should leave her here," said Talon. "She'll be safe enough."

Brien glanced down at me.

I straightened and gazed proudly back, trying not to shiver. I would *not* let them see the panic clawing at my intestines. "At least get me some dry clothes."

"No," he said. "She accepted my blood bond. Her loyalty is to me now, isn't it Twilight?"

That's when it hit me. My loyalty *was* to him now. Not Slayers, Inc.

I blinked rapidly. "Yes." The word came out raspy. I cleared my throat and tried again, more clearly this time. "Yes."

22

BRIEN

Back in my apartment, I pulled Twilight aside. "The blood bond is permanent. You can never leave. You understand that, right?"

I'd pressured her into accepting the bond. Prosper had backed me into a corner—if she hadn't agreed, she would've been executed.

Maybe I should've felt guilty, but I didn't. Instead, I felt a fierce satisfaction. Twilight had accepted my blood bond in front of witnesses. She could never leave me now.

"Only I can break the bond," I added. And I'd take a knife to the chest before I'd do that.

"I know." She touched my cheek. "I'm not going to leave. I knew what I was doing, and I said yes."

My gaze snagged on her mouth. Gods, I wanted her—even like this, dirty and tired, with dark smudges under her eyes, my shirt so big on her she looked shapeless.

Even when I wasn't sure she could be trusted.

Mine.

I gave her a hard kiss and turned to where Cain, Talon and Jasper were huddled on the other side of the room, carrying on a low-voiced discussion.

She halted me with a hand on my bicep. "What about the challenge?" she demanded.

"What about it?"

She didn't relax. "Prosper is smart and fast—are you sure you can beat him?"

She stated it warrior-to-warrior, and I did her the courtesy of responding in kind.

"He is. And he knows my moves—we've sparred on and off ever since I was a kid. But that means I know his moves, too. And I've gotten faster in the last couple of years. I don't think he's aware of that."

Her eyes moved between mine like she was trying to see into my brain. Then she gave a short nod and let go of me. "Good. Because if you don't—." She bit her lower lip. "Just don't lose, okay?"

My brow furrowed. The woman was fucking confusing. Maybe she hadn't lied when she'd said she loved me?

Then I recalled how she'd been concealing the fact that someone had passed her a switchblade for close to two weeks, and my mouth turned down. "I don't intend to."

I turned and caught Jasper's eye. He broke away from Cain and Talon. "Yes?"

"Go to the war room and search the video feed. Someone left that switchblade for Twilight—possibly an intruder. I want to know who."

"It was a Sunday," added Twilight. "Not last Sunday—the Sunday before. Sometime between midnight and dawn."

"I'm on it," Jasper said, and left.

Next I phoned Avril and asked her to arrange for someone to send dinner and clean clothes for Twilight to my apartment.

"Is everything all right?" Avril asked. "I haven't seen Twilight all day."

"Twilight's fine, but the primus has gone to his grave."

She sucked in a breath. "So you're primus now?"

"Acting primus," I corrected. "Lieutenant Prosper has issued a challenge."

A pause. Then my typically unflappable PA burst out, "No! He wouldn't—"

"Just bring the food and clothes," I said and cut the connection.

Twilight had stayed nearby, leaning against the wall like it was the only thing holding her up.

I frowned. I hadn't forgiven her, but I hated seeing her so listless and defeated.

She glanced at me and straightened. "Thank you. For the food and clothes, I mean."

"Sit." I jerked my chin at a couch.

Her shoulders seemed to collapse into her chest. "Brien...I didn't have a choice. My halmoni—"

"You did have a choice," I interrupted. "I'm a fucking syndicate prince. You think I can't keep one human female safe? *Now sit.*"

She stopped arguing and sank onto the couch. "Then you will send someone to guard her?"

"Yes," I gritted.

She gave me a searching look. "Promise?"

My jaw worked. This was a god-awful time to send any of our allies in the syndicate off-island, but this was Twilight's family—and an elder. I was damned if I'd let anyone mess with her.

"Talon," I said, and he and Cain joined us.

"Twilight's grandmother is in danger," I told him. "I want you to send a couple of soldiers to guard her."

Talon immediately pulled out his phone. "Name?" he asked Twilight.

"MinJi Park. She lives in a condo." She rattled off the address.

He noted it on his phone. "I'll get a couple of soldiers on it ASAP."

Twilight's face lit up like I'd given her a diamond necklace. "Thank you." She swallowed thickly, tears shimmering in her eyes. "I...thank you. She's all I have. I've been so worried." Another shiver shook her, and her teeth clicked together.

I expelled a breath and strode into the bedroom for a blanket. "Here." I draped it around her shoulders.

"Thank you," she said so politely I wanted to shake her. "May I have some water, too?"

Talon got her a bottle from the wet bar. Meanwhile, Cain opened a bottle of blood-whiskey and poured double shots for the three of us.

Cain and Talon raised their glasses to me. "To you wiping the floor with Prosper's ass," Cain said, and Talon murmured assent.

It wouldn't be easy, but I appreciated their faith in me. I touched my glass to his and Talon's. "Fuck, yeah."

"May Lilith be with you," Talon added.

"To Lilith," Cain and I echoed.

I tossed the shot back. The whiskey burn was followed by the warm glow of the blood.

"You've got this," Talon said.

"I'm not worried. I'd hoped to avoid a challenge, but—" I shrugged and set the glass on the bar.

He nodded. "This might be for the best, actually. Beat Prosper and the rest of the hierarchy will fall in line."

"Exactly. That's why I pushed him."

Talon grunted. "Thought so."

"What about her?" Cain cut his eyes at Twilight, who wasn't even pretending not to listen.

I dropped my voice. "If I lose, I want your promise that you'll both do whatever it takes to get her off the island. If you don't, she's dead." That's if Prosper was merciful enough to kill her quickly.

Cain replied in the same subvocal tones. "Don't worry. We'll see her safely out of Canada."

"If it's at all possible," Talon added, always the truth-teller, because we all knew they might not be able to spirit Twilight away in time, especially if Prosper gave them a direct order not to help her.

"Get her a passport and money." I named an amount that made them both lift their brows. "And a phone," I added. "That's a priority—have it ready by the morning."

Cain glanced at Twilight. "You sure that's a good idea?"

"She knows if she runs, I'll only hunt her down. And if things go south, I want her to have options."

"Consider it done, then," said Cain. "Meanwhile, let's get a description of this man she says is blackmailing her. And I'd like to know more about those notes she received."

"You believe her, then?"

Cain lifted a shoulder in a shrug. "She got that switchblade from somewhere."

Talon's dark brows came together. "What man was blackmailing her? And what's this about a switchblade? She didn't have any weapons. I made sure of that."

Cain brought him up to date with a few terse sentences.

Talon scowled. "How the fuck did someone get into her bedroom without us knowing it?"

"That's what I'd like to know." I started across the room to Twilight.

She tensed and straightened her spine, her gaze jumping between the three of us like we were the Inquisition. "What?"

"Relax." Cain leaned a hip on the opposite end of the couch from her, arms folded over his chest. "We're trying to figure out how this SOB got to you. You received the first note while you were still on the jet?"

She nodded. "That's right."

"Tell us about it," Cain invited as Talon and I took the chairs across from them. "Anything you can remember."

"There's not much to tell." Twilight spread her fingers, rubbed them up and down her thighs. "Like I said, I found the note in my back pocket. I have no idea how it got there. I suppose it could've already been in the pocket when I got dressed."

"I rode in the SUV with you to the airport," I said. "And on the jet, you were next to the window with me on your other side."

"But you didn't board with me," Twilight pointed out. "I got on in a group with Pinky, Lesa and Eden."

"You think one of them put it in your pocket?" Talon shook his head. "They've all been with us for at least a couple of years."

"I'm not accusing anyone. Just telling you what happened. But—" She glanced at Talon and folded her lips in.

"Tell us," I told her.

"It's Eden. Every time I step out of my suite, she's there. It's like she's waiting for me."

Talon drew a harsh breath.

"I don't have any proof," Twilight added. "Just a gut feeling."

I squeezed my nape. "Eden grew up right here on the island. We've known her since she was a kid."

"So did Lesa and Pinky," murmured Cain.

"Right," said Twilight with a glance at Talon's set face. "Forget I said anything."

"No," he said. "I'll question her myself."

Avril's knock interrupted us. Cain let her in, and she entered with a tray of bread, cheese, fruit and a steaming bowl of seafood chowder. "I'll just set this down and get Twilight's clothes."

I thanked her without looking at her, my mind on Twilight's blackmailer.

"Even if it was one of the thralls," I said to Cain and Talon, "it doesn't explain the switchblade or the second note threatening Twilight's grandmother. The other thralls didn't have access to Twilight's suite."

Avril made a small, sharp sound. She lowered the tray onto the coffee table in front of Twilight.

"Sorry, sir." Her pale skin reddened. "I—I spilled some chowder on my hand."

"Get some cold water on it." I turned back to Cain.

"Yes, sir." She hurried toward the open door.

Twilight watched her go, a small frown between her eyes. Suddenly, she was on her feet. She shot across the living room, pulling Avril to a halt. "What do you know?"

Avril looked at me over Twilight's shoulder—and crumpled against the doorjamb. "It wasn't supposed to be him."

"Who?" Twilight shook her. "Brien?"

Avril's throat worked. "Yes." She cast me an agonized glance. "I'm sorry. I didn't know. I'd never do anything to hurt you. I—"

I came to my feet. "Get back here. *Now.*"

When she didn't move fast enough, I stalked across the floor and jerked her back into the living room. Twilight shut the door.

"Talk," I told Avril. "*What* didn't you know?"

Tears ran down her cheeks. Her red hair was escaping its neat bun and the buttons on her gray silk blouse hadn't been buttoned up correctly.

"The cook told me just now that Twilight was here to stake you. But that's not what *he* told me. I swear I wouldn't have done it if he'd said she was here to slay you. I'm so sorry."

I gripped her arm more tightly. "Who did you think she was supposed to stake?"

Her throat worked. "The primus," she said in a small voice.

Cain and Talon had moved up to stand on either side of Avril.

Cain growled. "That's treason."

"I know." She swiped a hand across her face, smearing her mascara. "He offered me money, but I didn't take it. I swear I didn't."

"Who?" I demanded. "I want his name."

"I don't know his name. I swear I don't. He said he was with Slayers, Inc. He said Twilight knew about the switchblade, that she was expecting it to be delivered to her."

"How did you get into my apartment?" asked Twilight.

"I'm Brien's PA," Avril said. "I have access to all the thralls' apartments. Sunday night, I took fresh flowers to your room. I had the blade hidden in them. If anyone had asked, I would've said Brien had sent them."

I swore under my breath and released Avril. "Get her out of here," I told Cain. "Put her in a cell, then come back. I'll deal with her later."

He took her arm in a hard grip. "Will do."

Avril let Cain turn her toward the hall, but as he opened the door, she swung around, raking a fierce look over the three of us.

"You know something? I'm not sorry I helped him. Not if Twilight used the switchblade to slay the primus. Gwen was my best friend, and he killed her. He fucking mauled her like she was *meat*, not a person—and you didn't do anything." Her voice caught. "Any of you." Her tear-drenched eyes fixed on me. "You just threw money at her family, like that would bring Gwen back."

My jaw tightened. "I'm sorry about Gwen. If I could've stopped it, I would've. But I trusted you, Avril, and you passed a blade to someone you thought was here to slay one of us. That, I can't forgive."

Avril shrank back. The aggressiveness leaked from her. "Yes, sir."

"Get her out of here," I told Cain. "But keep quiet about why we've detained her—I don't need another reason for people to question my ability to lead."

Avril wrung her hands. "Can you do something for me? Please? Tell my mom where I am? She'll worry, otherwise."

"I will," offered Cain.

"Thank you." Her breath shuddered in, and she started crying again. This time, she didn't resist when Cain urged her out the door.

Hades. I stared after them for a beat, then shook my head.

Twilight made a small sound but didn't speak. I was pretty sure she was on Avril's side, though. My back teeth clamped together. Twilight was right, which was why I hadn't slit Avril's throat right then and there.

After the challenge, I'd wait a few days, then banish her from the island. For a longtime local like Avril, being cut off from her family and friends would be punishment enough.

I turned to Talon. "The first thing we need to do is locate this Kuro. See what you can find out about him, including is he really a member of the SI Board.

Twilight spoke. "He's on the island. I saw him right here in the castle. At least, I think it was him—I didn't get a good look."

I rounded on her. "The hell you say. When?"

"A few days after I got here."

"And you didn't tell me?"

Her firm little chin jutted. "I couldn't. Because of my halmoni."

I inhaled through my teeth. "Okay. Tell me now. Where did you see him?"

"In the ballroom. He was watching me." She described how she'd seen a man and followed him outside but lost him. "I can't be positive, but I think he went into the shadows to hide from me."

"So he's a vampire," Talon said. "But an older one, because this was during the day, right?"

She nodded. "But my guess is he's a dhampir. If he's a member of the Board—and I'm almost sure he is, because he knew things about me only they would know—then he's probably a dhampir. Most of the BOD is."

Talon scowled. "How in Lilith's name is he moving around the island without any of us knowing?"

"Maybe he's one of us," I said.

"A double agent? Describe him," Talon told Twilight.

"About medium height with short brown hair. Slim, with Asian features—Japanese, maybe. But he's American, at least his accent is. I suppose he could be Canadian—maybe even French-Canadian. Probably a martial arts expert—he moves like one, you know?"

"We have a couple of Asian men in the syndicate," I said. "That's if he's a syndicate man. He could be a member of our support staff."

Talon nodded. "I'll talk to Kerry and William, see if we have any recent hires." Pulling out his phone, he showed Twilight a photo of a Japanese-Canadian soldier who'd been with the syndicate about five years. "That him?"

She shook her head. "No."

"What about him?" Talon pulled up another photo, this one a man of French and Vietnamese descent. "Although he's off-island and has been since early August."

Twilight frowned at the photo. "No. That's not him either."

"He could be using a glamour," I said. "Did you ever spend an extended period of time with him?"

She heaved a breath. "No, I didn't. Never more than a few minutes. And I was blindfolded when they gave me the tattoo."

"So he might not even be Asian," Talon said.

Twilight's shoulders slumped. "You're right."

Her stomach growled. She darted a glance at the bowl of chowder.

"Go ahead and eat," I told her. "Talon, you talk to Kerry and William. And for now, have them lock down the thralls so they can't talk to each other. When you get around to it, you can question them about Twilight and Kuro. If you have to, compel them to tell the truth. We need to get to the bottom of this."

Talon nodded, his expression grim, and left the apartment.

"A glamour." Twilight sank onto the couch. "I should've thought of that myself, but there aren't many dhampirs who can power a glamour."

"Eat," I said. "You'll feel better."

"I *am* hungry." She looked at the food without moving.

Sitting on the couch next to her, I dipped a spoon into the chowder and brought it to her mouth.

"Mm." Her eyes closed in that look of pleasure that always made me hot. "Your cook makes the best chowder."

"That's what they tell me." I fed her another spoonful. "They catch the fish and lobster right off the island."

"You don't know what you're missing." She took the spoon from me and began feeding herself.

"Yeah?" Maybe not, but then she didn't know what she was missing by not being a blood drinker—the flavors, the nuances from one human to the next. No two humans tasted the same, just as no two humans had the same scent.

Twilight finished the chowder, then broke off a piece of bread and ate it with a hunk of cheese. "You were right," she said with a tentative smile. "I did need to eat. Thank you."

I grunted, irritated that she kept thanking me. I wasn't a monster, after all. She was hungry, so I'd fed her.

"The sooner you're better, the sooner I can fuck you."

Her smile faded, and I felt a little like that monster after all.

Cain returned with the news that Avril was safely in a cell. "Make sure she's fed," I said. "And give her blankets, that sort of stuff."

"Already done. I told William to make sure she's taken care of. But she swears she knew nothing about the first note, and I believe her. Her words had the taste of truth."

"So this guy, Kuro, somehow got to Twilight on the plane?"

"Either that or someone else is working with him," said Cain. "Maybe Twilight's right and one of the thralls is helping him."

"He could've bribed someone to pass the note," said Twilight.

Fuck. I had to regain control of the situation, and fast. "Text Talon and tell him to come back. I want him to hear this."

Cain nodded and took out his phone.

"What can I do?" Twilight yawned and scrubbed at her eyes.

"Get some sleep." I scooped her off the couch, blanket and all, and started toward the bedroom.

She groaned and I stilled. "Did I hurt you?"

"Not really. I'm just a little stiff."

Which meant she was probably very stiff, and sore, too. Not only had she fought off my father, she'd sat in wet clothes for hours on a cold stone floor.

"Put me down." She pushed at my shoulder. "I can't sleep—not yet. You need me to help find Kuro."

"You're no use to me like this." Closing the bedroom door with my foot, I lowered her onto the duvet and stripped off her clothes.

She wrinkled her nose. "I need a shower. I smell like wet basement."

"You can take one when you wake up." I tucked the blanket around her.

"'Kay." She yawned and rolled onto her side. "But don't let me sleep too—" Her eyes closed and she was out.

That's when it hit me. I'd almost lost her. She could've died.

I stared down at her, stomach knotted. I was actually grateful that Kuro prick had slipped her a blade. If he hadn't, Jules would've tortured and drained her like he had Gwen.

And in retaliation, I would've torn my father's fucking head off. I wouldn't have stopped to consider the consequences.

It might have been me in a cell right now.

Talon returned. I gave myself a shake and pulled on a clean shirt, then returned to the living room, closing the bedroom door behind me.

Talon and Cain were seated on a couch, speaking in low voices. Talon's knowing look made me frown.

I sank onto a chair catty-corner to them. "What?"

"She's your mate," he said.

My frown increased. "She accepted my blood bond. Of course, I'm going to take good care of her. Doesn't mean she's my mate."

Cain's mouth had dropped open. He shut it with an audible click. "Actually, that explains a lot."

"Like what?" I demanded.

"Like why you blood-bonded yourself to a slayer when you knew it would give Prosper the perfect excuse to challenge you."

Talon looked at Cain and gave a tiny shake of his head.

I ground my back teeth together. "She's. Not. My. Mate."

Cain lifted a shoulder. "You would know."

"Of course I would. And I wanted Prosper to challenge me. I didn't want to spend the next six months dancing around him. Better to settle this now before it splits the syndicate apart."

"Makes sense," Talon said as if he were humoring me.

"She's human," I said, goaded. "Purebloods don't mate with humans."

"Blood goes to blood," murmured Cain. "That's what the old ones say, anyway."

"Exactly," I said.

Vampires might fuck humans, but when it came to forming a permanent bond, we looked to our own kind.

Talon snorted.

My mouth tightened. "You have something to say?"

"The old ones also say we should've never stopped trafficking in humans when the money's so easy, but like you say, the world's changed. We can make plenty of money with legit investments—and without the hassle. So what if Twilight's human? You can always turn her. She won't be a pureblood, but I'm not, either."

"Or me," Cain muttered.

I glanced between their impassive faces. "Hell, I didn't mean to insult you. You guys are my brothers. You know that."

"We know," said Cain.

"No insult taken," said Talon.

"Good." I put my hands on my thighs. "Cain, I want you to work on tracking down Kuro. See if you can find out if he's really on the SI Board of Directors, and if there are any dhampirs on the SI Board who can power a glamour. Rafe Kral might know—tell him that you're asking for me. His father's on the Board now."

As Twilight had said, not many dhampirs had enough magic to generate and hold a glamour. If we could discover who on the BOD had the ability, it might be a way to nail the bastard.

Cain nodded. "Should I talk to Kerry and William—see if they've hired any staff recently?"

"I already did," said Talon, "and the answer is no."

"Okay," said Cain. "I'll contact Kral then. And I'll also get online, see what I can find on the dark web."

I nodded and turned to Talon. "Find out who Prosper is using as his seconds and do what you have to do—check the weapons, verify the meeting place. Oh, and make sure the enforcers who are currently off-island are informed that Jules has gone to his final grave."

"Will do. I'll let them know about the challenge, too. Which daggers are you going to use?"

"The blades we got in Switzerland." They were sharp and strong, with stainless steel handles and a clean heft that made them my favorite weapons.

"Got it. And about Eden—" Talon's dark brows met over his nose in a scowl. "She has nothing to do with this. I know the woman, and if she has a problem with you, she tells you straight out. She wouldn't spy on us."

"I'm not asking you to single her out," I returned. "Question all the thralls."

They rose to their feet.

"If you need me," I said, "I'll be here." After what had happened to Twilight, I was going to stick to her like glue until after the challenge, and probably longer.

My friends left, and I opened my laptop to see what I could dig up about a dhampir on the SI Board. However, there was almost no intel of use on the internet, just a bland Wikipedia article about how heroic the slayers were. Hopefully, Cain could dig up something on the dark web.

Next, I went online and special-ordered a blood-bond bracelet from the island jeweler, adding a note that if she delivered it by dusk tomorrow, I'd pay her double.

I checked on Twilight again. The blanket had slipped down to her waist, and she'd curled into a tight ball, her hand tucked under her cheek.

My throat clogged. She looked so fucking fragile. She might be a badass, but she was a human.

Kuro must've known how risky it would be for her to try and slay me. I wasn't an old, blood-mad vampire; I was a pureblood in his prime. And even if she had managed to stake me, she'd never have gotten off the island alive.

The SOB had sent her here to die.

My jaw hardened. As far as I was concerned, Kuro—or whatever his name was—was a dead man walking.

I eased the duvet and the top sheet out from beneath her, tucked the blanket around her again, and covered her with the sheet and duvet as well.

Twilight's eyes popped open. Her hand shot out and grabbed my wrist, her heartbeat fast and fearful.

"Oh." She released me. "It's you."

I smoothed the backs of my fingers over her cheek. "Go back to sleep. You're safe."

It was a vow, one I meant to keep.

"Maybe just a few more minutes..." She curled up on her side and went still again.

An odd ache started in the vicinity of my breastbone. Talon's statement reverberated in my brain. *"She's your mate."*

Twilight's accusation the other night had been uncomfortably accurate. I did have a plan, one that included mating with a vampire princess or at least a pureblood like me. Not Zoe—she was the kid sister I'd never had—but someone like her. I'd been pissed off that Zaq Kral—a dhampir—had snatched up Princess Renata before the rest of us even knew about her.

I pressed the heel of my hand to my chest, trying to massage the ache away.

"You can't be my mate. I'd know, wouldn't I?"

But if Twilight wasn't my mate, how had I known she was in trouble and needed me?

And why was I hovering over her now like a mated man determined to protect his woman no matter what the cost?

❧ 23 ❧

TWILIGHT

I jerked awake, breathing hard.

Back in the cell, chained to a wall and wondering whether they'd kill me cleanly or torture me first.

"Hey, take it easy." Brien's voice. His earthy green musk enveloped me.

Memory flooded back. I wasn't trapped in a windowless cell. I was in Brien's bed, cuddled up with him under the duvet, his long body curved around mine, spoon-fashion.

I dragged in oxygen. "Sorry. It's dark and I—"

"Bedroom—ambient lights on," he said, and small LEDs lit up along the baseboards and the bed's teak headboard.

Grabbing his hand, I focused on a round copper vase on a shelf across from me and drew a few calming breaths, grounding myself in the here and now.

"Can I get you something? Water, maybe?"

"Water? Yeah. That would be nice."

He tried to tug his hand from mine. My fingers tightened.

"You'll have to let me go." His voice was soothing. "But if you're not ready, I can stay—"

"No. It's okay." I forced my fingers to release him.

He unwound himself from me and left the bed with a vampire's easy, animal grace, returning with a glass of water.

"Thank you." I sat up and took it from him. The water was cool and welcome to my parched throat.

Brien climbed back into bed, drawing me between his bent legs and leaning back against the headboard. I felt his arousal against the small of my back, but he seemed content to simply hold me. He was being so nice, when guilt was a hard lump in my stomach.

I finished the water and looked down at the empty glass. "I'm sorry," I said lowly. "That I didn't tell you sooner. I wanted to, but—"

I gave a little shrug. He didn't need to hear my excuses. In the end, I hadn't told him and that was on me.

"It's done. You should've told me sooner, but I know you had your reasons."

"I was going to tell you tonight. I was waiting for you to wake up. You don't have to believe it, but it's the truth."

"Like I said, it's done. I accept your apology, if that's what you want to hear. Forgiving you is going to take a little more time."

"Fair enough." I sighed and put the glass on the night table. "What time is it?"

"Three."

"Three in the morning? The night's almost over. You should've woken me up." The challenge was in less than twenty-four hours, and even if he won, there was still Kuro.

"You needed the sleep."

"I should get up. I can help." I pushed at his arms, but he kept me where I was.

"Relax." He nuzzled my loose, disheveled braid. "Cain and Talon are looking into it. There's nothing any of us can do until we have more intel."

"You don't understand. Kuro is still on the island—I'd bet money on it. He'll know I accepted your blood bond. There might even be another slayer on the island—a backup plan. SI always has a backup plan."

"You're worried about me?" He sounded perplexed.

"Of course, I am. I told you, I...care about you."

I would *not* tell him I loved him again. It made me too vulnerable, like pulling up my shirt and inviting him to stab me in the heart.

Especially when he hadn't said it back.

He didn't say it now, either, but he did kiss my shoulder.

"I'm a vampire, angel. We're safe here in my apartment, and security is on alert that we may have been infiltrated by a dhampir slayer. And even if the dhampir somehow makes it this far, they won't take me. I don't care how good they are. I'm a pureblood—faster and stronger than any dhampir, and most vampires, too."

His tone was matter of fact. He wasn't boasting, simply stating the truth as he saw it. That didn't mean he wasn't vulnerable.

"Just...be careful, okay?"

"Of course. Now, how about a bath?"

I was abruptly conscious of how rank I smelled. To Brien, the odor would be even stronger. "If you're sure there's nothing I can do right now..."

"I'm sure." Gathering me in his arms, he carried me into the bathroom.

Like the bedroom, it was decorated in copper and black and teak. "Bathroom candlelight ambiance on," he said, and tiny lights embedded in the black marble walls glowed on like stars in the night-time sky.

He set me down on a fluffy rug so he could turn on the faucet of a sunken jacuzzi bathtub. The muted lighting painted his sleek muscles a warm gold. Even for a vampire, the man was beautiful. Ripped abs. Toned ass. Shark tattoos snaking around his cut right deltoid.

I swallowed. "Brien?"

He crossed the tiled floor to me, stopping a few inches away. "What?"

He was fully erect, his craving palpable, like he needed me so bad it hurt. But he kept his hands by his sides.

I stroked my palms over his hard pecs. "Touch me."

He took me by the upper arms and pulled me up on my toes. His mouth came to mine, but instead of kissing me, he caught my lower lip between his teeth, hard enough to make me suck in a breath, before releasing it. "Is this your way of apologizing?"

"No. I already apologized. This is my way of making it up to you."

His face hardened. "With sex?"

"No." I smoothed his hair back from his face. "I mean, it's not just about sex. I'm not trying to manipulate you. I just need to touch you. Okay?"

It was the truth. I did need to touch him. I ached to repair the connection between us, and sex seemed like a good place to start.

He released my arm and stepped back, raking his gaze down my body. A gush of heat dampened my panties.

I wasn't quite certain what he'd do next. But the not knowing—that edge of danger—added to my excitement.

"You're overdressed," he said flatly.

I immediately dragged off the T-shirt he'd lent me. But when I started to remove the cropped tee underneath, he brushed my hands away.

"Let me." He drew the tee up and over my head. My bra followed a second after.

He brushed his thumbs over my nipples, sending more heat rippling through me. Then, to my shock, he lowered to his knees and touched his lips to my stomach above the waistband of my shorts.

"You're my weakness," he confessed against my skin. "I'd do just about anything to keep you."

My heart clenched. I dug my fingers into his shoulder muscles. "You'd better win this fucking challenge."

He nipped my belly. "I will."

Leaning over, I wrapped my arms around his shoulders and rested my cheek against his temple. "I wouldn't have done it, you know. Not even for my halmoni. If I'd really wanted to, I could've done it that night up on the curtain wall. We were alone, and no one knew where we were. But I couldn't. I just...couldn't."

His arms tightened around my hips. "You should've told me. I have to be able to trust you."

"But you understand why I didn't."

His chest heaved. "I'm trying to."

For a vampire, that was a huge concession. But then, most vampires in his position would've left me to rot in that cell.

I hugged him. "Thank you."

"Never again, though." He brought a hand to my face, angling my chin so he could look into my eyes. "Understand? This is your one chance. Don't blow it."

I gripped his wrist, willing him to feel my sincerity. "I understand, and I won't blow it."

"Good." He gave me a hard kiss, then returned his attention to undressing me. My shorts and panties joined my other clothes in a heap on the floor.

He nuzzled my mound. One long finger dipped into my sex, testing my wetness. He gave a hum of satisfaction and closed his lips around my clit, sucking lightly.

My knees turned to rubber. I grabbed his head to keep my balance, and he let me go with a last, tantalizing lick.

He smacked my ass and stood up. "Get in the tub."

I dragged a hand over my hair to steady myself. "I have to pee first. And brush my teeth—my mouth tastes like a mouse crawled inside and died."

He chuckled. "You have such a colorful way of putting things."

"That's why you like me."

His smile faded. "I do like you. Too much."

My breath snagged in my chest. "Same here."

We stared at each other for a good ten seconds, then he pointed to a cupboard. "Toothbrushes are in there."

He sauntered to the jacuzzi—and yeah, he sauntered, knowing I was watching—and down the steps into the steaming water. Turning off the faucet, he leaned back and rested his arms along the rim of the tub. Water droplets slid down his neck and over his smooth, powerful shoulders. Other drops clung to the light brown hair on his chest.

I licked my lips.

He lifted a brow, amused. "I thought you had to pee?"

"Right." I lurched into motion.

The toilet was in a small, enclosed stall off the main bathroom. I used it and washed up, then brushed my teeth and slipped into the jacuzzi.

I tried to crawl on top of Brien, but he turned me around and pulled me between his outstretched legs. My eyes drifted shut and I relaxed against him.

His fingers trailed up my thigh. "The water's hot enough?"

I nodded. "Yeah. It feels so good."

Dark strands of my hair floated around our shoulders. He undid what was left of my braid, combing it with his fingers.

"I should wash it," I said without moving.

"Let me wash you first." Picking up a bar of soap, he lathered up his hands and stroked his soapy fingers over my breasts. The clean scent of lemons spiced the air. His fingers moved to my stomach, then my arms. Massaging, caressing. "Should I turn on the jets?"

I shook my head. "I like it quiet like this."

It was so hushed, I heard the low slap of the water against the bathtub when he changed positions, drawing his knees in so they supported my bent legs.

"How about some music?" he asked.

When I nodded, he gave a voice command and low Celtic music filled the room. The singer had a voice like an angel, the kind that tugs at your heart.

He soaped up his hands again, gently cleaning the scratches on my throat.

"I owe you an apology, too. I thought you were safe in the garden. My father shouldn't have been able to get to you. Like I told you, he was supposed to be confined to his apartment."

"You were aware he was going blood mad?"

"Yeah." A sigh. "You heard Avril—he killed a thrall last month."

"Why didn't you call us—I mean, Slayers, Inc.?" I corrected myself because I was no longer a slayer. Which felt...odd. Not bad, just odd.

"I don't trust them, and I don't want them on my island. And he was my sire—it was a tricky situation. But I thought we had it handled." He shook his head. "I wish I knew how he got out of his apartment and made his way to the garden. I control the only entrances."

"I'm pretty sure he dropped down from the ground floor level. But Lieutenant Prosper came in through my door."

"Hell. Prosper overrode the security, then. He has the clearance to do it. I'll have to do something about that."

I traced a circle on his wet knee. "D'you think he let your father out?"

"I'm not sure. We had an agreement—an agreement Prosper initiated. I've never known him to break his word."

"Then someone else released him. But why?"

"I don't know. But whoever it was, I'll find them." He scooped up a palmful of water and rinsed the soap from my neck. "I can lick the scratches for you. They'll heal faster."

"They're fine. Really."

He grunted but didn't argue. His hand slid down my stomach.

I took it and placed it between my legs. "Touch me."

"You're tired," he objected, but his fingers slipped lower, toying with my clit.

Heated prickles filled my belly. I hooked an arm around the back of his head and turned my head to kiss the corner of his mouth.

"Not that tired. I need this."

I did. In this, at least, we were a perfect match.

And I ached to reconnect with him. To find a way back to where we'd been before tonight.

"Twilight." My name was a groan. He pressed an openmouthed kiss to the side of my neck.

I nipped his earlobe. "Don't make me beg."

He gave my nipple a reproving tug with his free hand. "You're not in charge here. I am." His fingers dipped inside my sex, stroking me like he owned me. "And you like to beg."

I moaned and shook my head, my attention on his magic fingers.

He hit a particularly sweet spot and my whole body went taut. The strain of the past day, the danger and fear, combined with pleasure in a powerful adrenaline cocktail that fizzed in my blood like a drug.

"But I won't make you beg," he decided. "Not tonight."

"I'll do anything you want. Just—"

"Do this?" He flicked a fingertip against my clit, then circled it.

My insides tightened. "Yes...that. But more."

His hands encircled my waist, lifting me from the water and

setting me on the ledge of the tub. He lowered to his knees between my legs. "Spread for me."

I put my hands on the ledge and eagerly widened my thighs. Then his tongue was against me, alternately coaxing and lashing me into a spiraling storm of sensation.

My head dropped back against the wall. Without stopping the wonderful things he was doing with his tongue, he pushed two fingers inside me and curved them, stroking my sensitive inner tissue.

My mind blanked. The singer's angelic voice reached a crescendo. The tiny amber lights seemed to explode into a thousand golden stars, drenching me in heated sparks of pleasure.

I cried out, my body undulating against the marble wall as I climaxed, my inner walls clamping around his fingers.

Brien wasn't finished with me. From somewhere far away I was aware of him lowering me back into the hot water, this time facing him, my legs draped over his. I was still catching my breath when he thrust inside me with a primal growl.

I groaned and constricted around him. It was almost too much, but I wanted it so bad.

I craved the feeling of him, thick and hard, inside me. I wanted to fuck over and over. To make us both hurt so good.

I wanted to feel him tomorrow.

To know that he was feeling me, too.

He lifted me a couple of inches, his eyes holding mine, and brought me down, a sharp, sudden movement that sent an electric shock up my spine.

I drew a sobbing breath and he said, "That's it. Take me, sweetheart."

I gripped his shoulders and kissed him. Our tongues tangled and slipped over each other. I raised and lowered my hips in sync to the rhythm he'd set. He met me on each downstroke. With each contact, pleasure slammed through me.

"Sweet Lilith," he muttered, his face tight with need. "You feel so good. So hot and wet."

Water sloshed around us. I drew back, watching where we were joined together. When I glanced up, Brien was looking back at me, his gaze drinking me in like I was the most beautiful woman in the world.

Emotion clogged my throat. This was more than sex for me, and I'd known it from the night he'd fucked me against a bathroom wall in the Tremblay Chateau.

Maybe that sounded insane, but who said it couldn't happen that fast, a lightning bolt to the heart?

Leaving him had been so hard. I'd hated SI for weeks after that, hated that my job didn't allow me any lasting personal relationships.

Now that I knew Brien better, my feelings for him had grown.

He got me, the badass slayer who also happened to love pretty clothes and steamy novels.

He *saw* me.

And I saw him.

The man who wasn't so perfect after all, but who thought he had to be to have any worth.

The man who craved love, even when he didn't really understand it.

"Is that good?" His fingers circled my clit in time to his strokes, making me forget everything but the two of us and what he was doing to me.

"Oh, yeah." The words came out rough and needy. "So, so good."

Wrapping an arm around my waist, he pulled me up against him. We were cheek to cheek, his night-beard abrading my skin, my nipples rubbing his chest with each thrust.

Sharp teeth nipped my earlobe; he'd extended his fangs. He pressed harder until he broke the skin.

I moaned and arched my back, rubbing myself against his lower abdomen. "More, more, more."

He hummed low in his throat and sucked the lobe into his mouth, tasting the tiny amount of blood, and giving me back the aphrodisiac.

"Come for me, angel." He rocked his hips up in a hard thrust.

My skin heated. I was so sensitized, so near the edge. Pleasure balled in the base of my stomach.

I rasped his name and ground myself against him.

"*Mine*," he said, and the dominant way he said it sent me over the edge again.

This time, he followed me, thrusting hard several times before groaning out his release and stilling deep inside me, his face buried in my neck. "So. Damn. Good."

I stroked his head. He shuddered and tightened his grip on me.

He was right. This—the sex—was so damn good. And it could be mine for as long as I lived. He'd never release me from the blood bond.

I swallowed back tears. Because it wasn't enough.

I loved him, and I wasn't a half-assed kind of woman. I couldn't be content with just a blood bond.

I wanted to be his partner, not his thrall. Wanted to be his mate.

But first, I'd have to regain his trust.

"Say it again," he said. "Say you love me. Even if you don't really mean it."

Oh, Brien.

He was so screwed up in some ways. I was starting to understand why. With parents like his, he knew nothing about love. He only knew power, possession, control.

But then, what did I know about it myself? I'd never relaxed my guard enough long enough to let myself fall in love.

My father had loved my mother, but he'd hated that she was a slayer. They'd argued about it whenever she was home. She'd agree to quit—after the next job. But then there was another job and another, ops that only Shade could handle. It took her dying for me to realize she would've never quit. That she hadn't loved my dad—or me—enough to give up being a slayer.

I figured if that was what love was, I was better off without it.

So when I'd felt that punch in the heart when I'd first met Brien, I'd been scared to death. So I'd run. But it hadn't worked. I hadn't been able to forget him, and now I had a chance for a do-over.

How many times does life give you a second chance?

I traced my lips down his cheek to his mouth. "I love you," I said against his mouth. "And I *do* mean it."

He didn't say anything, just gave me a hard hug. I kissed him, slow and deep.

He pulled back to cup my face. "Whatever happens, you'll be fine. If anything goes wrong, Cain and Talon will get you off the island. And you'll have a passport and a phone by morning—and some cash. They're yours no matter what happens."

My heart squeezed. It was his way of saying that he trusted me, that he believed I'd keep the blood-bond agreement.

I set my forehead against his. "Thank you."

He eased me off him and resettled me on his lap with my legs to the side.

He idly played with my hair, combing his fingers through the strands and toying with the ends. "Should I wash it now?" he asked, and when I said yes, massaged a lemon-scented shampoo into my hair, rinsing it off with a hand-held shower. He repeated the process with a palmful of conditioner.

When he was finished, he pressed his lips to the back of my neck. "Ready to get out?"

I heaved a reluctant breath. "Not really. But I guess I'd better before I turn into a prune."

Brien chuckled and came to his feet, bringing me with him. As we exited the tub, he grabbed two towels from the warming rack and we took turns drying each other off.

I dried my hair and rebraided it. Brien got dressed in a long-sleeved T-shirt and black nylon utility pants, and stood in the doorway, watching me.

"Your clothes are in the walk-in closet," he said when I was finished. "I had a maid transfer them while you were sleeping."

The closet was off Brien's bedroom. His clothes took up three-quarters of the space: rows of shoes; shelves with neatly folded T-shirts and pants. A three-sided island jutting from the wall displayed several levels of dress shirts arranged in color-coordinated groups. His suits were on the second side and the third side held neckties, belts and small cubbyholes for cufflinks and watches.

It was like walking into an exclusive men's shop. I blinked. "When do you have time to wear all these?"

A shrug. "You'd be surprised. This is your section." He led the way around the side to where an entire wall had been given over to my clothes—shoes, dresses, jackets, sweaters. He touched a built-in dresser against the wall. "The rest is in here."

I swung to face him. "You moved me in with you."

"It's safer that way."

"So it's just until after the challenge?"

"We'll see." He lifted a brow in an *are you questioning me?* look, which might've pissed me off if I hadn't been still processing that he'd moved me into his personal space.

"I thought you didn't trust me to sleep with you."

"I have a secret room I can sleep in."

"Oh." Stupid me, to think his moving me into his apartment meant something.

I turned away to choose some clothes. I sensed his gaze on me.

"Well? Do I need to use the vault?" he asked.

I glanced at him over my shoulder. "The vault? That's what you call your secret room?"

"Yeah. Do I need to use it?"

"No." I met his eyes. "You're safe with me. But I'll understand if you don't want to sleep with me."

"Mm," he said noncommittally and headed for the living room. "I'll order you breakfast."

When I joined him a few minutes later, dressed in jeans and a thick cotton sweater, a fresh tray had appeared on the coffee table— an egg and cheese sandwich, freshly squeezed orange juice, a salad of ripe blueberries and succulent peaches.

My mouth watered. Suddenly, I was starving.

Brien took a chair opposite the couch. He brushed off my thanks, saying, "You had a rough night. I need you in top shape."

But I saw how he watched me eat, like feeding me satisfied something in him, and it gave me hope.

After I'd devoured the entire contents of the tray, he offered me a box of chocolate truffles. "Want one?"

"For breakfast?"

He shrugged and started to place it on the table, but I snatched it from him. "I never turn down chocolate," I said with a grin.

He poured himself a glass of blood-wine and settled onto the opposite end of the couch, watching with that same intent satisfaction as I ate a truffle.

I picked up a bottle of ice water and unscrewed the lid. "Do you have to be somewhere?"

"Why?"

"Because." I took a gulp of water and put the bottle back on the tray. "I want to tell you everything."

I want you to trust me.

24

BRIEN

I straightened. "Go ahead," I invited Twilight. "If anything critical comes up, Talon and Cain will get me."

I'd suspected there was more to this than she'd told us earlier. I could've compelled her to tell me everything, but I'd wanted her to do it of her free will. And yeah, that was probably fucked up, but I couldn't help myself.

Like I'd told her, she was my weakness. The woman I needed to believe in. The woman I just plain *needed*.

She turned sideways so she faced me. Opened her mouth. Shut it.

I draped an arm along the couch's back, affecting a calm I didn't feel to put her at ease. "Why don't you start at the beginning?"

"The beginning?" She shook her head. "I'm not even sure where that is."

"Then start with the Quebec City auction. Why were you there?"

"That was Kuro. He got me the job singing at Le Dahlia Noir. Told me to play along when a vampire showed interest in me." Her mouth thinned. "I thought he meant I'd have to accept a thrall contract. He forgot to mention that the coven has a side hustle selling blood slaves."

My hand tightened on the couch back. "This was Fleur's coven?"

"Yeah."

"When I've taken care of this challenge, I'm going to pay her a visit."

Our eyes met.

"Take me with you," she said.

I grunted. "We'll see. It may come down to war."

Twilight tilted her head to one side, considering me. "I'm good," she said matter-of-factly. "Vampires tend to underestimate me, and that works in my favor. I want to go. You owe me that much."

I moved a shoulder, unconvinced. She might be a trained fighter, but she was human. A full-out vampire fight took place at speeds a human could barely see, let alone defend against.

She switched gears. "But why a war?"

"Because I think Fleur knew you meant something to me and was deliberately trying to provoke me."

Twilight pursed her lips. "Kuro. He seemed to know everything there was to know about me."

"So why did you do it?" I asked. "You keep saying you're not still a slayer. So why take orders from Kuro? Was he threatening your halmoni even then?"

She shook her head. "He didn't bring her into this until last week. It was me he was threatening. He...has something on me. Something big."

"Go on."

"It goes back two years, to that summer in Montreal. I was assigned to slay Rafe Kral."

When my brows shot up, she said, "Zoe didn't tell you? That's why I was at the Tremblay Chateau. After Zaq Kral was kidnapped, SI somehow knew Rafe would come to Montreal to ask her for help."

"No, she didn't tell me. All she said was that you were a slayer, and she only told me that because I asked where you'd gone."

"I see." Twilight chewed her lower lip. "I'm going to tell you something, but it can't go any further, okay? It's not my secret to share, but I think it will help you understand things."

"Understood."

"Princess Renata was a slayer, too."

My brows shot up. "Zaq Kral's mate?"

She nodded. "We were assigned to the same operation. That's how she and Zaq met."

"Huh." It explained why no one had ever heard of the Paris Syndicate princess until she'd mated with the middle Kral brother. Also, like Twilight, Renata gave off a badass vibe, although hers was quiet, watchful.

"Anyway," Twilight continued, "Renata and I couldn't understand why the Kral brothers were being targeted by SI. I mean, it was obvious they weren't blood mad, and they hadn't done anything to deserve being staked. The Krals don't even keep blood slaves. What we didn't know was that the SI Board had been bribed by the Tremblays to slay Gabriel, Zaq and Rafe. It was an easy sell, because the BOD wanted to strike at their father anyway—he was asking too many questions about SI and how things are run these days."

I gave a low whistle. "That's fucked up."

"Yeah." She shook her head. "We're not supposed to take sides in syndicate vendettas. As far as I'm concerned, if you guys want to off each other, that's your business. As a slayer, my job was to protect the humans. And Renata felt the same way."

I eyed her, grudgingly impressed. From where I stood, Slayers, Inc. was a group of holier-than-thou do-gooders who, if not for the syndicates, would've cheerfully wiped out every vampire on earth. But to Twilight, being a slayer was a noble calling. She'd seen herself as fighting on the side of right.

"It seemed like everything had been settled," she said. "The vampires who'd hired us to slay the Krals were in their final graves, and SI even gave Karoly Kral a seat on the Board. But here's what no one else knows, or at least, I thought no one else knew it. I was at Zaq Kral's mating ritual along with my alpha."

I straightened. "The hell you were. I would've known."

She moved a shoulder. "I told you I'm good. I was disguised as one of the caterers. I dyed my hair, made up my face so I looked twenty years older, and wore a false belly to make me appear heavier. Most people don't pay attention to the hired help anyway. They see the uniform, not the person."

"But I would've sensed you. Smelled you."

"Heavy perfume." She took a sip of water. "Works like a charm. You guys go out of your way to avoid it."

She was right. Like most vampires, I found a human drenched in strong scent, whether perfume or aftershave, distasteful. And of course, the perfume would've disguised her natural scent.

"And I think you did sense me. During the ceremony, you rubbed the back of your neck—just like that—and looked around, like you felt someone watching you. I was crossing my fingers that you wouldn't realize I was there."

"So, why were you at the ritual?"

"To slay Princess Renata."

My jaw slackened. "But why?"

Her mouth pulled into an odd little smile. "Because when you're a slayer, you don't just leave. And if you join a syndicate, it's even worse. You'd better watch your back for the rest of your life."

"But it's been two years, and Renata's okay."

"They managed to bury the fact that she used to be a slayer. But my alpha knew, of course."

"So what happened?"

"I couldn't do it. My alpha said SI had ordered it, but by then, I wasn't sure what to believe. Crow—that was my alpha's code name— had gone off the deep end. She was paranoid, questioning everyone's loyalty. And Renata's good people, you know. My best friend, really." She gave a wry little shrug. "So I staked Crow instead."

"Your alpha?"

"Yeah."

"And Kuro found out," I said slowly.

She nodded. "And Kuro found out. I went off the grid immediately after, arranged things so it looked like I'd died, too. I thought I'd gotten away with it until he tracked me down. He threatened to inform the SI Board of Directors that not only was I alive, I'd killed my alpha."

"So that's what he's got on you."

Kuro was dead, regardless, but she'd just given me another reason for eliminating the man. Slowly and painfully.

"He shouldn't know. Crow and I were alone. No one else was

there, damn it—and Crow was a dhampir, so her body disintegrated. But he somehow found out or guessed what had happened and came looking for me. And he didn't just threaten to expose me to the Board of Directors." A humorless laugh. "He's too smart for that. He promised me something, too. If I worked with him, he'd vouch for me to the Board. Bring me back into SI."

"He wouldn't have." I'd never been more certain of something. "The motherfucker has his own agenda. He would've kept blackmailing you into doing questionable jobs for him until you slipped up, and then he would've abandoned you."

"You're probably right." She pressed her lips together. "Hell, I know you're right. He made me get that damn tattoo, after all. What use would I have been as a slayer with such an easy-to-identify mark? He might as well have tattooed a big 'S' on my forehead."

My chest tightened. I pulled her onto my lap. "If Kuro had sent you on a different job..."

My arms tightened convulsively around her. I'd come so close to losing her all together.

She craned her neck so she could see my face. "Then you believe me?"

I nodded. I didn't even have to think about it. "And yeah, I believe you because I can read you better now. But I'd believe you anyway."

"Why?" Her brows pinched together. The answer mattered to her.

"Because your story fits everything else I know. You even knew I was at Zaq and Renata's ceremony."

"Oh." Her face fell. "Well, good, because it's the truth."

"If you're asking do I believe you because I trust you..."

"It's okay. I understand why you don't."

"Hey." I gave her a shake. "That's not what I meant. What I'm trying to say is that I'm not there yet, but I'm getting there. The fact that you told me the whole story helps."

She dipped her chin. "Fair enough. And Kuro's bound to approach me again. Now that we're working together, maybe we can out the bastard. Actually, maybe you shouldn't have moved me into your apartment—it makes it harder for him to get to me."

"We'll get him," I said, hard-voiced. "But I'm not risking you to catch him. In fact, maybe I should send you off-island until this is over."

"You really think I'd be any safer? Kuro could be anyone, you know. If he's able to power a glamour like we think, there's a good chance he's someone you know—a soldier, a member of your staff. If you send me off-island, he might follow."

She was right. At least this way, I could see to her protection myself. "By now, word will have spread that you accepted my blood bond. The syndicate will know that touching you would be an unforgivable insult to me."

She snaked an arm around my neck. "And I want to stay here with you."

I nodded. "If you stay, you're confined to my apartment until after the challenge. The only people allowed in will be William or Kerry, and they'll have orders not to let you out."

"All right."

I cocked a brow. "All right? You're not going to fight me on this?"

She shook her head. "I think it's smart for me to lay low. And it's only for a day, right?"

"Yeah." By midnight tonight, things would be settled one way or the other.

My phone buzzed. I shifted on the couch so I could take it out of my pocket.

"It's Cain," I told Twilight and accepted the call. "What have you got?" I asked.

Twilight leaned her head against my chest, listening. I ran my hand down her braid. I was probably allowing her too much access to intel, but it felt like she was my partner in this.

And from one heartbeat to another, I realized I did trust her. Her story rang true, and maybe she'd been right not to tell me everything before now. When I'd first brought her to the island, I'd been angry and suspicious of her. I probably would've figured she was playing me in order to get me to release her.

"This guy's good, whoever he is," Cain said grimly. "And he's definitely got access to the castle—either he's in here himself, or he's working with an insider."

"Explain."

"That day Twilight was in the ballroom? The footage of the exits on that side of the castle has been wiped. Thirty minutes of it in the middle of the afternoon."

I muttered a curse. Twilight pulled back and met my eyes, frowning.

"Yeah," said Cain. "We have to consider the possibility that he's working for Prosper. Not many people have that kind of access."

My hand tightened on the phone. "I know."

"So that's a dead end," Cain said.

"Still, it verifies Twilight's story. She did see the man. There's no good reason for wiping the footage except to cover his tracks."

"Yeah. Anyway, I just wanted to update you. I'll be in touch if we turn up anything else."

"Good." I ended the call and glanced at Twilight. "You heard all that?"

"Yeah." She made a face. "He's got everything covered, doesn't he? I wonder how long he's been planning this?"

"That," I replied, "is a very good question. It may even go back to my mother's assassination. My father was fine up until then."

Kuro would've known that when a vampire loses their mate, it wrecks them, body and soul. And of course, Prosper knew that too.

Twilight's chest heaved. "If SI was behind your mother's slaying, I'm sorry. But if they were, I'm betting someone in your syndicate brought them in."

"You're saying we have a traitor."

"Well, yeah."

"I'm starting to think the same thing." My jaw hardened. "One thing I can promise—if we do, I will hunt them down and make them wish they'd never been born."

❦   25   ❦

TWILIGHT

When I woke up later that morning, Brien's body was curved around mine, his arm draped over my breasts. I smiled to myself and snuggled closer.

It was a relief to have told him everything, and after, he'd been less guarded with me, more open. Before falling asleep near dawn, we'd made love a second time—and it *had* been making love, slow and beautiful, his eyes holding mine until we climaxed at the same time.

I stroked a hand down his forearm. That's when it hit me; he hadn't left me to sleep in his vault. He'd slept in his bed with me.

Rolling over, I nuzzled his chin, shadowed with sandy brown stubble. Strands of wheat-gold hair trailed across his cheek, and his lashes formed thick semi-circles on his sculpted cheekbones. Even asleep, the man was beautiful, a slumbering demigod with broad shoulders and six-pack abs.

I heaved a breath. "You had to make me fall in love with you, didn't you? I'm a sucker for alpha males, especially when they've got that protective thing going on. I mean, you made sure Avril had blankets and food, and I'll bet you'll quietly send her off-island with a new name and some money. You'll tell yourself that cutting her off from her family and friends is punishment enough—won't you?"

Of course, he didn't answer.

228

But I couldn't stop. I'd been bottling up a lot of feelings, and now that the cork had been removed, they spilled out.

"And I'm a freaking stereotype—the slayer who fell in love with her target." I traced a fingertip down his straight nose to the cleft in his perfectly chiseled jaw. "Except in the real world, we don't do that sort of thing—well, Renata and Zaq did. But he's a dhampir and you're vampire-born, which is so far above a human slayer I must be bat-shit crazy to want more."

I gave a sad little laugh. "But guess what? I do want more. You think I'm yours? Well, it goes both ways."

I came onto all fours, glaring into his face like I could make him love me through sheer force of will. "You're mine now, and I'll do whatever it takes to keep you. Because I think we're mates, and I'm not going to settle for second best. I want more than a blood bond. I want your fucking heart." I took a deep breath. "I want you to turn me into a vampire."

My heart thumped. I sat back on my heels.

There, I'd said it aloud.

The idea that had been knocking around in my brain ever since I realized I'd fallen in love with a vampire prince. The only way I could have Brien—all of him—was to become a vampire, too. Renata and Zaq worked because like Zaq, she was a dhampir.

But Brien was a vampire. For this to work, I had to meet him as an equal.

I grimaced. Yeah, I'd definitely gone bat-shit crazy—or maybe it was more accurate to say I'd gone over to the dark side.

Me, Nikki "Twilight" Kim, one of a long line of famous slayers.

But Brien would never fit into my world. Hell, I didn't fit into my world any longer. The slayer part of my life was over, and yet I couldn't see me re-entering the mundane human world even if I managed to evade SI's long arm. These past couple of years, I'd felt like a fish out of water. When other humans had been in high school hanging out with their friends, I'd been in training morning to night to assassinate the world's most dangerous creatures.

And the part of me who'd always secretly envied a vampire's powers would get her wish. I'd be superhuman—faster, stronger, able to heal from almost any wound—but that was just icing on the cake of the life that Brien and I could build together as vampire mates.

I drew a shaky breath. "I *want* this."

Now I'd just have to convince him.

❦

When I got out of the shower, a Canadian passport and a phone were on the table next to my breakfast tray. I opened the little blue book first. It was issued to Susan Kane, with my photo and a made-up birthdate and place of birth.

Beneath the passport, I found a debit card in my new name with a bank statement showing a sum had been deposited for me. I had to read the amount twice because at first my brain couldn't take in the stupid amount of zeroes at the end.

It was enough money for me to go anywhere in the world. Enough money that I'd never have to work again.

My eyes stung. I squeezed them shut, digging my teeth into my lower lip. For Brien to provide me with a passport was huge, but to give me that much money was even bigger.

He was saying he trusted that I'd keep my word and stay with him. But if he lost the challenge, he'd provided me with the means to save myself.

It was the best gift he could've given me.

❦

The afternoon inched by. I got my cellphone up and running. A sticky note on the back had included my new phone number and that the bill would be paid by the Maritime Syndicate. For now, I held off contacting anyone, even Renata. It was enough that I could.

William stopped by to report that my halmoni had been stashed in a safe house in northern California. "She put up a fight," the beefy dhampir told me, "but the men insisted."

In other words, they'd kidnapped my grandmother. The next time

I spoke to her, she was going to chew me a new one. But at least she was alive.

I tried to read a book, but even a sexy paranormal romance by one of my favorite authors couldn't hold my interest. Things were coming to a head, and my gut told me we didn't know the whole of it. This entire op had been like feeling your way through a dark tunnel without a light. A shitshow, in other words, and I felt powerless to fix things.

I fucking *hated* feeling powerless.

I tossed the paperback aside and worked out instead, an hour of martial arts followed by an hour of yoga.

Demon meowed at the hallway door. When I got up to let her in, Kerry opened the door. "Here's lunch." She shoved a paper bag at me and turned to go.

I took the bag and grabbed her arm. "What the hell's your problem?"

"You." She rounded on me, her narrow face livid. "This is all your fault—the old primus's death, the challenge. The prince isn't ready. And if Prosper stakes him, the syndicate will be without a true heir. Everything my lady worked for—the planning, the preparation—will be all for nothing. Maybe you even had something to do with her assassination."

Her lady.

This was about Brien's mother?

"Okay." Letting her go, I lifted an index finger. "First, I had nothing to with the prima's assassination. I've never even been to Nova Scotia, let alone Lilith Island." I raised another finger. "And second, the primus attacked me. The man was blood mad. He'd already killed one thrall."

Kerry's eyes flickered.

"Yeah," I said. "I know about Gwen. If I hadn't staked Leclerc, who knows who else he would've killed?"

The housekeeper folded her arms over her flat chest. "Maybe so, but your people were behind the prima's death, and Jules would never have gone mad if he hadn't lost his mate. How do I know the slayers didn't send you to finish things? Everyone knows you were here to stake the prince."

I flinched. "That's true, but I was being blackmailed—"

"So you say. But you're a slayer. Lying for you people is as easy as breathing. If you ask me, the prince is thinking with his balls, not his brain. And the challenge is because of you. William told me that the prince forced a challenge to save you from Prosper."

I gave a helpless shrug. It was more complicated than that—Brien had *wanted* Prosper to challenge him. On the other hand, I couldn't deny that he'd done it partly to protect me.

"Well?" Kerry demanded. "Aren't you going to tell me that's not true, either?"

I lifted my chin. I refused to feel guilty about staking Jules Leclerc. "What matters is that you're wrong about Brien. He's ready. He'll win."

She sniffed. "The lieutenant wouldn't have issued a challenge if he didn't think he could win."

My heart sank. "Brien will win," I repeated, a little less firmly.

Her lip curled. "You'd better hope so, because if he loses, the syndicate vampires will pass you around until you're dead—or wish you were. Now if you'll excuse me, I have work to do."

The door closed behind her with an angry click.

"Jesus." Putting the paper bag with my lunch on the coffee table, I sank onto the couch.

Demon leapt onto the cushion beside me. "Meow?" She butted her head against my arm.

"Yeah, things kinda suck right now."

I shifted her to my lap and rubbed her behind the ears, my face buried in her fur, until she'd had enough and wriggled free again. She settled onto the opposite side of the couch and, lifting an already pristine white leg, began to groom herself.

My appetite had fled, but I made myself open the paper bag. All it held was a sandwich and a can of soda. I unwrapped the sandwich—a thin slice of roast beef between two pieces of bread—and ate it, washing the dry, unappetizing meal down with sips of Coke.

Then I balled up the paper bag and put the remains of the lunch in a trash can.

It was time to get off my ass and take action. I'd spent most of the afternoon waiting for Brien to wake up like some pampered thrall. If someone attacked him—or me, for that matter—I didn't even have a weapon.

The blade in the garden was out—Prosper had confiscated it last night. And Brien would notice if I helped myself to that dagger he liked to strap to his ankle. However, I'd never met a vampire who didn't keep at least a couple of blades close at hand. Most had a whole arsenal stashed somewhere in their quarters.

I started in the bedroom, lifting paintings and running my hands over the walls, searching for a hidden safe or cabinet. No luck there, but in the walk-in closet I found a hairline crack in the wall behind Brien's dress shirts.

I pushed them out of the way and ran my fingers around the crack. It was a two-by-three-foot rectangle.

Gotcha.

It took another few minutes to get inside, but eventually I figured out that I had to press the upper left and lower right corners at the same time. The door swung open to reveal two shelves of silver daggers and switchblades arranged in neat rows on black velvet.

I eyed the shiny array like Demon eyed the koi. The handles ranged from vintage wood, stag horn, and mother-of-pearl to the more modern stainless steel, fiberglass, and acrylic. I took my time, picking them up one by one so I could examine them, but in the end, I limited myself to a single switchblade from the back row on the bottom shelf. With any luck, Brien wouldn't notice it was gone until after the challenge.

Closing the cabinet door, I pulled the dress shirts back over the opening and took my treasure into the living room to examine it. The handle was mother-of-pearl etched with Brien's initials and a crescent moon. Releasing the blade, I practiced thrusting with it—forward, back, circling right or left—accustoming myself to its weight and feel.

Demon scrutinized me from the couch, her black ear flicking from time to time. Then, apparently deciding I wasn't doing anything interesting, she put her head on her paws and settled down for a nap.

When I was comfortable with my new blade, I lay on the couch with her, wrapping myself around her warm, furry body. The next thing I knew, I was opening my eyes and sunset was just two hours away.

I indulged myself with a long, hot bath. After, I dug through the clothes Avril had bought me until I found an outfit I could fight in, if necessary.

Silver jeans. A slim-fitting ribbed henley. Low-heeled ankle boots.

Demon joined me in the walk-in closet, yellow eyes gleaming with what I could've sworn was approval. I rebraided my hair into a tight, no-nonsense French braid, then tucked the switchblade into my sock next to my ankle.

I caught sight of myself in the full-length mirror.

My smile was sharp-toothed. For once, my outside matched how I felt on the inside. Even here, where I'd been able to be more myself than the roles I usually played, I'd still been dressing the part of a sex kitten.

This, though, was the real me. Stripped down and tough.

I'd come out of the shadows—and it felt good.

Demon twined herself around my ankles, meowing loudly.

I bent down to scratch her behind the ears. "You must be hungry."

She twitched the white ear at me. "Rrow."

Brien kept a couple of ceramic bowls behind the wet bar. Opening a can of cat food, I dumped it into one bowl and refilled the other with fresh water. Demon crouched on her haunches, devouring the meal with a dainty greed.

A few minutes later, Kerry arrived with my own dinner. At least this time the meal appeared edible—a leafy green salad, a grilled salmon steak, a baked potato and a bottle of mineral water.

She put the tray on the coffee table, her mouth pursed like being forced to wait on me caused her actual, physical pain.

I heaved an exasperated breath. "I'm not going away, you know. I love him. You don't have to like me, but you'd better get used to me."

No response.

I rolled my eyes and waited for her to leave, but instead she shoved her face into mine. Okay, now she was pissing me off.

I placed my hand on her chest and pushed her back a few inches. "Back. Off."

Cold fingers clamped around my wrist. "Listen to me, Twilight," she intoned, staring into my eyes.

"What the fuck? Let me go." I slammed my free elbow into the side of her neck.

She grunted and recoiled but came back at me. Blue fire flickered around her irises. "*Listen to me.*" Her voice crackled with magic.

I stiffened. This wasn't Kerry. The housekeeper was a human.

But whoever it was, she was trying to compel me.

I stopped fighting and pretended the compulsion had worked.

The grip on my wrist tightened. When the mystery woman spoke again, she kept her tone low and gritty, like she was trying to disguise it. "Are you listening? Say *yes* if you are."

I let my face go slack. "Yes. I'm listening."

"Good." She dug a brown glass bottle from her uniform pocket and pressed it into my hand. "Spray this liquid into Brien's mouth and nose. It will make him stronger, so he wins the challenge. You want that, don't you?"

I didn't believe for a second that whatever was in the bottle would help Brien, but I shoved my doubt down deep so she wouldn't pick up on it and closed my fingers around the bottle.

The intruder repeated the statement two more times, infusing it with a strong compulsion that an ordinary human wouldn't have been able to resist.

"Do you understand?" she demanded. "Tell me your instructions."

"I will spray this in Brien's mouth and nose."

"To help him win," she added.

"To help him win," I repeated.

Smart, to frame the instructions as a way to help Brien. Compulsion is like hypnosis—it's easier to compel a person to do something they're already inclined to do.

"Do it now," she commanded. "And say nothing to Brien. It's important that he doesn't know you helped him. When you're finished, throw the bottle away and come back to the living room. You'll eat your dinner and forget I was here."

"Yes." I turned toward the bedroom, the bottle clenched in my hand.

"Go," she said sharply.

I obeyed. She waited until I was leaning over Brien, pretending to spray the liquid into his face, then walked to the door.

I watched her leave out of the corner of my eye, careful to keep my gaze on Brien. The air shimmered around her, and she seemed to shrink a few inches and develop curves. And then to my shock, a shark tattoo appeared, curving around the side of her neck. An instant later, the tattoo disappeared, and her body narrowed and elongated again.

I jerked my gaze back to Brien.

The door shut behind her. I straightened from the bed, the little brown bottle in my hand.

I was almost certain that had been Clarisse Dumas, the enforcer I'd met in the Bite Club. But was she working with Kuro or on her own?

I took the bottle into the bathroom so I could examine the contents. The liquid inside was odorless and nearly colorless, but I'd bet all the money in my new bank account that it contained colloidal silver.

The bitch had tried to compel me to poison Brien.

It was fucking diabolical, actually. A small dose of silver acts on a vampire like a flu virus on a human. If I'd sprayed it into Brien's mouth and nose, within an hour he would've been feeling sick and feverish. But if he'd called off the challenge, he would've appeared weak.

A lose-lose situation.

In the bedroom, Brien mumbled something under his breath. I hurried back to him. The recessed lights were growing brighter; he apparently had them timed to come on at sunset.

"Brien? You up?"

He grunted and rolled onto his stomach.

I put the bottle on the nightstand and shook his shoulder. "Wake up."

"Twilight?" he muttered without opening his eyes.

"Yeah, it's me. Wake up."

He caught my wrist and before I could stop him, pulled me onto the bed and nuzzled my neck. "Mm." He rolled so I was beneath him. He was naked and aroused, his sexy musk filling my head. "You smell good."

"Wake up. I have something to tell you." I shoved at his shoulder, but it was like trying to move a granite cliff.

"I am up." His hard body pushed mine into the mattress. His eyes were open now. He settled his hips into the cradle of my thighs, rubbing his cock against my jeans and teasing my throat with his fangs. "Very...up."

I swallowed and turned my head. "Stop it, Brien. This is important."

"So's this." He came to his knees so he could undo my jeans. "Too many clothes."

I let out a frustrated laugh. "Listen to me, damn it!" I smacked his chest. "While you were sleeping, someone tried to compel me to poison you."

He closed his eyes, then reopened them, the irises a brilliant green in the low light. "Someone tried to *what*?"

"Compel me to poison you," I repeated. "With colloidal silver."

He withdrew his hand from my waistband and sat up. "You left the apartment?"

"No. It was Kerry, when she brought my dinner. At least it *looked* like her—"

"Not Kerry." He shook his head. "You're wrong. She wouldn't."

"That's what I'm trying to tell you." I rebuttoned my jeans and sat up as well. "Whoever it was looked like Kerry, but as she was leaving, I saw a shark tattoo on her neck. The air wavered, and for a second the shark was visible. You know, like she was holding glamour and lost control for a few seconds."

"You're saying someone glamoured themselves to look like Kerry?"

"Yeah—a woman. In fact, I think it was Clarisse Dumas." I quickly explained what had happened, then indicated the nightstand. "See for yourself. There's the bottle she gave me."

He snatched up the small brown bottle and held it to the light, then pulled out the spray pump and sniffed the contents. His face tightened as he replaced the pump.

"You're right." He returned the bottle to the nightstand. "I can smell the silver. You say this woman was disguised as Kerry? That's how she got inside?"

"I think so, yes. After I sprayed the liquid into your mouth and nose, I was supposed to throw the bottle in the trash."

A muscle jumped in his jaw. "They wanted your fingerprints on the bottle so that if I realized I'd been poisoned, you would've been blamed."

"Yeah." I grimaced. "And I wouldn't have known what happened. The compulsion included instructions to forget all about the bottle."

"Gods. So Clarisse may be part of this? I thought she was neutral." He scrubbed a hand over his face. "Sometimes I get so damn tired of not knowing who I can trust."

I touched his leg. "You can trust me. And Talon and Cain. And Jasper thinks you're the next thing to God."

That elicited a small smile. "He'll learn. But thank you."

I took his face between my hands and stared into his eyes, willing him to *hear* me. "I've never told another man I love them, Brien—and when I was a slayer, I had to say a lot of things I didn't mean. But I'm not a slayer anymore. When I say you can trust me, I'm saying that not just as Twilight but as Nikki Kim."

He jolted almost imperceptibly as I spoke my real name—or at least, the one I'd been born with. I felt a comparable jolt as the final layer of secrecy peeled away.

Not even that detective of his could've discovered I'd been born Nikki Kim; my family had lived under an alias to protect all of us. Even my birth certificate was registered under a different name.

"That's your real name?" he asked slowly.

I nodded, adding, "I'm on your side. You may not believe it, but I am."

I released him and sat back. Brien knew everything now. I'd laid myself bare. It was up to him, now.

Way back in his eyes, something warmed. His hands came to my shoulders, squeezed. "You know something? I think I do believe you —Nikki."

❧

While Brien showered and shaved, I went back to the living room to eat dinner. When he reappeared, he was dressed for the challenge in a T-shirt and gray stretch tactical pants, his hair in a short blond ponytail. He got himself a glass of blood-wine and sat on the couch with me.

I took out the phone. "Thanks for this. And the passport and money, too—which is way too much, by the way."

He lifted a shoulder in a negligent shrug. "The money's nothing. And you don't have to thank me. It was an asshole move, keeping you here without a phone or passport."

My mouth tugged into a grin. I slid the phone back into my pocket with the passport and debit card.

"Yeah, it was. But I wanted to thank you anyway. It means a lot, that you trusted me enough to give them to me."

I leaned forward to brush my lips over his. When I started to pull away, he curved a hand around my nape, keeping me there so he could kiss me back. A slow, thorough melding of mouths and tongues that almost made me forget the danger we both were in.

"So." Sitting back with a very Brien smirk, he draped an arm along the couch. "Why don't you walk me through what happened, starting from when this woman brought your food?"

I nodded and, in between bites of grilled salmon, walked him through what had happened from the time fake-Kerry had entered the apartment.

"And you're sure it was a woman?" he asked. "You said yourself you didn't get a good look at whoever it was."

"It wasn't just her body—it was her voice. You know how a

glamour doesn't change your voice, just your appearance. She disguised her voice, but it was a woman's."

He sipped his wine. "Only a few people are cleared to enter my apartment—Cain. Talon. Kerry and William. Not even Avril can enter without my permission. So if it was Clarisse, how the fuck did she get in the door?"

I cut into my baked potato, thinking. "She couldn't have overridden the security system?"

"Unlikely. My apartment isn't connected to the main system, and I'm the only one who can make changes to this one. I'll run a check, but my guess is that whoever it was compelled Kerry to open the door for them."

I drank some of the mineral water. "So this person waited in the shadows until they came inside? Because the hall cam should've picked up another person, right?"

"It's the only thing that makes sense, but whoever it was must be powerful. It takes a lot of energy to compel two people and hold a glamour at the same time."

"Someone high in your hierarchy, then."

"Yes." His mouth thinned. "Which Clarisse is. She's the highest female, actually."

I frowned. "Maybe Kuro doesn't even exist. Maybe it's been someone from your syndicate all along. Someone who doesn't want you to succeed your father—Lieutenant Prosper, for example."

"It could be Prosper, but why challenge me then? And why throw you into the dungeon in the first place? He could've let you go free and hope you'd stake me, too." Brien shook his head. "It doesn't fit. He's a cold sonuvabitch, but it's not his style. He challenged me because his honor demands he beat me in a fair fight. But yeah, I'm more and more convinced that Kuro's a member of the syndicate."

"What about the main video feed? Maybe you can catch Clarisse— or whoever it was—meeting up with Kerry earlier."

"I'll have someone take a look, but so far, the feed has been worthless. Whoever's behind this, they're smart with tech. And if it's one of us, they know where the cameras are—it's not hard to avoid them if you know where they're located. Can you describe the tat?"

"I didn't get that good of a look. All I can tell you is that it was one shark, not two. And the body was curved like a C." Which described most of the tats I'd seen. "I think it was dark blue," I added, "but it could've been dark gray."

Brien put his wine glass on the table. "So, here's what we have so far. Someone, probably Clarisse Dumas, tried to compel you to poison me and set it up so that when the bottle was discovered, the blame would fall on you." His face hardened. "With me sick, you would've been dead by morning. Talon and Cain would've taken you out the moment the bottle turned up in my trash. There'd be no evidence you'd been compelled."

I blew out a breath. "Good thing it didn't work."

"Yeah." His gaze sharpened. "And why is that, Twilight? You said someone tried to compel you. I assume they included an order not to tell anyone, and yet the first thing you did was inform me. None of the intel I have on you says you can't be compelled."

"Oh." I grimaced uneasily. "That."

"Yeah, that." A low growl. "I thought we were done with all the fucking secrets."

I paused in the act of bringing a forkful of potato to my mouth. "We are." I gave a hard swallow and put the fork down without eating anything. "But everything's happened so fast, you know? And it doesn't come naturally for me to be so open. Plus, this is a family secret, one I buried so deep, it honestly didn't even occur to me to tell you until now. Even my alpha didn't know I can't be compelled."

"It runs in the family, doesn't it?" His eyes narrowed. "That's why so many of you are slayers. Even back in Korea, your family was prominent in SI. In fact, you guys are famous among other slayers. Some of the best slayers in the world have come from your lineage."

"Jesus. That detective you hired was good."

"I kept digging," he said between his teeth. "I was determined to find you. And when I did, you wouldn't have liked what I did with you."

"Brien." I scooted closer and touched his thigh. "I didn't mean to hurt you. You and me—it was like a hand grenade to the heart. It just...blew up. I didn't expect it. It's never been like that before for me. And when Prima Victorine ordered me to leave with her, I had to go. I was on an assignment. If I'd refused to go, SI would've considered me AWOL, and they'd have hunted me down."

He stared at my hand on his thigh. "I wanted to forget you—Lilith knows I tried. But I couldn't. There's something about you." His eyes lifted to my face. "I...need you. And I've never said that to any other woman."

I straddled him and caught his face between my palms. "I'm here," I vowed, "and I'm not leaving. But—" I sighed and pulled up my pant leg to show him the switchblade tucked into my sock.

His gaze went from the blade to my face. "Where did you get that?"

"Your cabinet."

"That's one of mine?" His head fell back against the couch. "Fuck. What am I going to do with you?"

"You're still thinking of me as a thrall." I forced his head up again so I could look into his face. "But I'm a slayer, Brien. I spent my teenage years living and breathing every fighting technique ever invented so I could hunt and kill vampires. Maybe the blood bond makes me yours, but as far as I'm concerned, you're mine, too. And that means I'd to die to protect you—understand?"

I snagged his gaze with mine, willing him to believe me.

To believe in us.

A beat passed, then his arms came around me in a bone-crushing hug.

"I can't lose you." He swallowed. "It would...break me."

"I know." A rock-sized lump filled my throat. "Because it's the same for me. This thing between us goes both ways."

He nodded without speaking.

I touched my lips to his. He angled his head, his mouth taking mine in a hard kiss. He didn't stop until I was breathless.

I laid my forehead against his. "So you have to win this challenge, understand?"

"Oh, I understand all right," he told me.

I nodded and sat back. "But I've been thinking—as far as Clarisse knows, the compulsion worked. So she thinks I poisoned you, and she also believes I won't remember doing it—which gives us the upper hand. My guess is that Kuro is working with Clarisse. Watch her, and chances are we find him, too."

"You're right. The sonuvabitches finally went too far." The corners of Brien's mouth tugged up in a smile that would've iced the Artic. "We've got them, now."

"About that." My answering smile was as frigid as his. "I have an idea…"

A knock on the door interrupted us. "Who is it?" Brien called.

"William. Your package is here, sir."

Brien went to the door, returning with a small box from which he took a gold cuff. Seating himself on the couch again, he slid the bracelet on my wrist and kissed my palm.

"To celebrate our blood bond. I had it specially made last night. It's tradition," he added when I just stared at it without speaking.

"Oh. Right."

The cuff was a simple design of sand-blasted, hammered gold with tiny pink diamonds scattered across the surface. The lump in my throat was back. I ran my thumb over the rough surface.

"You don't like it," he said flatly. "No problem—I can order another one."

"No fucking way." My fingers closed over the cuff. "I love it. It's perfect—exactly what I would've picked out myself."

And it was. That wasn't the problem.

"Yeah?" His mouth turned up in a quick, boyish grin.

I nodded. He seemed so pleased that I didn't have the heart to tell him that I wanted more than a blood bond. I wanted to be his mate.

"It's beautiful." I leaned forward and kissed him. "Thank you."

"I thought you'd like it," he said. "Now tell me about this idea of yours…"

26

BRIEN

idnight arrived. I waited in the hall outside the ballroom with Twilight.

Inside the ballroom, a soldier started ringing a gong. *One. Two. Three.*

I mentally ran through fighting moves and strategies. The syndicate's future depended on me, not to mention Twilight's life. I had to win this.

Four. Five. Six.

She nudged me with her shoulder. "You're going to kick his ass."

I smiled despite myself. "Thanks. And you stay close to Cain and Talon, understand?"

"Will do." She gave me a thumbs-up.

Seven. Eight. Nine.

I hadn't wanted Twilight at the challenge, but she'd pointed out that until we unmasked Kuro, she was safer with me, Cain and Talon in the ballroom than alone in my apartment.

And if I lost, we both knew she'd be running for her life. Better to know as soon as it happened than to lose time waiting for word to reach her.

Ten. Eleven. Twelve.

"Showtime," murmured Twilight.

Drawing myself up to my full height, I squared my shoulders and strode through the door, Twilight following a little behind. Candles flickered in the gold-leaf sconces mounted on the dark red walls, their flames reflected in the mirrors that ringed the ballroom floor. Across the room, Prosper entered through the opposite door.

In addition to our seconds, all the syndicate enforcers were present—two women and six men. Those who hadn't already been on the island had flown in earlier tonight. They'd formed a ring in the middle of the floor, everyone in dark suits except for the women, who'd both worn red.

Cain and Talon and Prosper's seconds, Matthew and Donald, stood in the center of the ring, facing each other. Prosper and I joined them.

Per Twilight's plan, Cain and Talon had let themselves be overheard earlier worried about my supposed "poisoning." The rumor had flashed like wildfire through the castle. Matthew had even texted Cain to ask if the challenge was still on. If Prosper had been involved in the plot to poison me, he was in for a nasty surprise.

Now, I sent a look around me at the enforcers. I let my gaze linger on Clarisse, elegant in a chic red pants suit cut low over a lacy black bra, her dark hair swept into an updo that displayed the dark-blue shark tat on the side of her neck.

Her eyelashes flickered, a small tell that she was worried. She clearly hadn't expected me to show up at the challenge looking healthy and fit.

Clarisse didn't know it yet, but she was going down. She must've been the woman who'd given the poison to Twilight. She was the right height, and the tattoo matched. And as Talon had pointed out, she was ambitious. When she'd realized I wasn't interested in mating with her, she'd apparently decided to throw in her lot with whoever was trying to overthrow me.

Twilight slipped into the circle near Talon and Cain, and every head in the room swung in her direction.

Clarisse licked her lips in another small, nervous movement.

Seeing Twilight with me—clearly unharmed instead of dead or in the dungeon for poisoning me—must be quite a shock.

Matthew took a threatening step in Twilight's direction. My muscles locked, but he stopped well away from her, snarling, "No thralls allowed. This is syndicate business."

Several people, including Clarisse, nodded.

"That's my father's rule," I countered, "not mine. And I say the woman stays. This concerns her as much as me."

Matthew curled his lip. "Thralls have no rights at a challenge." He raised his voice slightly. "Eugene. Remove the human."

A ballroom door slammed open and a dhampir soldier raced inside, heading for Twilight. She spun to face him, feinting left, then going right, but he was too fast for her.

He grabbed her and dragged one of her arms up behind her back, urging her ungently toward the exit. "Out, woman."

The lethal look she sent him over her shoulder should've shriveled his balls. "Go to hell."

I stalked toward them. "Let her go, Eugene."

Instead of releasing her, he glanced at Prosper for confirmation. Several of the other vampires turned to Prosper, too, like it was up to him.

My back teeth set. As acting primus, my wishes should be enough for Eugene, Matthew and everyone else in the syndicate. That they were waiting for Prosper's approval demonstrated why this challenge was necessary.

"Lieutenant?" Eugene prompted. It was the last word he ever spoke.

I leapt, jerking him off Twilight and wrapping an arm around his head. "I said, *Let. Her. Go.*"

His garbled apology turned to a scream that died in his throat as I ripped his head off. Blood spurted everywhere. His headless body stumbled forward, dropping to its knees before crumpling to the floor.

I tossed his head on top of the still-bleeding remains. It bounced off his chest and rolled onto the black-and-white marble tiles, rocking back and forth before coming to a halt on one cheek, eyes open, mouth gaping.

The ring of enforcers had gone statue-still. Twilight had managed to avoid being splashed with the fool's blood, but I wasn't so fortunate. Pulling off my spattered T-shirt, I wiped my face and dropped the crumpled material on top of Eugene's smoking, rapidly blackening body.

"Any other objections?" I glanced around me, letting my gaze linger an extra beat on Matthew.

Twin spots of color burned in his cheeks, but he dropped his gaze to the floor and kept his mouth firmly shut.

I smiled coldly. "Good." Taking Twilight by the arm, I inserted her back in the circle and returned to the center. "Now, can we get on with this fucking challenge?" I asked the room at large.

The assembled vampires muttered agreement.

Prosper and I faced off. Like me, he wore tactical pants. His dark brown hair had been freshly cut. He appeared determined yet saddened; even the pouches under his eyes seemed deeper. I knew he genuinely mourned my father—the two had shared a special bond.

"Prince Brien." He gave me a curt nod.

"Lieutenant," I returned.

Neither of us offered to shake hands. That sort of hypocritical civility was for humans. A challenge for primus was a brutal, no-holds-barred fight. Cheating wasn't only allowed, it was encouraged. If you could get away with it, then your opponent didn't deserve to win.

Still, there were rules, which varied from syndicate to syndicate. Per Maritime Syndicate tradition, you were allowed two silver weapons. Also, a challenge was fought bare-chested. It provided a clear view of the target—the area over the heart—and proved you weren't wearing protective gear. Most of us opted to fight barefoot as well, for balance and better awareness of our surroundings.

Finally, no one could aid the combatants in any way. It was the seconds' task to ensure that.

Prosper stripped off everything but his pants, handing his T-shirt, shoes and socks to Matthew. I removed my shoes and socks and gave them to Cain.

I sought out Twilight for one last look. In the dimly lit ballroom, she stood out like a vibrant star, her inky hair smoothed back from her stunning oval face into an intricate braid, her slender form clad in a cream-colored henley and shimmering silver jeans.

My heart fisted in my chest.

She was air. The blood in my veins. My own personal goddess.

Of course, she was my mate.

I was an idiot not to have realized it before now. But I'd been too blinded by what was expected of me—mate with a vampire, preferably a princess like Zoe Tremblay—to recognize my mate when she was literally standing in front of me.

Twilight winked at me. "Kick some ass," she mouthed.

I was still reeling, but I felt the corners of my lips tug up. Yeah, this was the woman for me.

Talon held out the box with my daggers. Dragging my gaze from Twilight, I selected one and turned back to where Prosper waited, dagger in hand.

The vampires fell silent. We ritually touched the blades together. In the hush, the quiet clink sounded unnaturally loud.

I took a last look at Twilight and drew a breath, centering myself. Reminding myself one last time what the stakes were.

Prosper raised a sardonic brow. "I see you've recovered."

"Disappointed?" I returned.

"I didn't have anything to do with it, if that's what you're thinking."

"But you know who did?"

He moved a shoulder noncommittally. "I have an idea, yes."

"Ready?" Talon asked us.

"Yes," I replied, my gaze on Prosper.

I extended my fangs, allowing my vampire full rein. All my senses sharpened—my hearing, my sense of smell, my sense of touch, and most of all, my vision.

The lieutenant bared sharp white fangs, his irises shining blue. "Yes."

With my senses cranked up, I caught helpful nuances. His heart rate had increased and he was breathing harder than he should've been.

My lips pulled back in a feral smile. He wasn't as confident as he wanted me to think.

Matthew raised a hand over our heads, then slashed it down. "The challenge for primus has commenced!"

❧ 27 ❧

TWILIGHT

The other vampires eyed me with varying degrees of anger and dislike. I'd invaded the inner sanctum—a mere thrall—and they weren't happy.

I let a slight smile curve my lips.

Up yours, bloodsuckers. I'm here, and I'm staying.

Then they forgot about me as Brien and Prosper started circling each other, hard-faced and intent.

Brien's hair was secured with a leather tie, his chest smudged with Eugene's blood. In the flickering light, the twin sharks curving around his upper arm seemed almost alive. He wasn't the largest vampire in the room, but his raw dominance overshadowed everyone else.

A primitive arousal heated my belly. Having him defend me like that was so fucking erotic.

My man.

My lover.

Mine.

The ring of vampires edged closer, their faces gleaming in the candlelight like a circle of the damned.

Prosper struck first, a sharp thrust aimed at Brien's side. Not a killing blow. More like he was testing Brien's defenses.

Brien knocked the dagger aside and countered with a jab at Prosper's throat. The lieutenant danced backward. Brien's blade whipped past him, missing Prosper's jugular vein by a hair.

Brien settled back into a crouch, and the two men resumed their circling.

Striking out. Retreating. Circling some more.

A minute passed, then another, with neither managing to cut the other.

The vampires muttered and growled.

Cain and Talon had taken a place in the circle on either side of me. Now Cain called, "You can take him, Brien," and someone from Prosper's side yelled, "Hamstring him, Lieutenant."

Brien lashed out, his movements a blur, at least to me. This time, he took a chunk out of Prosper's shoulder. Blood spurted, spraying the marble tiles with ruby droplets.

"First blood to the prince," Cain called.

He and Talon exchanged a victorious grin over my head.

The fight picked up pace. Grunts sounded and daggers clanged.

Prosper lunged at Brien, slicing the silver blade across his face and nearly taking out his eye, bringing home to me that this wasn't over.

Not until Brien won.

Brien jumped back as Team Prosper applauded and hissed encouragement.

Prosper lunged at him again. I didn't even know he'd moved until his blade carved a gash out of Brien's abdomen. Brien took a stumbling step backward and fell on his butt.

I gasped and instinctively started for him, my hand going to the switchblade in my pocket.

Cain's hand clamped on my upper arm, halting me. Pale blue eyes blazed into mine. "Interfere and I'll toss your ass out of here."

"Fuck, I'm sorry." I jerked my hand from my pocket like I'd touched a hot poker. "I wasn't thinking."

Brien was back on his feet now. Cain released me and turned back to watch the fight.

"You're on thin ice as it is," he said out of the side of his mouth. "The old vampires don't like knowing a human bested the primus. My advice is to be humble and submissive—at least in public—even if it kills you."

He was right. I had to play the part of a thrall—for now, anyway.

"Understood." Without taking my eyes from Brien, I clasped my hands in front of my body, shoulders rounded.. "Sir," I tacked on meekly.

Cain glanced at me. "You're good. I can see why you've survived so long."

I smothered a smile.

The moment I was back on my feet, I dodged right, expecting Prosper to take advantage of my slip.

But he didn't. Instead, he moved back, breathing hard. Vampires don't sweat, and we normally take only four or five breaths a minute. But Prosper's breathing was ragged, heavy.

I was breathing deeper, too, but he sounded exhausted. Was he really tiring, or was he faking it?

I pressed harder.

He lashed out with his blade, slashing a line over my left eye to match the one he'd made on my right. I would've been blinded by the blood if the cut over my right eye hadn't already closed up.

A nasty bit of strategy, one his side applauded. I backpedaled and swiped the blood away with my arm.

Prosper followed, breathing hard but still fast. I faked right, kicking out with my left foot and catching him in the elbow. His dagger flew out of his hand.

We both lunged for it, but I reached the dagger first, snatching it up. Prosper swore and spun toward Matthew, who slapped the second blade into Prosper's hand.

Prosper spun back to me, but I parried the thrust with his own blade and struck out—once, twice—cutting deeply into his side and then stabbing him in the neck. Then I backpedaled, quickly putting a few feet between us.

He was bleeding from multiple wounds now. A strategy he'd taught me himself. The more he bled, the more slowly his wounds would heal.

His chest expanded. I sensed him drawing on his magic. He launched himself at me, his fangs gleaming in the candlelight.

I sidestepped—and slipped on a pool of blood. My feet shot out from beneath me and I landed hard on the marble floor. Worse, in the split second I'd been distracted, trying to catch my balance, Prosper slashed his blade across my inner elbow, cutting through tendons and rendering my left arm temporarily useless. The blade in my left hand clanged to the floor several feet away from me.

I cursed myself under my breath. I should've seen that coming. It was a classic Prosper move.

The lieutenant stomped on my right wrist, grinding his bare heel into the tendons to make me release the dagger I still held. Without my willing it, my right hand opened and the dagger slipped to the marble floor. I drew my knees up to kick Prosper away, before I could, he'd dropped to his knees on my chest, hard enough to knock the breath out of me.

One hand gripped my chin, forcing it back. His fangs gleamed, his gaze on my throat. Then the motherfucker shifted on my chest so he could dig a knee into my balls.

The pain nearly blinded me. Then it got worse, spreading from my nuts to my groin to my stomach, wave after wave of it, until all I wanted to do was curl into a fetal ball and wait for it to pass.

Prosper raised his free arm to stake me. Somehow I managed to shove his knee away from my groin and bring up my own leg to protect myself.

Way back in my brain, my father's voice whispered.

You don't have what it takes to be primus.

Twilight moaned and I flashed on what would happen to her if I lost this challenge.

Like fuck I don't.

A growl erupted from deep inside me. I got a foot between us and kicked Prosper in the stomach with all my strength. He flew through the air, landing five yards away from me.

Despite my still-aching groin, I leapt back to my feet and quickly licked the crook of my left elbow to speed its healing. But for now, I'd have to fight righthanded.

I drew on my own magic with everything I had and came at Prosper.

Time to end this.

We fought hand-to-hand, hard and dirty, but he'd used up the last of his strength in that final push. I, on the other hand, still had energy to spare. The pain in my gut had subsided, and my right wrist felt good as new.

His gaze flicked to mine. He kept fighting, but I think we both knew I had the upper hand now.

I slashed his wrist, forcing him to drop his second dagger as well, and swept my leg behind his. A shove, and he slammed onto his back.

I straddled him and raised the dagger to deliver the killing blow.

"Do it." He stared up at me without a trace of fear. "I'm ready."

The circle of vampires hissed and snarled. Blood does funny things to us. My gaze locked on the bright red, life-giving fluid oozing from Prosper's chest. I had to fight the urge to lick it off him, especially given my own wounds.

Stake him. Prove you're dominant to him. Only a weakling shows mercy.

My fingers tightened around the dagger's stainless-steel handle. I lifted it high above my head, preparing to drive it down into his heart.

Staring down at Prosper's grim face, it was almost like I could see my father's face superimposed over Prosper's.

And it would feel so sweet. So fucking sweet.

Stake him. Prove to everyone that you're worthy of being my spawn.

But that was Jules's voice talking, not mine, and I'd already proved I was Prosper's dominant.

And that's when it finally hit me. My father was gone now.

And I had nothing to prove to anyone except myself.

Prosper's face swam back into focus. He bared his teeth. "Do it, damn you."

Losing him would be a blow to the syndicate. He was smart and cunning, and he had the confidence of the older vampires. If he was willing to yield to me in front of the upper hierarchy, I could still use him, although not as my lieutenant.

Prosper's chest heaved. His gaze slid from mine.

I snarled. "Look at me."

He obeyed, helpless to do anything else.

I locked gazes with him. One by one, the vampires fell silent. I spoke into the hush, my voice pitched so everyone could hear.

"Yield. Or I'll send you to the Dark Lady."

❦ 29 ❦

TWILIGHT

The challenge seemed to last for hours, although in reality, it probably wasn't more than fifteen minutes. There was a final flurry of activity and then Brien straddled Prosper, demanding he yield.

The ballroom went still as a graveyard. A syndicate challenge almost never ended in one of the combatants yielding.

Cain glanced over my head at Talon. "What's Brien up to?"

"Hades if I know," the curly-haired enforcer muttered.

I caught my breath, teeth digging into my lower lip, right hand curled into a fist at my side.

Across the circle, Matthew's eyes met mine. Something about his compressed mouth and fixed gaze sent an icy shock over my nerves. I'd seen the exact same expression on Kuro's face when he'd informed me that I worked for him now.

I wrenched my gaze from Matthew and back to Brien and Prosper. Both were wounded. Beneath the red splashes, Brien's torso gleamed with a savage beauty.

Prosper dipped his chin. Somehow, it wasn't a surrender so much as an acknowledgment of Brien's fighting skill.

"Yes," he said in a carrying voice. "I yield."

Brien rose and offered his hand to Prosper. The lieutenant took it and came to his feet. The cuts on Brien's face and elbow had already healed over. Prosper's wounds were healing, too, although not as fast.

My breath whooshed out.

Brien had won. He was officially the new primus.

Instead of releasing Brien's hand, Prosper raised it high above both their heads. "Hail to Primus Brien Leclerc."

Talon and Cain took up the cry, and so did most of the other enforcers.

But not all of them.

Talon and Cain went to Brien to congratulate him. I'd started after them when something sharp touched my lower spine. I stiffened.

"Don't move," Matthew said in a barely-there rasp, "and say nothing. Or I'll carve your fucking liver out. Nod if you understand."

I lowered my chin in a tiny nod.

"You might think you can figure a way out of this," Matthew said in an undertone. "Especially now you've removed your grandmother from the equation. But Kuro worked for me. I know everything he knew."

"Kuro's gone?" I asked to give myself time to think.

From her position in the circle a few yards away, Clarisse's eyes flicked at us, a tiny smile on her lips.

"Yes. I miscalculated there. I didn't think the prince valued you so much."

Something in his tone—anger mixed with regret—helped me connect the dots. My gaze jumped to the ashes that were all that remained of the dhampir soldier Brien had slain.

"Kuro was Eugene," I breathed.

"My only spawn," he confirmed tightly. "Which is why slitting your throat will be the easiest thing I've ever done. An eye for an eye, so to speak."

My eyes widened.

Matthew's spawn?

"You were the one in the shadows," I said. "Not him."

That had been Matthew slinking around the ballroom that day. Kuro—or Eugene—had a similar way of moving, and that's what had confused me.

Matthew grunted, neither admitting nor denying it. "Your grandmother might be stashed away somewhere safe right now, but we'll find her, sooner or later. The Ghost is a dead woman, Lainey Q—and so are you, unless you do exactly as I say."

My bowels iced. He knew my last alias and that my grandmother had been known as the Ghost. Even if he hadn't mentioned Kuro, it would've been proof that he was working with SI. How else would a Maritime enforcer know all that?

More dots connected. Kuro/Eugene must have been a double agent, pretending to work for SI when his real loyalty had been to his sire, Matthew.

"What do you want from me?"

"Here's my offer, and you should know it will expire by sunrise. Stake Brien before then, and you're free, and I'll call off the hit on your grandmother."

He'd put a hit out on my halmoni?

My whole body went taut with anger. "You SOB," I said between my teeth, not caring who heard me.

But everyone's focus was on Brien, who was surrounded by several enforcers, including Talon and Cain, accepting their congratulations.

Matthew wasn't finished. "I'll personally send you off the island before anyone knows, and let SI know you're ready for another assignment. I will not let that *'boy prince'*"—he hissed that last part, and it took me a second to realize he meant Brien—"spoil everything."

I glanced at Brien again, and suddenly, I knew. It was the final dot, the event that had set off everything which followed.

"You staked Prima Lenore, didn't you? You or Clarisse. You two meant for this to happen—all of it. Jules going blood-mad, then a challenge between Brien and Prosper. Except you thought Prosper would win and you'd end up his lieutenant. Or maybe you were also going to stake Prosper—and blame that on SI, too."

Matthew's furious growl told me I'd nailed it. "Enough talking." The blade's point bit deeper into the small of my back. "Now, do we have an agreement?"

I dipped my chin.

"Slide your hand behind your back," Matthew ordered, and when I complied, he pressed a switchblade into my palm.

I closed my fingers around the handle.

"Sunrise," he murmured next to my ear. "Or your halmoni will die a slow, painful death."

I slipped the blade into my back pocket. He must have faded into the shadows, because a few seconds later, he reappeared on the opposite side of the circle.

Brien raised his hand for quiet, and the room went silent. The enforcers stepped back into the circle, Talon and Cain retaking their places on either side of me.

Brien invited Prosper back to the center of the circle. "You've served the syndicate well," he told his father's longtime lieutenant. "It would be a waste to lose you. Swear a loyalty oath to me, and you can stay. But if you can't serve me as you served my father, then I want your promise that you'll leave the island and never return."

Prosper didn't hesitate. He inclined his head and said, "I'd be honored to serve you, Primus."

The circle of vampires were clearly surprised, but I saw nods of approval. Prosper obviously had their respect.

Prosper held his hand out to Brien, his inner wrist facing up. Taking the wrist, Brien carefully slashed his dagger across it, opening up a single vein. Blood welled out.

Prosper dipped his fingers in it and drew a scarlet line diagonally across his chest. "I swear on my blood and all I hold sacred that I will be a loyal member of the syndicate under our new primus, Brien Leclerc."

"So be it," said Brien.

The vampires muttered approval.

"It was a test, you know," said Prosper.

Brien's brows drew together. "A test?"

"The challenge," Prosper explained. "To be honest, I wasn't sure you'd have the balls to accept."

"Are you saying you let me win?"

"No. If you'd lost, I would've sent you to the Goddess."

Jesus. My mouth dropped open; sometimes the ruthlessness of vampire syndicates surprised even me.

But the other vampires seemed impressed, and Prosper had extended his hand to Brien to shake. "Congratulations, Primus Leclerc."

"Hail the new primus!" shouted several vampires, including Cain.

A chill tightened my shoulders. Unlike everyone else, Clarisse wasn't paying attention to Prosper and Brien. No, she was eyeing me like the vampires at the auction had, as if I was cattle, not a person.

It was now or never. My halmoni was safe—for the time being, anyway. Frankly, I didn't trust Matthew worth a damn. Who knew if he'd really call off the hit on my halmoni? Plus, I had a feeling he wouldn't let me leave the island alive—I knew too much.

And I was so done with being pushed around by these motherfuckers.

I nudged Cain and Talon. They glanced at me, surprised.

Clarisse's smooth brow creased, so I nodded and grinned at the two men like I was excited Brien had won the challenge.

Cain frowned. "What?"

I dropped my voice to a thready whisper. "Matthew was working with Kuro. While you were congratulating Brien, he gave me a switchblade. Don't look, but it's in my back pocket."

Matthew was glaring at me now, too.

I talked faster. "He was the one who staked Brien's mother—he practically admitted it to me. Or if not him, it was Clarisse; they're working together."

Cain and Talon exchanged a glance. "Matthew gave you switchblade?" Talon asked.

"Yes—he wants me to stake Brien. Now, *hurry*. They're both looking at us."

Talon tilted his head to the left, and Cain nodded. They dropped back, Talon circling left toward Matthew, and Cain sidling right toward Clarisse.

Brien spoke again. "But before we open the circle, I have one more item of business." He stretched out his hand to me. "Step forward, Twilight."

My gaze snapped back to him. What the fuck?

He stared back, unsmiling, every inch a vampire primus.

I had to obey him; we both knew that. A thrall didn't ignore a direct command from a vampire, especially the primus.

His hand was still stretched out, and even though he hadn't moved or spoken since calling me to him, I saw it as it was. A plea to trust him.

I went to him.

His fingers closed around mine.

He didn't drop to his knees. His expression was severe, even a little cold. He was half-naked, bloodied, barefoot. But there in the dimly lit ballroom, surrounded by the top people in his syndicate, he met my eyes and it felt...perfect.

"I claim this woman, Twilight, as my mate."

A shockwave rippled around the circle of vampires. Jaws slackened. A couple of the enforcers actually rocked back on their heels. But no one spoke up to object.

A similar shock hit me right in the heart. I gripped Brien's hand as the connection between us opened fully, linking me to him in a way that I knew could never be broken, like our souls had somehow joined.

"Well?" Brien prompted, and I realized I was staring at him without speaking like my mouth had been glued shut.

I managed to pry my lips apart. My face split in a grin.

"I accept," I said in a voice that was probably too loud, judging by the way Brien blinked.

He recovered quickly, though, and with a low chuckle, pulled me into his arms for an open-mouthed kiss that almost made me forget we were in a ballroom surrounded by a dozen cold-eyed vampires.

A commotion made us break apart. Talon and Cain had reached Matthew and Clarisse, and the pair were fighting back.

Brien swore. "Matthew's part of this?"

I nodded. "He just tried to get me to stake you."

Prosper's bushy brows lowered. "What in Hades is this?" he asked Brien.

"Enforcer Smith's a traitor," Brien stated in a carrying voice. "As is

Enforcer Dumas. They're hereby stripped of their ranks and their rights as made members in the Maritime Syndicate."

Prosper's scowl deepened. It was clear he wanted an explanation.

I held my breath. It was Brien's first test as primus. His word was law now. He didn't have to explain himself unless he chose to.

Prosper's jaw worked, but he bowed his head. "As you say, Primus."

"Take them," Brien ordered.

Two vampires started forward, but instead of helping Talon and Cain, they attacked them, dragging the two men off Matthew and Clarisse. It was like touching a match to a bonfire. The adrenaline and testosterone in the ballroom was already high. People ran forward to help, including several soldiers who'd been guarding the doors out in the hall, and within seconds, the room had exploded into a full-out brawl.

Brien's daggers jumped into his hands. "You still have that switch-blade?" he asked me.

"Two." I grinned at his raised brow, brandishing the one Matthew had forced on me. "I'll explain later."

He grunted. "Stay close," he ordered.

I nodded. I would've done it anyway; I was more use guarding Brien's back than fighting on my own.

I retrieved the second switchblade and dropped into a crouch, one in each hand. I pressed the catches and the blades slid out with a satisfying snick.

The vampires split into two factions. Most took Brien's side, including Prosper, but a third person joined the vampires fighting on Clarisse and Matthew's side. Talon was fighting both Matthew and the new attacker now. In the uproar, Clarisse wrenched herself free of Cain and faded into the shadows.

"Bloody Lilith." Brien shoved me toward the nearest door. "Go! You'll be safe in my apartment. Lock the door and don't come out for anyone but me."

I stumbled a few steps in the direction he'd pushed me, then caught myself. No way was I going to cower in Brien's apartment while he—*my mate*—fought for his life.

The fight picked up. The air swelled with unearthly snarls and hisses, like a swarm of demons had broken out of Hell. Goosebumps popped up all over my body, but the fear was mixed with exhilaration. Adrenaline surged in me. I darted around a couple of battling vampires, a switchblade in each hand, heading back to Brien.

Meanwhile, Matthew evaded Talon and lunged for Brien with a wicked-looking silver dagger. He halted long enough to taunt Brien, a sneer on his coyote-lean face.

Matthew's mistake—it allowed me to slide behind him.

"You were supposed to be in your final grave by now," the enforcer told Brien.

"Guess you backed the wrong man," he retorted.

Slipping one switchblade into my pocket, I crept closer to Matthew, the second blade gripped in both my hands. Brien noted me with a brief flicker of his eyelashes.

Raising the switchblade above my head, I brought it down, stabbing the sharp silver point with all my strength into Matthew's nape. I dragged downward, severing his spinal cord. He jerked and dropped to his knees. My only regret was that he'd never know it was me who'd slain him.

Brien was there as Matthew hit the floor. He drove his dagger into the older vampire's chest as insurance.

"Sonuvabitch." Matthew's mouth gaped like a startled fish. "Should've staked...you...the day...you were born."

Brien smirked. "Too late now," he said and came back to his feet. His gaze swung to me. "Why am I not surprised you're still here?"

I rolled my eyes. "You're welcome."

His jaw tightened. "D'you think I give a fuck about surviving if it means I lose you?"

Matthew's body was smoking. His eyes had already burned up, leaving him with two empty sockets in his rapidly blackening face. Putting a foot on his shoulder, I wrenched Brien's dagger from his chest.

"Here." I tossed it to Brien. "And by the way, I love you. That means I don't want to lose you, either."

He snatched the blade out of the air in a movement too fast to see. "*You*—." He crooked an arm around my neck and gave me a hard kiss, then released me. "You do realize that I'm your primus now. That means when I give an order, you obey it."

I snorted. "Good luck with that."

His lips twitched, and I could tell he was trying not to smile. "Stay, then," he said, half-growl, half-laughter.

"Yes, Primus," I said with a grin.

He just shook his head as Clarisse dropped out of the shadows a few feet behind him.

"Brien!" I pointed over his shoulder, and he spun to face her.

Clarisse's dark hair had pulled free of its chic updo, and she'd kicked off her high heels and lost the jacket, leaving her in a black bra and crayon-red pants. She evaded Brien with a vampire-fast move and stalked toward me, murder in her eyes.

Brien grabbed her shoulder, and she turned on him, rage twisting her fine features. "Mate," she spat at him. "A human? You must be soft, to want her when you could've had me."

He dropped into a fighter's crouch. "She's got something you'll never have."

I moved a few feet back, guarding Brien from another attack. Although to be honest, if a vampire came at me, I'd be dead before I knew I was being attacked.

I'd never wanted so badly to be a vampire myself.

Brien wasn't weak. I was.

"What?" Clarisse mirrored Brien, dagger out.

She began to move her upper body from side to side, feet planted and knees bent, in a hypnotic, cobra-like movement. I focused on her feet so I wouldn't get drawn in.

"Integrity," Brien replied.

It took me a few seconds to realize he was talking about me, then I blinked. I'd lied to Brien from the day we'd met.

"If she makes me a promise," he stated, "I know she'll keep it. Can you say the same thing? You swore loyalty to the syndicate, and I'm your new primus. So what in Lilith's name do you think you're doing?"

"Challenging you." Clarisse struck at Brien's chest, sharp and vicious, but Brien knocked her thrust aside and she almost lost the blade.

"You've lost the right to challenge me, Dumas. But I accept."

She regripped the dagger handle and bared her teeth. "You and your honor and integrity. Like I said, *soft*. Jules was right."

She went for him again. The fight was short and vicious, a flurry of slashing blows too fast for me to follow. But when Brien straightened, lungs heaving, his dagger was buried in Clarisse's chest.

Shock slackened the former enforcer's jaw. She wrapped her fingers around the handle, her gaze traveling past Brien's shoulder to where I stood, gripping my remaining switchblade.

Hate flashed over her face. "Bitch," she hissed.

Then her fingers slipped from the dagger's handle. Her eyes rolled up in her head and she slumped to the marble floor.

Brien smiled. "You lose."

He jerked the blade from her chest and stepped back, glancing around for me. I went to his side, and his arm came around me like an iron band.

The battle was over. The two vampires that had attacked Talon and Cain were ashes, as well as the vampire who'd gone to their aid. Brien's side was nursing a few serious injuries—Prosper was holding his detached right hand to his wrist, waiting for it to reconnect—but they'd only lost one man.

"You okay?" I asked, although as far as I could tell, Clarisse had barely touched him, and his earlier cuts, while still visible, were healing rapidly.

Brien's green eyes seared me. "I'm fine. You?"

"I'm good."

"Good." Something about the way he said it—all growly and sensual—made my inner thighs clench.

Keeping me tucked against his side, he raised his voice. "All of you, it's over." He sounded cool, in control. If he hadn't given me that single, searing look, I wouldn't have known how revved-up he was. "There will be a meeting tomorrow at midnight to discuss the new hierarchy—my war room."

The remaining vampires either saluted or murmured, "Yes, Primus." They were bloodied and disheveled, their eyes hyper-alert and ringed with blue. The testosterone and adrenaline in the room was still sky-high.

"And have someone dispose of the ashes in the ocean. These bastards don't deserve an honorable burial."

Brien turned back to me. This time, his gaze lingered on my throat.

My blood heated. I recognized that look. He was hungry.

I gave him a slow smile. "Congratulations, Primus."

"Mm." He nuzzled my cheek. "Let's get the fuck out of here."

"Now," I agreed.

As we left the ballroom, Cain and Talon came up on either side of us.

Cain had conjured up a bottle of blood-wine. He shoved it at Brien. "Congratulations, you two."

"Thank you." Brien took the bottle and chugged some down without moving his arm from my shoulders. "By the way," he said as he handed the bottle back to Cain, "you two are my new lieutenants. I'll make it official at the meeting tomorrow night."

Cain removed the bottle from his lips without drinking. "Both of us?"

"Yeah." Brien's mouth edged up. "You think you can handle it?"

Cain puffed his chest a little. "Of course."

Talon simply inclined his head. "You honor us."

A grin split Cain's face. "To the new primus." He lifted the wine bottle above his head, and with a wink at me, added, "May he kick ass."

I grinned back.

"Give me that wine." Talon leaned around Brien and grabbed the bottle from Cain. "To the new primus." He took a swig and lobbed it back to Cain, who snatched it out of the air without spilling a drop and drank the rest of it down.

A couple of vampires appeared with more blood-wine, and those bottles got passed around as well.

The thralls were in the passage now, too, talking excitedly. I caught a few openly envious looks. I felt kind of like Cinderella after the prince showed up with the glass slipper.

Pinky handed me an open bottle of champagne. "What's this I hear about you and Brien? You fucking *mated?*"

"It's true." Brien caressed the back of my neck. "She's my mate. I claimed her, and she accepted."

I took a drink of champagne and handed the bottle back.

Pinky was staring at me, open-mouthed. "Holy crap." She raised the bottle to me. "You work fast, girl."

I grinned ear-to-ear. I couldn't seem to stop smiling, actually. Joy fizzed in me like the champagne I'd just swallowed.

"Not that fast. We actually met two years ago at Princess Zoe's birthday ball."

Pinky's brows shot up to her hairline. "Seriously?"

"It's the truth," Brien said. "One look and I knew I had to have her. It took her a little longer, though."

"That's not—" I was still sputtering a denial when he pulled me into a kiss that ended with me bent over his arm as he scraped his fangs down my throat. The onlookers hooted and cheered.

We continued winding our way through the tunnels. People kept stopping us to toast Brien's win and our mating, so it was a good thirty minutes before we reached his apartment.

Brien turned to face the small crowd of well-wishers, his fangs still visible. "Thank you, everyone. Now fuck off."

There was more hooting and cheering. Cain said something crude, and I gave him the finger. Talon's mouth twitched in amusement.

"Let's go to the Bite Club," said someone.

"Yeah," said Cain. "This calls for champagne. Brien, you sure you don't want to come? Excuse me, I meant to say *Primus.*"

"No," said Brien. "But you mofos go—and don't come back."

"Rude," I said, laughing, and he dragged me inside, shutting the door and engaging the lock. I had time for a single breath, and then my back was against the door.

"Holy Dark Mother." He slapped his hands to the wood on either side of my head, his irises encircled with a hot blue, his expression darkly sensual. "I thought we'd never get rid of them."

I feathered my fingertips over his nape. "You must be hungry."

"Starving." He nuzzled my throat. "I want blood and I want you. My mate," he added with bone-deep satisfaction.

The connection between us was still open. His need and hunger poured through.

And suddenly, I understood. He *did* love me, he just didn't know how to tell me. In fact, I'd bet no one but me had ever said the words to him.

"I love you." I gave him a hard hug, willing him to not only hear it, but *feel* it.

"My heart," he returned gruffly, which was all the answer I needed.

He caressed my throat with one hand, tilting my head up with his thumb so he could kiss me. His tongue swept into my mouth, tasting every corner.

His fangs slid out, a reminder that I was playing with a dominant alpha predator. My nipples tightened. Heat pooled in my lower belly.

"I'm going to fuck you," he said against my lips, his tone gravelly.

"Yes." Pressing my mouth to his, I ran my tongue around his fangs. He groaned like I'd licked his cock. I rocked my hips against his, desperate to seal our mating in this way. "*Now*."

His hands came to the hem of my shirt. He dragged it up, breaking the kiss so he could pull it off and toss it aside. He jerked down my bra straps, exposing my breasts and binding my arms to my sides. He rolled the nipples between his thumb and forefinger, pinching them into hardness.

He licked each one in turn, wetting them with his tongue. "So pretty," he muttered, his gaze on the tingling tips.

He dropped to his knees and undid my jeans. "I need a shower," he said, working them down my legs along with my panties, leaving them balled up around my ankles. "But first, I have to taste you..."

"I don't mind you dirty." I ran my eyes over his blood-smeared torso. "In fact, I like it. You look so freaking hot."

His response was an animal-like growl, which made me even hotter.

He put his thumbs between my thighs, encouraging me to widen them as far as I was able with the jeans binding my ankles, then paused, greedily taking me in from my thighs to face.

I pictured what I must look like. Mouth swollen from his kisses. Nipples flushed and puckered from his handling. My arms partially bound to my sides by the bra straps, and my sex slick with arousal.

He blew a warm stream of air against my clit. "What do you want, angel? Tell me."

"You. Licking me." Freeing my arms, I reached for his head so I could guide his mouth where I wanted it.

A hard look up from under his eyelashes. "Hands on the door."

I swallowed, completely, irrevocably under his spell, and pressed my palms to wood again.

His gaze returned to my thighs. "Gods, I need this."

"Yes," I said. "Please, Brien."

His mouth touched me again. His tongue glided into the V he'd made.

I was so primed, it was like he'd lashed me with an electric current. Pleasure sizzled from my core to my brain. I made a low, unintelligible sound and arched into the wet heat of his mouth.

From there, it just got better.

He tongued and sucked my swollen clit until I was writhing against the door, my eyes squeezed shut against the pleasure, my palms open against the wood. He worked two fingers into me. I clamped around him.

"That's it," he ground out. "Come for me."

He gently scraped his fangs over my clit.

I gasped. "Fuck."

He chuckled lowly. "You like it."

And I did like it. The hurt mixed with pleasure, especially when he licked the small wound he'd made. The rush of the aphrodisiac blew through me, turning me inside out and upside down.

His fingers worked inside me while he kept licking and sucking my tender, sensitive nubbin. It was too much. I moaned, low and needy, and broke apart in an explosive orgasm.

My knees had somehow been replaced by rubber. I slid partway down the door, lungs heaving, but Brien was there, sweeping an arm under my thighs and standing with an easy, inhuman grace.

He carried me into the bathroom. "Can you stand?"

When I nodded, he set my feet on the marble floor. I valiantly pried my eyes open. "I'm okay. Just..." I flapped my hand, words failing me.

"Good, because I'm not done with you."

Resting a hip against the counter, I met his dark smile with a wicked grin of my own, and took off my shoes, dropping them on the floor. The rest of my clothes followed.

Brien was already undressed. He grabbed me, threw me over his shoulder in a fireman's carry and stepped into the shower.

"Hey!" I smacked his hard butt, and he retaliated with a slap on my ass before whipping me around and in front of him.

I wrapped my legs around his waist and laughed into his eyes. "This is how you treat your mate?"

He tapped a control and hot water pounded our bodies from multiple directions. "Just showing you who's boss."

I punched his shoulder, and his mouth curved in one of those tiny Brien-smiles I'd come to love. The water washed away the remaining blood and slicked down his hair. The cuts on his face were thin red lines now.

His erection nudged my opening. "You know you like it."

"Maybe," I allowed.

I shifted my hips, lining us up, and his tip slid into me. My breath rasped in, and he halted.

"Ask me to fuck you. I want to hear you say it."

Tangling the fingers of my right hand in his hair, I eagerly obeyed. "Fuck me, Brien. Please."

"How?" He pressed a little deeper.

"Hard."

"Say please." He pulled almost all the way out.

I tightened my thighs around his lean hips. "Please." I paused, then added, "My lord."

His throat vibrated with something that was almost a purr. He turned us so my back was up against the marble tiles and thrust into me, deep and hard.

His fangs touched the turn of my neck. "I like you like this. All soft and warm and submissive."

I dug my fingers into the sleek muscles of his shoulders, grinding against him, my wetness sliding against his cock.

"Don't get used to it," I said, panting.

He thrust into me again, pinning my back to the wall, his fingers digging into my ass. "Lock your legs around me," he ordered against my throat, and I did.

I thought he was going to bite me then, but he didn't. Instead he looked up at me with burning, blue-encircled eyes.

His emotions poured through our bond, fierce and dark and deep. More powerful than desire. Stronger than need.

He was holding nothing back, and I fucking loved it. Because I felt the same way.

He looked back at my throat, and he seemed to catch himself. His thrusts slowed. "I shouldn't."

I cupped his nape and urged him back to me. "I want it."

His Adam's apple bobbed. "I don't want to hurt you."

I gave him a little shake. "Don't."

"Don't what?"

"Hold back. I want all of you, understand? You're my mate."

His lashes came down, veiling his eyes. Then he licked my throat. Something in me uncurled and pulsed, eager for what he could give me.

"Do it, damn you. I want it."

He groaned out my name. Sharp points touched my throat. He drew his hips back and thrust deep inside me at the same time his fangs broke my skin, sinking into the vein, sending a jolt of pleasure straight to my sex.

He drew hard on my throat in time to his pumping hips. Fire licked at my throat, burning a path over my nerves to my nipples, my clit.

"That's it," I said against his temple. "Fuck me. Take me. Don't stop. Don't. Ever. Stop."

My sex tightened around him. He gave a last suck and released me, licking the small wounds to close them, while his hips continued to thrust.

The fire raced up my spine to my brain. Through the bond, I felt his pleasure, and knew he also felt mine.

The sensations ratcheted up. From somewhere far away, I heard myself make a high, keening sound. I gulped oxygen, my entire being vibrating with the wild sweetness of it.

He thrust, hard and fast. We both stilled, then groaned as we climaxed simultaneously. It was as if we'd broken free of our bodies and hurtled into a special space where it was just the two of us, twined together in endless, mind-blowing pleasure.

Then we were back in the shower, Brien's face buried in my throat, hot water raining down around our heads.

$$\text{❦} \quad 30 \quad \text{❦}$$

BRIEN

When I woke up the next evening, Twilight was perched on a chair next to my bed, her dark hair falling forward over her face, her arms around her knees, contemplating her bare toes.

My mate.

My stomach clenched, but in a good way.

I could hardly believe this beautiful, passionate woman had agreed to be mine for the rest of her life.

But she had. She'd accepted to the mate bond. She really did love me.

I propped my head on my hand. "Hey, angel."

"Hey." Lifting her head, she offered me a half-hearted smile.

Okay, that wasn't like Twilight. And now that I was more awake, I sensed something was bothering her. In fact, I'd been feeling her turmoil even in my sleep.

I sat up. "What's wrong, sweetheart?"

She hitched a shoulder. "Nothing. Just...thinking about our mating and everything."

"And?" I reached out a hand and she came to me. I pulled her onto my lap. "Tell me. You're my heart. Whatever's bothering you, I'll make it right. Are you worried about the syndicate accepting you? Because they'll come around. Vampires know how it is with a mate. It's not fully under our control."

And those who didn't come around would answer to me.

"It's not that." She wrapped her arms around me. "You've got this. It was smart, the way you handled Prosper."

I shrugged. "He helped make the syndicate what it is today. It would've been a waste to lose him."

"I guess so." She leaned her cheek against mine. "But he was also the last link to your parents, wasn't he? That's why you didn't stake him."

I shook my head. "That's not why—" I sucked a breath through my teeth. "Well, maybe it was part of it. You know, all I ever wanted was Jules's respect. Not his love. Just his fucking respect. And the bastard made Prosper promise to challenge me. A final test."

She sighed. "I know."

I set my jaw. "I was never enough. No matter what I did, I was never enough."

"I get it." Her arms tightened on me. "And I'm so sorry. It's like me and my mom. I was always trying to live up to her reputation. Even when they shoved me into a coffin-sized box to see how long it would take until I broke, I took it. I fucking gritted my teeth and stuck it out until I passed out from lack of air."

"Why the hell didn't you leave sooner?"

Her mouth twisted wryly. "They were my family. But hey, you won. You beat Prosper. You passed your father's test. You're the primus now, so to hell with Jules."

My chest expanded with a sense of rightness. Not pride, although that was part of it. Rightness.

"Yeah, I did pass his fucking test. My father would've staked Prosper, you know. He would've said that only a weak man would let him live."

"But you knew Prosper still had something—some worth to the syndicate—so you allowed him to make his own choice. That's not weak, Brien—that's a kind of strength Jules wouldn't have understood. I didn't know your father, but I've seen enough vampires like him to know how they think."

I considered that. "You're right. To him, everything was about balancing the scales. An eye for an eye, a tooth for a tooth, a life for a life."

"Fuck Jules." She nuzzled my cheek. "You're going to make a good primus. I know it."

I combed my fingers through her hair. "Thank you."

She still hadn't told me what was bothering her, but one thing I'd learned from Jules was patience. I could wait. And then we were kissing.

Slow, deep kisses that were almost like a conversation.

I want you. I want to hear you make those moans. I want to make you beg. And I want to be inside you when you break.

Yes. Now.

Not yet.

You're so—

Sexy as fuck?

A low chuckle. *Yeah. That.*

We couldn't actually read each other's minds, but we were so attuned, emotionally, through our new bond that it felt almost like we could.

I pressed her onto the mattress, stopping only long enough to remove her clothes before taking her in my arms. She twined her arms and legs tightly around me.

Now that I could sense her emotions, fucking her was an endless smorgasbord of sensuality, her pleasure adding to mine. I kept her on the edge for long minutes, teasing us both, and when I finally pressed into her, she climaxed almost immediately.

I rounded my back so I could suck her nipples. When I sensed her starting to climb again, I sank my fangs into the smooth curve of her breast, sucking hard. Her blood filled my mouth, rich and spicy with the special essence that was Twilight.

She breathed my name and arched up to me, her slick inner walls squeezing my cock.

"Mine," I ground out.

The small of my back tightened. I thrust a last time and emptied myself into her.

I hung over her, feeding, my dick pulsing inside her. Then I licked the tiny punctures and withdrew from her, rolling onto my back and bringing her with me.

Neither of us stirred until her stomach growled. We got up and she ordered some food from the kitchen, then we showered.

While Twilight was eating, Talon texted me that Eden had left the island.

I immediately called him back. "What do you mean, Eden's gone?"

"She left—snuck away in the middle of the day when most of us were sleeping. Said goodbye to her parents, packed a bag and hitched a ride with a fishing boat to the mainland."

An emotionless recitation of facts, but I knew Talon had a special affection for the curvy blonde.

"You're sure she left of her own free will?"

"I'm sure. The fishing boat captain confirmed it."

I swore under my breath. "Let me know if you hear anything."

"I will—I sent Adrian to Halifax to see if he can pick up her trail."

"Good choice." Adrian was a young, tech-savvy dhampir soldier.

Talon heaved a breath. "Look, I've got it handled. I wouldn't have bothered you, but I thought you should know. Now forget about Eden and enjoy your new mate."

"Thanks." I hesitated, then added, "I'm sorry."

"Don't be," he replied in a hard voice. "She's only a thrall—and when I find her, she's the one who's going to be sorry."

I grunted and ended the call. He was right. We'd have to make an example of Eden.

Twilight screwed up her nose. "So Eden was involved in this somehow?"

"Looks like it."

Twilight worried her lower lip. "Something was wrong, though. I found her crying in the Bite Club bathroom one night."

"Then she should've been honest about it, whatever it is." I shook my head. "No, she broke the rules; she knows the consequences. Are you done eating?" I asked, firmly changing the subject. "Because I thought we could go for a walk on the beach."

She looked like she wanted to say more about Eden, but one look at my set face and she swallowed whatever it was and got to her feet. "I'd like that."

Outside the night was crisp and clear. We took off our shoes and walked barefoot along the shore, holding hands, our pants rolled up so we could kick our feet through the surf. When a pile of rocks blocked our way, we scrambled over it, leaping down to the beach on the other side.

Twilight sparkled up at me. "It's so beautiful out here tonight."

I had to kiss her—her face was so alive, so beautiful in the moonlight—so I did.

We continued walking along the water's edge, our linked hands swinging between us. "I want to hold our mating ritual as soon as possible," I said. "Make it official."

She nodded. "It will send a message to the syndicate—and the other syndicates. We should invite the primuses who are your main allies."

"That's what I was thinking. But it's important to me, too. I want to have the whole island at the reception—I want everyone to know how proud I am that you accepted my claim."

She released my hand. "About that..."

"Yeah?" I prompted.

"I can ask for a mate-gift, right?"

I bit back a smile. "So you want jewelry after all?"

"Well, I would like a ring to seal our vows. One that matches my cuff." She lifted her hand so she could admire the gold bracelet I'd given her. The diamond chips caught the moonlight, twinkling like tiny stars.

"It's yours. Hell, I'll buy you a ring for every day of the month. And a necklace and earrings to match."

She brought her arm back to her side. "I just want the one ring. But that's not what I meant."

"Anything. Just tell me and it's yours."

"Promise?" She stopped and looked up at me, her eyes dark pools in her face.

I faced her, my back to the ocean. A spike of wariness made me add, "If it's within my power to give it to you, then yes, I promise."

"It's within your power." She drew a breath, then said the rest in a rush. "I want you to turn me."

"Turn you." My insides chilled. Behind me, the surf surged toward the shore, sucking at my ankles. "Into a vampire?"

"Yes," she said. "And yeah, I know it's risky, but I want this. I want to be a true mate to you. Otherwise, when I'm an old lady, you'll just be hitting your prime."

"Twilight. It *is* risky. You might not make it through."

"But if you don't do it, I'm going to die hundreds of years before you. Do you really want to live that long without your mate? If you stay sane, that is. Look what happened to your fa—"

She broke off, but we both knew she'd meant Jules.

My hands came to her shoulders. "I can't lose you."

"You won't. I'm young, strong. People like me almost always make it through, don't they?"

I hesitated. "Yes. But not all of them."

She put her hands on my chest, her eyes moving between mine. I knew my expression was stony, but inside, fear clawed at me.

It was too soon. My mate was human. I knew I wouldn't have her for long—not as a vampire counts years. But this, this was too soon. I couldn't risk losing her now, not when I'd only just found her.

"Listen to me," Twilight ordered. "Are you listening?"

I reluctantly lowered my chin in a nod.

"I *need* to do this. It's not a sudden decision, if that's what you're worrying about. I was thinking about it even before I accepted your blood bond—almost since I came here, in fact. Clarisse Dumas was right. I am weak, and that's not what you need."

"Clarisse was a liar and a traitor. Don't let that bitch push you into doing something you don't want to do."

"Yeah? What about the tattoo on my back? You think I wanted that?"

"Of course not." I caressed her shoulders. "I know that was forced on you."

"Because I couldn't stop them." She huffed a breath. "It's not the tattoo so much. It's that it's a symbol."

I furrowed my brow. "Of what?"

"That I'm a human. Even in SI, I was one of the weaker ones. Yeah, I worked my ass off to make up for it. But most of them were dhampirs, and no matter how hard I tried, I could never be as fast and strong as someone who's even a quarter vampire."

I was starting to understand. "I see."

"So, believe me when I say I want to do this." She swallowed, then added, "SI is going to come after me, Brien. You can't just leave like I did. I've been AWOL for two years—and at least one person knew I staked my alpha. As soon as I resurface, they'll put out a kill order on me."

My back teeth clenched so hard my jaw hurt. "They'll have to go through me to get to you."

"But if I was a vampire, it would make it a helluvalot harder for them. In fact, we could make sure Karoly Kral knows. The Krals owe me a favor."

"Do they, now?"

She nodded. "In fact, if you don't want to turn me, I could always ask Karoly."

"Like fuck you will." My mouth tightened, the possessive animal in me rising to the fore. No one, even a mated male like the Kral primus, was getting anywhere near Twilight's pretty throat. "You're my woman. I'll be damned if I'll let him drink from you. You can't be turned without my permission. You know that, don't you?"

"Because of the blood bond?"

"Yeah. Also, as your mate, I'm your primus, too."

Her spine went rigid. "Are you going to play the boss-man card every time we disagree? Or do you want a partner, someone you can talk things over with?"

We glared at each other. Then she sighed.

"I'm a weakness. It's not just your people. The other syndicates will know it, too. They'll try to take me out to weaken you, like Matthew and Clarisse did with your mother. You'd have to put so much protection on me, I'd go insane. And I will not live in a fucking cage, not even for you."

My fingers dug into her shoulders. "Ask me anything but this. If I lose you now..."

"But you will lose me." She stroked the back of my neck. "Even if I stay, even if I let you put me in a cage, I'll get old and die and you'll still be a young man."

"Angel." I buried my face in her hair. "Please don't ask me now. Give us some time together. Then in ten, maybe twenty years, we can talk again."

"No. Right now is when you need a vampire mate the most."

"Damn you," I rasped.

Her throat worked. "I'm right. You know I am."

I closed my eyes. Because she *was* right. Turning her was risky, but now that we'd mated, letting her remain a human was even riskier.

Yeah, she was a kickass fighter, but as a human, she was vulnerable. As my mate, she might as well have a target painted on her back because taking her out would be the best way to get to me.

And I'd known that, even last night when I'd claimed her in front of everyone in the ballroom. I could say the emotions of the moment had overwhelmed me, but that wasn't entirely true. I'd judged it was the ideal time to bind her to me in front of the syndicate's inner circle.

In the back of my mind, maybe I'd even hoped that eventually, she'd agree to be turned. Just not so soon.

"Say yes," she said. "You don't have a choice and we both know it."

She'd showered recently. I gathered her closer, drawing a lungful of her fresh, clean, necessary scent.

"Fine," I said through a mouth that felt like it had been filled with sand and gravel. "I'll turn you."

❧ 31 ❧

TWILIGHT

"You understand what's going to happen, right?" Brien stroked the line of my throat from my jaw to my collarbone.

We were on the curtain wall, the stars glittering in the midnight sky, the ocean a velvety dark cloth as far as the eye could see. I was barefoot, my hair in a loose braid, the wind whipping the skirt of my sleeveless red dress around my thighs.

I'd chosen to be outside when Brien turned me. Alone with him in this wild, open place where the two of us had first dropped our defenses.

"Yes." I brushed a strand of wind-blown hair back from his tense face. "Do it. I want this."

He kept talking, his tone as clinical as a doctor's. "I'll have to bring you near death. Your heart will stop—and that's when I'll feed you my blood. The magic will be what sparks the transition, and it's not the same for any two people. But it hurts. Even if you don't die, you might wish you had."

"I understand."

A week had passed since the challenge for primus. Brien had spent hours each night consolidating his power and cleaning up his father's messes.

I'd helped where I could, especially with social media. When I was through, the Maritime Syndicate was going to be as popular as the Krals. Growing a syndicate these days was all about spin. Already, key human influencers were hailing the transfer of power to Brien as a step forward.

As for Brien and I, we'd snatched whatever time we could for ourselves: making love, taking walks, getting to know each other. We talked for hours, telling each other things we'd never told anyone else.

The better I got to know Brien, the more I realized how much he hid behind his Perfect Prince persona. The real Brien was darker and more complicated than the cool, self-assured syndicate prince. A man who could be ruthless when he had to and yet with an innate fairness that had earned not just my love, but my respect.

After all, I wasn't exactly little Miss Sunshine myself.

He'd been acting a part as much as I was, which made it even more special when he dropped the mask and let me see the real man beneath. A Brien who was far from perfect...but he was perfect for me.

And I knew that right now, that clinical manner concealed a very real fear.

"You'll be buried for a week," he said. "Then when you wake up again, you'll be so hungry for the first five or six days, you'd eat your own flesh if you can't have blood."

I swallowed dryly. That—the buried-alive part—was what I would've given anything to avoid. "You said it's only a shallow grave, right?"

The grave he'd prepared was in a secret cavern beneath the castle so he could stay with me even during the day. He'd stocked the cavern with blood-wine so he wouldn't have to leave. Only Cain and Talon knew the location so they could keep him in the loop about syndicate business.

Brien's clinical manner fractured. He pulled me to him in a hard hug.

"I dug it myself," he said against my hair. "It's less than a meter deep and the only thing covering you will be sand. You won't have any trouble getting out of it yourself, but if you do, I'll be right there, helping you. I won't leave your side the entire time."

I briefly closed my eyes. "I know you won't."

We rocked back and forth, hugging each other like you do when it might be the last time.

Brien released me. He had one more thing to tell me, but at least he'd dropped the Dr. Leclerc façade. "You won't be able to go out in the sun for years—I'm talking forty, fifty years, maybe longer. And I know how much you enjoy your food. You won't, anymore. If you try to eat anything other than alcohol or chocolate, you'll vomit."

"Brien." I summoned a wry, Lainey-Q smirk. "I know the risks. And living on wine and chocolate isn't the worst thing in the world. Now do it already, before you talk yourself out of it." *Before you talk me out of it.*

"You called your halmoni?"

"I did. She's not...happy about this." I made a face. "I'm hoping she'll come around."

She'd let me know straight out how insulted she was that I'd felt she needed protection. And where had I been the last two years?

After she wound down, I'd given her the CliffsNotes version of what had happened, then told her that I loved her and had mated with Brien. Then, like a coward, I'd promised to call her soon and hung up before she'd had time to do anything more than growl, "Have you lost your mind, Nikki?"

"Good." He smoothed his fingers down my braid. "Just in case you don't make—"

"I'm not going to die, understand? This thing between us—" I thumped first his heart, then mine—"will keep me alive. *You'll* keep me alive."

His Adam's apple worked. "I will," he said like he was taking a sacred vow.

"But I will miss the sun," I admitted.

"I know, angel." I felt his sorrow through our bond. "If I could make it up to you, I would."

"Hey," I said. "You have nothing to make up to me. This is my decision—I want to be turned. Everything comes with a price, and if I have to give up sunshine to have you, then I choose you. Now, c'mere already."

I curved my fingers around the back of his skull and guided him to my throat. His fangs scraped the skin. He breathed out a curse—and sank them into my carotid artery.

The familiar pain, followed by a rush of adrenaline, flashed through my body. Brien inhaled deeply, drawing in my scent, a sound so erotic I shivered.

His hand stroked beneath my dress. I knew the moment he discovered that I wasn't wearing panties. He made a sound low in his throat and tapped my mound, a small spank that made my inner thighs clench.

He sucked harder. My skin was on fire, my nerves on the edge between pleasure and pain. The aphrodisiac was in my blood now. Heat slammed through me, wave after wave of it.

I moaned, and then I climaxed, fast and hard, babbling, "Don't stop, don't stop, don't stop," over and over.

I dragged in a breath, my body still humming but wanting more. The sky shifted, the stars streaking crazily across the night-dark surface, and then I was on my back with Brien's body pressing me to the cold stone floor.

He stopped drinking long enough to tear his clothes off, his skin gleaming in the dark, his eyes rimmed with electric blue. He licked the blood spurting from my throat and began to suck again. With one hand, he caressed my breasts, pinching the nipples into hardness while he pressed inside me, slow and firm.

He slipped his hand under my shoulders, holding me to him while he fucked me in time to the surge of the ocean against the cliffs.

A heavy, drugging pleasure flowed through me. I wrapped my arms and thighs around him. "I love you. So much."

He hugged me closer in a wordless response.

Drinking. Thrusting. Drinking.

The pleasure increased until a second orgasm screamed through me. I tightened my grip on him and sobbed out his name.

He made a guttural sound low in his throat and pressed deep, then stilled, coming inside me in warm gushes of heat.

I was fading now, his hard body my only anchor to consciousness.

As I grew weaker, my arms and legs fell away from him. Fear licked at me.

"Easy," he murmured at my throat. "I've got you."

"Yes..." My agitation settled. I wanted this, and I trusted him to do it right.

Darkness edged my vision.

Brien framed my face in his palms. "Look at me, badass."

When I forced my eyelids open, he brushed his mouth over mine. "I love you."

I gave a faint chuckle. "*Now* you tell me."

"You *will* make it. Promise me."

"Hell yeah," I managed to say.

A second later, a bright light exploded behind my eyes. The sky rushed toward me, then everything went black.

From a distance, I heard Brien swear.

A warm liquid filled my mouth. I sputtered and choked. I tried to turn my head but firm fingers kept me where I was, my lips pressed to Brien's wrist.

"Swallow," he muttered.

This was part of it, I reminded myself. I had to drink or die.

So I did. The blood tasted of Brien and salt, like he'd mixed his essence with the ocean.

I sucked harder, greedily, mindlessly.

"That's enough," Brien said.

I made a sound of protest, but he was too strong. He pulled away, but only so he could lift me.

Like a lightning bolt, pain struck out of nowhere. I screamed and arched my back in agony.

"Twilight." Brien's voice was as agonized as mine.

He sped up. I was dimly aware of him running with me through the castle and down the stairs again and through the tunnels. I must've passed out for a short time, because I came to as he deposited me on soft, sandy surface.

A grave.

My grave.

We must be in the secret cavern.

A shovel scraped. Sand hit my legs. I moaned, my skin so sensitive it felt like hundreds of tiny insects stinging me.

Breathe. You can do this.

But I couldn't breathe. I was dead.

Panic clawed at my brain like a small, furry animal.

"No!" I managed to force the words past my numb lips. "I can't."

"It's too late." Brien's tone was raw with regret. "The transformation has already started."

Another wave of pain slammed into me. I groaned and thrashed on the sand.

Another wave hit, then another and another.

I could no longer move. A scream built in me, louder and louder, but my vocal cords weren't working anymore so it reverberated in my head without the relief that would've come from releasing it.

Brien touched my face. "Let go, sweetheart. Let it take you."

The sand struck my face. I was covered in sand now.

I braced myself for another surge of panic, but it didn't come. In fact, I felt...nothing. No panic, no pain, no fear at being buried alive.

Just endless, blessed nothingness. A void with no end.

I let go and welcomed it with open arms.

❧

I was a lotus, dreaming under the starry night sky, my roots in the mud, my petals unfolding like angel wings to reveal a series of mysteries too much for any one mind to contain.

Pain.

Death.

Oblivion.

Exhilaration.

Rebirth.

I drifted for hours, days, centuries. I was smothered in sand, but it didn't matter. Light and oxygen weren't necessary.

Survival depended on my inner power, and now I drew on it.

I'm Twilight, daughter of Shade, granddaughter of Gho....

But no. I wasn't my mom, and I wasn't my halmoni. Being heir to their legacy was important, but it wasn't the source of my power.

I'm the source.

Yes. That was it.

I dreamed some more. But I was back in this world now, on Lilith Island. The ocean surged; seagulls shrieked; Brien spoke in a low murmur to Cain, or maybe Talon.

Another day and night passed. For the first time ever, I sensed the setting sun.

And my mouth was so dry, my stomach hollow with hunger.

It was time to wake up. My new life was waiting for me.

Brien was waiting for me.

With a growl, I pushed at the sand until my head and shoulders popped free. Everything was blurry, my fingers clumsy, my body still transforming itself—but Brien was right there as he'd promised, helping me out of the shallow grave.

"Twilight." His voice was choked with joy.

He pulled me onto his lap and brushed the grit from my eyes and mouth with a clean cloth.

My gaze locked on his smooth, tan throat. Beneath the skin, I heard blood pulsing in his jugular vein. "Hungry."

"Let me wash you off in the ocean first."

I barely heard him. The fangs I hadn't yet realized I had extended for the first time, and my fingers clamped around his nape.

Pulling him to me, I sank the sharp point into that tempting vein and sucked hard.

BRIEN

"How is she?" Cain poked his head into my bedroom.

A newly made vampire sleeps both day and night, waking only long enough to drink before slipping back into unconsciousness. I glanced at the bed where Twilight lay, her dark hair spread across the bronze silk pillowcase. Her creamy skin was flushed, her mouth a bright, unnatural scarlet from the blood she'd ingested.

"She—" I cleared my throat of the grit that seemed to have filled it again. "She's had a tough couple of nights. But she seems a little better now."

It was dawn of the second night since she'd crawled out of her grave. After washing her clean in the ocean, I'd brought her to my apartment and given her a sponge bath to remove the salt from her skin before tucking her into bed.

Since then, I hadn't left her side. She needed me now even more than she had that week she'd been buried underground. I'd bathed the blood-tinged sweat from her body, changed her sheets, soothed her when she groaned with pain. And when she was hungry, I'd fed her from my own veins.

"Good, good." Cain's hard face softened. "She made it through the first week—that's the hard part. She's tough. My bet's on her."

"Yeah." I turned back to Twilight, staring at her as if my will alone would bring her the rest of the way through the transition.

Cain knew better than to get any closer to the bed—Twilight was still too weak for my vampire to allow that—but he stood in the doorway for another minute, silently offering support. Throughout that first, never-ending night, either he or Talon had checked in with me every couple of hours, asking how I was and plying me with blood-wine to replace the blood Twilight had taken.

Behind me, I heard Cain yawn. "You need anything?" he asked.

"No," I said, my gaze on Twilight.

"Okay, then. I'm going to bed."

A few seconds later, I heard the outer door close. I made sure it was locked, then carried Twilight into the vault and laid her carefully on the mattress. I locked that door as well, then slid beneath the sheets, my body curled protectively around her.

When I awoke at dusk, she was twitching. Her eyes popped open. "Brien?"

"Right here." I kissed her cheek. It was cooler now than a human's, and she'd stopped sweating. "How are you?"

She zeroed in on my throat. Tiny fangs peeped out from between her crimson lips, and for the first time, I saw a sparkle of blue in her eyes. "Hungry."

I slid my hand under her head and guided her to my jugular vein. "Drink."

Her fingernails dug into my shoulders. "Don't...want to hurt you," she said against my throat.

"You won't. Now drink." I lay back on the pillows and she climbed on top of me, thighs open and curved around my hips.

"Yes..." She sank those sharp little fangs into my neck like a ravenous animal and sucked hard.

I grimaced. "Easy now, badass. You want to make the experience good for the person you're drinking from."

"Sorry," she said in a garbled voice, fangs still locked on me. But she eased off.

"That's it," I murmured.

She was more vampire than human now. As she fed, the aphrodisiac from her saliva entered my bloodstream and for the first time ever, I felt the rush. My dick jerked. I was instantly, painfully aroused, my tip pressed against her slick sex.

I ached to push inside her. But she was a newborn, her body tearing itself apart and remaking itself as a supernatural being. Sex was off the table for at least another week—her delicate body couldn't take it—so I gritted my teeth and bore it.

Her sucking slowed. Her muscles went lax and a minute later, she was asleep, sprawled on top of me.

I indulged myself by stroking her back, her bottom. Then I stood up, bringing her with me, and let us out of the vault. Back in my bedroom, I tucked her into bed and headed into the shower to rub one out. It was the only way I was going to get any work done that night.

※

"Twilight was right." Talon stalked into my living room, Cain behind him. "Eden was a spy."

Cain nodded agreement, his mouth a thin line. "All the evidence points to it."

"Fuck." I rose from the chair near my bedroom where I'd been seated, keeping eye on Twilight.

A third day had passed, and she seemed to have made it through the worst of the transition. Her fangs had reached their full length, and at night, her skin shimmered with an inner light.

I wasn't ready to relax my vigilance yet, though. She was too precious to me.

The funny thing was, I understood things about my parents I never had before, like why losing my mother had driven my father half-mad. He must've felt like his soul had been torn out of his body.

I dragged my gaze from Twilight's unmoving body to Talon. He'd stopped nearby, fists clenched, his body vibrating with a very un-Talonlike tension.

"You have proof?" I asked.

Up until now, the only thing we'd had against Eden was that she'd broken her contract with us.

Cain answered. "I hacked into her Halifax bank account. The morning after she left, she withdrew all the money and closed it. She must've saved every penny she earned as a thrall. But the clincher is that three weeks ago, she received a hundred thousand Canadian from an offshore bank."

My mouth tightened. "What about Adrian?"

A vein pulsed in Talon's temple. He wasn't just pissed off, he was frantic in his laconic, understated way.

"Adrian's got nothing," he said. "She's apparently using cash and a fake ID. The trail's cold, so I told him to abort and come home. I want permission to go after the bitch myself. And when I find her—and I *will* find her—I'm going to explain exactly what it means to break faith with the syndicate."

"Agreed," I said. "But you'll have to wait—I can't spare you for another month, maybe two. Too much is in flux right now. I need both my lieutenants on site."

Cain wordlessly poured a double shot of blood-whiskey and handed to Talon. He tossed it down.

"Fine." He set the glass back down on the bar a little too hard. "But as soon as things are under control here, I'm going after her. And when I finally track her down, I'll make her wish she'd never been born."

"Of course. Meanwhile, as far as the syndicate is concerned, Eden had my permission to leave."

"Why cover up for her?" Talon's mouth twisted. "Let everyone know what a lying bitch she is. It's not like I—*we*—want her back anyway except to make an example of her."

"We don't need the distraction right now." And I wasn't convinced Talon didn't want her back.

"Brien's right," Cain told Talon. "The less said about Eden right now, the better. For the Lady's sake, she's just a thrall who got greedy. She didn't do any real damage. We were spying on Twilight ourselves."

Talon snarled. "She is *not* just a thr—" He broke off and muttered a curse. "You're right. Both of you. The woman's dead to me."

A knock on the outer door interrupted us. Cain answered it while I shut the bedroom door. It was Prosper, asking to speak with me.

"In private," he added with a glance at Talon and Cain.

I hesitated, aware of Twilight asleep and vulnerable behind the closed door.

"It's important," said Prosper.

"Come in, then." I nodded for Talon and Cain to leave us alone.

Prosper had recovered from the challenge, but an inner weariness clung to him like a thin gray fog. "Your mate is okay?"

"She's fine."

"That's good." He drew in a breath. "I'm requesting a leave of absence from the syndicate."

I considered him. To be honest, I'd been considering how best to handle Prosper without offending him. On the other hand, I liked having the man where I could see him.

"You swore an oath of loyalty to me," I reminded him softly.

He stiffened. "And I meant it. I was loyal to your father. I will be loyal to you."

"Then why?"

"I'm...tired. I want to go north, find a place where there aren't so many people. I've given hundreds of years of my life to the Maritime Syndicate."

"You'll return to the Mi'kmaq?"

He lifted a shoulder. "I'll visit, maybe spend a few weeks with the elders in my old village. But I'm not of them anymore. So, do I have your permission?"

His face was expressionless, but it had to grate that he had to ask my permission.

"You do," I told him. "But Lilith Island is your home. You're welcome to return at any time."

"Thank you." His brown eyes warmed slightly. "But for now, this is better for both of us. You need to set your own stamp on the syndicate."

"That's what Twilight says."

He nodded. "She's good for you," he volunteered to my surprise.

I glanced at the closed bedroom door. "I know."

"I didn't let Jules out of his apartment," he said abruptly. "It was Clarisse. But I swear I didn't know until right before the challenge when Matthew told me. They meant Jules to kill Twilight. They told him she was special to you and that he could find her in the garden suite. My guess is they did it to force you to slay your own sire."

My mouth flattened. "I figured it was something like that. And if I'd staked Jules to save a thrall, I would've lost the hierarchy's respect."

"But Twilight got Jules instead." Prosper shook his head. "If I'd known those sonuvabitches had set you up, I'd never have issued the challenge. Only a coward hides behind a thrall. If they wanted you and Jules gone, they should've challenged you both themselves. The syndicate's better with them in their final graves."

I smiled coldly. "Saved me the trouble."

"There is that." His answering smile held a hint of his usual self. "By the way, Donald would like a transfer off-island, too. I suggest you agree. I'm not saying you can't trust him—you can. But with your father in his final grave, he'd prefer to work for the syndicate in another capacity."

I nodded, unsurprised. Other than my father, Donald was the closest thing Prosper had to a friend in the syndicate. "I could use a good man in Quebec City."

"Fleur's coven?"

"Yes. Did you know they're trafficking in blood slaves?"

"I've heard rumors. But Jules wasn't interested in investigating further."

"They had Twilight on the block. Nazaire was the top bidder." I grimaced, remembering. "If I hadn't been there..."

"Jules would've said she wasn't a fitting mate for you."

My jaw hardened. "Jules isn't primus anymore."

Prosper inclined his head. "No, he isn't. And just so you know, I think he would've been wrong." He glanced at the door. "Donald's waiting in the hall."

"Let him in then."

Prosper opened the door and beckoned Donald inside. I explained what I had in mind for him, and the tall, lanky vampire seemed quietly pleased at his new assignment.

"Gather all the intel you can, especially on Fleur and Lemaire," I told him, "then contact me. I want to be there when you move in. I'm going to stake those sonuvabitches myself. And Twilight wants to be part of it, too."

"What about Régis?" Donald asked.

"If he gives you any trouble, refer him to me."

Strictly speaking, Régis didn't answer to me, but we were twice the QC Syndicate's size. It was past time we flexed our muscle.

"Very good, my lord," said Donald.

"In fact," I added, "tell him I said the auctions are to end as of now, and that the blood slaves his syndicate has been holding are to be returned to their homes with a suitable bonus—and treatment for blood addiction, if necessary. If Régis objects, give him this message: The woman I bought at his auction was an undercover slayer, and if I find out he had anything to do with the plot to slay me, I'll come after him with everything I've got."

I hadn't forgotten that Twilight had been offered up at an auction on the one night I'd been in attendance—at Régis' invitation.

Donald gave a thin-lipped smile. "I'll leave for Quebec tomorrow night."

We went over a few details, then he left. Instead of following him, Prosper lingered.

"That's an intelligent use of Donald's skills. Jules underestimated you."

"So did you."

"I let him influence me," my father's former lieutenant admitted. "He convinced me it was better for the syndicate to keep you in your place and him in power. After he went to his final grave, I believed I was the best man to succeed him. I told you the challenge was a test, but what I didn't tell you was that Jules begged me to challenge you. In fact, he made me swear an oath that I would."

I'd thought I'd outgrown my hunger for my father's approval. That with him in his final grave, he couldn't hurt me anymore. I'd been wrong.

"I see," I said flatly.

Prosper met my eyes. "Your father was wrong about you—and not because you bested me in the challenge. Because everything you've done in the past year—including how you handled yourself these past few days—shows you have both the guts and the control to lead the syndicate into the next phase."

He meant it; Prosper didn't suck up to anyone, even my father. He was the ultimate syndicate man—everything he did was for the good of the syndicate—which made his approval all the sweeter.

"You and Father never gave me enough credit."

"No," said Prosper. "That's not true."

I lifted a brow. "No?"

"Jules was always a little afraid of you. That you'd best him some-day." A corner of his mouth quirked in an odd little smile. "I suppose you did, in a way." With a crisp nod, he headed for the door, pausing with his hand on the doorknob. "As for your mate, I have a feeling she's going to surprise us all."

The door closed behind him.

I rubbed my hands over my face. What the fuck had just happened?

Apparently, I'd earned Prosper's respect, at least. That was some-thing, anyway.

That's when it finally sank in. Jules was in his final grave. Prosper and Donald were leaving Lilith Island, and the worst of the older vampires had been staked in the challenge.

I'd gotten my wish. I was primus now. The syndicate was mine to direct, the hierarchy stacked with people loyal to me.

But my satisfaction was tainted by bitterness. It wasn't Prosper's respect I'd craved, it was my father's, and now I'd never have the chance to win it. To get some fucking closure.

"Jules begged me to challenge you."

My fingers curled into tight fists. I looked down at them. I'd never wanted so badly to punch something, but that would be letting my father have the last word. I forced my fingers to straighten.

The sound of footsteps made me turn. Twilight stood in the bedroom doorway, a wobbly smile on her face. "I feel...different."

I immediately went to her side. "You should be in bed."

"No, I'm fine." She put a hand on my chest, holding me off. "Better than fine. Everything is so beautiful." Her gaze roamed the room before returning to my face. "So intense. I heard you and Prosper talking, and he's right. You're going to make the best primus ever."

"That's not what he said."

"That's what I heard—and it's what your father should've realized."

I fingered a lock of her hair. "Jules was jealous of me. I'm vampire-born, and he wasn't."

"So maybe he did realize it. He just didn't want to admit it."

"My mother said something like that once. Not to me—to him. But I overheard."

"Well, if Prosper believes in you, then that's almost as good, right? He's like your father without the emotional baggage."

"I never thought of it like that," I said slowly.

"It's good that he's leaving, though. Prosper's right. He was your father's righthand man for a helluva long time. If he stuck around, people might be tempted to go to him behind your back. This way, you can run the syndicate your way—and deal with other syndicates without having to worry about him."

I nodded, still absorbing that I'd received Prosper's seal of approval.

I'd wanted closure? Maybe I'd gotten it after all.

Twilight slipped past me into the living room and twirled in a circle like she had that day in the ballroom.

I forgot my father and watched my mate, enchanted all over again. "You sure you're all right?"

"I'm fucking awesome." Her smile spread like moonshine across her face. "I want to do all the things—dance all night, swim with the sharks, climb to the top of the castle and dive into the ocean..."

It was too soon. She shouldn't be looking so healthy or have this much energy, but she did. She'd made it through the transition.

Thank you, Lilith.

Twilight's joy was contagious. It swept through me, shining light into all my cold, dark, imperfect places. I broke into an answering smile and lifted her by the waist, swinging around in a circle.

"You *are* fucking awesome."

"Damn right," she said with a chuckle. She arched her back, arms spread like she was flying.

Our gazes caught and we stared at each other, arrested. I slowed down, sliding her down my body, then stopping all together. One lean leg twined around my hip, pressing her naked crotch against mine.

And then we were kissing, soul-deep and urgent.

Twilight broke away first. "I have an idea…"

"Yeah?" I nuzzled her cheek.

Her mouth curved, revealing a sexy hint of fang. "Why don't you show me how a vampire primus makes love to his vampire mate?"

So I did.

It was mid-October, the first night after the new moon. A paper-thin crescent, the symbol of hope and new beginnings, hovered above Castle Leclerc's dark towers as I exited the courtyard in a red silk slip dress and spike-heeled ankle boots.

Princess Renata (I was still getting used to calling her that instead of Ridley) strode alongside me, wearing the same slip dress in black, her short platinum hair a shiny cap around her elfin face. Her ankle boots had a short heel, though; I knew better than to ask her to wear four-inch heels like mine.

"Hang on." Renata stopped me to adjust my ruby-and-diamond tiara, then stepped back with a satisfied nod. "Nice. You clean up well."

I grinned back. "So do you. Zaq's good for you—and just not because you're wearing a silk dress."

My best friend seemed easier in her skin these days. Happy. She hadn't even objected to the girly dress I'd put her in for my mating ceremony.

"Yeah." A corner of her mouth tugged up in a smug smile. "He is."

"I'm so happy for you." Shifting my bouquet of jasmine and white roses to the crook of my arm, I gave her a one-armed hug.

She hugged me back. "Back atcha. Brien would do anything for you."

"As he should," I joked, because if I didn't, I was going to tear up and ruin my makeup.

We both chuckled, then I expelled a breath and stepped back, the bouquet gripped in front of my waist. "Okay. Let's do this."

Renata nodded and, long-legged and graceful, led the way to a path of crushed oyster shells. Demon materialized out of the night and fell in beside me.

"Good of you to show up," I muttered, and the cat responded with an *of-course-I'm-here* meow.

We crested the cliff and I paused, drinking in the moonlit ocean. My nerves settled. Happiness hummed in me.

God, I was lucky. I'd come to love this wild, beautiful island almost as much as I loved the man, and now I'd have both.

We followed the oyster-shell path along a high cliff. On either side of the path, syndicate members stood, faces shimmering above their mating-ceremony finery. As we passed by, they joined the procession until we were strung out in a long line with Renata in the lead.

We rounded a bend, and there was Brien, waiting under a glittering canopy of fairy lights in a gray sharkskin suit, snowy white shirt and skinny red tie. Cain and Talon stood with him, gorgeous in matching black suits and red ties, but I barely saw them, my focus on my mate.

To my vampire senses, he was as radiant as the stars. His blond hair shone, his eyes glowed, the green outlined in a faint blue.

My heart bumped into my throat. My mouth pulled into a wide, uncontrollable smile.

His lips curved in response.

I felt his satisfaction, his wonder.

His love.

I dragged my gaze from his and handed Renata my bouquet. She took her place next to my halmoni, standing a little apart from the three men, her wiry body elegant in a chic pink pantsuit.

My halmoni's gaze raked over me, then her chin dipped in approval. She'd been in the castle when I'd emerged from those first few days of insane vampire cravings. In that short time, she and Kerry had already come to an understanding and were running the household as a team. I'd been thrilled to learn that for now, she was staying on Lilith Island. In fact, she'd taken over Avril's second-floor suite.

When Brien had brought her to me in the secret garden, she'd placed her hands on her slim hips and shaken her graying head. "A vampire? Have you lost your mind, Nikki?"

The old me would've been defensive, would've apologized for letting the family down. But I reminded myself that my life was my own. That I wasn't my mom or my grandmother, and this was what I'd chosen.

"I love him, Halmoni. He's my mate. I know this is a shock—"and that was probably an understatement—"but I hope you can be happy for me."

She pursed her lips. The silence stretched. Then she sighed. "At least he's rich."

"He's standing right behind you," I said.

"I know." She raised her voice slightly. "And he'd better treat you like a princess, or I'll put a stake in his heart myself."

Brien came to my side. "I'll treat her like a queen." He ran his thumb and forefinger down my braid, his expression tender. "That's a promise."

My halmoni gave a ladylike sniff. "You'd better, or I'll hunt you down myself. It's not your money I care about, you understand. It's that you treat her like she deserves."

"Yes, ma'am," he said.

"All right, then." Gripping my head in her strong fingers, she pulled me down to her and kissed me on the forehead. "I love you, cupcake."

I gave her a careful hug. She was thinner than I remembered. Another woman might've appeared frail, but not Minji Park. She might've lost weight, but what was left was one-hundred-percent grit and guts.

"I love you, too—so much. You don't know how much I missed you, these past couple of years. And I can do as much good as his mate as I could in SI—you'll see."

"About the last two years," she started to say.

I released her. "I'm AWOL," I admitted. "I—"

"So you did stake Crow?"

My mouth dropped open. "You know? How?"

"People tell me things. I only found out a few months ago, or I would've done something sooner." She patted me on the cheek. "But now that I know, I'll fix it, don't you worry. I'll be damned if I'll let them take my only granddaughter from me. They got my daughter— they'll have to be satisfied with that."

Brien shifted on his feet. "Perhaps a sizable donation would speed the negotiations?"

They exchanged a look. "How sizable?" she asked.

"Very. Set up a meeting and we'll talk."

My halmoni's smile was downright evil. "I believe I'm going to like you, young man. And I'll set up a meeting as soon as possible."

"Meanwhile," I said, "I'll contact Rafe Kral. He owes me a favor, big-time. And you know his father sits on the SI Board now. He'll bring them to the negotiating table."

"The Krals owe you a favor?" Her brows climbed up to her hairline. "You *have* been busy, cupcake."

I wrinkled my nose. "It's a long story."

"And you'll tell me all of it. But not tonight." She looked from me to Brien, her expression stern. "I expect the mating ceremony will be soon, understand? My granddaughter doesn't shack up with a man. I don't care who he is. Is that clear, Leclerc?"

The corner of Brien's mouth twitched. "Yes, ma'am," he said meekly.

Now a stir went through the assembled syndicate members. The night priestess who was officiating our ceremony had arrived. Delphine was stunning in a dangerous, Lucrezia Borgia kind of way, her sleek body poured into a silver dress, her auburn hair braided into a crown intertwined with diamonds.

She welcomed us all to the ritual, then turned toward the ocean and raised her hands to the sky, speaking an ancient prayer that ended with, "We call on the Goddess Lilith to bless this special night."

As if on cue, the wind picked up and clouds raced across the sky, alternately revealing and concealing the crescent moon.

Delphine brought her arms down and turned eerie blue eyes on me. "You may give the primus your hand."

A gust of wind caught my hair, whipping it into Brien's face. Laughing up at him, I caught it in one hand and gave him my other hand. His fingers closed around mine. His lips barely lifted, but I felt his joy through our bond.

Delphine raised her arms again and the wind died as suddenly as it had picked up. From the woods, an owl hooted. Below, the surf boomed.

When the priestess spoke again, her low, resonant voice seemed everywhere, as if it were echoing off the sky itself. "Do you, Nikki Twilight Kim, bind yourself to Brien Leclerc to be his mate as long as you both have life?"

My smile faded. My gaze snagged on Brien's as I spoke the phrases I'd memorized.

"By the Lady Lilith and the moon She rules, I, Nikki Twilight Kim, take you, Brien Leclerc, as my mate. The mate bond is as old as the stars and as new as the crescent moon. My body is yours. My heart is yours. And my soul is yours. This oath I swear on the sacred blood of the goddess."

Brien slid the ring he'd had specially made for me onto my finger. He'd kept the design a secret, telling me it was a surprise.

My eyes prickled. I hadn't cried since transitioning to vampire, but now I came close. He'd remembered what I'd said about missing the sun, and he'd given me a handcrafted gold ring made of two sharks that met in the center, balancing a sun between their open mouths.

"You like it?" he murmured.

I raised my eyes to his. "It's perfect."

His smile held the warmth of a hundred suns.

Then it was Brien's turn. He spoke his vows loud and clear, his gaze locked on mine. Like my ring, his was composed of two sharks, but instead of a sun in the middle, there was a crescent moon.

The priestess pronounced us bound for all eternity and we turned to face the crowd. They broke into applause. Champagne corks flew and fireworks exploded over the castle, a surprise from Cain and Talon.

The party that followed was epic. Only syndicate members had witnessed the ceremony, but the entire island showed up for the reception in the castle courtyard. A band made up of Tremblay Syndicate dhampirs played fast, fun club music.

Servers circulated with trays of canapés, and the serving tables were piled high with platters of roasted chicken, lobster salad, steak tartare, crispy Korean dumplings and a raw oyster bar, among other foods. Fountains spouted champagne, both plain and spiked with blood, and a thousand handmade chocolates were arranged into mouth-watering tiers in a vampire version of a wedding cake.

Cain prowled through the crowd like a lean, white-blond wolf, dancing with both thralls and vampires alike. Talon withdrew into the shadows beneath an oak tree, tossing down one blood-champagne after another. If I had to guess, I'd say that Eden had broken his heart.

Donald had returned from Quebec City in a stylish new suit to witness the ceremony. He wound his way through the dancers and raised his champagne glass to us. "May you enjoy many moons of happiness together."

"Thank you," Brien said, and we touched our glasses to his.

"The clean-up operation is on schedule," he told Brien. "Whenever you're ready to go, just say the word."

Brien glanced at me. "What d'you think? Want to spend your honeymoon kicking some ass?"

I grinned. Yeah, this man got me.

But I had more interesting things in mind for the next few days. "Not for our honeymoon. How about two weeks from now?"

Donald inclined his head. "I'll make preparations," he said and faded into the crowd. A few minutes later, I saw him dancing with Lesa's mom.

Zoe and Rafe came up on either side of us. After congratulating both of us, Zoe nodded at the mixed crowd of vampires, dhampirs and humans.

"Your father wouldn't have invited the island humans to a ceremony like this."

"No," said Brien. "He wouldn't have."

Zoe broke into a broad smile. "Long live the new primus." She touched her glass to Brien's.

The other Kral brothers meandered over with their mates—Zaq and Renata, and the oldest brother, Gabriel, with his hand resting on his mate Mila's ass. I had a brief, disorienting sense of surrealness.

Was this really me, laughing with the famous Dark Angels, one of whom I'd been assigned to stake?

And I couldn't have been enjoying myself more.

My halmoni danced with both the guards who'd gone into hiding with her. After that, she took a seat at a table and regally entertained both vampires and dhampirs alike.

That was my halmoni. I swallowed a chuckle. In a few short weeks, she had the entire castle sucking up to her.

Brien's arms came around me from the back. "What's so funny?"

"My halmoni." Turning to face him, I interlaced my fingers around his nape. "She's an alpha if I ever saw one. Even the vampires try not to piss her off."

A corner of his mouth hooked up. "I'm guessing you're going to turn out just like her."

I grinned back. "Be afraid, Primus. Be very afraid."

"Oh, I am." His fangs slid out. Cupping my nape to hold me still, he dragged the points down my throat. "But I have a plan."

Excitement danced over my nerve endings. I pressed my inner thighs together. "What's that?"

"Get a room, you two," growled Rafe.

"Let's dance," Zoe suggested and dragged him away. That's when I realized the other two couples had already moved off.

Brien didn't even look to see if they'd left, just bit me hard enough to draw blood, then licked it. Arousal rocketed through me.

"This." He palmed my ass, pulling me up against his erection.

Laughter fizzed up in me. Reaching behind me, I set my champagne glass on a table. "That's the plan? Sex?"

"Hot sex." Withdrawing his fangs, he kissed his way up my neck. "Hot, hard sex." He traced the shell of my ear with his tongue.

"Whenever I want it. However I want it. In case you forget who the real alpha is."

My whole body heated. "That works," I managed to say.

He smiled, slow and so wicked I'm surprised I didn't spontaneously self-combust. "I thought it might."

Scooping me into his arms, he strode with me back to the castle. But when we reached the lower level, instead of heading for his apartment, he turned in the opposite direction.

"Where are you taking me?" I nibbled on his earlobe, not really caring as long as it was private.

"I had the primus's apartment renovated for us. If I don't take it over, people will wonder why, but I wanted to bring you somewhere new. Somewhere decorated just for us."

"But I liked your old apartment."

"Good, because I had them move the furniture." Opening the door with one hand, he carried me over the threshold and set me down.

"Oh!" I brought my hand to my mouth. "I love it."

It was like his apartment, but larger with the same plank floors and wood-and-metal furniture. The walls were a robin's egg blue that reminded me of the sky over the island, and the wet bar was carved with a big sun and crescent moon.

He shrugged, but I could tell he was pleased. "My parents had a lot of musty French antiques. I figured that wouldn't be your style."

"No. And you moved the paintings."

"I remembered how much you liked them."

I gave him a quick, happy kiss. "I love it," I said again. "The color you painted the walls, the wet bar."

I started for the bedroom, but he caught my hand and drew me toward a room off the living room. "I have something else for you. Your mate gift."

"My mate gift?" I looked around, puzzled.

"I've had people working on it around the clock. You go first."

He gave me a small push over the threshold. A soft pink light glowed on and gradually increased in intensity. Other lights joined it until the room was awash in pink and lavender and orange.

"It's a sunrise," I breathed.

The rest of the room was an indoor garden of leafy green plants and cozy couches and chairs. There was even a reading nook supplied with plump pillows and a stack of books.

Brien was looking at me. "If I could give you the sun, I would. But I can't, so..."

"Oh, Brien." Tears filled my eyes. I gave him a hard hug. "You couldn't have given me a better gift. I love you so much."

He buried his face in my hair. "I love you, too. You're my light, my heart. Without you, nothing seems to matter. If you left me now, I wouldn't survive."

Emotion welled up in me. He sounded so humble, so...human.

"You know I won't," I said around the constriction in my throat. "That's how it is for me, too. I promise, I'll never leave you again."

"I wouldn't let you," he said.

And just like that, my arrogant vampire prince was back.

Not that I minded.

"I haven't shown you the bedroom," he murmured.

I swallowed a smile. "No, you haven't."

"Right this way." He put his hand on my lower back and guided me to a room past the reading nook. The walls were citron with a massive platform bed of smooth teak. Our clothes practically fell off, and then we were naked.

"Get on the bed," Brien said in a rough-tender voice.

I obeyed and he crawled on top of me. We kissed, our hands moving over each other. Touching, stroking, learning each other like it was our first time.

He rose up over me, but I stopped him with a hand on his chest.

"What?" His brow furrowed.

"I have a gift for you, too."

"Give it to me later. It's been too long."

"No, now. Get off, please."

He heaved a very male, what-the-fuck sigh but rolled off me. I turned to show him my back.

The transformation to vampire had faded my tattoo to almost nothing. But I'd decided I wanted something to replace it, so I'd secretly gotten a new tat last week, then informed Brien that I wanted to wait until our mate night before we had sex again and moved back into my old suite.

Fortunately, vampires regenerate quickly. My back had already healed.

"I don't know what to say." Brien traced one of the two gray sharks the artist had twined around the newly inked black dagger.

"But you like it?"

"Of course. I love seeing the syndicate's mark on you. But...why?"

I slanted him an over-the-shoulder smile. "So you'd know I'm all-in."

"Twilight." He pressed a line of kisses down my spine. When he reached my tailbone, I shivered.

With a low growl, he flipped me over. His hand went around my nape, and he pulled me to him and kissed me hard. Then he was inside me, his palms framing my face.

"I love you," he said with each thrust. "I. Love. You."

My hands tangled in his hair. "Keep going."

A low chuckle. "Keep fucking you? Or keep telling you I love you?"

"Both."

And he did.

We crested together. By then he'd stopped talking to kiss me. Deep, wonderful kisses that were better than words.

My sex spasmed around his, sending jolt after jolt of pleasure through me. With our bond wide open, I felt his enjoyment along with mine.

"I love you," I moaned against his mouth. "Love you, love you, love you."

He buried his face in my throat and thrust one last time. "Forever," he said on a groan.

We stayed like that for a long time, his forearms on either side of my head, our bodies intertwined.

I stroked his powerful back, smiling at the ceiling.

I was home at last.

❧ 34 ❧

BRIEN

MARITIME SYNDICATE OFFICIAL
Paris, France. The new Maritime Primus and his vampire love were spotted out and about in the City of Lights. The primus looked fine in a William Fioravanti suit, and his mysterious new mate, who goes by a single name, Twilight, was rocking a leopard print dress by Dolce & Gabbana.
#perfectprince #vampirelover #vampiresyndicate

I growled and put my phone down. "It was you."

"What?" Twilight glanced up from where she reclined on the couch of our hotel room, sipping blood-wine and eating chocolate.

"You're the one who started that hashtag."

"Me?" She gave me an innocent look from beneath her lashes.

"Don't even think of lying about it." Plucking the wine glass from her hand, I set it on the coffee table and pulled her onto my lap, her ass in the air. "I should've figured it out before now."

A giggle escaped her. "Guilty."

309

"You—" I rained down several hard spanks on her skirt-covered bottom.

"Ow!" She was still laughing.

I pulled up her little pleated skirt, jerked down her panties and caressed her reddened cheeks. "I promised myself that when I found out who started that hashtag, I'd hurt them."

She turned her head and grinned up at me. "I'm sorry, okay? You're not perfect."

I couldn't resist kissing that sassy mouth. "No," I said. "I'm not."

Flipping her over, I pulled off her panties, then unzipped my pants, releasing my erection, and eased her down onto me. "Ride me." I dragged off her cashmere sweater and gripped her bottom beneath the pleated skirt.

Her fingers were busy with the buttons of my shirt. She got it undone and pulled it open, pressing a kiss to my throat.

"You're not perfect," she said again as she began to move on me. "And that's why I love you."

Emotion filled me. "Love you, too," I returned thickly.

"I know. I can feel it—here." She touched her breast over her heart, then leaned forward and brushed her lips over mine. "Now shut up and fuck me."

Placing her hands behind her on my thighs, she arched her back, fierce and sensual and beautiful.

My woman.

My love.

Mine.

ALSO BY REBECCA RIVARD

Want to be the first to hear about my vampire romances and other steamy paranormal romance books?

Sign up for my newsletter: rebeccarivard.com/newsletter

In return, I'll gift you with "Lir's Lady," a sexy short story from my Fada Shapeshifters world.

THE VAMPIRE SYNDICATE

Sexy, twisty vampire mafia romance

Tempted

Pursued

Craved

Taken

Fallen

Hunger

VAMPIRE BLOOD COURTESANS

Steamy vampire romance set in Michelle Fox's Blood Courtesans World

Ensnared

Compelled

Learn more: rebeccarivard.com/vampires

THE FADA SHAPESHIFTERS

Dark shifters, seductive fae...

Stealing Ula

Seducing the Sun Fae

Claiming Valeria

Tempting the Dryad

Lir's Lady

Shifter's Valentine

Sea Dragon's Hunger

Saving Jace

Charming Marjani

Adric's Heart

Learn more: rebeccarivard.com/shapeshifters

ABOUT REBECCA RIVARD

USA Today bestselling author Rebecca Rivard read way too many romances as a teenager, little realizing she was actually preparing for a career. She now spends her days with vampires, shifters and fae—which has to be the best job ever. When she's not writing, she walks and bikes in the Chesapeake Bay area with her guitar-playing, story-telling husband.

Rivard's stories have received numerous awards, including the RONE (*Tempted* and *Craved*); the PRISM (*Charming Marjani*); and the Paranormal Romance Guild Reviewer's Choice Award (*Saving Jace*).

In addition, eight of her books have been awarded the coveted Crowned Heart Review from *InD'Tale Magazine*.

www.ingramcontent.com/pod-product-compliance
Lightning Source LLC
Chambersburg PA
CBHW050754190726
48285CB00005B/1655